# THE SHADOW OF THE SUNSTONE

SIERRA BYRD'S AIRBORNE ARCHAEOLOGICAL ADVENTURES

LUKE RICHARDSON

JOHN HOPTON

# 1

**Mazar-e-Sharif Airbase, Afghanistan. Seven years ago.**

"Whatever people wanna say about this place, nowhere else has a sky quite like that." Nora 'Sierra' Byrd stood with her hands on her hips, looking up at the huge expanse of unbroken blue. The sky was, after all, where she spent so much of her life. Over eight thousand logged flight hours, to be exact, with the highest mission completion rate in her squadron. Not that Byrd was counting—but others were. Now, after fifteen years of service, she could read the Afghan sky like a weather map.

"Briefing started two minutes ago." The voice that boomed from behind her failed to permeate Byrd's thoughts as her gaze drifted back to the heavens.

Some days, when she took off into that beautiful sky, it was almost impossible to believe the horrific things taking place on the ground below. But horrific things *were* taking place, and that's why she and the United States Air Force were here at all. Just yesterday, her squadron had provided close air support for a convoy that came under heavy fire. Three weeks into this deployment, and already the pattern was familiar: the peaceful serenity of high altitude being shattered as muzzle flashes and hostile heat signatures lit up the ground below.

"If it weren't for these damn sandstorms," Byrd muttered, her gaze dropping to the harsh beauty of the surrounding sun-bleached plains and agricultural fields that faded into the hazy silhouette of the Hindu Kush mountains. The airbase itself was a jarring contrast of concrete and steel against the ancient landscape, surrounded by blast walls and razor wire that glinted in the afternoon sun. Where the usually precise line delineated the mountain ridges from the sky, there was now a smudge, like the dragging of an artist's thumb across the canvas.

"Now that one is moving fast," she muttered to herself, knowing the power that was coming their way.

"Byrd, you're about thirty seconds from being AWOL," the voice came again, this time loud enough to catch her attention. "Get in here now, or I'll have you reassigned to weather reconnaissance out of Minot!"

Exhaling a long sigh—the kind of insubordinate display that would've landed others in front of an officer faster than they could say Article 15—Byrd spun and double-timed it across the gravel.

Byrd approached Major Halloran, standing at the door, his face set in a grimace of frustration. His expression was so familiar to Byrd that it might as well have been carved into his timeworn face, crossed with lines like leather binding on an aging book. Without a word, he spun around and led Byrd through the maze of corridors and into the briefing room.

Fluorescent lights buzzed faintly, casting a cold glow across a table covered with maps, mission folders, and a few untouched cups of coffee. Around the table, propped up on mismatched folding chairs, Byrd's squadron mates waited, lounging with an indifference that only came after several thousand hours spent waiting for instruction.

"About time," Captain 'Vegas' Rodriguez muttered in Byrd's direction while spinning a pen between his fingers.

"I hear that's what your wife says when your deployment starts," Byrd retorted in her sun-kissed Southern accent before sliding into a chair at the back of the room.

"Hey, you know Byrd likes looking at the sky," Second Lieutenant 'Dice' Marshall quipped from the other side of the room, baring yellow teeth as he grinned. "I guess there wasn't much else to do back home in Alabama."

"Nice athletic body on her," Captain 'Hawk' Peterson drawled in reply, "but her daydreamin' mind needs some training."

"Leave her alone," an authoritative voice rumbled in the compact space. "Her mind's sharp as a bayonet when she's in the air. Down here, most of us would rather stare off into space than have a conversation with you boys."

Byrd glanced across at Bourdell, who sat with his feet up on the back of the chair in front of him. One of the older members of the crew, Bourdell should probably have been riding a desk at the Pentagon by now—and his stubbly, slightly disheveled appearance suggested he had given up on active service already. Three passed-over promotions told the story of a man who'd never learned to play nice with brass.

"I was 'daydreaming' about the small matter of a sandstorm coming from the southwest," Byrd shot back, running her fingers through her jet-black hair. "I first mentioned it an hour ago, and now visibility will be zero within ten minutes, maybe less. If we want wheels up before it hits, we need to go now and pin down mission details over comms—instead of having this coffee meeting." She snapped her fingers like it would bring everyone back to reality.

Halloran's fist crashed into the table, the crack exploding through the room like a gunshot.

The room froze—even Vegas stopped his perpetual pen-spinning. Halloran's jaw worked beneath his skin, a muscle twitching at his temple.

"I decide when we move!" Halloran bellowed, speaking as though he were addressing a thousand, not half a dozen in an enclosed space. He pointed at the grainy satellite image projected on the wall to his right. Taking a deep breath, the major continued at normal volume. "Steven Johansson. An American journalist captured one hundred and thirty-seven days ago. You think this place is grim? Try spending a night in his shackles."

"You know where he is?" Byrd said calmly and rocked forward in her chair, unfazed by Halloran's dominance. The last intel they'd received had been three weeks ago and pretty much amounted to nothing—fragments of comms chatter and grainy drone footage that led nowhere.

"It seems that Langley finally came through for us," Halloran said, pointing at the image.

"About time," Hawk muttered.

"They've got reliable intel that Johansson is being held in this compound, and as of two hours ago, we've confirmed a Taliban commander is en route. At the outside, he'll arrive before dawn."

"You know what that means," Bourdell said, his feet

hitting the floor as he leaned forward to eye his superior. "It's an execution."

"We need to go *now*," Byrd said, shaking her head in frustration. "Get out before the—" The sandstorm rattled the windows. Byrd glanced at the glass as the storm rolled in like a tidal wave of red-brown fury.

The whole group followed Byrd's lead and watched through dusty windows as the base's perimeter buildings disappeared into the wall of sand. Grains peppered the pane like machine-gun fire, the most persistent finding their way through the cracks in the concrete structure. The sun dissolved into nothing, plunging the room into amber twilight.

"It would seem that the senior commander is likely arriving to oversee an execution," Halloran repeated. A vein in his neck bulged as he shouted over the wind—the major certainly wasn't the sort of man to let a simple thing like the weather interrupt him. "We need to move. Anyone got an opinion on how long this storm might last?"

"Shouldn't we have moved when I first reported the incoming weather, *sir*?" Byrd said, loading that last word with enough venom to drop a camel. She slumped back into her seat. If the major spent half as much time in the air as he did polishing his oak leaf insignia, maybe he'd understand what it meant to waste perfect flying conditions.

As though echoing Byrd's frustration, the wind howled again. Somewhere across the compound, a door banged with wartime violence.

Halloran tucked his fingers through his belt and rocked back on his heels. He looked down his nose at Byrd as though sizing her up for a fight.

"Answering a question with a question. Not as smart as

you think you are, are you?" Halloran said, eliciting a dry laugh from at least two of the crew.

"Here's another question," Byrd replied. "How much more time are we going to waste?"

"We'll never get airborne in this," Halloran said and flicked a thumb toward the window, at which the sand continued to claw. "Wind speed must be pushing seventy knots—"

"Sounds more like eighty-five to me," Byrd said.

"Visibility is dropping too. So please, do tell us how you plan to get off the ground when you can't even see the runway?"

"You'd struggle to rescue yourself out there, Byrd, let alone anyone else," Captain 'Vegas' Rodriguez said, drawing more contemptuous laughter.

"This is a man's life we're talking about," Byrd spat back, rounding on the men and eying each of them in turn. Her knife-blade gaze darted from face to face, calling each man to account. The laughter stopped as quickly as it had started, replaced by the uncomfortable shuffle of boots and the sudden fascination with coffee cups. Even Vegas, who had a smart-ass comment for everything, found something interesting to study on the ceiling.

"If we don't act, a man will be dead, and you're here laughing about it like it's happy hour at the Officers' Club." Byrd turned back to Halloran, squaring her shoulders. "With respect, sir," she said, her tone containing none of the aforementioned respect, "these sandstorms don't last long. It'll pass over within the hour. I suggest we get ready and take off the moment the wind—"

"We go at first light," Halloran interjected, striding to the wall and tapping the projected image. "That is our best shot.

That'll give us time for the storm to pass and visibility to improve. Moving in before this is far too dangerous."

"Dangerous for who?" Byrd said. "Waiting is a death sentence for Johansson."

"I will not risk this team or the hostage on a half-blind op!" Halloran shouted. "We gear up at five. That gives you a few hours to rest. Take it. You'll need it."

## 2

**Cancun, Mexico. Present day.**

Lucian Sallas threw another sideways glance at the man beside him in the Audi Q5. He ran his dark, narrowed eyes over the big man's heavy features, following the scar that snaked from one side of his face to the other. *Like an ogre*, he thought. *A big craggy mess. Like a face on Mount Rushmore when they were just getting started with the chiseling.*

"I can hear you breathing," Sallas muttered. "Every bit of phlegm. You sure you're up to this?"

"I'm just drivin', boss," The Ogre said in his rumbling voice. "Skinny guy is doing the catching. He's even more toned than you. Why is everyone we know so good-looking? Except for mysel—"

"Quiet." Sallas looked through the windshield and across the street. He watched the 'skinny guy' pouting, appearing relaxed as he sat on the terrace of a bar called the Green Frog Cafe. The young girl beside him smiled, twirling a finger through her red hair.

"Get on with it, Carlo, you idiot," Sallas hissed. A small

group of revelers staggering their way down the Cancun Boulevard blocked his view as they passed in front of the car, washed in neon light. Tourist girls in summer dresses mixed with locals hawking tours and timeshares, while taxi drivers leaned against their white cabs, calling out to potential fares.

Through gaps in the passing crowd, Sallas could still make out the bar's terrace, where overhead fans fought a losing battle against the tropical heat. String lights crisscrossed above the tables, casting soft shadows that did little to help his surveillance.

"He'll make a move soon," The Ogre said. "She'll be ours before—"

"Get ready, then," Sallas snapped. "Hand on the stick. Sit up straight. Come on."

The Ogre turned his chunky head toward Sallas. "You okay, boss? You're edgy. Is it your brother?" A green neon hue patterned across the big man's craggy skin, making him look even more Hulk-like. Sallas glanced in the rear-view mirror and saw the same glow highlighting his own high cheekbones. But even the sight of his tanned, catalog-model face couldn't cheer him up right now.

"What? What are you talking about?" he asked.

"I saw the news this morning. The Congressional Medal."

"So?"

"Just. He's doing pretty well," The Ogre mumbled. "And you're doing...this."

"Nobody ever made it to the top by playing nice," Sallas said, his voice as bitter as raw coffee. "Now shut up and watch the girl."

Across the street, Carlo stood up from the table. The girl followed, reaching across and touching his arm. Her fingers lingered on his sleeve as they started toward the exit.

"She's ready," The Ogre said, his massive paws tightening on the wheel.

"Move," Sallas instructed as a gap appeared in the traffic.

The Ogre started the car and eased out onto the boulevard, threading between a packed tourist bus and a line of honking taxis. A group of drunk springbreakers stumbled across their path, oblivious to the danger. The Ogre tapped the brakes, and Sallas swore.

"Side street behind the bar." Sallas gesticulated, catching another glimpse of Carlo leading the girl down the sidewalk. "Same as always."

"Same as always," The Ogre confirmed, swinging around the corner.

They pulled into the side street and slowed beside an overflowing dumpster. Some creature or other scurried in the gloom. Steam leaked from a rusting air vent on the wall above, and a single security light threw a pallid glow over stacks of empty beer kegs and abandoned pallets.

Sallas turned and watched Carlo lead the redhead arm in arm toward the car. Carlo weaved slightly, clearly playing up his drunkenness. She giggled.

Sallas grinned to himself at how easy they had this. Time after time, they came—lambs to the slaughter, accepting their fate. For a moment, he wondered if it should bother him how simple it was, how predictable these tourists were, stumbling willingly into their trap.

The Audi's back door clicked open, and Sallas glanced in the rearview mirror, waiting to get a better look at the girl as she slid into the backseat. The seat remained empty.

"What are you doing?" Sallas heard the redhead ask, still outside the car.

"Get in," Carlo instructed. "It's just my friends. They're gonna give us a ride."

"I'm sorry, I'm not comfortable with—"

"Get *in*," Carlo growled.

"No!" the girl returned, immediately defiant.

An impact shook the car as Carlo attempted to push the girl inside, the Audi's suspension rocking with the force of bodies hitting metal. Through the side mirror, Sallas caught glimpses of the struggle—Carlo's hands clutching fabric, the girl's red hair whipping around as she lashed out, clearly realizing the trap she'd walked into. Anger and nervousness made Sallas' skin prickle.

"Never touched her damn drink," he muttered to himself. "I knew she'd be trouble."

"Hey!" The yell pierced the night, deep and powerful. Sallas whipped around to see a chef bursting through the bar's back door, still wearing his whites, drawn by the sound of the struggle.

The Ogre exploded out of the driver's seat, but the distraction was all the girl needed. She wrenched free from Carlo's grip and bolted toward a dark passageway.

Carlo spun and sprinted after her, his longer strides already closing the distance.

The Ogre slammed the door closed and followed, his huge frame lumbering into a dimly lit alleyway.

Sallas jumped into the driver's seat, then looked in the mirror as the redhead darted into the shadows. He gripped the wheel and hit the gas, the engine powering up loudly. Leaning forward, he picked up speed and swung the Audi around two quick corners, then into the narrow cobblestone passageway. The engine's low growl grew into a high-pitched roar. He sped past Carlo and The Ogre as they gave chase on foot.

The girl glanced back as she ran, her face bright in the Audi's headlights. Terror flashed in her eyes before she vanished around a corner. Sallas floored it, fishtailing through a puddle that was more likely to be urine than rainwater. He took the turn hard, tires squealing. The headlights swept across grimy walls and dumpsters, turning the alley into a stark maze of light and shadow. Cancun glamor soon disappeared away from the main drag.

A dog burst from behind a mound of garbage, forcing Sallas to wrench the wheel left. The Audi's side mirror scraped against brick, sending sparks into the darkness. He swore, then powered around the next corner.

"There you are, honey," he said as the headlights caught a flash of red hair fifty feet ahead. Sallas smirked and then hit the gas.

The girl's figure came into full view, framed by dim light spilling from a window above. She glanced over her shoulder again, her eyes wide and tears glistening on her cheeks. For a moment, she stood paralyzed, a red fox caught in the headlights. Sallas felt that familiar rush of power as he eased the car forward, his hand sliding toward the door handle.

The girl bolted again, wheeling toward another street on the left. She darted between the trash cans that lined one side and the stacks of wooden crates on the other.

Sallas angled the Audi between the crates. He smiled and thanked his luck when the car fitted with just an inch or two to spare.

"Nowhere to go, girl," he said quietly, closing in on the running figure. "You have a whole new life waiting for you."

The girl turned her head in all directions, clearly desperate for a way out that did not materialize. As she zigzagged, she slipped. She tumbled left and collided with a stack of trash cans. The impact sent her sprawling, and her chin smacked hard against the cobblestones.

Smirking, Sallas eased off the gas, the car rolling slowly toward his prey.

The girl lay crumpled on the ground, motionless, surrounded by scattered garbage. She then groaned and rolled over onto her back. Sallas saw blood trickling from her chin, staining the collar of her white *I Love Cancun* T-shirt. She gingerly turned herself and pushed up onto her hands and knees, her body visibly trembling with the effort. She staggered to her feet, swaying left and right before forcing herself to take a step, then another, away from the Audi. She made it to the end of the alleyway, but the exit was blocked.

She came to a stop as The Ogre and Carlo stepped forward, blocking her escape. Their massive silhouettes loomed against the street lights beyond.

She took a retreating step, her head whipping between the men and the car—a rabbit realizing it had run straight into a poacher's trap.

Sallas leaned back in the seat, observing the scene with cold detachment. The redhead sank to her knees, her hands raised in surrender. "We won't kill you, honey," he whispered to himself. "We need that body of yours."

Through the windshield, Sallas locked eyes with The Ogre and jabbed his finger in the direction of the girl. The Ogre nodded, hooked a huge hand under her armpit, and dragged her toward the car. He yanked open the door and flung her inside like luggage.

"Stick a needle in her," Sallas hissed when everyone was inside the vehicle, the girl jammed between the two men in the back seat. The redhead's anguished howl only lasted a few seconds, cut short by unconsciousness. "Close her eyelids," Sallas added. He sighed. "Too much chaos. Way too much."

"I'll do better next time, man," Carlo said.

"Next time? There is no next time for you, Carlo. You let her run."

"This is why it's better to grab people on the island," The Ogre said. "Nobody goes to the island."

"So we should try to grab people where no people ever go?" Sallas replied. "Cretin." An awkward silence filled the vehicle, leaving only the sound of the engine as Sallas drove carefully away.

"What about the boats?" The Ogre asked glumly. "The people we take from the boats that get too close?"

"A few small boats, here and there," Sallas said with contempt." We need bodies. Guinea pigs. Lots of them. Plus, our island has a new neighbor. She'll need to be dealt with too."

# 3

**Mazar-e-Sharif Airbase, Afghanistan. Seven years ago.**

Byrd lay on her hard bed, staring at the ceiling and listening to the sandstorm ebb away. As she'd expected, within the hour, it was down to the occasional gust. The familiar sounds of the base gradually returned—the distant whine of generators, the shuffle of movement drifting through thin walls. Although the end of the storm should have brought relief to Byrd, each second was a reminder of the precious minutes ticking away. Each minute like a nail in the coffin of an innocent man.

She could picture the scene playing out at the compound—vehicles arriving under cover of darkness, their target being dragged from his bare cell, and then...

Intelligence had a shelf life measured in minutes out here, and they were squandering it because Halloran couldn't pull his head out of his regulation manual long enough to see what was at stake.

A knock sounded at the door, pulling Byrd from her reverie. She groaned, frowned, and then the knock came again—three raps, loud enough to alert her but not to draw anyone else's attention.

Through the thin walls, Byrd heard the night shift moving around—the muffled thud of boots, the clatter of someone dropping something in the hallway, followed by creative cursing.

"What is it?" Byrd said, slipping out from beneath the sheets and stalking across the room. She swung the door open and peered out.

Bourdell stood in the corridor, his gaze as bright and alert as it had been in the middle of the day. Even at this hour, he had that coiled energy about him that younger pilots tried to imitate but never quite managed.

"I'm taking the mission now. I need you," Bourdell said quietly, looking left and right along the corridor. The silver at his temples caught a distant light, shining in a way that commanded more respect than any amount of brass on the collar ever could.

"Get in here," Byrd said, standing aside and then closing the door behind him.

"You know as well as I do, if we don't go now, it'll be a mission to rescue a corpse," Bourdell said, his voice hardening. "Remember Kandahar? We waited fourteen hours for Pentagon approval. Fourteen hours to decide whether one life was worth the risk."

"They found pieces of that kid scattered across three provinces," Byrd said, snapping on the light and stepping back into her flight suit. That mission continued to haunt the entire squadron. "How much time do we have?" she asked, already knowing the answer.

"If the convoy traveled through the night, then they're about three hours out. Once he arrives..." Bourdell let the sentence hang in the air like smoke. "They'll want to make an example of the hostage. They always do."

"They'll film it," Byrd said, her voice barely above a whisper. She'd seen too many of those videos—grainy footage of men in orange jumpsuits, dead-eyed speeches forced at gunpoint. "Broadcast it across every network that'll carry it. Make sure his family sees exactly what happened to him."

"Which is why we're going now," Bourdell said. The steel in his voice matched the look in his eyes. "While Halloran's filling out his risk assessment forms in triplicate, the journalist's got a bag over his head wondering if each breath is going to be his last." He checked his watch—the same battered Casio he'd worn since Desert Storm. "But I can't do this alone; clock's ticking."

"You don't have to tell me that, buddy," Byrd said, already dressed for the mission. Her jaw clenched as she zipped up her flight suit. "You ready to go?"

Bourdell gave Byrd a proud smile and a firm nod. "I knew I could count on you, Byrd. If we fail, we lose our careers, but if we succeed, Halloran will be more interested in taking the glory than in any kind of discipline."

"Better make sure we don't fail, then," Byrd said, giving Bourdell a wink as she strode past him and out the door. "Come on. *Clock's ticking.*"

The AH-64 Apache powered up with a distinctive whine as its turboshaft engines spooled to life. The rotor blades began their lazy arc, gradually picking up speed until they merged into a single blur against the night sky.

"All set," said Lovan through comms, and the young ground crew member gave a thumbs-up gesture from the asphalt in front of the chopper. He disconnected the external power unit and pulled the heavy cables clear of the rotor wash, then ducked under the nose to remove the last safety pin from the chain gun.

"Lovan, I didn't know you had it in you," Byrd said, running through the launch sequence. "You've saved a man's life tonight." The cockpit came alive, displays casting a green glow across the instrument panel as systems initialized.

"You're doing the lifesaving. God Speed," Lovan replied before backing away through the gloom.

"Don't worry, your name stays out of this," Bourdell said, watching the engine temperature gauges climb.

"I'd appreciate that, Captain," Lovan said. "You're on your own now." A click signified that the younger man had closed the connection as he sneaked his way back to the accommodation block.

"Let's Shake, Rattle and Roll," Bourdell said with a smile, clearly knowing Byrd would enjoy the old-time reference. He was right. For Sierra Byrd, midcentury music was almost as great as classic midcentury planes.

Bourdell eased up on the controls, and the Apache lifted smoothly into the night. The dark mass of the helicopter moved like a panther high in the trees, the rotor blades churning sand that swirled around the chopper. The nose tilted forward, and they powered away over the perimeter fence and toward the desert, lights of the base falling to nothing.

"Okay, Byrd," Bourdell said. "We're in this now, until the end or death... whichever comes first."

"I like to complete my missions," Byrd replied. "So here's my plan. We'll take out the commander while he's en route to the compound, make sure he never gets there." Byrd loaded the map onto the heads-up display. The overlay appeared in ghostly green lines against the

*The Shadow of the Sunstone*

darkness, showing the winding path through the mountains.

"How are your acting skills?" Bourdell said. "You reckon you can keep a straight face when Halloran takes the credit for his rescue mission being a success?"

"It's not my face I'm worried about, it's my right hook when he starts gloating," Byrd said. "But if that's the price to save a man's life, then so be it."

"High risk, for no reward whatsoever," Bourdell said. "That's my kinda fun."

"You masochist," Byrd quipped, throwing Bourdell a glance.

The pair dropped into a comfortable silence as the landscape rose from desert plains to the rocky ridges. Bourdell worked the controls, keeping the Apache within the valleys where possible to avoid detection.

"If our intel and calculations are correct, we should pick up the convoy in the next twenty miles," Byrd said, scrolling through the map. "We're now following their path, so we'll approach from the rear." Her fingers danced across the thermal imaging controls, adjusting the sensitivity. At this range, even a cigarette ember would show up like a beacon. "They'll be using these mountain passes—it's the only way to move vehicles through this section."

The Apache's nose dipped slightly as Bourdell brought them lower. The helicopter raced perilously close to the rocky ground below, skating over the moonlit landscape. Each ridge and valley offered a potential hiding place for the enemy, each cluster of rocks a possible ambush point. They'd both flown enough night missions to know that the Taliban owned these mountains, especially after dark.

"Watch that ridgeline at two o'clock," Byrd said, marking it on Bourdell's display. "Perfect spot for one of their heavy machine guns if they're expecting company." She scanned the ridgeline where the weapon's muzzle flash could appear at any moment. "And keep us above one hundred feet—rocket launchers are like a fashion accessory out here."

"Vehicles ahead, three o'clock," Bourdell said as a cluster of ominous heat signatures appeared on the display. The shapes crested the mountain pass and then started down the other side. A tense silence followed his words, both pilots becoming even more alert.

"Four vehicles, tight formation," Byrd confirmed, zooming the targeting system in. Through the thermal imaging, the convoy appeared as bright white shapes against the cool black of the mountain road—engine blocks and exhaust systems glowing like embers. "Jeeps, I think, set up to appear like a trading convoy. Two have tarpaulins over their backs." She adjusted the magnification, picking out more details through the green-tinted display. "Lead vehicle's got extra antenna arrays—probably for communications. The tarps are stretched tight, but I can't see heat signatures underneath."

"You sure it's them?" Bourdell said, dropping the chopper as low as he dared to mute the noise of their approach.

"The compound is less than fifteen miles ahead," Byrd said, checking the map. "There's nothing else out here for miles. Plus, look at their formation."

"Exact distance between the vehicles," Bourdell said. "Only combat training gives you that sort of precision."

"Exactly," Byrd said. "I'm certain we've got our target."

"Roger that," Bourdell confirmed. "Take out the jeep that has the comms system first. Last thing we want is them to get a message to the compound." He eased the Apache slightly higher as they approached, giving Byrd a better firing angle. "Your call on the weapon. But whatever you choose, make it count—we won't get a second chance at surprise."

Byrd's fingers moved across the weapons management system, cycling through their options. The Hellfire missiles would be guaranteed kills, but the explosion would echo for miles through these valleys. The chain gun was quieter but required Bourdell to fly closer.

"Chain gun," she decided, her thumb resting on the trigger. "We get in close. I'll hit that comms vehicle first and then work my way back."

"Great choice," Bourdell said, his voice as casual as though he were complimenting her selection of dessert. He powered the Apache up and across the crest of the hill, dipping the nose to give Byrd the perfect attack position.

On the thermal imaging system, the lead vehicle's engine blazed white-hot against the dark mountain road. The targeting computer overlaid precision boxes around each vehicle, distance and speed calculations updating in real-time.

"Eight hundred meters," Byrd called out, the gun tracking with microscopic precision as the targeting computer adjusted for wind, speed, and distance. "Seven hundred... Six hundred...." Her thumb tensed on the trigger. "Five hundred meters."

The lead vehicle's brake lights flared in the darkness, the driver clearly realizing they were no longer alone. But the mountain pass offered nowhere to turn, nowhere to hide.

"Looks like they've spotted us," Bourdell said.

"It doesn't matter," Byrd said, taking aim. She was about to squeeze the trigger when the shape of the second Jeep in the convoy changed. The tarp whipped away, revealing a DShK heavy machine gun mounted on a rotating pedestal in the truck bed. The .50 caliber weapon might have been Soviet-era, but it could still punch a hole in the Apache at this range.

"Fire! Fire now!" Bourdell roared, turning his body to glance at Byrd. The chopper rocked slightly, mirroring Bourdell's movements.

Byrd squeezed the trigger, but her aim was now slightly off. A strafe of rounds drifted away and hammered into a rocky outcrop beyond the convoy.

"Damn it," Byrd growled through gritted teeth while setting up the shot again.

On the ground, the gun swung around as a hostile combatant brought it to bear on the chopper. Byrd saw every detail with haunting clarity through the thermal imaging system—the gunner's smooth movements as the DShK locked on their position. The man fired, the powerful machine gun lighting up the night. The muzzle flash exploded on Byrd's display, temporarily blinding the thermal imaging.

Byrd returned fire, but readjusting her aim had cost her time. The bullets ripped the comms Jeep to shreds...but did nothing to stop the rounds of return fire that cut through the air around the chopper. Byrd adjusted again, shifting her weight to roll with the helicopter's rocking movements.

"Safe to say we lost the element of surprise," Byrd yelled as her bullets slammed into the roadway around the remaining vehicles. Rounds kicked up geysers of dirt and stone, missing the convoy by inches. The Jeeps at the rear accelerated away, powering past the lead vehicle, which was now reduced to a fireball.

Bourdell threw the chopper into a hard banking turn as more tracers lit up the darkness. The g-force pushed them both back in their seats as the Apache rolled away from the threat.

"I should have gotten the first shot in," Byrd said through heavy breaths. "Panic would have affected their accuracy." Another stream of tracers arced through their previous position.

Then came the sound—like a sledgehammer hitting sheet metal. Byrd saw the spider-web crack of bulletproof glass and heard Bourdell's howl of pain. The cockpit filled with the copper smell of blood as shrapnel tore through the instrument panel, biting chunks out of the dashboard.

The Apache lurched violently to the left, entering a spin as Bourdell's grip on the controls went slack. Warning lights flooded the cockpit in crimson as the helicopter spun. Byrd's vision spun with the chopper as the night sky and the mountain road traded places in a sickening whirl.

# 4

**Isla de la Vida Eterna, Caribbean Sea. Present day.**

"I swear to God, that is the most beautiful thing I have ever seen."

In the late afternoon sun, Professor Ralph Wall dropped to one knee, staring down into a six-foot-deep hole at the twisted, grotesque remains of a person who had surely been at their most beautiful several thousand years earlier. Jungle rot and black sludge caked the remains, but unmistakably human features pushed through the decay—rigid fingers, the dome of a skull, the outline of a ribcage.

"It looks like a zombie that fell into a septic tank," said Hans Hutchins, Wall's much younger assistant, "but I agree with you. It is truly beautiful. Is that an insect in its mouth?"

"You'll get to find out soon enough, young Hans," Wall said in the polished British accent that Hutchins so admired. Wall ran a hand through his white beard. "You're going down there."

Hutchins frowned but immediately changed his expression into a smile. "You're right. You've certainly put in your time doing the dirty work over the years."

Hutchins wiped his eyes with the back of his wrist, leaving a grimy streak across his forehead. He wrapped a length of rope around his waist, tested the knot twice, then stepped up to the edge of the pit. He looked around in all directions at the remote tropical island. Then, confident that they had only lush jungle and loudly squawking wildlife for company, he flicked his floppy, uncombed fringe away from his long, thin face and scrambled down.

"Careful," Wall said, looking over the edge. "We mustn't damage the remains!"

"I don't plan to damage myself either," Hutchins groaned in reply.

He reached the bottom of the pit and dropped to his knees beside the skeleton, releasing a rich scent of soil. He moved his hands toward the bones, then froze.

"You're going to have to touch the remains," Wall called out from above. "Don't be hesitant. Brush off the soil and see what she's holding."

Taking out his field brush, Hutchins cleared debris from around the hands. The damp air grew heavier as he brushed at the dirt. Despite its age, the skeleton was in good shape.

Brushing around the fingers, Hutchins touched something soft—different from the gritty earth and brittle bones elsewhere. He crouched in close and recognized the distinctive texture of ancient parchment, somehow preserved in the tomb's microclimate.

"Professor," Hutchins called, his voice barely above a whisper as if speaking too loudly might disturb whatever he had discovered. "I think I've found something."

He slipped on a glove and pinched the corner of the parchment. The ancient document came free without struggle from its resting place of several thousand years. Hutchins turned, his eyes wide in amazement, and looked up at his senior.

"What... what is it?" Wall called out with uncontrolled excitement.

"It's some kind of parchment," Hutchins said, looking in awe at the object. "It's delicate, although incredibly well preserved."

"Good lad," Wall said, grinning widely. "Bring the parchment up here now. Anything else can wait until later."

Hutchins secured the parchment inside a protective plastic wallet, then tucked it away and scrambled out of the pit. The climb was harder than the descent. Several times, his boots slipped on damp stone, sending cascades of loose soil down into the pit. Near the top, a chunk of limestone crumbled under his foot. He swung wildly for a moment before finding purchase on a thick tree root. Wall held out a hand, and Hutchins grabbed it, letting the older man haul him back into the blinding sunlight.

"Here," Hutchins said, sitting up and passing the parchment across. Wall wiped his hands on his red University of Minnesota Twin Cities T-shirt and the beige shorts that hung over his bony legs, then slipped on nitrile gloves.

"This could be it," Wall said, his voice little more than an inhale. He removed the parchment from the sleeve with tweezers. He lifted the ancient document to his eyes, trembling.

"Maya glyphs," Wall mumbled, after what felt to Hutchins like a really long time. "This language hasn't been used for thousands... fair to say, I'm rusty."

Hutchins scooted around and looked over the professor's shoulder, trying to work out what the red, orange, and blue pictographs might mean. "What does it say?" he asked finally, impatience getting the better of him. "Tell me!"

"You should be able to work it out yourself, boy," Wall muttered, eyes still locked on the parchment. "Think of it as a code, not an alphabet. Have I taught you nothing?"

"I know, but you'll decipher before me. Please, just tell me!"

Wall ran his finger over the hieroglyphs one more time, tracing each symbol with the reverence of a priest reading sacred text. His hands shook—something Hutchins had never seen in all their years working together.

"This is it. It's real. It's all real," Wall said. The evening light caught his face, and Hutchins saw something almost maniacal in his mentor's eyes—a fever-bright intensity that made him look twenty years younger. Wall's standard British reserve had cracked completely, replaced by the raw enthusiasm of a man who'd spent his entire career chasing a dream and finally caught it.

"The Mayan Sunstone! Does it reveal the location?" Hutchins said, looking again at the parchment but making no sense of it.

"No. Of course not," Wall said.

"Oh."

"Don't expect things to come that easily, boy," Wall said, a strange smile playing across his face. "How many times have I told you that? Your instant-gratification generation is not used to a narrative lasting thousands of years."

"*Right*, all I ever do is stay home doom-scrolling. That's why I'm on this remote island covered in filth."

Wall ignored the sarcasm, still peering at the parchment. "This is good news. This confirms our beliefs." Wall ran his gaze over the ancient document once again. "This reveals a cave, located in a canyon in the shadow of a 'demon rock.' That must surely be where the Sunstone is hidden."

"So it *does* reveal the location?" Hutchins asked, frowning again.

"It describes a cave beside a rock that looks like the face of a demon. The problem we have is that it does not reveal the location of the canyon."

Hutchins leaned in and squinted at the parchment. "Because the lower section is missing?"

"Exactly. The place where we now stand is precisely what we hoped it would be. The grave of Ix Tz'akbu Ajaw, the Queen of King K'inich Janaab. The King originally made notes of the Sunstone's location so that his most trusted followers could find it after he passed on. More importantly, they could find the location of the fabled plant we seek. The Sunstone is said to have detailed not only the location of the plant but also how to use it."

"Linium. That legendary plant *does* exist. It's real!" Hutchins said, leaning in close to get a better look. "Admit it, even you thought it was a myth."

"The most health-giving plant ever to have existed," Wall said, his tone now level. "It's a shame K'inich Janaab did not want the world to know the only location it grows in."

"But he buried the notes?" Hutchins said.

"He did. In the end, he decided the plant was too powerful." Wall looked up at the younger man. "Would good people benefit from its powers, or would bad people misuse them? The way his reign ended, he was right to believe that bad people may use the Sunstone to their own end. So, he buried it with his wife."

"But half of it went missing? Grave robbers?" Hutchins

looked back down into the pit, a shudder working its way through his body.

"Unlikely. They would have taken the whole thing. Most probably, the parchment disintegrated naturally, and nature also played a part in disturbing the grave. Earthquakes, floods, who knows. But later generations may have rebuilt this grave without knowing what it contained."

"Which is why the lower half of the parchment was found buried on another part of this island?"

"Right. And which is why it's now alone, buried in the archives of the National Museum of History in Mexico City. They seem unsure what it is or what to do with it, especially without the piece we just found. But now I'm sure the two parts must fit together."

Silence fell over the two men, leaving only the lapping of waves against rocks on the beach nearby.

"We need to get that lower half," Hutchins said finally, speaking quietly as if museum staff were eavesdropping nearby. "We need to know where that canyon is."

"We can't rob a museum, boy," Wall said. "I tried all my contacts but got nowhere. We'll have to do this the hard way."

"You're gonna search every canyon in Mexico, maybe even beyond, for a rock that looks like a demon?" Hutchins said, rubbing a hand across his stubbleless jaw. He shook his head, dust falling from his floppy hair.

"If I have to. As I said, we will do this the hard way." Wall straightened up and slipped the parchment back into its protective case. "But for now, let's celebrate. Focus on today's many positives."

Hutchins got to his feet and helped the aging professor do the same. They unfolded their camping chairs and positioned them beside the grave, facing the sea, their backs to the dense jungle that spanned most of the island.

Hutchins looked out across the sparkling Caribbean Sea toward the hazy form of another island a short distance over the water. "What's that place?" he asked. "It seems to be pretty built-up compared to our paradise here."

Wall looked in the same direction. "I believe that island is called Isla de la Fortuna. Those buildings are big enough to be aircraft hangars, and the place is certainly occupied. But it doesn't matter. We'll never bother them, and hopefully they'll never bother us."

"We're lucky to be here instead," Hutchins said, looking from the crystalline water to the lush forest. He had already forgotten about the other island and its occupants.

"Yes, yes, we are," Wall said, slipping into the tone of a seasoned lecturer. "It was local people who named this place the Isla de la Vida Eterna."

"The Island of Eternal Life," Hutchins said, swatting away a fly.

"Very good. During the 1950s, a Mesolithic skeleton was discovered on the island. Radiocarbon dating put the remains at around almost twelve thousand years old."

"Like the 'Cheddar Man' discovered in southern England?" Hutchins said.

"Yes, quite, although this person was different. The Cheddar Man died in his twenties."

Hutchins noticed Wall glance at him to make sure he was paying attention. Apparently satisfied, Wall continued. "The woman who was found here was over one hundred years old."

"That's incredible," Hutchins said.

"The locals had stories passed down for centuries about

people on the island living unusually long lives—most dismissed it as folklore."

"But now it's deserted," Hutchins said. Something cawed and then shuffled through the trees just behind them. "Other than monkeys, maybe."

"Yes, the population was most likely wiped out by disease during the colonial era. But the grave we found today may begin to provide us with answers."

"Our discovery will add to the knowledge of humankind," Hutchins said with a lofty tone.

"Indeed," Wall said, leaning back in the chair and pulling his hat down over his eyes.

"Think about it—this discovery could revolutionize both medicine and archaeology," Hutchins said, his voice rising with excitement. "We could be looking at the key to human longevity."

"Yes. But discoveries like this can be a blessing and a curse," Wall replied. "The kind of discovery that brings fame and f—"

Wall's words died in his throat as a massive hand clamped around his neck. His eyes bulged, his face purpling as he clawed desperately at the fingers crushing his windpipe like an iron vise.

Hutchins swung around and gasped. A giant of a man stood behind the professor, holding him aloft like a trophy. Wall's feet kicked helplessly in the air, his face now a desperate shade of crimson.

"Run!" Wall managed to splutter, his fingers scrabbling against the giant forearm.

Hutchins leapt to his feet but stood frozen, transfixed by the horror. His eyes landed on the parchment, now held by the thug—the priceless artifact in one hand, Wall's throat in the other.

"Get out of here!" Wall's words came as a desperate hiss, snapping Hutchins from his trance.

Hutchins pivoted, ran across long grass, and dove into the undergrowth just as two more figures emerged from the jungle shadows, rifles raised.

# 5

**Afghanistan. Seven years ago.**

"Bourdell!" Byrd shouted over the screech of tortured metal and discordant wail of warning alarms. She fought with the spinning chopper, gripping the controls that were duplicated on her side in preparation for events like this. The aircraft twisted back and forth in jerking movements. Byrd glanced at Bourdell, his head slumped forward and his body weight pulling at the straps over his chest.

"Trust you to sleep on the job, Bourdell," Byrd said. "I'll have to worry about you later, buddy. We're both dead if I don't land this thing."

She pulled back on the cyclic, sending the engine into a frenzy. The horizon tilted, the ground a blur. The torque meter red-lined as the rotor system fought against the unnatural forces.

"I dunno about you, but I definitely don't feel like dying today," Byrd said as she eased back on the collective to reduce power. The Apache's nose continued to dip, ignoring her commands. She needed more power to pull them out of this, but too much would tear the rotor head right off the aircraft.

"Come on, old man, talk to me," Byrd shouted, shooting a look across at Bourdell's still form. The ground and sky traded places with nauseating speed. The warning systems screamed louder still, each critical failure competing for attention. The altimeter unwound as though an invisible cord had been cut.

"Yeah, I don't feel like dying today either, thanks for asking," Bourdell groaned, slowly lifting his head. "But you're gunna have to take this girl down."

"Welcome back, old pal," Byrd said through clenched teeth. "Me? Take over? What a good idea. I hadn't thought of that."

Byrd pushed forward on the stick. The Apache fought against her like a wild horse, shuddering and bucking. The massive machine pitched and yawed, and she needed every toned muscle she had to battle against it.

"Not like that," Bourdell said, his voice weak but steady. Blood dripped from somewhere above his left eye. "You're fighting her. Let her spin, use the momentum. Quarter turn more, then opposite rudder. Hard."

Byrd stopped fighting against the spin, letting the helicopter rotate further.

"Now!" Bourdell shouted.

Byrd slammed the rudder in the opposite direction. The helicopter shuddered violently, but the spin slowed.

"Now collective, pitch the blades gently," Bourdell wheezed, each word clearly painful. "She wants to fly, just let her."

Byrd eased the controls, feeling the rotor blades bite into the air again. The horizon steadied, then leveled. The ground stopped rushing toward them quite so fast.

"They don't teach you that sort of recovery in flight school," Byrd said, her hands trembling on the controls.

"That's because almost everyone in a spin like that comes out in a body bag," Bourdell said, the strength in his voice recovering somewhat. "You did good."

Now that the spinning had stopped, Byrd saw muzzle flashes from the rear of the Jeep as the gunner attempted to finish what he started. The rounds cut trails through the darkness, but the Jeep now accelerated away. With a manually aimed gun, they were too far for an accurate shot.

"I'm not going to miss twice," Byrd shouted, flipping up the cover that sheltered the most lethal control on the chopper. With just a simple squeeze using one finger, Byrd released a pair of the Apache's destructive Hellfire missiles. The two missiles streaked away from the Apache's underside, their laser guidance system already locking onto the thermal signature of the convoy's rear vehicles.

The missiles closed in on their prey, covering the distance in seconds. The first missile slammed into the gun-mounted Jeep, the explosion lighting up the night like an artificial dawn.

"Well, I guess I drew attention this time," Byrd said. "Maybe everyone from here to Kabul will get the message not to point their weapons at me."

Another Jeep slammed on its brakes—a fatal mistake. The middle vehicle crashed into it, bunching them together just as the final Hellfire struck. A ball of fire consumed the vehicles, sending shards of metal in all directions and lighting up the landscape. Burning wreckage lay scattered across the mountain road as chunks of shattered vehicles rained on a nearby cliff face.

"Why didn't you just do that first time around?" Bourdell

said. "Would have saved us a lot of bother, to put it lightly. Maybe even saved our careers."

"I promise you, next time, that's exactly what I'll do," Byrd said. "If there ever is a next time."

They exchanged knowing looks.

"Let's get this thing down," Byrd said, scanning the terrain below for a suitable landing spot. The Apache continued to groan and lurch, hydraulic fluid painting a fine mist across their windscreen. Warning lights still flashed across the instrument panel, and the port engine was making a sound no engine should ever make.

"There, beside the road," Bourdell said, nodding to the right.

"Bringing her down," Byrd announced, easing the collective down with one hand while keeping the cyclic steady with the other. The ground grew closer, but the Apache drifted to the left, the damaged systems making even this simple maneuver a challenge. "Come on, baby, work with me here."

Byrd glanced at the airspeed indicator. The needle climbed into the red, pushing the chopper toward its limit. Suddenly, the Apache nosedived. Byrd pulled back on the control, searching for the right balance before the ground crushed the aircraft like a paper cup.

"Rudder first," Bourdell said, his eyes fixed straight ahead.

Byrd pressed her feet against the rudder pedals and counted to three. Reluctantly, as though the aircraft were enjoying the unpredictability, the craft dropped level.

"Nicely done," Bourdell coaxed. "Now, will you please sort out this dive?"

Byrd grasped the stick with both hands. Pulling back slowly and steadily, she fought not only the malfunction but the chopper's own momentum. The aircraft rattled and shuddered, sounding damaged and weak yet still traveling at deadly speed.

Streaks of sand whizzed past the cockpit like lasers, the downward velocity increasing as death neared. The chopper shook, threatening to break apart in the air before it even had a chance to slam into the ground.

"That's it," Bourdell said. "Coax it, don't fight it."

"You can do it, baby," Byrd told the chopper soothingly in turn.

As if hearing her pleas, the chopper's nose swept upward. Gradually, the horizon righted itself, leveling off. The chopper still trembled, but it was steady.

"Talking to inanimate objects is the first sign of madness," Bourdell said.

"It seemed to work," Byrd replied, taking a moment to read the vital gauges: oil pressure stabilizing, airspeed back within safe limits. "She's under control."

"Yeah, but for how long?" Bourdell asked.

"Long enough to get on the ground, I hope," Byrd said. "I'm afraid this is a one-way kinda flight."

"I have a family. Get me down safely," Bourdell said.

"No you don't," Byrd said, throwing him a look.

"I know, but people like to say things like that in dangerous situations," Bourdell quipped. "I do have a bottle of Eagle Rare 25 I've been saving for too long."

"That would taste great right about now," Byrd said as she squinted down at the terrain below. The helicopter's stabilizers groaned in protest as she fought against the turbulence. She focused down on the sand's pale outline, her training guiding her as the chopper inched closer to the ground.

"That dirt track will have to do," she told Bourdell. "I've

been getting a little bored with regular flat and level ground anyway," she added.

"Not funny," Bourdell replied.

The skids hit the sand and then bounced, sending a shockwave through the aircraft and making every part of Byrd's body shake. Airborne again, they drifted to the side. Byrd corrected, remembering to let the aircraft find its own balance rather than forcing it. The second touch was gentler, but the Apache wasn't done fighting. It slammed down again, and eleven tons of metal skidded across the dirt, scraping and screaming like the demons of hell begging for release. It finally settled, the rotor blades clunking as they slowed.

Byrd unclipped her harness, suddenly feeling as though she weighed eleven tons herself. She leaned across to check Bourdell's vitals. His breathing was labored, and his face was wet with blood, but he spoke calmly.

"Top pocket?" Bourdell said, trying but failing to reach for something in his pocket. He took several more short, sharp breaths. "I need you to get something from my top pocket. It's important."

Byrd inspected his wound. A bit of shrapnel passing through the windshield had made an unsightly mess but didn't seem to be life-threatening. "You're not going to die, and I'm definitely not taking some love letter to a long-lost sweetheart."

"Me? I never had a long-lost sweetheart." Bourdell wheezed back. "I just want my damn cigar."

# 6

**Isla de la Fortuna, Caribbean Sea. Present day.**

Sierra Byrd felt just like her feathered namesake, gliding with grace and freedom through the air as the Caribbean Sea twinkled like topaz gemstones beneath her. For just a second, she allowed herself to be thankful that she was in this joyful situation and not spinning in the skies above Afghanistan.

The engine of her Piper PA-18 Super Cub purred contentedly as she steadily guided it toward a runway flanked by coconut trees on the lush, bright green island she had selected as the home for her new flight school.

The wheels touched down with little more than a shudder, and she taxied over to the brand-new buildings at one end of the airstrip. Byrd had visited this part of Mexico several times in recent months to meet with architects, communicating exactly what she needed them to do in order to turn her vision into concrete and steel. This was to be her second attempt at a little piece of paradise. Her first go, taking over an old airstrip just north of Mexico City, hadn't worked as she'd hoped. Pollution, traffic, and people getting in her way had tainted the experience. In all honesty, it wasn't just the pollution and traffic she wanted away from, but people in general. Most of them, at least. Those who paid her handsomely to share her experience on the flight deck were tolerable, just.

She rolled to a stop outside the pristine new hangar and killed the engine. Grabbing her flight bag, she climbed out of the Piper Cub and then looked up at the hangar. The vast structure gleamed in the sun. Behind the hangar, curving along the beach, a series of smaller buildings housed maintenance facilities, offices, and accommodation blocks.

It was certainly more comfortable than the old military buildings she'd used up in Mexico City and would take a lot of highly paid hours up in the sky to pay off. It would be worth it, that Byrd knew for sure.

After stepping down from the aircraft, Byrd paced into the hangar and ran her hand through her hair's jet-black bouffant. Although the towering fifties hairstyle wasn't the most practical hairdo for a pilot who often had to squash it down with a helmet, Byrd wouldn't have it any other way. She hadn't dealt all that well with rules and opinions in the military, so she certainly wasn't interested in them as a civilian.

"It's hotter than an oven in here," she said to herself, unzipping her flight suit. She shrugged it off her shoulders and tied the sleeves around her waist, her red tank top now visible beneath.

She jabbed her finger into a button on the stereo that sat on a dusty desk in the corner, sending a scratchy version of "Rock and Roll is Here to Stay" blasting out into the cavernous hangar.

Turning her attention to the occupants of the hangar, the smile of a proud mother lit up her face.

"How are you settling in?" she said, walking over to her P-51 Mustang and patting the nose as though the craft might respond. Known in full as the North American Aviation P-51 Mustang, the single-seat fighter and bomber had flown Allied forces to victory in World War Two, and it had also been used in the Korean War. Its grace and majesty was everything that Byrd loved about the forties and fifties. Originally developed for the Royal Air Force in the United Kingdom, the aircraft used an engine by Rolls-Royce, another symbol of formidable British engineering during the mid-twentieth century.

"Now will you look at that," Byrd said, noticing herself in the reflection of the Mustang's highly polished fuselage. She stepped back, admiring the muscles that now flanked her toned arms and shoulders. "Certainly more there than two months ago. Good to get the training regime back on track."

She had been working out quite a lot recently, trying to improve her strength so that she could get back to training hapkido when time allowed. The Korean martial art based on throws and striking required strength and athleticism.

Byrd wandered around the Mustang, and her pride and joy came into view. She froze, a tingle of excitement working up her spine.

"Now you really are a thing of beauty," Byrd said, looking up at her favorite piece of machinery in the whole world—a Douglas C-47 Skytrain. It was almost god-like in its size and presence. Byrd had restored the craft herself. Although *Byrd Force One*, as she jokingly referred to it, was now more or less capable of flight, keeping her sky-ready was the work of a lifetime.

Byrd picked up a rag and ran it across the aluminum

fuselage. Here, alone and working on the Skytrain, she felt something akin to a first date with a dream suitor—as far as she could remember what that felt like.

"Nora Byrd!" A voice boomed from the door, cutting through the music like the shattering of glass. Byrd cut the song and turned to see a dark figure standing in the doorway, backlit by the blinding sun.

"It can't be. I think I'm hearing things," Byrd said, straightening up and planting her hands on her hips.

"You're hearing things because I'm saying them!" the visitor said, stepping into the gloom.

"As I live and breathe." Byrd dropped the cloth and stepped toward the visitor. "Bourdell?"

"Guilty as charged, ma'am," Bourdell drawled, offering a mock salute. He stepped forward, and the pair embraced. "Good to see ya, Nora Byrd," Bourdell said, stepping back and wiping sweat from stubble that was now more grey than black. "With that hair and those full red lips of yours, you look like a cross between Earhart and a fifties pin-up girl."

"Keep the compliments, cut the Nora," Byrd snapped back, jabbing a fist into Bourdell's shoulder. "Sierra is the nickname you gave me. Are you drunk?"

"Of course not. Just flew in on a gorgeous Mooney M-18 Mite, all the way from Alabama." Bourdell rubbed his shoulder dramatically.

"That doesn't mean you're not drunk," Byrd said, an eyebrow raised.

"Byrd, on the life of someone's children, I am not drunk."

"*Someone's* children?"

"Well, I don't got kids, so I gotta swear on someone's."

"You're gonna have to do better than that, Bourdell."

"Okay, okay. I swear on this great bottle of bourbon I got

here." Bourdell dug around in his flight bag and pulled out a bottle that was certainly not full. "Okay... this half bottle."

Byrd cocked her head and shot Bourdell the sort of look that could shear through metal.

"You didn't ask if I *had* been drinking," Bourdell said, offering her the bottle. "You asked if I was drunk. It's a good—"

Byrd snatched the bottle and eyed the label. "Listen, I know we've been out of the Air Force a few years, and a lot of veterans turn to drinking when they're at a loose end. Just keep it under control, yeah?" She shoved the bottle back into Bourdell's flight bag and looked him up and down. She had to admit, if he was drinking too much, it didn't show. "You're on my trusted list. You know there ain't many on my trusted list."

"I know." Bourdell nodded.

"Good. Well, make sure your name don't get scratched off."

"Sure will. Proud of my place on that list, Byrd," Bourdell said, his gaze shifting beyond Byrd and locking on the Skytrain. "Now that is a thing of beauty. I heard you were fixing up one of these—"

"She's been airworthy and certified for a few years, but you know how it is with these old birds—always something that needs attention," Byrd said, turning as Bourdell paced up to the craft.

"A good woman takes love and care," Bourdell said, running his fingers across the fuselage.

"Like you'd know what a good woman needs," Byrd muttered under her breath.

"I heard that," Bourdell replied with a rasp, moving to inspect the engines. He traced the edge of the prop blade. "Twin Wasps, fourteen cylinders, if I'm not mistaken. These engines could take a beating and keep on turning. What's her story?"

"Built in the late forties. Used in the Berlin Airlift in forty-eight," Byrd explained, folding her arms and looking up at the aircraft's nose. "After that, she bounced around Europe for a while—cargo runs mostly. Some oil company bought her in the seventies, flew her all over Alaska until the engines gave out. She sat in a barn in Anchorage for twenty years before I found her."

"And brought her back to life," Bourdell said admiringly.

"Took three years and every penny I had," Byrd said. "But she's original—right down to the Wasps." She pointed at the engines. "Had to track down parts from six different continents. The instrument panel came from a wreck in New Guinea, if you can believe it. Found the landing gear in some farmer's barn in Kansas."

"Worth every cent," Bourdell said. He turned to Byrd with the look of a hungry puppy in his eyes. "Hey, what do you say you let me take her for a spin. I'd love—"

"Hell no. Nope. Negative. Nein. Non. One-hundred-percent that's never, ever going to happen."

"You can co-pilot," Bourdell said hopefully, looking longingly up at the craft. "It'll be like—"

"Absolutely not," Byrd said, stepping forward and sliding her arm through Bourdell's. "But I sure can show you the prettiest spot on this whole island for watchin' the sun go down while we sample that fine whiskey you brought along."

"Second best option," Bourdell said, his head craning to look back at the Skytrain as Byrd led him away.

# 7

**Isla de la Vida Eterna, Caribbean Sea.**

Hutchins plunged into the jungle, branches whipping at his face as he crashed through the undergrowth. A bullet shrieked past his head, so close that the air displacement ruffled his hair. The shot slammed into a nearby tree with a crunching thud, splintering and scattering the bark.

"I told you not to shoot at *weaklings!*" a voice like rolling thunder exploded from somewhere behind him. "Just capture them like vermin!"

Hutchins dove forward and hit the deck, flattening himself to the ground and clasping his hands around his scalp. Wet soil filled his mouth and nostrils. He sucked in dirt while trying and failing to breathe. Grimacing, he clambered to his feet and spat the soil into the air.

Another zipping sound pierced the air, loud and angry. Hutchins waited for the pain. Mud kicked up like a fountain between his legs as the bullet drilled into the soil two inches from his feet.

"Need to get out of here," he gasped, heart hammering

as he scanned the surrounding jungle. "Got to get back to the truck." Orienting himself by the sun, which was now dropping toward the horizon, he plowed on through the undergrowth. Thorns ripped at his clothes, and vines snared his legs. Each branch he shoved aside snapped back with a vengeance, slashing at his face like a blade.

He froze as another strafe of bullets snapped through the air, paralyzing him in terror. Someone plowed noisily through the jungle behind him, clearly fighting with the dense undergrowth in desperation to get hands on prey.

"Keep moving, keep moving," he told himself. "Get back to the truck."

His lungs burning, Hutchins fought through the jungle, but he couldn't shake the images seared into his mind—Wall's white beard against that monstrous hand, the professor's eyes bulging as the life drained from his face. The sound of those desperate gasps seemed to echo with every ragged breath Hutchins took.

No time for grief. Not now. He forced his legs to keep moving, sprinting when he could, scrambling when he had to. His boots slipped on rotting vegetation, found purchase, then drove him forward again. The truck was his only chance—if he could reach it, he could put some distance between himself and the attackers.

"Got to get to the other side of the island, meet our boat pilot," he said in a low growl. "Wall's discovery can't be lost to these murderers."

His breath suddenly burst from his lungs as a sharp object dug into his ribs. He sank to his knees and then stuck his elbows out, an inadequate attempt to protect himself from the attack.

But the attack didn't continue. His eyes focusing in the gloom, he saw that instead of a knife, a sharp branch had dug into his ribs. Relieved for just a second, he shoved the branch away and listened in to the sound of the jungle.

He heard a rhythmic rustling not far away, like someone moving methodically through the foliage. He crawled into a dense patch of undergrowth and tucked his knees up under his chin. Remaining still, he slowed his breathing, trying everything he could to stay silent.

The sound of movement came closer. Listening hard, he realized that it wasn't just footsteps but someone hacking away vegetation as they neared. The hacking grew louder and more urgent, like the beeping of a metal detector getting nearer to a priceless find.

Hutchins squeezed his eyes closed. The swishing moved closer and closer. It sounded so close that the next stroke could sweep away the greenery that was hiding him. His trembling body rustled the vegetation around him. He stifled whimpers, attempting to remain quiet.

Then, the approaching sound stopped. Insects buzzed. Hutchins' heart pounded somewhere inside his throat, where it certainly had no right to be.

The sweeping sound came again, although now it sounded as though it was heading in the opposite direction. Hutchins held his breath, hoping that he was not wrong. He remained motionless, listening for what felt like an hour as the sweeping faded into the soundtrack of the surrounding jungle. As certain as he could be that the pursuer had moved away, he crawled from his lifesaving hiding place.

He peered up at the purple sky through gaps in the leaves. As he looked up, he heard the sound of an aircraft engine. He turned toward the noise and saw the lights of a small plane as it took off into the sky. He was sure Wall was on that plane, being carried away to heaven knows where. Cold terror flooded his chest as he feared for Wall and for himself. He was now alone with any criminals who remained on the island.

Time to move. He spun around, assessing the identical walls of jungle surrounding him on all sides. Vines and branches formed a maze of shadows, playing tricks with his sense of direction. He was losing light, losing time, and somewhere in this green hell, killers were hunting him.

In the distance, he saw a glinting red light atop a tall, dark silhouette. For a second, he stared at the light, not understanding what it was. Then, hope surged within him as he recognized the radio tower. Wall, a font of knowledge on all topics, had explained that the tower was part of Mexico's coastal navigation network, helping cargo ships and fishing vessels navigate the dangerous reefs and islands that dotted this area. Most importantly, it marked the spot where they'd left the truck.

Hope and adrenaline flooded through him as he charged toward the tower. Energy renewed, he kicked aside leaves and branches. When the branches became thicker overhead, he did his best to follow the right direction on instinct, moving toward the light. Emerging into a less dense patch of trees, he stopped and checked the sky again. The radio tower reared up ahead.

He pushed on, no longer feeling the tangle of plants that clawed at him. The dense canopy gradually thinned, letting shafts of dying sunlight pierce through. Eventually, the strangling vegetation gave way to waist-high grass and open sky. He paused in the cover of the undergrowth, ribcage heaving, sweat streaming down his face as he surveyed the scene.

Spotting their battered Land Rover exactly where they'd left it, parked in the shadow of the radio tower, relief flooded through him. He dug through his pockets and pulled out the keys, ready to leap inside the truck just a short distance away. Not that he remembered locking the Land Rover in the first place—they hadn't expected to see another person during their whole time here.

Hutchins broke into a sprint, his feet tearing chunks of grass from the ground as he accelerated toward the Land Rover. The grassland became a dusty track as he neared. He swung to the side to avoid a fallen tree—and slipped. His feet slid across the gravel, his arms windmilling wildly as he fought to stay upright. At the last moment, he caught his balance and powered on.

"Hey!" a shout reverberated from somewhere behind him. "You can't run!"

"Try me," Hutchins muttered, ignoring the fear in his guts. He reached the door, flung it open, and hurled himself into the driver's seat. With shaky hands, he stuffed the key into the ignition and twisted. The engine roared to life as he glanced in the mirror and saw a pair of men emerge from the jungle cover, running his way.

Hutchins slammed the stiff gear shift into first and floored the gas. Gravel sprayed from beneath the tires as the Land Rover lurched forward. A bullet slammed into the side mirror and cracked it, sending fragments of glass into the vehicle.

Ducking his head, Hutchins yanked the wheel hard, swinging the Land Rover into a ninety-degree turn. As he powered away, Hutchins watched the men in the rearview mirror, taking aim. They fired, but were already too far away to be accurate. They lowered their guns and watched the Land Rover go.

Hutchins turned his attention back to the dirt road ahead and barreled around the next curve, a slight smile on his face. Then, the smile fell away, and his blood ran cold. He heard the distinctive click of a pistol being cocked.

"Stop, now," a voice rumbled from the seat directly behind him.

Hutchins turned and watched in horror as a massive figure rose from where he'd been lying flat across the rear bench. The figure raised the gun and pressed it against the back of Hutchins's head. "Do what I tell you, or your life will end on this island."

# 8

**Isla de la Fortuna, Caribbean Sea.**

Byrd sank into one of the beach bar's deckchairs and looked out at the sinking sun. She dug her feet into the warm sand as a light breeze rustled the palm-leaf thatch above her.

"There's one thing I can agree with you about," Byrd said, raising the glass to her lips and taking a deep sip of the whiskey. Ice cubes clinked inside the amber liquid. "That's not a bad drop of bourbon at all. Smooth as silk and more comforting."

"You're questioning my drinking, but you have your own private beach bar," Bourdell said, settling into the striped deckchair beside her. He looked at the beach stretching out before them in a perfect crescent of white sand, melting into turquoise waters. Pelicans skimmed the waves, diving occasionally for their evening meal, while frigate birds circled lazily overhead.

"Built by the previous owner, but I gotta say, I'm not complaining," Byrd said, placing the glass on the rickety wooden table between them.

"I like how you've hidden it behind the aircraft hangar," Bourdell said, lighting a cigar with one hand while topping up his whiskey with the other.

"That's what you get from years of working throttle and stick," Byrd said, nodding at her companion's surprising dexterity.

"I could do that at Mach 1," Bourdell said, puffing the cigar alight. "Probably."

Byrd spat out a laugh. "That's something I definitely don't wanna see."

"You gunna keep this Officer's Club secret from the new recruits?" Bourdell asked, nodding at the kiosk-style bar that appeared to have been fashioned from driftwood.

"To begin with," Byrd said, taking another sip. "You know me; I need my alone time. The ones I like will be invited for a drink. Eventually."

"That won't be many, then," Bourdell said, chuckling. "But it is a good spot, I'll give you that. If you don't mind me askin', how d'you afford all this? I sure as hell know my Air Force pension don't stretch that far."

"I do a bit of private work every now and then," Byrd said, thinking of the jobs she'd done for Eden Black and the Council of Selene. Whilst she trusted Bourdell, some things were just better not shared.

"Like that, is it?" Bourdell said, throwing her a wink.

"You've got no idea," Byrd replied, remembering the various times she'd performed an off-the-books flight to rescue Eden, Baxter, and Athena. Eden had, in fact, funded the build in exchange for Byrd keeping her craft fueled and on standby, and allowing the council to use the airstrip if needed. All off the record, of course.

"Well, here's to whatever top-secret stuff you're up to," Bourdell said, raising his glass. "I gotta say, I'd hate it.

Beach and sunshine—that's a recipe for boredom and sunburn." He clamped the cigar between his teeth and fanned the air with his hand. "I'm happy that you're happy, though."

Byrd appreciated her companion dropping the subject and not probing for details. Meanwhile, Bourdell's eyes followed a passing yacht with a pair of bikini-clad women on the deck.

"Really, you'd hate it? Could'a fooled me," Byrd said, choking back a laugh. "You already look a touch overheated, but I wouldn't say bored."

"Maybe I spoke a little too quickly there," Bourdell said, tearing his eyes away with slow reluctance and looking at Byrd. "Seriously, though, after what we went through..."

Byrd looked down into her glass and swirled the bourbon. "Yeah. No need to go back over that."

"I know. But you never found out the full story. After we were discharged, I did some investigating. I tried to tell you, but you'd gone underground."

"I needed some space," Byrd said, unable to look away from the liquid in the glass as the memories of that horrific day spooled back through her mind's eye.

"I get that, I really do. But you should know the truth," Bourdell said.

"What truth?" Byrd sat forward.

"Halloran delayed on purpose. The sandstorm was just an excuse to wait."

"Why would he need an excuse?" Byrd asked.

"It turned out the journalist and hostage, Johansson, had a story on Halloran," Bourdell explained. "It seems losing an American to the Taliban wouldn't have been such a tragedy for the major."

Byrd closed her eyes, hung her head, and took a

moment to breathe. She then took a long drink, allowing the spark of the bourbon to bring her back to the present.

"What was the story?" she asked quietly.

"The journalist was working in a rural village near Kandahar, and Halloran ended up there after a malfunction with an aircraft brought him down for an unplanned landing. After a meeting with elders who apparently did not like the intrusion, Halloran apparently lost his mind...with a weapon in hand." Bourdell sighed, then added. "The past needed burying."

Byrd stayed silent for a moment while Bourdell glugged a heavy measure of liquor into both glasses.

"That incident in the village cost us our careers, and we never even knew about it," she said finally.

"No," Bourdell said firmly, turning to look at Byrd while shielding his eyes with his rough hand. "Halloran cost us our careers. And a damn fine Apache. We should have had support and live intel on that mission."

"I dunno. Maybe my missed shot cost us our careers," Bird said, choosing not to mention Bourdell's momentarily unsteady piloting.

"Don't talk that way," Bourdell said. "I mean it. You know that's not true. And we saved Johansson's life, albeit not very efficiently."

Narrowing her eyes, Byrd looked out across the sea as she thought back to the long, bloodied trek from the Apache crash site back to base, only to be received with derision by her supposed comrades. Tropical birds called from the trees around her, bringing her back to the present.

"This is my paradise," she said quietly. "My new home. My new life. If this place can't save me and take away the memories, nothing can."

Bourdell nodded slowly. When he spoke, his voice was

harder and more serious than Byrd had heard in a long time. "You may be right. Bourbon may be a lot cheaper than building this place, but it only helps a little."

Byrd turned to her old friend and smiled. "Maybe we should stop relying on the booze so much, then. Just as soon as this bottle's finished."

"Just promise me one thing," Bourdell said, smiling in return. "Don't hate yourself, or the Air Force."

"I don't hate the Air Force…"

"Byrd. Come on."

"It's okay. I'm okay. I just need a little alone time. A few weeks. Months. Years."

"Well, I'm the only one here, and I'll be leaving soon," Bourdell said, scanning the sea remorsefully as the yacht with its female cargo slid out of view. "Liquor store owners in Alabama will be wondering where I've gone. You'll have plenty of alone time with your planes between sessions with recruits."

"You're right. You can stay a while longer. We can hide from the world togeth—"

The shrill sound of a ringing phone cut through the whispering waves. "Who in the name of the Almighty—this ain't office hours," Byrd said, turning to look at the hangar where she knew the phone was.

Thrusting herself up from her chair, Byrd stomped into the hangar. Her bootsteps slapped against the hard floor as she trudged into the gloom. She snatched up the phone.

"What is it?"

"Are you the proprietor of the island?" The voice was deep and rich. *Sounds like he comes from money*, Byrd thought.

Byrd pondered for a moment. "The proprietor. What does that even mean?"

"Are you the proprietor of the island?" the man repeated.

"I do not own the island," Byrd said flatly. "I own the only property on the island."

"Would you be willing to sell said property?"

"I only just built the damn place!"

"You would be paid well," the caller purred, his voice growing even smoother at the mention of money.

"I know. That's what usually happens when you sell a property. But I don't want to. Good day now."

"Enjoy paradise while you can..." the man said, his tone suddenly darkening.

Byrd slammed the receiver down, the sound of metal-on-metal echoing around the hangar.

"Everything okay?" Bourdell asked when Byrd emerged.

"Yeah," she replied, accepting a new glass of bourbon. "But clearly, it's impossible to be left in peace on this island. Who knew paradise was such a damn hassle."

Bourdell smiled, but Byrd did not return it. The ominous tone of the caller's last utterance weighed heavy in her guts.

# 9

**Mexican desert, north of Cabo San Lucas.**

The late afternoon sun beamed down on the Mexican desert, casting angular shadows from the tangled metal sculptures that jutted from the earth like car wrecks. As Sallas walked across the rough sand of his remote compound, he glanced at the sculptures, shaped by wannabe artists who had looped the metal into impossible shapes. The air shimmered, distorted by the heat, making the landscape seem alive, gyrating like the movement of bodies at a drug-fueled rave.

Sallas turned and looked at a group of his faithful disciples roaming the compound, their skin streaked with bold swirls of red, orange, and black paint. Some wore robes patched together from mismatched fabrics; others moved freely, their bodies almost bare save for the paint. In a far corner of the compound, five of his followers sat cross-legged in a circle, swaying in unison and chanting in low voices.

Nearby, a young woman with unbrushed blonde hair sat

on the ground, stacking small stones in careful towers, her lips moving in inaudible prayer or chant. The strap of a white singlet, now dirty, fell from her tanned shoulder, leaving it exposed. Silently, Sallas wondered what the best use for her might be.

He nodded with satisfaction at how healthy, slim, and full of vitality his faithful followers all looked. Glancing down at his own tanned torso, the thin hairs glistening, he felt even more satisfied. He breathed deeply and eyed the contours of his muscles.

Smiling to himself, he watched as their new and involuntary recruit—the redhead they had obtained from the Green Frog Cafe—stumbled forward. Having been given more drugs to keep her sedated, there was no risk of her escaping. She took a step and almost tripped over her own feet. The Ogre grabbed her, yanking her back up again. Sallas stepped in to help, and the two men led her away from the dusty main compound and down a path lined with potted plants and other greenery.

"In there," Sallas said, pointing at a small wooden structure, its exterior stubbled by sand and faded almost gray by the sun. "Let's show her to my Gloriette," he added with a wry smile.

The Ogre shoved the door open and led the girl inside. Sallas followed them, his nostrils immediately picking up on the medicinal scent hanging in the air. He took a seat in a dusty armchair, its soft upholstery erroneous amid the sand and dirt. He crossed his legs, then brushed a few grains of sand from his white linen shorts. Catching a glimpse of his reflection in a smeared window, he noted how long his dark, curly hair was getting. Down past his shoulders. He briefly formed it into a bun with his hands, flexing his biceps at the same time.

The Ogre shoved the girl into another, equally tatty chair opposite Sallas's. Sallas nodded at the big man, indicating that he wished to be alone with the new recruit. The Ogre nodded and lumbered back out the door, where Sallas knew his goon would wait until he was next summoned. That was the good thing with men like The Ogre; as long as their basic needs were met, they never felt the need to argue.

"What's your name?" Sallas said, looking at the girl now slumped in the chair opposite him.

She gurgled something, her head lolling forward like a teenager reticent to get up in the morning.

Sallas rose to his feet and dug a cold bottle of water from a cooler box by the door. He snapped the bottle open, sending droplets of water flying through the humid air. He crossed back to the girl, tilted her head back gently, and poured a stream of liquid into her mouth. After waiting for her to swallow, he poured in some more. When she'd consumed almost half the bottle, he returned to his seat.

"What's your name?" he asked again, leaning forward to catch her eyeline.

"What... where am I?" she said, blinking several times and looking around the small wooden structure, her eyes landing on a pile of plants and dried roots stuffed onto a shelf along the wall.

"The answers will come soon. First, tell me your name."

"It's Lucy," she said, her voice croaky. "I'm Lucy. Wait, I remember. The Green Frog Cafe." She jerked upwards as though an electric current had just passed through her body. Her hands dropped to the arms of the chair, and she made to push herself up, then glanced at the door. Clearly remembering the man mountain waiting just outside, she settled into a suspicious silence.

Sallas rested his elbows lightly on his knees. Noting her

average looks and physique, he immediately marked her as a target for experimentation. She would be no use as a breeder.

"Lucy," he said calmly. The girl's head snapped toward him, her eyes now searching his face with a strange kind of recognition. "You are about to become part of something extraordinary. I can't promise that there won't be pain, but it will be worth it. You have been selected, and you are one of the lucky ones."

Lucy sat rigid. Now fully conscious, she had fury in her eyes.

"What are we doing here?" Lucy said, looking down at the tatty armchair. "This is the worst therapy session *ever*." She folded her arms and lifted her chin as though Sallas was beneath her.

Sallas smiled. The phrase and accent told him much about his new recruit. She was from New England, probably. She had the inner confidence that came from being raised by a lovely family. She was clearly well-educated but probably not very rich.

"It's funny you mention therapy," Sallas said, raising an eyebrow. "Hours of talking, then at the end of it, they give you drugs to swallow. Drugs that are much more powerful than talking." Sallas held her gaze and was impressed to see that she didn't flinch. Perhaps she was more confident than he had expected. "Humanity is at a tipping point," he continued, taking on the tone of one of the aforementioned therapists. "Our bodies are failing us, poisoned by our own greed. The toxins we've poured into the earth and into ourselves are killing us all. But there is hope. I know of an ancient plant, long believed to be mythical, with properties unlike anything you can imagine. It can heal, restore, enhance. It's more powerful than any medicine, any food, any miracle cure humanity has ever known."

Lucy shifted in her chair, her gaze so narrow that her eyes were almost hidden.

"Not impressed?" Sallas said.

"You're talking about humanity as if you care about it," Lucy said. "But as far as I can remember, you've *kidnapped* me. Did I ask to be here? Did I get a choice?"

"The path to salvation is paved with sacrifices," Sallas said, a smile creeping across his lips. "With me as your mentor, you'll come to understand this soon enough."

"What kind of sacrifices?" Lucy asked quietly.

"Most possessions are not needed here. They can be sacrificed. *Other* sacrifices too."

Lucy looked as though she were about to say something, then clamped her jaw shut. She tapped at the pockets of her shorts.

"You'll get your stuff back. Eventually. Probably," Sallas added.

"You... you rifled through my pockets like some kind of common criminal. But you talk like you're a rich kid gone wrong." Lucy looked hard at Sallas, as though seeing him for the first time.

"Wait a second," she said, leaning back in her chair. "I've seen you somewhere before."

"Unlikely," Sallas replied, trying to hide any frustration at the conversation's direction. "You think you know me, do you?"

"Yes, you come from one of those rich and influential families. Your brother, he's the really famous, successful one."

Sallas dug his fingernails into the upholstery.

"He's successful. *Really* successful," Lucy added. If she

was trying to annoy Sallas, it was working. Her gaze swept the room, lingering on the insect-ravaged furniture and worm-ridden walls. "I'd say he's more successful than you, by the look of this place."

"Go on," Sallas said, projecting serenity. "Tell me what you think you know."

"I read about you and your family in *Good Living*. You have a mansion on Herring Island, near the Cayman Islands."

"Wrong. It's Herd Island," Sallas spat back, driving a finger into the arm of the chair. "The only property on the island. I told the magazine it was Herring Island to, well, throw them a red herring. But I'm happy to correct you. Maybe you can figure out why."

Lucy said nothing, clearly sensing that she had rattled her captor.

Sallas took a long, slow breath.

"It doesn't matter what you think you know," he said, letting a few seconds pass to show his obvious superiority. "Soon, you won't be able to think at all. Meanwhile, I'll have the ear of every powerful person in America. I'll be a national treasure."

"And how exactly am I supposed to help you with that?" Lucy said, the final word catching in her throat.

Sallas could hear the confidence in her voice melting away, no matter how hard she tried to hide it. He raised his right hand and clicked his fingers. The door creaked open, and The Ogre stomped inside, his massive frame filling the small room.

"Show our new guest to her room," Sallas said, looking from the giant man to his new recruit. "And make sure she's fully settled in."

The Ogre stepped toward Lucy, ready to lift her from the chair.

"Wait!" Lucy shouted, her eyes wide with panic. "You didn't answer me. I demand to know what you want from me. What am I here for?"

Sallas grinned, reveling in the fear that now oozed from his captive, especially after her brief burst of bravery. He inhaled slowly as though the fear came with its own unique scent. He nodded once. The Ogre leaned in and grabbed Lucy by the shoulders.

"No!" Lucy cried as the brute hauled her from her seat and dragged her out of the room.

Sallas gave a casual wave as her protests turned to screams. The door slammed, and her pleas became muffled.

Sallas waited until the noise of the woman's torment faded to nothing, then reached into his pocket and pulled out a small, soft object resting inside a protective plastic bag. He caressed the surface of the thing, showing a tender affection that wasn't usually part of his DNA.

"What does it mean?" he whispered, looking once again at the red, orange, and blue pictographs drawn on the brown parchment. "It's just a damn mess. Makes no sense to me, but I'm sure I know someone who can help..."

## 10

**Isla de la Vida Eterna, Caribbean Sea.**

"Out," the man growled, keeping the gun pressed against Hutchins' skull. The intruder reached forward with his other hand and yanked the keys from the ignition. The engine died, leaving only the tick of cooling metal and the distant chorus of jungle insects.

"Listen, you've got the wrong—" Hutchins started, but a massive hand clamped around his shoulder, fingers digging into his flesh.

The man swung open the rear door and then rounded on Hutchins.

Hutchins looked frantically around the interior of the Land Rover, searching for something, anything that might offer options.

As though sensing his prisoner's intentions, the man swung open the driver's door and dragged Hutchins out with terrifying strength. Hutchins winced as his hip slammed to the ground, sending a jolt of pain through his body. The brute dragged Hutchins away from the Land

Rover like roadkill.

After what felt like a mile, but was probably no more than thirty feet, the thug picked Hutchins up and slammed him up against a tree trunk. Hutchins gasped as the impact knocked all the wind from his lungs.

"What do you want with—" Hutchins stuttered, his vision swimming from the impact.

Headlights swept through the jungle behind them, cutting white beams through the darkness. For a moment, they illuminated his captor's face—the same brutal features Hutchins had seen when the man crushed Wall's throat. The giant's eyes reflected the light but were distant and lifeless, devoid of humanity.

The approaching vehicle rounded the corner—a Toyota Hilux, its mud-splattered sides marking it as a local vehicle. These trucks were the workhorses of every remote region Hutchins had ever visited, perfect for the kind of people who wanted to operate far from civilization.

The thug barked something to the driver, but Hutchins could barely focus on the words. His head throbbed, every muscle screaming from his desperate charge through the jungle. Before he could gather his thoughts, the giant's hand clamped around his neck again, dragging him toward the Hilux.

"Wait... no..." Hutchins gasped as the brute yanked down the tailgate with his free hand. The metal clanged against its chains.

"In," the giant ordered, lifting Hutchins as if he weighed nothing. The young archaeologist scrambled into the truck bed, acutely aware of how few options he had left. The tailgate slammed shut behind him, and his captor indicated that Hutchins should sit with his back against the cab.

The thug produced a length of rope from a pile of stuff

in the flatbed and yanked Hutchins' arms up behind him. The giant's fingers dug into Hutchins' wrists as he bound them to the metal frame at the back of the cab.

"You make a noise, I shoot," the brute said when his work was done. "You move, I shoot. Understand?"

Hutchins nodded frantically, the movement sending a fresh wave of pain through his battered body. His captor grabbed one corner of a filthy tarpaulin and dragged it over Hutchins. He secured it at the corners, then climbed into the cab, leaving Hutchins with the scent of damp soil and mold.

The engine growled, and the truck bounced forward. It rounded a corner and accelerated, sending Hutchins swaying painfully against his bonds. Through gaps in the covering, he caught fleeting glimpses of the jungle canopy, then open sky, then jungle again. They were taking a route he didn't recognize—no longer on any marked road.

The truck's suspension groaned as they hit a particularly deep rut, pulling at Hutchins' bonds and sending waves of agony through his shoulders. For a moment, he wondered whether the driver was being purposefully erratic just to cause him pain and discomfort.

Minutes stretched into what felt like hours. The temperature under the tarp rose to suffocating levels, and the exhaust fumes made his head swim. To take his mind off the pain and the growing nausea, Hutchins tried to work out where they were going. Roughly north, probably, based on the shape of the island.

He caught a glimpse of the sky now filled with stars. The sun had set at some point during his ordeal, although Hutchins hadn't noticed. He thought back to the spellbinding sunsets he and Wall had witnessed since first arriving on the island.

The young academic closed his eyes and tried to focus. He once again pictured Wall, held by the throat, telling him to run with what could have been his last breath. He realized he didn't know if the professor was dead or alive, but the fact that he wasn't also in the truck didn't bode well.

Wall had been kind and patient ever since Hutchins had joined his team after graduating. The appointment had been a dream job for the young Hans Hutchins. A memory of the day he told his parents he was going to Mexico on a dig with one of the world's most renowned professors spooled through his mind. His mom's face lit up when he mentioned Mexico, her eyes sparkling with pride as she handed him a nutritious packed lunch to start his journey off well. He shook his head vigorously, casting off memories that were of no use to him right now.

The truck hit a rut and bounced hard, lifting Hutchins from the metal and then slamming him down again. Fireworks of pain whizzed and popped through his back. The driver made a turn, and the truck clattered down another dirt track.

Hutchins's stomach bounced like salt in a shaker. They turned a corner and then slowed. The truck chugged, crunching forward a few more feet, and then squealed to a stop. The engine died, and the doors swung open. A moment later, the tarpaulin was unceremoniously yanked from him.

Without a word, the man-mountain tugged on the rope securing Hutchins to the flatbed. The knots, now slick with blood from his raw wrists, gave way with a single brutal tug. Before Hutchins could even attempt to restore circulation to his hands, the giant seized him by his shirt collar and hauled him over the side of the truck like a sack of grain.

He hit the ground hard, face-first into thick mud. His chin bounced off something solid beneath the muck—a rock or root—setting his teeth clacking together painfully. The impact knocked out what little air remained in his lungs, sending a spray of wet earth into his mouth and nose.

"Up," the thug spat, massive fingers digging into Hutchins' bicep as he yanked him vertical. The archaeologist's legs, senselessly numb from the ride, buckled beneath him. The world tilted and spun as Hutchins' circulation struggled to adapt to the sudden change in position.

The brute didn't wait for Hutchins to find his feet. He dragged him forward, each stumbling step sending fresh waves of pain through the young academic's body as feeling returned to his limbs.

After a few steps, Hutchins's vision stopped swaying, and he saw that they were heading toward a squat concrete structure. It looked like some kind of bunker or storage facility. As they got closer, the structure seemed more ominous. It had only tiny windows and just one heavy metal door.

The big man yanked open the door, which groaned on rusted hinges. The brute shoved Hutchins through the doorway, sending him stumbling into darkness. His hands, still tingling from the rope burns, shot out instinctively to break his fall. They found cold, dusty concrete.

A light flickered to life overhead—a single bare bulb swaying gently, casting shifting shadows across the barren room.

One man shoved Hutchins against the wall while the other threaded a length of thick twine through an iron hook set into the concrete. They bound his hands behind him, the twine already digging into his raw wrists. The larger man gave the bonds one final yank, testing their strength.

Without a word, the men turned and marched out of the room. The door squealed shut, followed by the heavy clunk of a bolt sliding home. As fear ran through Hutchins' body like a gulp of antifreeze, the one light bulb fizzled out.

# 11

**Isla de la Fortuna, Caribbean Sea. The following day.**

Sierra Byrd's stomach felt as if the propeller on an old Supermarine Spitfire was whirring away inside of her.

"These people paid for your help," she reminded herself, picturing the faces of her new recruits while hoping the soothing words would ease her frustration. She glanced up at the Skytrain, its silver skin shining in a bar of light beaming through the hangar door. Maintaining a C-47 Skytrain wasn't cheap. Nor was the Barton 1792 bourbon she loved to drink to celebrate each long, sweat-streaked, oil-stained day. But right now, she had customers, so her time with her loved one would have to wait.

Using the aluminum fuselage as a mirror, she ran her fingers through her bouffant locks and raised the zipper on the flight suit right to the top. "Don't wanna give any red-blooded males in the class the wrong idea," she said to herself.

With a pang of regret, she turned away from the noble C-47 and paced out of the hangar.

"Get the thing done; it's a means to an end," Byrd quietly reminded herself, eyeing the three people assembled on the tarmac. Fortifying herself with a backward glance at the Skytrain, she crossed the tarmac and strode into the center of the group.

"Good morning," she announced, clapping her hands together and putting all her effort into forced enthusiasm. She'd flown missions that pushed the limits of both pilot and aircraft, logged thousands of combat hours in the Air Force's most dangerous operations, yet somehow, forcing out these two cheerful words felt more challenging.

"If y'all don't know who I am," Byrd continued, "then I reckon you best pack up and get on out of here."

An awkward laugh rippled from two of the three. The third stood motionless as though he were there in body but not in spirit.

"But, just in case you've forgotten, I'm Nora Byrd. But only my mama and the doctor call me Nora, and I ain't seen either in a dog's age. It's Sierra Byrd to you, and that's all you need to know. Twenty years in the Air Force, fifteen in combat roles. Three tours in Afghanistan, two in Iraq, and a handful of operations I still can't talk about." She paced in front of the group, sizing them up. "Point is, I've trained pilots in conditions that'd make most of y'all quit before sundown. I've brought aircraft home that had no business still flying. So when I tell you something about aviation, you can take it as gospel."

She shifted her gaze from one person to the next. "But enough about me. I want to know a bit about you. Don't be shy; if you're scared to introduce yourself, you've got no business battling gravity in one of these metal birds. You first." Byrd pointed at a tall, square-shouldered man with tanned, healthy skin. He had the appearance of an insurance salesman who relied on his looks over his product knowledge. She hated to admit that he suited his silvery gray hair perfectly.

"Name's Tom, originally from Weston, Massachusetts," he said, his deep and gravelly voice matching his polished appearance. "My background's on Wall Street, but I want to get out of the corporate world and into the skies. I have some flying experience as a hobbyist, and now I want to learn from the best." His eyes sharpened as he flashed Byrd an intelligent smile. Byrd found herself reaching for the zipper on her flight suit with the intention of pulling it down slightly. She stopped herself.

"Nice to meet ya, Tom," Byrd said, turning her gaze on the woman beside him.

"Me? I'm Candi, born and raised in Long Beach, California," said the blonde, grinning in a way that said, *The world was made for me.* "I love sun, sky, sand, surf. Anything that gets my juices flowing!"

Byrd raised an eyebrow. "Well, I can't speak for your juices, but I can promise you you'll learn how to fly. Do you have any experience?"

"Very little, ma'am. Just what my dad showed me once or twice. Watercraft is more my thing." Candi pointed at the Jet Ski bobbing alongside the small pier. "Arrived here by Jet Ski bright and early!"

"Well, at least we know you're not afraid of a little adrenaline. Welcome to flight school." Byrd allowed herself a smile.

"And you?" Byrd said, pointing at a young man who was so unmuscular that he looked as if his drooping body was melting in the heat. His shoulders slanted diagonally downwards like ski slopes, and his baggy clothes were seemingly made for somebody else.

"I'm... I'm Zane," the man said, twiddling a piercing in his left ear filled with a penny-sized piece of cork. Watching the movement made Byrd feel a little bit sick and angry all at the same time. "I come from, well, kinda everywhere and nowhere. But I'm sure you don't care about that."

"If I didn't want you to introduce yourself, I would not have asked you to introduce yourself," Byrd said coldly.

"Okay," Zane said bluntly. "Let's say I'm from Greenwood, Indiana. And I came here to get out of there."

Byrd paused for a moment, allowing the silence to admonish Zane for his attitude. She made a mental note to keep a close eye on this guy. Finally, she said, "Okay, that's the hard bit done." She eyed the students one after another, letting each gaze last a moment longer than was comfortable—the lack of comfort was purely on the part of the students.

"Now we've got the simple task of turning a lump of metal into a well-oiled machine that'll dance through the air like it was born there. You'll learn every system, every gauge, every warning light. You'll understand air pressure, wind vectors, and engine torque like they're the pulse in your own body. The pre-flight checklist will become as natural as breathing."

Byrd paced to one side of the group and then spun on her heel.

"It won't be easy. Flying isn't just pulling back on a stick and hoping for the best. The hard work starts now. Who's ready to get to it?"

"Absolutely," Tom said, his smile bright enough to persuade someone to get their shoelaces insured. Byrd smiled back, winked at him, then silently reminded herself to stop winking at people.

"Ready, ma'am!" Candi announced in her rasping, well-bred voice, the kind that spoke of private schools and debutante balls.

Byrd turned to Zane, who seemed fascinated by his own shoes, scuffing patterns in the dust.

"And you, young man? Are you ready to get your wings?" Byrd eyed the kid, a troubling suspicion working in her gut.

"Sure." Zane shrugged. "Nothin' else to do around here." He looked up but still failed to meet Byrd's gaze, instead focusing somewhere past her shoulder toward the horizon. His eyelids drooped, matching his slouched shoulders and general air of disinterest.

Recognition hit Byrd, bringing with it an all-out rage. She'd seen eyes glaze like that before and had grounded pilots for far less. The thought of this rich kid thinking he could stumble into her cockpit while high made her blood boil.

"Are you stoned?" Byrd snapped, her voice as violent as a viper.

"What? No, I—" Zane started, finally making eye contact.

"Don't you dare lie to me," Byrd cut him off. She looked at him with the precision of a radar lock, her targeting system already engaged. "I've flown combat missions where one mistake meant death. "I've carried wounded soldiers while taking anti-aircraft fire. I've seen good pilots—better men than you'll ever be—die because someone's reflexes were a split second too slow."

She sidled up to the man until they were toe to toe. She inhaled deeply and smelled the tell-tale odor on his breath. "And you have the nerve to show up to my flight school high. Pack your stuff; you're going home."

"Wha—?" The final part of the word tumbled away

down Zane's tongue as it lay lifeless at the bottom of his mouth.

"Flippancy and flying are a bad mix. Marijuana and flying are a very bad mix."

"If I damage anything, I'll pay for it." Zane shrugged.

"I'm damn sure you ain't got a job, so you mean your parents will pay for it?"

"Same difference," Zane said.

"This is not the military," Byrd said, her tone icy. "But military discipline is required to keep everyone safe. You are dismissed."

Zane raised his hands in protest.

"Call the office in the States about getting your money back," Byrd added unemotionally. "Minus what I'm going to call a wasting-my-damn-time-fee."

"But…I only just got here."

"And that's my problem because?"

Zane's top lip curled. Then, clearly sensing an argument would get him nowhere, he turned on his heels and sloped off.

Byrd backstepped and eyed the two remaining would-be pilots. She noticed that Candi was standing to attention with her chin in the air and her arms stiff by her sides. Byrd couldn't help but smile.

"You don't need to be afraid of me," Byrd said gently. "Just be polite, focus, and don't put corks in your ears. Then, we'll be the best of buddies."

Tom chuckled with more amusement than the comment really deserved.

"You may be disappointed to learn that we won't be in the air today," Byrd continued. "The first day is about learning to respect your aircraft. Best way to learn respect for your plane? Clean it."

## 12

**Isla de la Vida Eterna, Caribbean Sea.**

Movement outside his makeshift prison cell jolted Hutchins awake. He hadn't slept—he'd crashed into unconsciousness, his body surrendering to the harrowing events of the past few hours. He bolted upright, his bound wrists screaming at the movement, and squinted into the gloom. The one tiny window was covered over with what seemed to be cardboard, and only a slim halo of light appeared at the edges of the frame.

The bolt on the door slid open with a metallic clang, followed by the piercing shriek of rusted hinges. A flashlight beam sliced through the doorway, the light washing over stained concrete walls and illuminating the cluster of rotting crates huddled in the corner. The harsh light locked onto Hutchins' face, blinding him. He jerked his hands up instinctively, forgetting his restraints, and fire tore through his raw, chafed wrists.

"*Despiértate, cabrón.* Time to talk." The Spanish-accented voice cut through the darkness, gravel-rough and raspy, probably from decades of cheap cigarettes. A silhouette materialized in the doorway, more overweight than muscular. Not so overweight to make the thug slow and tired, though, just enough to put some power behind his blows.

The man stepped inside, giving Hutchins a better look at him. The brute grinned, showing gaps between his yellowed teeth, like the bars in a prison window. He wore farmworkers' overalls stained with a whole variety of substances, and his thick, square head was topped with a military-style crew cut. The man's deep-set eyes studied Hutchins with the cold calculation of a pitiless predator sizing up wounded prey.

Hutchins pushed himself back against the wall, hoping to increase the distance between himself and the newcomer, but achieved nothing more than another stabbing pain from his wrists.

The man dragged a small wooden stool across the room and dropped it a few feet from Hutchins. He placed the flashlight on the floor, its beam casting across the dank room, and sat on the stool. He grinned, showing even more monolithic teeth, and his eyes glinted in a way that made Hutchins' skin tingle with fear.

"I am your friend," the man said, resting his hands on his knees. His face remained contorted, unnaturally, and he bared his Stonehenge smile again.

"Don't play games with me," Hutchins said, the final syllable a high-pitched squeak as the word extinguished itself in his throat.

"I play no games. I am your friend," the man said.

"I've seen this. Good cop, bad cop," Hutchins said, thinking of cop shows he'd grown up watching in his parents' living room. Thoughts of his previously comfortable life brought a ball to his throat. He tensed, determined not to sob in front of his grinning captor.

"Where is bad cop?" The newcomer held out open palms, looked around the room, and pushed up his bottom lip. Despite his broken English, he appeared to be aware of the game. "Only me."

"Then why am I tied to this wall?" Hutchins asked, shaking his wrists. "You wanna act nice, untie me."

"What?" The man's mouth hung open as he apparently tried to figure out what the scrawny kid in front of him was talking about.

Inhaling, Hutchins caught the unmistakable stench of Tequila on his captor's breath. Sensing a tiny, almost microscopic advantage, Hutchins realized that this guy had knocked back several drinks in the last hour. A slow, calculating smile tugged at the corner of his mouth as a flicker of hope emerged.

"Say, if you're the good guy, why don't you get us a drink?" Hutchins said as casually as he could. "Everyone gets along better after a little drink."

"Water?" the brute replied, his bushy eyebrows bunching together.

"Yuck, no!" Hutchins spat, attempting to sound amused. "What sort of friends share a drink of water. You like Tequila, don't you?"

The Stonehenge smile returned to the brute's face.

"Sure, let's drink!" The man's face lit up with sudden enthusiasm. He lurched to his feet, stumbling slightly as he found his balance, then snatched up the flashlight. The beam swung wildly across the cell, momentarily blinding Hutchins again. "Don't move, amigo. I bring the good stuff, eh?"

The guard staggered outside, then closed and secured the door, returning Hutchins to the darkness of his prison, which was dingy despite the teasing sliver of sunlight at the edges of the window.

*If I can get even one hand free*, Hutchins thought as he listened to the man's uneven footsteps thudding away, *at least it gives me options. Though not many.*

Once again, the desperation of his situation crashed over him in waves. Here he was, wrists bound and bleeding, promising to take shots with the same man who had helped kidnap him. But an inebriated captor who had lost some of his faculties to Tequila might just be easier to take on.

Hutchins berated himself for the glimmer of hope as he heard the footsteps returning. The bolt clanged back, and the door once again screeched open. The brute staggered back into the room with a bottle of Tequila in one hand and two filthy, clouded glasses in the other. He returned to his stool, filled one glass, and then the other. He placed one glass on the floor in front of Hutchins and lifted the other to his lips.

"My hands," Hutchins said, looking from the drink to his captor and back again. "Unless you plan on pouring liquor into my mouth for me?" The brute moved forward, then hesitated, clearly thinking through his next course of action. Reaching a decision with the speed of a 1980s computer, he lunged forward and untied just one of Hutchins' bonds, leaving one hand free for drinking and one as a reminder of captivity.

Hutchins nodded thanks, then reached down and grabbed the glass. He lifted it to his lips, trying not to think about how filthy the glass was, or how the last time he'd drunk Tequila, he'd seen it again about twenty minutes later. He thought about trying to discard the liquor somehow, but with his captor watching his every move, that would be impossible. He prepared himself and then downed the glass. The liquid slithered down his throat like molten metal.

"Nice, *si?*" the man said, sitting on the small stool at an angle like a capsizing ship in a storm.

"Yes, thank you," Hutchins said, placing the glass back on the floor. "What do you want with me?" he added, trying his luck with getting some answers from a man whose inhibitions had been lowered by grog.

"Don't worry," the brute said, waggling his finger. "You not going to die."

"That's good to know, I suppose," Hutchins said, not reassured.

"Yes. Good. We... we need you," the brute stuttered.

"For what?"

"To find the..." he paused, clearly searching for the word. "The Sunstone. We need you to find the Sunstone."

The Tequila swished around in Hutchins' guts, turning from warmth into nausea.

"The what?" Hutchins asked, trying his best to look confused.

"You know what I talk about. Don't play dumb, eh? Is no good." The thug waggled his finger, the gesture more suited to an angry mother than a battle-hardened gangster. "You know more than me, *comprende?* I am only hired..." The captor stopped talking mid-sentence as though he'd completely forgotten what he was saying.

"Hired to take care of people?" Hutchins said.

"Yes, of course." The big man shrugged, smiling. "I take care of people who are useful." The smile then melted away, and the eyes hardened. He picked up the bottle and filled the glasses once again.

"Sunstone is the path to eternal life," the big man said, thrusting the refilled glass toward Hutchins. "It's the key...

the key to..." Clearly struggling to find the words, he waved both hands along the length of his chest as if removing imaginary crumbs.

*...to the plant of the gods*, Hutchins thought, although he wasn't going to let on that he knew anything about that.

The thug huffed out a few wheezing breaths and then continued. "You follow what is written on the Sunstone and live forever."

*First, it's not eternal life. It's long life*, Hutchins thought, silently correcting his captor. *The promise of eternal life has been sold like snake oil for millennia.*

The brute swallowed down the shot, exhaled what was probably mostly alcohol vapor, then wiped his mouth before saying, "First, there will be great pain. Next, there will be great joy. Finally, there will be eternal life. That is what The Mentor says."

"The Mentor?" Hutchins said.

"The leader. Sallas. Rich. Powerful."

"Who is Sallas?"

"A man you should try to please. People shouldn't come to this island. It holds treasures that only Sallas should possess. Those who get too close are wiped out. Or worse..."

Behind closed lips, Hutchins gritted his teeth in anger. "He would never have found those treasures without—"

"You work for him now," the thug interrupted. "We all do."

"No," Hutchins said with as much authority as he could muster. "I work for the University of—" The big man shot forward and seized Hutchins by the collar, the force cutting his sentence in half and knocking him off balance. Hutchins fell sideways, only saved from smashing into the floor by his bound wrist.

The brute dragged him upright, shoving him hard

against the wall. With his other hand, the criminal grabbed the Tequila bottle and swung it through the air, breaking it on the wall. He shoved the jagged edge right up to Hutchins' cheek.

Hutchins froze, every muscle locked as he looked into the bloodshot eyes of the man he thought would end his life. Tendons on the tattooed neck protruded, and the red eyes were wide with booze-fueled rage.

"I the good cop, and bad cop," the brute snarled. "I be anything, any time I want. Because I am in control."

Shaking, Hutchins nodded his understanding. The thug pushed him hard again, and Hutchins heard his ribs crunch like they had been cracked. Now wild with rage, the brute slammed Hutchins' head three times against the wall, leaving his brain pounding.

"Tomorrow," the criminal said, jabbing a finger into Hutchins' stomach, "you feel great pain. No long life for you."

The thug stood tall, his figure filling the room. He swayed left and right, clearly drunk. But his eyes told Hutchins there was still meanness inside of him that had to be released before he could sleep off the booze.

As Hutchins watched the man draw back his fist, he felt powerless. Frozen. He had barely begun to raise his hands to protect his face when the blow landed with a savage crunch, and darkness fell over him.

## 13

**Isla de la Fortuna, Caribbean Sea.**

"You're okay, baby. I'll fix you," Sierra Byrd told her Skytrain soothingly as long rays of evening sunlight slid into her hangar, bathing her beloved plane in angelic light. Her oily fingertips caressed the exposed tip of the aging spark plugs. "You're a demanding girl, but worth every cent."

Byrd balanced on the maintenance stand, gripping the plug with the wrench. The thing had been firing out of sequence for the last two flights, causing the big radial engine to run rough above two thousand RPM. She'd noticed the slight miss—a subtle shimmy in the engine's normal rhythm that most pilots might have missed. But to Byrd, the sound of those Twin Wasps was better than anything Mozart, Bach, or even—if today's kids could be believed—Taylor Swizz ever produced. She was pretty sure that was the young singer's name...

Byrd applied pressure to the wrench, but the plug refused to budge. She looked up at the fourteen-cylinder radial engine and decided right then and there that she needed to take each plug out and reset it as soon as possible. Nothing was too much for her girl.

Byrd adjusted her grip on the wrench and focused on her unlikely adversary. If the plug sheared off in the cylinder, she'd be looking at hours of careful extraction work, maybe even having to pull the entire head. On a seventy-year-old engine, that kind of operation was about as fun as performing surgery blindfolded.

"You're as old as my favorite records," Byrd said as the song "Whole Lotta Shakin' Going On" popped into her head, and she silently noted how it was a fitting title for the experience of flying in aging planes. "Come on, sweetheart," she whispered, applying steady pressure. "Don't fight me on this." The wrench creaked ominously. A bead of sweat rolled down Byrd's temple despite the cooler evening air. Then, with a sudden crack that made her heart skip, the plug broke free. Byrd let out the breath she'd been holding as she carefully backed it out the rest of the way.

"There's my girl." She wiggled the plug free and inspected the threads with relief. "No wonder you were unhappy." The electrode was completely fouled, caked with carbon deposits that had been causing the misfires. Left unchecked, it could lead to cylinder damage—something these old engines didn't forgive easily.

"Now that's a sight for sore eyes!" The voice boomed across the hangar, making Byrd flinch. The wrench slipped from her fingers, clattering down the maintenance stand and hitting the concrete floor with a gunshot-crack.

"Perfect timing," Byrd muttered through gritted teeth. At least she'd kept hold of the spark plug. "Read the sign," she called back, nodding toward the MAINTENANCE IN PROGRESS - DO NOT DISTURB sign she'd deliberately placed on the hangar door.

"You're extremely lucky to have one of these in your private collection," Tom said, sidestepping the sign and striding into the hangar's cathedral-gloom. He paced up to the Skytrain, his neck bent to take in the full wonder of the vintage craft.

"That's right. I paid a huge amount of money to... have this thing all to myself." Byrd picked up the rag from on top of her toolbox and set about cleaning away some of the detritus from the cylinder head.

"Gooney Bird," Tom stated, apparently having failed to get the hint.

"It's lucky I know all about this aircraft, or I might have thought you were insulting me," Byrd replied.

Still focused on the engine, Byrd saw the reflection of Tom's gleaming smile in the polished metal.

"Known to Americans as the Gooney Bird, but named the Dakota by the Royal Air Force," Tom continued with his stream of geeky knowledge. Byrd hated to admit that she suddenly found herself quite liking it. "Probably based on the acronym DACoTA for the Douglas Aircraft Company Transport Aircraft, rather than the American states."

Byrd spun around, fixing Tom with a glare that could strip paint. "Fine. You know your stuff," she said, hating to admit it.

"Sorry," Tom said, kneeling and picking up the fallen wrench. He passed it back up to Byrd, their eyes locking for a second longer. "I am intruding on your moment with your baby." Tom broke off the stare with a look of what appeared to be genuine regret.

"Big old baby," Byrd said as she smiled weakly.

Tom slowly rotated his shoulders, seemingly about to leave.

"You got kids, Tom? Family?" Byrd found herself saying,

knowing she should at least try to show some interest in her paying customers.

"Had a family once, but I made a mistake. Lost 'em."

"Oh. Sad. You looked under the couch?" She offered another diluted smile. "Sorry."

"No need to apologize. We have to laugh once we get to our age, don't we?"

"Sure do," Byrd said, biting back the urge to point out that his 'our' age comment was a stretch.

"So, how about you, Ms. Byrd? Any kids?"

"This plane right here is my only baby. I think it's borderline child abuse to bring a kid into a world like this. They even have news channels playing in family planning clinics, like people didn't get the message yet."

"Well, if you're giving all your love and affection to this beautiful bird right here, that's a pretty good outlet for it." Tom stroked the fuselage like he was stroking a dog's belly. "So, when do you think she might be airborne?"

"Technically, she's good to go, but there's still a lot of work to do. I want her back just as she was in her prime."

"I suppose, at least in that way, you can control the march of time," Tom said, a sadness passing over his expression.

"Something like that," Byrd said, still working on the spark plug.

"When the time comes, I'd love to co-pilot. It would be an honor, actually."

A scowl took hold of Byrd's face. "I won't be co-piloting with anyone who isn't suitable for it, and my guess is there won't be anyone suitable within a hundred miles of here. I'll train you up, Tom, improve your skills, but only with the right training exercises. I will never take anybody out on a flight they're not ready for."

"How can you really know if someone is ready until they put their skills to the test?" The slight tremble in Tom's cheek muscles gave away the fact that even he wasn't convinced by his own line of inquiry.

"Look, I don't need to justify my decision, but seeing as you're pushing the issue... I made that mistake before. And it was a big mistake. I allowed someone to convince me to get airborne with them, but ultimately, I have to take responsibility for anyone inside a plane that I control." Byrd let out a breath and then wrapped the spark plug in the rag and slipped it inside the toolbox. It was clear that she wouldn't finish this today.

"Who was that? A student?"

"No. Students are not supposed to be ready; that's why they're students. It was in the Air Force. But it doesn't matter. I shouldn't have even brought it up."

"I'm sorry to pry. It's just—"

"It's just the end of this conversation," Byrd said, stepping down from the maintenance stand. "Did you come here for a reason?

"Yes," Tom said, a hint of doubt in his usually confident and polished voice. "I've just seen the forecast, and there's a storm due to roll in overnight. I guess it happens often at the end of a long, hot day here, but I was wondering if it might affect our plans for tomorrow?"

"You lookin' for a day off already, Tom?" Byrd wiped her hands on her flight suit and eyed the man.

"Absolutely not," he said, his eyes twinkling. "Just thought you should know, is all."

"Thanks, Tom. I'll check conditions in the morning and make a decision."

Tom nodded once and then half-turned toward the door.

He froze and then turned back toward Byrd and the Skytrain.

"That really is a thing of beauty," he said, his gaze drifting up to the craft's majestic nose.

"That she is. Do you need anything else?"

"Just... I suppose watching the sunset with a cocktail is out of the question?" Tom said.

"Totally out of the question. Business and pleasure is a cocktail I don't touch," Byrd told him.

"Totally understand," Tom said, flashing that warm smile and heading out of the hangar. "See you in the morning, Captain."

Watching him go, Byrd found herself, for a reason she couldn't quite explain, curling her lips into a smile.

## 14

**Isla de la Fortuna, Caribbean Sea.**

Byrd flung open the door to her room and stepped inside. The space was spartan—bare walls and a metal-framed bed that others might compare to a prison cell. But to Byrd, this dark, minimalist room with its thin mattress offered exactly what she needed for a good night's sleep.

She stripped out of her flight suit and stepped into the shower, letting the warm water pummel her muscles and carry with it the oil and grease of the day.

Dressed in her bathrobe, she paced back into the bedroom and removed her trusted bottle of Barton 1792 bourbon from its shelf. She freed the cork with a pop and glugged a healthy measure into a glass—the sound as satisfying as pouring fuel into an engine.

Byrd brought the liquid to her lips just as the first thunderclap boomed across the sea—the sound sharp like the crack of a circus whip. She looked out the window just in time to see the lightning fizzle through the sky.

"It's going to be a big one," Sierra Byrd said, sitting down on the bed and taking another harsh sip of the spicy, oaky liquor.

She lay back, listening to the sound of the storm and letting any troubles of the day wash away from her. Although she found parts of the flight school operations frustrating, Byrd reminded herself that the students paid incredibly well, and she could take them on as and when she wanted. For a moment, she enjoyed both the warmth of the bourbon and the warm feeling of knowing that things were falling into place. She wondered if contentment might be possible after all. "It's only taken a few decades," she said with a wry smile.

As the bourbon got to work, she cleared her mind and listened to the ravages of the storm. To her, the nearing power of nature represented fate. It was like destiny prowling around the edges of someone's life before coming for them. As the next thunderclap shook the ground, there was a knock at the door. At first, Byrd thought it was just part of the cacophony, but after the thunder rolled away, the sound came again.

"What the...?" she said, shaking herself into focus and scrambling off the bed. "This is way past office hours." She tied her robe more tightly around herself and crossed to the door.

She positioned her foot behind the door—ready to slam it shut if needed—then turned the lock and pulled it open.

"I'm sorry to bother you," Tom said. "It's urgent; something's happened."

Byrd took one look at the man and noticed that his pallor was grayer than before. Rain dripped from his hair and clothes. This was clearly not a social call.

"Two minutes." Byrd shoved the door closed and dressed quickly, her relaxed mood disappearing like the calm day's weather. After quickly dressing in a clean flight suit—one of several she wore on rotation—she grabbed a flashlight, pulled on a waterproof jacket, and resentfully swallowed the last drop of her bourbon.

True to her word, two minutes later, she followed Tom out of the silent accommodation building and into the fury of the tropical storm. It hit her in the face like a slap. The wind howled between the buildings, driving sheets of rain sideways. Palm trees thrashed overhead, their fronds whipping and cracking in the gale.

The lights mounted around the buildings created eerie halos in the downpour, their glow diffused by curtains of rain. Lightning flashed across the sky, turning night to day for split seconds, followed by thunder that vibrated in Byrd's chest. Tom beckoned her toward the shore.

The path to the beach had become a series of growing puddles, warm water already reaching ankle height. Byrd snapped on her flashlight, Tom turned on his too, and the pair swept their beams through the deluge. The rain caught their lights like thousands of falling diamonds, making it hard to see more than a few feet ahead. The ocean's roar grew louder as they approached the beach, waves crashing with Hellfire force against the shore.

"What is it?" Byrd said, shouting over the din. "This had better be a matter of life and death."

"It is," Tom said gravely, wiping rainwater from his face. "Or you're half right, at least."

They emerged onto the beach—the same spot where she and Bourdell had watched the sunset. Now, the peaceful scene had transformed into chaos. The once-gentle surf had become a wall of white water as waves pounded the shoreline. Lightning illuminated mountains of black clouds advancing from the horizon. The beach chairs and umbrellas from her little palapa bar tumbled past and trundled along the beach, while palm trees bent nearly horizontal in the howling wind.

Tom led her across the sand, leaning forward to walk through the cutting gale. Salt spray stung Byrd's face as they made their way closer to the waterline. Through the rain-smeared beam of her flashlight, Byrd spotted what at first looked like a pile of ocean debris—the daily deposits of plastic bottles, fishing nets, and Styrofoam that plagued her little paradise.

But as they drew closer, something about this debris looked wrong. It was too large, too solid. The lightning flashed again, and in that stark moment of illumination, Byrd realized this wasn't the usual collection of sun-bleached trash. Her stomach tightened as Tom's flashlight beam settled on what she now saw as two distinct shapes, half-buried in the wet sand.

Another flash of lightning, closer now, seared the scene into her retinas: two bodies, face-down, their clothes sodden and dark. The waves lapped at them greedily as if trying to drag them back into the wash.

"Damn," Byrd breathed, the words stolen away by the wind. The rain streamed into her eyes as she forced herself to look at the scene. The larger body was clearly male, his broad shoulders unmistakable even in death. One arm lay trapped beneath his body, while the other stretched out as if reaching for help that never came, his fingers dug into the sand in a final, desperate grasp for safety. The smaller body appeared to be female, and the fabric of what looked like a medical gown billowed out around her like a distorted jellyfish. Long hair, possibly blonde under the grime, tangled with seaweed.

"They must've washed up from the island across the

water," Byrd said, nodding to where the neighboring island of Isla de la Vida Eterna was usually visible. She looked at the bodies more closely and noticed that they were both wearing medical gowns. "What the hell is this?" Byrd muttered to herself.

"You're calm for someone looking at two corpses," Tom said, his voice barely audible over the wind.

"Not sure what screaming would solve." Byrd glanced at Tom and noticed he was purposefully looking out to sea.

"What do you think we should do?" he asked.

"One thing's for sure," Byrd said, taking a step toward the bodies. "We can't leave them here. The tide's rising, and they'll be gone by morning." She took another step. "Grab his shoulders. I'll take the feet."

They struggled with the larger body first, their feet slipping in the wet sand as they dragged the waterlogged corpse up the beach. Lightning flashed again, illuminating their grim task.

"Here," Byrd grunted once they'd reached the tree line where the sand met the scrub. They lowered the body as respectfully as they could, but it still hit the ground with a wet thud.

The woman was lighter but somehow worse to move. Her long hair kept tangling around their hands, and the thin medical gown left little to the imagination. They placed her next to the man, just beyond the reach of the rising water. In the beam of their flashlights, the two bodies looked almost peaceful now, as if they were sleeping rather than victims of whatever horror had brought them here.

"There's nothing more we can do," Byrd said, turning to Tom, who wore the ordeal in a pained expression on his face. "We'll get back inside now and call the authorities."

"I know someone in the Federal Ministerial Police.

They'll get here faster than some overworked local cops." Tom said.

"Fine," Byrd said, leading the way back toward the buildings. The rain drummed against the sand with such force that it bounced back up around their ankles.

They stumbled back inside, bringing puddles of seawater and sand with them. The door clicked back into place behind Tom, muffling the howling wind. Byrd threw the deadbolt, paced into the kitchen, and snapped on the light.

Tom pulled out his phone and dialed as rain from his hair dripped onto the protective case. Despite the late hour, an answer came quickly. Tom spoke in fluent Spanish, then passed the phone to Byrd. She stuttered a few words in Spanish—although she had been trying to learn the language, with so much time dedicated to the Skytrain, progress was painfully slow.

"Tell me your problem, madam," said the officer in accented but clear English. His voice grated on her like a violin playing on a wartime gramophone. Byrd took a steadying breath and explained the situation as concisely as possible.

"Two bodies on an island only you inhabit?" the man said, his tone becoming sinister.

"They have washed up onto the island, yes," Byrd snapped in return. "It's obvious they came from the sea."

A long silence passed. The line hissed and popped. Byrd was about to check that the call was still connected when the man spoke again.

"May I give you some advice, unofficially, of course?" he said.

"Please," Byrd replied.

"Drag the bodies back down the beach and let the sea take them."

Byrd stiffened, her knuckles whitening as she gripped the phone. "What do you mean? They are people, with families. Something bad is going on here."

"Yes, I agree, something bad is going on here. Something you do not want to get involved in. In fact, miss, you seem like a nice person. If I were you, I would seriously consider moving somewhere more... welcoming."

Byrd's face tightened as anger and confusion took hold of her.

"I don't know what you're—" Byrd said, stopping mid-sentence as the line clicked and went silent. She removed the phone from her ear and looked at the screen—the call had been disconnected.

"That's the second person in two days told me to sell my property," she said quietly, handing the phone back to Tom.

"He's a good man," Tom said, tucking his phone away. "He's trying to do you a favor. They'll pin this on..." Tom paused, then took a breath. "You could spend five years in pre-trial detention just as a suspect," he said, more softly than before. "One thing you need to understand about Mexico: the weather is bright and sunny, but the law enforcement situation, not so much..."

"One thing you need to understand about me," Byrd replied, her gaze as hard as aircraft-grade aluminum. "Storms don't frighten me, and nor does Mexico."

Tom nodded. "Got it. Then I think we should get some sleep."

"You do what you need to. I need a drink."

## 15

**Mexican desert, north of Cabo San Lucas.**

"What were you promised? What did *they* promise you?"

The words cracked like lightning across the scorched desert where the compound stood. Dozens of sun-kissed people turned toward the sound, squinting through the glow of flickering fire torches that stood on tall wooden stands in the sand, surrounding the gathered people like guards. The self-proclaimed prophet stood atop a natural stone pulpit, his silhouette cutting into the night sky.

"I asked, what were you *promised*?" He slammed his fist down, sending dust spiraling into the air.

The crowd swayed in hypnotic unison. Smoke from the torches distorted the forms of the followers, making them appear to shimmer and dance on the sand that was still warm from the day's heat. Sweat carved muddy rivulets down dust-caked faces, yet not one person turned their attention to anything other than their mentor. They remained transfixed, moths to the prophet's dangerous flame.

"Freedom!" a female voice screamed across the sand.

Sallas, The Mentor, stretched out his arms, opened his palms toward the sky, and turned his face toward the stars. "Tell me again!"

"They promised us freedom!" the girl shrieked.

From his cage, Professor Wall observed the girl. She was small for someone packing such a powerful voice. A floral headband kept her hair from her eyes, and freckles dotted her tanned face.

The Mentor smiled and nodded, touching his hand to his forehead and shading his eyes as he searched for the face in the crowd.

"That's right, Tammy," he said, using the name in the way a shepherd would welcome the return of one of their flock. "And what did they *give* you?"

"Sedatives!" Tammy's voice exploded, the single word carrying years of bottled rage. Her face tightened up with fury as she drew another breath. "Nothing but sedatives!" she shouted again, her hands balled.

"I wish they would give you a few more," Wall muttered to himself, sticking his index finger into his ear and rattling it around to comfort his eardrum. The shrill woman stood way too close for comfort, and, locked inside the cage, there was nothing Wall could do.

"Consumerism!" yelled another voice, this time a man.

Wall sighed with relief as this voice mercifully came from farther away. He shielded his eyes from the torchlight and scanned the crowd for its source. There—a barechested man rose from the gathering, his long, hairy legs extending from a simple beige loincloth, his only clothing. Tribal markings covered his entire body like war paint, transforming what might have been a biblical figure into something resembling a piece of aboriginal art. After speaking, the man bowed deeply toward The Mentor before sinking back down onto the scorching sand.

Wall looked again over the crowd. These men and women in their twenties and early thirties all shared a similar appearance. At first glance, they could have been revelers at a desert music festival. The professor looked at one woman with intricate Celtic patterns spiraling down her arms, while a man had what looked like eagle wings across his chest. The next young man had something serpent-like spiraling up his neck. Sun exposure and dirt had weathered their skin into leather, and their eyes held the vacant, searching look of those who'd abandoned conventional reality for something more transcendent.

"Here is what *I* will promise you," The Mentor declared. "When we find the plant, and we are close, I can guarantee you health, well-being, and vitality. But there's much more that will result from the plant's life-giving properties. You may have been told that the meek shall inherit the Earth. That is wrong."

Even as Wall focused on his aching bones, he was aware of the irony of someone with such a biblical appearance deriding the Bible.

"The strong shall inherit the Earth," The Mentor continued. "The healthy. The *fittest* shall survive. You may have heard this theory before. But not only will we survive. We will prosper, procreate, and become rich. Now, go. Rest, create, make love. Tomorrow, our project continues."

As The Mentor descended from his podium, Wall shuffled in his cage, his joints screaming in protest as he sought a position—any position—that might bring him relief. The small metal box had clearly been designed to force a normal-sized person to bend their knees or hunch their shoulders. Wall had spent the last several hours alternating between tortures; now, even at night, the merciless desert heat added the fierceness of an oven into the mix.

Suddenly, the cage clattered hard as something—or someone—struck it from the outside. The impact sent Wall slamming face-first into the bars. He groaned as pain exploded in his head and fireworks of color danced through his vision. Blood filled his mouth, metallic and warm.

Before he could recover, the cage juddered again, more violently this time, nearly toppling onto its side. His body ricocheted from one side to the other, and this time, the impact smashed his shoulder.

"What... what are you..." Wall stuttered, turning painfully to see a giant man shaking the enclosure. The man had the face of an ogre and a scar that ran from the corner of his mouth to his eye.

"He wants to see you," the man grunted, removing a key and unlocking the padlock. He swung the door open and yanked Wall from his enclosure.

The big man seized Wall by the shoulder and dragged him across the sand toward a large tent in the center of camp. He stumbled as best he could, his muscles screaming with the movement after hours in the cage. Trying to push aside the pain, he took the opportunity to glance around and learn all he could about the place.

Now that the leader's speech had finished, his followers dispersed, going back to whatever bizarre activities they thought worthy of their time. Wall had not been able to see much from his cage, and he had still not quite figured out exactly what was going on here.

Wall looked around again, but aside from a few tanned bodies, the temporary structures, and a chain-link fence, the desert stretched out in all directions without any shade or shelter from the heat of long days. He realized with a chill, despite the heat, that making a run for it now would be futile.

Suddenly, weakness and exhaustion overcame him. He collapsed to his knees, but The Ogre tried to keep dragging him, ripping the skin from his legs. The big man turned and slapped Wall hard across the face with a huge, meaty hand.

"Stand," The Ogre instructed.

Feeling his legs trembling, Wall slowly got to his feet and continued in the direction the brute pulled him. They seemed to be heading toward a large, circular tent.

The big man pulled aside a piece of canvas and nodded for Wall to enter.

"Kneel," the brute boomed as Wall stumbled into the middle of the stuffy, humid tent. There was no flooring, and Wall dropped to his knees on the sand, which contained plenty of dirt and gravel that worked its way into his wounds. He glanced up and saw that The Mentor had already made his way into the tent and was sitting, bare-chested, on a large wooden chair. There was an air of regality about the man, making the chair seem like a throne. But Wall did not look for long. His gaze fell toward the ground. Staring into the eyes of the leader did not seem like a good idea.

The professor felt a breeze on his face, warm and strong. It brought a small amount of relief. Discreetly looking to his left, he saw a fan the size of a truck wheel. Beside it, a woman who looked to be about twenty years old was stretched out on a hammock, casually flipping through the yellowing pages of a paperback book that she rested on her long legs.

Wall could not help but notice how beautiful she was. She seemed young enough to be his daughter, if indeed he had ever bothered to have children, but her radiant perfection was surely obvious to anyone who might look upon her. Light brown hair shone as it ran in straight lines down each side of her symmetrical, elven face and over her feminine shoulders, caressing her healthy skin.

She seemed to be completely oblivious to the fact that Wall had entered the room, let alone the fact that he had been made to kneel on the ground as if he were about to be executed. She remained expressionless, and it appeared that the book was not providing much inspiration. Wall suddenly felt bad for staring at her. He thought about his wife back home in rural Suffolk, England. The white curls of her hair, which she refused to dye, forming ice cream swirls around her round and rosy face. *She* was the most beautiful woman he had ever seen. Not some zoned-out floozy who, for some reason, had found herself in this godforsaken place.

"Yes, she is beautiful," said a voice with rich tones like strong, sweet coffee. Wall still did not want to look. He knew who was speaking, but he was also aware that the first time their eyes met, the basis of their relationship would be established. The professor did not want to show any kind of exhaustion or fear, though his body was flooded with both.

"If you continue to look at her much longer, I might have to question whether or not you intend to steal her from me," came the voice.

Wall heard The Ogre laughing from behind him. The girl, however, was still unaffected by anything being done or said around her. For Wall, there was no choice left but to look the leader in the eye. He turned his gaze away from the young girl and slowly, reluctantly turned his head toward the man who thought he controlled everything.

The Mentor's thumbs and fingertips met and formed a diamond shape with his hands, which he held just below his nose. His intense eyes peered over the top of the diamond, narrowed as if he were focusing all of his attention on the inner workings of Wall's soul. With his dark, flowing hair and weather-worn skin, the man had a timeless appearance. He could have emerged from the deserts of ancient Mesopotamia, Wall thought, if it were not for his well-educated and modern American accent. Behind him, shadows from the torchlight outside writhed on the canvas.

## 16

"Radulf Andreas Wall," The Mentor said in his low, unhurried voice. Almost a drawl. "Ralph."

"Ralph to my friends," Wall advised. Silence.

"An icon in the world of archaeology," The Mentor said finally. "An academic great."

"That's not for me to say."

More silence. The gaps The Mentor left between sentences seemed to be a means of providing space for the other person to consider carefully whether they thought it was really a good idea for them to question, mock, or disagree with him. Wall glanced again at the beautiful young woman. She still appeared to be in a trance-like state, unaware that any other people were in the room.

"Well, I am happy to heap praise upon you, Ralph," came The Mentor's eventual response.

"Professor Wall, please," Wall replied.

"I know a lot about you, Ralph. Where you have conducted your work. The people you have influenced. Where your wife lives in England, waiting for you to return."

Wall's insides turned hard with tension, like he had swallowed a gravestone. "She is not involved in my work." The words scratched at his throat on the way out. The inevitable silence that followed was worse than any potential response.

The Mentor released his fingertips and then touched them back together again. "I am also interested in archaeology. It fascinates me."

Wall decided to give him back a dose of his own silence, which was helped by having no idea how to respond. The professor then heard The Ogre's breathing coming closer as the monster took a step toward him. Then another.

"I see," Wall croaked finally.

"If we were to work together..." The Mentor said, "...if you were to help me, you would be significantly rewarded. You would be treated very well here."

"Isn't everyone treated well here?" Wall asked. He waited for another step from The Ogre. It didn't come. He guessed the creature had not understood the subtext.

The Mentor had, though. It was obvious from the slight smile that tightened the right side of his lips. Except for the smile, the question was not addressed.

"There are clues scattered across this part of the world," The Mentor said instead. "It's like a treasure hunt, but the treasure is old bones, chipped teeth, scratched stone. The bodies that silently speak of long life. The artifacts that provide instructions on how to get it."

"Long life can be both a blessing and a curse," Wall said. "The same certainly applies to finding the clues—the treasure—you're talking about. I can assure you of that, as it applies to almost all aspects of archaeology."

"You're right. Smart man. Long life is a blessing for those who deserve it and a curse for those who do not. Long life for those who do not deserve it is also a curse for everyone they encounter, and for future generations."

Wall did not reply. The tension in the room was even more oppressive than the heat. The professor hoped his labored breathing could not be heard. It would give away the tightness in his chest.

The Mentor paused and took a moment to admire his own body. He gently stroked the skin tightened around each pronounced bicep, then looked down at the hair on his bare chest. Wall suddenly felt old. Everyone in this place was young and attractive. Everyone he had seen, anyway. That was except for The Ogre, who was obviously just a hired thug. A staff member, like the chunky security guard standing at the door to an exclusive party.

"You look concerned, Professor," The Mentor said, dragging his gaze from his own body. "I am just thinking out loud. Long life is not for everyone. I was agreeing with you. But for those who deser— for those who crave it, we could be the ones to provide it for them. Like the physicians and scientists who work around the clock to save lives."

Slowly and with great care, The Mentor pulled a piece of parchment from his pocket, cased in exactly the kind of small, clear plastic bag Wall used to protect such priceless artifacts. Wall already knew this could not be a coincidence.

The Mentor held the item in his hand, his outstretched arm pointing in the direction of The Ogre. The big man walked forward and took it, then stepped toward Wall and held it in front of his face.

"Help me to understand it," The Mentor said.

"I'm sorry. I can't help you," Wall replied meekly.

"You uncovered this in the first place, Professor. Of course you can help."

"I uncovered it. That does not mean I understand it."

"You certainly *could* help me." The vibrational tone of The Mentor's voice dropped slightly. "What you mean is, you do not want to."

"Yes, that is what I mean," Wall announced with as much assertiveness as he could muster. Then, a silent thought: *I find archaeological treasures; you can't even find a T-shirt. Why should I help you?*

"So, you would like to go back to your cage?" The Mentor asked.

"Of course not. I would not like to be caged like an animal, exposed to the elements, and nor would I like to be part of whatever weird social experiment you have going on here. That should be obvious to a great mind such as yours."

Wall noticed The Ogre's muscles twitch. He was ready for... something. The Mentor, meanwhile, was clearly trying to remain calm, but Wall could see the skin around his knuckles tightening as he gripped the armrests of his chair.

"If you go back into the cage," The Mentor explained, "I do not know when you will come out again. But, I do not believe a distinguished man such as yourself should be held in such a place. In fact, I will admonish the people who put you there. Allow me to offer you some comfort, without obligation."

"Without obligation? *Right*."

"Really. Basic politeness. That is all I ask of you. It is important that people here do not hear me being questioned or insulted. It disrupts the harmony. Be polite, and I will treat you well."

"Politeness, I can do," Wall replied, the words unplanned. He was hot and exhausted. He had spat out the words and allowed himself to be manipulated before he had even properly considered his response.

"Good. Take him to the White Rooms," The Mentor instructed The Ogre. "And take Briony with him."

For the first time, the beautiful woman's eyes flicked toward Wall. She appeared to be coming around from whatever psychoactive plant she had imbibed.

"Oh, really, there's no need..." Wall insisted.

"Be polite, Professor," The Mentor reminded. The Ogre helped Wall to his feet and showed him out of the tent. The girl floated along behind, following the professor like a bad memory.

## 17

**Isla de la Fortuna, Caribbean Sea. The following day.**

The sun was just rising as Byrd let the door to the accommodation block swing closed behind her and stepped out onto the warm, soft sand. Although the storm had moved on to terrorize shores anew during the night, it had certainly left its mark on the island. Pausing to look around, Byrd said a quiet thanks that all her building work was complete, and all the structures were designed to take the ravages of whatever the weather could throw at them.

The palm trees now hung motionless in the soft early morning light, their leaves hanging limp like unwashed hair. Debris lay across the beach: plastic waste, wood, and all sorts of other stuff Byrd didn't even recognize.

After her late-night drink with Tom—which had mostly been spent in awkward silence but had also been a necessary cure after the sight of the washed-up bodies—she had retreated to her bed, alone. Sleep, however, had not come willingly. Every time she closed her eyes, images of bloated corpses and aggressive police officers filled her mind. Of course, it wasn't the first time Byrd had seen someone whose days were numbered. She just hadn't been prepared for it to happen here, on her island paradise.

Still undecided what was best to do, Byrd crossed the sand toward where they had dragged the bodies far out of the reach of the waves last night. Sadness and nausea hit her at the same time, and she dreaded seeing the bodies in daylight.

As she had done so many times in the past, she buried her emotions and pushed on with her mission. She trudged over the sodden sand, kicking away fallen palm tree leaves that now lay flat on the beach. Then, Byrd froze. A sound drifted over the beach from the direction of where they had left the bodies.

She held her breath in an attempt to make as little noise as possible. She focused in on the sound, urging it to come again. Drifting on the breeze came the burble of a distant voice, low and rough. Another similarly rough voice joined in. Byrd heard the sound of scraping and shuffling mixed in with clipped, urgent chatter between at least two men—maybe more.

Byrd shuffled toward the sound, stepping back into the shadows of palm trees. Taking long, quiet breaths, she paused to look for better cover. A few meters ahead, where the sand met long grass growing around tree trunks, she spotted what looked like a whole side of a wooden rowing boat. Either it had been torn apart by the power of the storm, leaving the occupants in the churning ocean, or it had been washed in from a long way away on the mainland.

She moved along behind the curved chunk of wood and crouched, picking up the scent of dead fish that worked its way into the boat's wood planking and flaking blue paint.

Byrd edged forward and then peered out from around the remains of the boat.

She couldn't make out movement, but the sound was unmistakable—voices, low and urgent, punctuated by the shuffle of something being dragged along. The sounds became more distant, taking with them the possibility of gathering evidence on who might have brought this affliction to her island.

With an injection of adrenaline like nitrous oxide into an engine, she sprang up and ran across an area of open sand, then ducked in behind a fallen tree. Dropping to a crouch, she tucked in behind the fronds and looked out at the exact site where she and Tom had dragged the bodies the night before.

One man stood where the bodies had been left, looking around in a pattern of surveillance. Two more hauled the female corpse toward a speedboat, which bobbed in the shallows of a Caribbean Sea exuding incongruous calmness. Although the boat was fitted with a powerful-looking outboard engine, a pair of oars hung over the side. It looked to Byrd as though these men arrived silently on purpose.

Watching the men work, Byrd's nervous energy ramped up further, her eyes wide and her body now buzzing with alertness. These men weren't police or any official recovery team. That was clear from the filthy, torn jeans and filthier, once-white muscle vests that hung over tattooed bodies. These men had somehow learned of the gruesome deposit on the island, or they had taken a good guess as to where the bodies of their victims might have ended up.

Remaining still, Byrd considered her options. Although competent at self-defense thanks to her hapkido knowledge and standard combat training in the Air Force, she was alone against a group of criminals. And while she didn't know for sure, she suspected these intruders would be armed.

She reached slowly for her phone, then hesitated, questioning who she would even call—the same questionable police she'd reported this to last night? Plus, by the time anyone arrived, these men would be long gone—along with any evidence of what had happened to those poor souls.

The men reached the speedboat and unceremoniously dropped the body over the side. They moved on to the male victim, and Byrd heard grunts as the two men struggled with the heavier body, half-dragging and half-carrying the victim, leaving a trail in the sand behind them. Byrd winced at the lack of respect they were showing, but remained motionless in her hiding place as a trickle of sweat tickled the back of her neck.

The men reached the boat and shoved the man up and over the side. The body thudded down on the inside of the craft, rocking the boat from side to side.

The third man turned away from his surveillance and kicked the sand around, distorting the marks the bodies had left. He retreated slowly back toward the sea, kicking around the sand again to disguise their footsteps. Standing in the water, he looked around. For a moment, his gaze lingered near Byrd's hiding place. She held her breath, pressing herself flat against the fallen palm trunk. Something about the man gave Byrd a chill. His short but lean stature, with broad shoulders, reminded her of the kind of middleweight Mexican or Cuban boxers who don't give up until the referee saves their life. The tattoos and hard, narrowed eyes brought to mind gangs who tell prison officers how the prison is going to be run.

With a final look from right to left, the surveillance guy shoved the boat away from the shallows and then scrambled in. They dipped the oars and rowed away from the island, clearly wanting to avoid attention until they could get offshore and fire up their engine.

Byrd watched silently as the boat glided away, oars dipping rhythmically into the still, pond-like water. Only when they were a good distance from the island did one of the men pull the cord on the outboard motor. It sputtered to life with a low, unnaturally loud growl that sounded like a beast awakened from its slumber.

Byrd watched the boat picking up speed, carving a white trail through the water. She had expected it to cut right or left, heading back to one of the major islands on either side, but it continued straight ahead, making a beeline for the island directly across from hers.

Confident that the men were looking the other way, Byrd jumped up and ran down the beach to the small structure that housed her beach bar. The storm had done its work here—a section of the wooden roof had come down and hung over the serving area, while deckchairs and furniture lay scattered in all directions. Byrd ran inside and was relieved to find the binoculars still hanging beneath the bar —Byrd liked nothing more than to chill out watching passing craft with a bourbon in her hand, but this vessel-spotting session was far from chilled.

Running back to the beach, she lifted the binoculars to her eyes and watched the boat near the so-called uninhabited island of Isla de la Vida Eterna, which was just a mile away across the water. Reaching the shore of the island, the speedboat banked to the left and followed the coastline before disappearing altogether into a heat haze that surrounded the island like a security fence, warning trespassers to keep out.

# 18

**Isla de la Fortuna, Caribbean Sea.**

"Hey," Tom said, abruptly spinning around as Byrd strode into the hangar.

Byrd stopped and eyed the man, her gaze tightening just a fraction.

"Which one of these beauties will we be flying today?" Tom said, turning back to face the aircraft. He looked at the Skytrain, which, as usual, dominated the collection.

"None of them," Byrd said, taking a step toward the Piper Cub, which sat at the front of the hangar. "Unfortunately," she added in an attempt to soften the blow.

"What do you mean, none of them?" Tom said, placing his hands on his hips. "The weather's improved. It looks like a great day to get up in the sky."

"If you remember, Tom, we've had an incident or two to deal with," Byrd clapped back with a mixture of anger and confusion, swinging around to meet the man's gaze. "Look at this place; it's a mess." She pointed out toward the runway, urging patience into her voice. "It'll take a couple of days to clear up after the storm. Then we'll get back to normal. Maybe. I'm sorry, I know you've given your time to come down here, but you may have noticed things have changed a little."

Candi rounded the corner and jogged into the hangar with a spring in her step. "What's going on?" she asked, smiling.

"The captain here says that classes are cancelled today," Tom said, nodding at Byrd.

"Oh. Why?" Candi asked, her shoulders sagging. "Is there a problem?"

"No," Byrd snapped, shooting Tom a warning look to keep him quiet about their grim discovery. She turned to Candi. "I'm sorry, but it's going to take a day or two to get ready to fly safely again after the storm. You're welcome to relax here, or you can come back next week."

Byrd turned and strode toward the door control panel on the wall. She tapped a number into the keypad, and the vast door rolled open on well-oiled hinges. She paced across to her Piper Cub and swung open the door.

"Hold on a second. You're going up, and yet you say we can't learn today," Tom said, his voice carrying across the hangar.

"Yes, I'm sorry. I'm going to check the damage to the island—easier to see from the air," Byrd lied, climbing inside the compact cockpit and checking the fuel and pressure gauges. She reached for the ignition, but Tom's face appeared at the window, his expression hard. Her hand hovered over the instrument panel.

"What's going on? What about the bodies?" he hissed quietly.

Byrd glanced at Candi standing at the open hangar door.

Although the young woman was out of earshot, Byrd didn't want her getting suspicious.

"I've dealt with it," Byrd said curtly. "Now step back, please; the sooner I get these checks done and then hire the clean-up crew, the sooner we can get back to lessons."

Tom raised his hands in a gesture of surrender and backed away from the Piper Cub.

Byrd glanced at him and saw the skin beneath his silvery hairline tightening into a frown. He clearly didn't like being kept in the dark or being made to wait. A sense of disquiet fidgeted in Byrd's stomach. She decided not to let Tom in on any of her thoughts or plans for a while.

Byrd closed the door and started the Piper Cub, the sound of the Continental A-65 engine filling the hangar. The engine settled into a steady rhythm as she taxied out of the hangar and onto the runway. Having already checked the runway for debris, she pushed the throttle and angled the craft out onto the tarmac. The wheels bumped and shook as the engine's pitch climbed higher. Reaching takeoff speed, Byrd pulled back on the control stick. The Piper Cub responded smoothly, powering into a climb.

Banking east, Byrd kept her altitude low over the glittering sea. The engine maintained its steady pulse, occasionally changing note as she adjusted her course and speed.

Byrd took a moment to draw a deep breath and try to relax. Up here, with nothing but blue above and below, was where she felt at her best. This is what she loved to do and where she loved to be—up among the clouds. Even in the midst of a new crisis, it provided a little comfort.

Maintaining her altitude, she scanned the waters below for any sign of the speedboat. She quickly reached the other island and throttled back, slowing as much as possible to give her the best chance to see her quarry.

She passed low across the wide beach that extended along one side of the island, then out over the dense jungle that occupied the center. Only a pair of rocky outcrops and an old radio antenna, part of a now disused navigation system, broke the forest canopy. Byrd looked at the radio antenna, now so covered with vines that it was almost an extension of the forest itself.

She banked the Piper Cub into a gentle turn, following the western shore. Peering out through the canopy, it looked as though this island had also been ravaged by the storm. Fallen trees dotted the sand, and a gleaming white yacht rested at the edge of the beach.

Maintaining her altitude, she swung around the island's northwestern tip. The waves broke against rugged cliffs here, rising directly from the water.

Byrd continued the turn and followed the shoreline in the opposite direction. This side of the island was far craggier, with the forest hanging right over the surf. It appeared to have fared slightly better in the storm, too. At one end of the beach was a jetty with what she immediately recognized as a de Havilland Canada DHC-6 Twin Otter seaplane bobbing next to it. She then flew low over a small collection of run-down concrete structures and a tiny disused pier. Suddenly, she saw movement from beside the pier.

Byrd eased the stick right and adjusted the rudder pedals, throwing the Piper Cub into a turn. The aircraft responded in a move that would make most people instantly sick, banking at a sharp angle and then barreling toward the ground. The move gave Byrd the look she needed, bringing the speedboat into clear view.

She pulled back, descending for a better view. It didn't

look as though anyone was on the boat or visible on the beach.

"I gave you too long to hide the bodies," she muttered. "Probably buried them in the jungle and moved on to the next victim."

Then, she saw a narrow path had been trampled from the boat toward the forest. She looked toward the tree line and drew a sharp breath. She caught sight of two men just in time to see them dragging someone into the trees. Byrd was sure it was a woman, trying to kick and resist, but they all disappeared into the undergrowth before she could assess any further.

Byrd banked away quickly, climbing back to a safer altitude. The last thing she wanted was for whoever brought the boat here to look up and think she was doing reconnaissance. She swung the Piper Cub around and started in the direction of home, sensing she would surely need help dealing with the situation on the ground. The blocky shape of her hangar and the other buildings danced in the threads of heat. Her mind raced with the implications of what she'd just seen.

Her military instincts took over. *Leave no one behind.* She couldn't abandon whoever had been captured down there, and trying to return later with help would almost certainly be too late. Byrd puffed out her cheeks as she exhaled long and hard to calm herself for the coming mission. A mission with no support on the ground or in the air.

## 19

Byrd scanned the ground and identified a flattish stretch of beach that might just be workable as a landing strip. "It's far from perfect," she said to herself, "but nothing has gone perfectly since I arrived in this damn place."

She levelled out the Piper Cub and powered back out across the wide beach. The engine sputtered, sending a shudder through the fuselage. Byrd glanced down at the instrument panel, searching for any warning signs that something was amiss. She allowed herself a slight smile upon observing that all readings were normal—just in time to see the sky darken as the engine coughed out a cloud of black smoke.

"Don't do this to me, baby," Byrd muttered, tightening her face into a grimace as she adjusted the mixture control, then checked the instrument panel again. As she scanned, the engine sputtered, juddered, and died. An ominous silence swept through the cockpit. Byrd tingled with trepidation as she realized she would soon fall out of the sky like a penny falling into a well.

The engine coughed again, growled menacingly, and then roared back to life.

Byrd took a breath, easing off on the controls. She cursed herself for being so caught up with the Skytrain and the flying school that she hadn't checked the Piper Cub over in a few weeks. When—if—she got back, she would give the engine a full strip down.

Byrd hadn't even finished her thought when the engine sputtered again and became deathly quiet. Wind rattled the fuselage, which creaked and shook, reminding Byrd how fragile the plane was without its engine. Time seemed to slow in the harrowing silence, but readings on the dashboard quickly burst to life as the red hand on the altimeter flapped wildly.

Training kicking in, Byrd's mind raced with possibilities. The fuel gauge showed a quarter of a tank, which was plenty for this short flight. It didn't make any sense, unless someone had tampered with the aircraft.

Byrd thought about the men on the beach that morning, wondering whether they'd had time to get into the hangar and mess with the plane that was sitting there at the front and most likely to be used to assess storm damage. Then, she remembered the threatening call two nights ago. Could someone else have been sent to the island, visiting in the dead of night?

Byrd let the thoughts go and turned her focus to the emergency she had to deal with right now. With maybe only two minutes of gliding time available to her, every second was crucial.

"She wants to fly, let her fly," Byrd said, remembering Bourdell's advice all those years ago.

She trimmed the aircraft for best glide speed, keeping the

nose at the precise angle to maximize her distance. She looked out at her island and decided that it was too far away at her current altitude. That left two options—down the plane in the sea or crash-land on the island over which she'd just flown. She glanced over her shoulder and eyed the beach below her. Although strewn with debris from the storm, it was certainly wide and flat enough to make the landing.

Byrd gently banked the aircraft, lining up with the beach. Without the engine humming away, the controls felt unnaturally light. A gust of wind shoved the plane sideways like a man plucking a mosquito out of the air. Byrd squeezed the controls and jerked with her full body, using all her strength to fight back against nature. She levelled up, but the plane's vulnerability was now all too apparent.

"Come on, girl," she whispered, easing the Piper Cub into its best glide altitude. "Ready to hit the beach?" Now lined up for the best landing she could hope for, she let her altitude drop. "We only get one shot at this," she told her plane.

Five hundred feet. Four hundred. The beach stretched out below, a great section of it covered with storm debris. Dropping nearer and nearer, she saw chunks of driftwood and bubbles of plastic. The yacht she'd seen a few minutes before was right on the edge of the beach and would be engulfed in a catastrophic collision if Byrd didn't get her landing right.

She glanced at the altimeter—three hundred feet. She looked at the airspeed indicator and then out at the rapidly approaching shoreline. If she came in too fast, she'd risk being crushed or flipping on impact. If she let the Piper Cub slow too much, she'd drop like a stone.

Another gust of crosswind caught the wing, swinging the aircraft out over the sea. Tensing every muscle, Byrd corrected, fighting to keep the plane aligned with a section of sand that looked to be free of large debris.

Two hundred feet.

She deployed the flaps to their maximum extension. The nose dropped, and the Piper Cub began its final descent toward the beach. Clear skies gave way to a landscape of green and yellow-gray sand that careened closer through the canopy. Collision with the ground was now seconds away.

"It's gonna be a rough one," Byrd said to herself, gritting her teeth. She had to trust that the landing gear would take the impact. It would either hold or not—there was nothing she could do about it now.

One hundred feet. Falling toward the beach at a sickening speed, Byrd saw a fallen palm tree trunk lying directly in the path, having been obscured from the air by the sand whipped onto it by the storm. Narrowing her eyes with surgical focus, she nudged the stick, re-angling for a narrow gap between the tree and a pile of debris.

Fifty feet.

The wind shifted again, pushing her toward the water's edge.

Twenty feet.

Taking short, sharp breaths, she pulled back gently on the stick, raising the nose to slow as much as possible. The beach filled the windshield. Shock from the impact traveled up Byrd's spine as the Cub's wheels landed with a jarring thud, shaking the fuselage so hard that Byrd's helmet clattered into the back of her seat. The momentum then pulled her into a heavy jerk forward, but her muscular frame kept her upright.

Sand sprayed up high on both sides of the cockpit as the aircraft bounced once, twice. The plane's shock absorbers took the impact as best they could, but the jolting movements were disorienting and sickening. A piece of driftwood clipped the left wheel, swinging Byrd into a skid.

Byrd fought the controls, desperately trying to keep the wings level as the Piper slewed across the beach.

The right wingtip dipped just inches from the sand. Byrd countered, her body tense with the effort. She yanked the stick hard to the left, the muscles in her arm screaming. The Piper Cub responded sluggishly, missing another chunk of debris on the left-hand side. The tail wheel caught a ridge of wet sand, spinning the aircraft forty-five degrees. The nose now pointed directly at a solid tree trunk standing tall.

Byrd stomped on the heel brakes while also applying extra back pressure on the stick. The tree loomed larger. With the brakes screaming, the plane finally shuddered to a stop, the nose still pointing toward the jungle edge. Steam hissed from the cowling as Byrd sat frozen. She had her hands still locked on the controls, but she was on the ground and alive.

Byrd shoved against the door, but it didn't move. She shrugged off her harness, placed her shoulder against the door, and shoved again. With a groan and then a pop, it swung open. Shakily, she climbed out and scrambled down to the sand. She placed a hand against the fuselage and took a second for her legs to adjust to solid ground.

"Not my best work," she said, pacing away from the Piper Cub and then looking back at the craft, which sat slumped on the sand. She paced around the aircraft, assessing the damage. The left wheel strut was bent at an awkward angle, and one of the wingtips twisted up toward the sky. A propeller blade had shattered on impact.

"She's not a total write-off," Byrd said, searching her

flight suit for her phone. "But she sure ain't going anywhere for a while." Finding her phone, she dragged it out and glanced at the screen. "Well, ain't that typical." The phone showed no signal, just as she'd feared in such a remote place without the gadgets she had installed on her own island. She tried the emergency call function anyway, but the device couldn't connect.

She pocketed the phone and turned in a slow circle, taking stock of her surroundings. The beach stretched in both directions, littered with storm debris. To her right, about half a mile distant, a rocky outcropping at the end of the island jutted into the sea. To her left, the beach continued for perhaps a mile before curving out of sight around another headland. Behind her, dense tropical vegetation formed a green wall, and in front of her, the sea lapped lazily against the sand.

"Sure as hell ain't flying out of here," Byrd muttered, turning her attention to a stream of liquid running from the engine. She knelt beside the Piper Cub and reached for the latches to open the engine bay. She raised the panel and then leaned in closer, scanning the familiar plugs, wires, and fuel lines for any obvious sign of mechanical failure. Nothing immediately caught her eye—until she noticed the fuel filter.

"What the—?" she whispered, reaching toward the component. The filter housing had been tampered with, its seal broken and hastily reassembled.

She grabbed the multitool from beneath the pilot's seat and carefully removed the filter element. Fine metallic powder spilled all over her hands.

"Well, I'll be," Byrd said, looking at the powder. Despite the heat, a chill ran down her spine as she realized that the powder could only have been put there deliberately. "Someone's packed the filter with iron filings. No wonder she conked out after a few minutes." She paused, trying to assess who might have tampered with her plane.

A gunshot boomed across the beach, full and fierce. The bullet zinged off the metal of the fuselage, right next to the engine and inches from Byrd. She crashed to the ground belly first, her mouth filling with sand.

## 20

**Isla de la Vida Eterna, Caribbean Sea.**

Hutchin's eyes shot open, and he jerked back against the wall. Gasping, he took stock of his surroundings. A barbaric blow to the head and total exhaustion had left him blacking out for long periods. He tried to figure out how long he had been here. A day? Two?

Fragmentary memories came back to him. Since his surreal drinking session with the guard, the man had only been back once for just a few seconds, to bring water and utter the words, "You're next." Next for what?

Then he remembered the screaming. The awful howling and shrieking. He'd wondered at the time if it was part of his concussed dream, but he knew now that it was real. It came again. The sound pierced through the nearest wall, projecting terror through the concrete.

"I've got to get out of here," Hutchins said quietly, now more alert than he had ever been in his life.

Still tied to the wall in the tiny concrete building, he felt the pain of the twine that bound him. But he only felt it around one wrist. Excitement and hope mixed with his dread.

Given that his captor had savagely knocked him out cold, he could not say that his drinking plan had been a complete success. But at least the captor, in his rage, had neglected to tie Hutchins's drinking hand again. That part of the plan had worked.

He took a few deep breaths and tried not to think about the cruel irony of his bladder feeling as though it was about to burst while his tongue was as dry as a desert sandwich. Twisting his aching neck, he turned and could just about see his shackles behind him.

The unusable hand was tied to a rusting metal hoop set into the wall. The hoop looked to be as old as the building itself, stained with decades of rust. He assumed the hoops were probably set there to secure some kind of equipment, conveniently reused by his captors. He pulled against the twine that bound his wrist to the hook. Although the twine was old, it was clearly too strong for him to break through with brute strength alone.

With his free hand, he felt around for a knot that kept his other hand bound. He thought he could feel a small bump in the twine, and he began picking at it.

"Come on, damn it," he whispered. The knot didn't seem to be budging. He was sweating now, and his free hand kept slipping every time he thought he had a grip on the knot. Hope turned to cold desperation as the flayed skin on his fingers screamed with agony. He also felt a sting around his eyes as tears welled.

He closed his eyes and took a deep breath. *If you allow it to*, he told himself silently, *your weakness will kill you.*

He turned his attention to the objects scattered around the room. At first, he considered the stack of crumbling crates in the far corner. He shuffled toward them and kicked out, trying to reach them with his legs. His feet swung hopelessly through the air a couple of feet short of the crates.

Turning back to look at the floor, he saw several shards of broken glass. Remembering how the thug had smashed his own Tequila bottle in order to threaten him, Hutchins grinned at the irony of what he was about to attempt.

He stretched as far as he could in the direction of the glass, but the closest shard was still out of reach. Refusing to give up, he pressed himself to the ground flat on his back and shoved himself across the floor. More sweat started to pour from his brow.

He shuffled until the twine around his wrist dug in deeper and stung harder, but he still wasn't close enough. He stretched his legs until he felt as if the tendons were about to snap. He had to prevent himself from groaning with the strain. Glancing down, he noticed that his toe was now right beside one of the largest shards. He rolled his foot as hope flooded his body.

With an urgent movement to hook the glass with his toe cap, he accidentally kicked it away. He slapped the stone floor in frustration. He then lay still, hoping that his outburst had not alerted the guard to the fact that he was up to something.

He took a breath and tried again. His body was now so stretched that he wheezed whenever he breathed. He could feel the glass on the tip of his boot. With another agonizing stretch, he managed to get his boot around the object and drag it across the floor toward him. He then danced his fingers across the ground like a scuttling spider as his digits inched toward the tiny piece of shrapnel that might save him. He got his free hand around the object. He pulled it in, flipped over, and sat up straight while drawing in long, quiet breaths.

Tucking his hands behind his back, he worked away at the twine with the sharpest side of the piece of glass. Sweat now streamed from every pore, and the glass became slippery in his fingers. He cursed under his breath, knowing his survival depended on that tiny shard. He pinched and prodded the twine to see if it was getting weaker. He could not tell if it was or not.

The shard of glass slipped from his grasp and fell to the floor. He couldn't see it anywhere. With panic rising in his chest, his fingers tapped around once more, searching for the object. Now, there was only dust and dirt beneath his fingertips. He continued to feel around for the precious shard, knowing it was his only hope. It made its location known with a sting, a bite in the dark, digging so hard into his skin that blood flowed. But he did not care. His fingers closed lovingly around the broken glass.

He worked at the twine again, harder and faster. Snap. He fell forward as the energy transferred to his body. He was free. But only of his bonds. Next, the guard.

He took a moment to assess the situation. He looked up at the window, which was only a few inches square and certainly not big enough to get through, even for a scrawny academic.

A few larger shards of glass lay scattered around. But was there really any possibility he could use one of these pieces of glass to cut into the skin of his captor? Violence was an alien world, or it had been until two days ago.

*This guy has probably been in hundreds of fights in his life. I've been in none,* he thought. Hutchins had to hope that the guard's Tequila addiction would lead to bouts of daytime unconsciousness.

He stood, rubbed his wrists, and stepped with the lightness of a ballerina toward the door. The door to his room was not secured. The place was not a cell block but apparently a building for keeping livestock or storing tools that had been made into a makeshift prison. However, the slightly ajar door came with problems of its own. Hutchins knew it was going to creak loudly as soon as he pushed it. He hated it for its creakiness. Right at that moment, that door was his enemy.

Sure enough, the slightest touch released a loud creaking sound. As soon as there was enough room to squeeze through, Hutchins stopped pushing. From the other side of the door, he heard a growl. He stood still. After a second, the growl turned into a snore. Hutchins turned sideways, flattened his arms to his sides, and took a sidestep through the door.

In a wooden chair beside a wooden desk, the guard was slumped, seemingly fast asleep, with saliva dribbling onto his shoulder. Resting close to the man's thumb and index finger was a large brass key. Hutchins took a step toward the desk, then stopped. He looked at the door next to the one he had just come from. The room from which the screams had come.

Hutchins did not allow himself any more time to think. Quickly but steadily, he stepped over to the desk and reached down toward the key. He curled his fingers around it and picked it up first time. He gripped it tight, making sure sweat would not deny him again. With the key in his left hand, he turned away from the desk. A hand gripped his wrist.

"Hey!" the guard yelled. Hutchins tried to move his right hand, but the guard's strength pinned it to the table. Rage took hold of the captor's face, his nostrils flaring and his eyes bulging wide. Hutchins tried again to pull his hand free, desperately tugging and twisting, but it did not move an inch.

Hutchins rotated his hips and swung his free left hand through the air, surprising himself as much as the guard. The same fist plunged into the guard's pudgy, leathery face, and Hutchins heard the squelch of flesh and the snap of breaking bone.

The guard released Hutchins' wrist. As the brute reached for his own jaw to assess the damage, Hutchins darted for the main door and thrust the key toward the lock. It thudded against wood. He tried again. The key clattered and clunked and finally entered the lock. He twisted the key, and the door sprang open. He heard furniture clattering as the guard got to his feet to give chase, but Hutchins had a head start and sprinted into the fresh air with no clue as to where he was headed. The guilt of leaving a victim behind already weighed heavily with each step.

# 21

**Isla de la Vida Eterna, Caribbean Sea.**

Instinct kicked in as Byrd dropped to the ground. Three more bullets hammered into the fuselage, pinging off and plunging into soft sand that parted like flesh. Byrd rolled beneath the plane just before a geyser of sand erupted where she'd been a second ago.

"Playing target practice is not my favorite game," she said, pulling herself up behind the fuselage.

More slugs zinged from the other side of the engine block, raining sparks down onto the beach.

Byrd crawled to the Piper Cub's tail, breathing hard. Standing with her back against the fuselage, she risked a look over the tail.

Two men paced down the beach toward her, both shirtless and covered with tattoos that swirled across their torsos. They walked with their heads ducked and their guns extended in a two-handed grip. The fact that they were out in the open meant they had assumed Byrd wasn't armed.

Unfortunately, other than the knife she always carried strapped to her ankle, they'd assumed correctly.

"Why is it always me bringing a knife to a gunfight?" she groaned as another shot whizzed through the air before kicking up sand near the Piper's wheel, close enough to spray onto Byrd and remind her that death stalked nearby.

She turned and looked at the surf. Just a few strides away, the sea sloshed against the hull of the yacht she'd seen from the air, the vessel seemingly having been stricken by the storm. Byrd risked another look over the plane's tail section just as two more shots glanced from the exposed engine, sending another shower of sparks into the now fuel-soaked sand.

"Oh, man," Byrd muttered. She pivoted and broke into a run before the deadly fire could consume her.

With an ominous whoosh, flames quickly sprang up across the sand where the fuel had soaked in. Fanned by a breeze floating in from the sea, the flames soon grew larger, licking toward the plane's belly.

The first explosion was deceptively small—little more than a muffled thump followed by a brilliant flash of orange as the fuel tank ignited. For a suspended moment, time seemed to slow. Byrd felt the heat on her back before the sound reached her ears.

She took two more steps before the shockwave slammed into her like a haul truck, lifting her clean off her feet and hurling her forward. The world tumbled in a blur of sky and sand. The roar was all-consuming—a physical force that pressed against her eardrums.

Byrd slammed into the surf with a colossal splash, the water breaking her fall just enough to avoid serious injury. Without looking back, she pushed up and ran the remaining few paces to the yacht. She dragged herself in behind the hull and peered out, watching fragments of metal and fiberglass rain down, hissing like tormented serpents as they peppered the sea.

"I really did like that plane," she said, looking up at the column of smoke, which would be visible for miles around. "And now I'm going to have to find another way outta—"

A bullet skipped off the water as the first of the thugs rounded the burning Piper Cub.

Byrd dropped in behind the hull and moved around the back of the yacht, staying submerged as much as she could. She reached the ladder and dragged herself up.

She hit the polished wood deck and crawled to the other side of the yacht. Taking a few deep breaths to force the smoke from her lungs, she peered out over the side.

One of the gunmen stood in the shallows a safe distance from the burning plane. He held the gun steady, pointing at the yacht. Thick black smoke now blocked out the sun, bringing artificial gloom, and Byrd could not see the other attacker anywhere.

She glanced down at the blade at her ankle, but immediately judged that throwing the knife would be unlikely to take out the assailant at that distance. More likely, she would simply lose her only weapon.

Trying to make another plan, she eyed the man again as he moved forward. His shaved head glistened with sweat, and his eyes were dark slits half-closed against the smoke. He swept a pistol from side to side, clearly seeking a clean shot. He took one more step and fired.

Byrd flattened herself against the deck as bullets zipped overhead, one glancing off the mast with a powerful clang that vibrated through the hull.

The attacker shouted something—a guttural bark of anger. He adjusted his stance, planting his feet more firmly.

He released another shot, hammering Byrd's eardrums again. Wood splintered behind her, and fragments splashed into the water.

Byrd shuffled backward and quickly searched the deck for something she could use as a weapon.

A glint caught her eye, and she noticed a speargun clipped to the console a few feet away.

She shuffled across the deck and lunged for the device. She gripped the stock and yanked it from the clip, which had clearly kept it in place during the storm. She took the two spears clipped beside the gun and slid one into place. With a satisfying click, the band locked into position, the weapon now primed and dangerous.

"Two shots it is," Byrd said, examining the weapon. "Two fish just got lucky; two criminals didn't."

The speargun was a high-end model. She tested its weight in her hands, feeling the balance.

Another bullet struck the yacht, sending Byrd ducking behind the console.

She took a deep breath, steadying herself. Unlike her attacker's gun, the speargun would give her only one shot at a time, with a painstaking reload between each.

"Let's even these odds," she whispered, raising herself just enough to spot her assailant through the yacht's railing. "It might be designed for fish, but it's sure enough gunna do some damage to a human being."

Byrd remained in position and waited for the attacker to slosh toward her through the waves. She rose slowly to one knee, pressed her shoulder against the metal, and carefully took aim.

"Gotta make it count," she muttered, making a final adjustment. She squeezed the trigger.

The spear whistled through the air, a blur slicing toward

its target. At the last possible second, the man twisted an inch to the side. The spear grazed his shoulder, tearing through his shirt and carving a line through his flesh. He roared but remained standing.

"Dammit," Byrd breathed, watching the spear splash into the surf. "Am I really going to die in paradise?"

Blood bloomed across the attacker's shoulder, but instead of deterring him, the wound seemed to fuel his rage. He marched forward, firing rapidly as he closed the distance.

Bullets hammered into the yacht's hull with increasing accuracy, sending splinters of fiberglass and wood exploding around Byrd. One round punched through the deck near her foot, the impact vibrating through the planks beneath her.

Her fingers slicked with sea mist, Byrd jammed the next spear into place before tugging the mechanism with a grunt of effort. She kept the weapon low while her eyes zeroed in on her target. Then, she swung the weapon high and fired.

The spear moved in a perfect arc, quick and true. It plunged into the man's body just beneath his collarbone. He released a strangled cry as the force of the impact slammed him into the surf. He clutched his wound, his weapon falling uselessly from his hand as seawater splashed up all around him.

Just as Byrd breathed a sigh of relief, she heard footsteps on the ladder behind her. She spun around, still clutching the now useless speargun as the other assailant scrambled up onto the deck.

As the assassin brought his gun to bear, Byrd threw the speargun to the deck and jumped in the opposite direction. The air exploded with gunfire as she leaped across the railing and plunged into the water. She hit the shallow water with a splash, bullets biting into the sea around her, sending up fountains of surf.

Waist-deep in crystal turquoise water, she crouched low, moving around the yacht to keep out of sight. She glanced back at the felled first assassin.

"Must be twenty feet away," she whispered, judging the distance. "By the time I get there, I'll have more holes in me than a political manifesto."

She pushed herself further down into the water and listened to the movement of the second assassin up on the deck. His footsteps created a hollow rhythm against the wooden planks—deliberate, unhurried. Hunting her.

The water lapped gently against her torso, its deceptive tranquility at odds with the deadly situation. The footsteps grew louder as the assassin approached the railing above.

"Take one more step, my friend," Byrd whispered. This close, one-on-one, the knife might just help her.

She took a deep breath and dropped beneath the water. She looked back up at the deck, now a hazy blue as sunlight broke through the smoke and fractured on the surface of the water. She pulled her hunting knife from the ankle strap, the handle fitting perfectly in her grasp.

Her lungs began to burn as she waited for her assailant through the distorted lens of the water's surface. A shadow moved across the water, then the man's silhouette loomed at the railing, his gun sweeping back and forth as he scanned the water for her.

The weight of the knife felt reassuring in her palm—seven inches of high-carbon steel that had saved her life more than once. She gripped it tighter, muscle memory positioning it for an upward strike.

Byrd counted the seconds, watching as the assassin leaned further over the railing. Just a little closer. The pressure in her chest grew more insistent as her lungs demanded air.

Sierra Byrd erupted from the sea like a missile. Water cascaded around her as she surged upward, her arm already in motion. The assassin's eyes widened in surprise as he tried to swing the gun down toward her.

Byrd was too quick—she hurled the knife with deadly force. Once the knife left her hand, she swung to the side, moving out of the way of the coming gunfire.

The blade shot through the air, catching sunlight. The polished steel flew upwards, straight and true. The knife cut into the man's neck with a sickening thud. He gurgled, threw his arms toward the sky, and then leaned forward, rocking the whole yacht. The gun sailed through the air while the attacker instinctively clutched at the protruding knife handle. A babbling sound escaped his throat as blood sprayed between his fingers.

His knees buckled, and he pitched forward, tumbling over the railing in an ungraceful arc. He hit the water with a heavy splash, sending a wave crashing against the hull. A cloud of crimson bloomed around him in the clear water. His fingers still twitched, clutching weakly at the knife in his neck.

"I didn't want to do it," Byrd said as the last bubbles of air escaped the man's lips. "But getting shot at is one of my little bugbears."

She waded over and pulled the knife from his neck, then quickly searched his body and scanned for the fallen pistol. She retrieved it from the water and opened the chamber, seeing that one bullet remained. Smiling, she splashed back toward the sand.

Reaching the other assassin, Byrd dropped to a knee and

searched him too. Finding his pistol was out of bullets, she slung the weapon into the sea in frustration.

"At least I still have one bullet," she said out loud. Suddenly, a wet, bloodied hand gripped her by the ankle. Byrd turned and met the man's wild, yellowed eyes. He snarled, showing blood running between his teeth. Byrd stood, and the man bolted upright, then pushed up as he lunged at her. Ignoring fear, she stood still, feet wide apart, and extended her right arm. She released her final bullet, and it landed right between the eyes.

Breathing hard, Byrd dropped the now-useless gun. The guy had wasted her only bullet, but he still turned out to be useful. In the back pocket of his jeans, she found a crumpled piece of paper that looked like it had been torn from a yellowing book on botany. Byrd flipped over the paper and saw the scribbled words:

*11:30am - symphyotrichum puniceum plant, by mouth*
*Observe and note the effects of the plant*
*1pm - white snakeroot, intravenous*

"What madness is this?" Byrd said, looking from the paper to her island across the water. The Dakota Skytrain inside the hangar was not visible, but Byrd could feel her precious time with it slipping away as life took a different path. "As Bourdell says," she said with quiet affection for her old friend, "you're in this now, until the end or death... whatever comes first. Damn you Bourdell."

## 22

**Isla de la Vida Eterna, Caribbean Sea.**

"It's a shame, I really did like that plane," Byrd said, glancing over her shoulder at the burning Piper Cub. "Can't say anything so nice about those two," she added, eyeing the dead thugs lying in the surf, tinting the waves pink. Shaking off the memory of the fight, Byrd turned and stalked off up the beach, into the jungle to search the island.

The calls of tropical birds and zinging insects surrounded her as she picked her way through the vegetation. She peered up onto the canopy and noticed a pair of dark eyes looking back at her.

"Hello there, now where did you get that beauty?" Byrd said, locking eyes with a macaque eyeing her suspiciously from a branch up above. The monkey tore a handful of flesh from a juicy-looking mango, then stuffed it in his mouth. Liquid from the fruit ran down the monkey's chin. Not taking his eyes off Byrd, he tore another fistful from the mango, looked at it thoughtfully, then shoved it home.

"Tell you what; you share that with me, and I'll get the

next round," Byrd said, realizing how appealing the fresh fruit looked.

The monkey tilted its head to one side, giving her a quizzical look. She noticed that ripe mangos surrounded the animal on all sides. The boughs of the trees hung heavy with lush fruit—ready to drop at the slightest nudge.

"Boooo!" Byrd shouted, baring her teeth and spreading her arms wide. Clearly no longer the biggest predator in town, the primate bounced away, disturbing the surrounding foliage. A ripe mango thudded to the ground beside Byrd's feet.

"Thanks very much," Byrd called to the disappearing monkey. "I owe you one." She took out her knife again, checked to make sure nothing remained from the grizzly task it had just performed, and then sliced the mango's skin. The exquisite juice burst forth, and Byrd clamped her mouth over the split. She swallowed, taking the liquid and sweetness into her body. Right then, it felt like one of the greatest moments of her life.

But as Byrd was learning fast, the greatest moments of a person's life rarely last as long as they should. Hearing movement in the jungle behind her, she whirled around, shaping instinctively into her fighting stance.

Instead of the muscular fiend she had expected—a comrade of one of those she'd encountered down at the beach—a skinny and bedraggled man emerged from the trees. Floppy hair partially covered his filthy face, and he moved as though his minimal muscles had just run out of gas.

"Can I have some?" the man said in a vibrato voice, pointing at the fruit that now leaked juice all over Byrd's hands. "Please?" he added when Byrd didn't immediately reply.

Slowly and with a raised eyebrow, Byrd handed over the fruit. This man certainly looked as though he needed it more than she did. He took the mango with both hands and pulled it toward his face like he was passionately pulling in a lover for a kiss.

Byrd assessed the newcomer while he was distracted with the fruit. Along with specks of mango juice and pulp, his shirt appeared to be flecked with blood. It looked as though he had been rolling around on a floor covered with human filth.

"What in the name of the Almighty is going on?" Byrd said.

The strange man looked at her and then took a sudden step toward her. He lunged, his arms raised in front of him. She was just about to bring her knife to bear when she heard an unexpected sound. The young man sobbed, sharp and high-pitched, like the call of the colorful tropical birds in the trees above.

The weeping man spread his arms wide and wrapped Byrd in a bear hug. His face fell into her shoulder as he collapsed into her embrace. It took all of Byrd's inner strength, and a good deal of human decency, not to drop him to the floor.

She found herself curling the right side of her top lip upward—like Elvis sending his audience into a frenzy during his comeback special. Only, Byrd's gesture was one of mild disgust.

"I... I escaped," the man said between sobs. "I thought I was going to die in there. They were going to kill me."

"Escaped from where?" Byrd said, waiting what seemed like an appropriate length of time—but was probably less than five seconds—before breaking the hug and holding the man at arm's length.

"These men... They took me and my partner. I think he might be..." The man's tears flowed forth again, and he was clearly unable to verbalize the trouble his friend was in.

"Probably the same vermin I ran into on the beach," Byrd said, thinking out loud.

"What?" the man asked, looking up at her. He rubbed a hand across his face, smearing mango juice into the filth.

"Don't worry. You said 'maybe' they killed him," Byrd said, her tone of voice going full *tough love*. "That means maybe they didn't. Shouldn't you be doing something to help him instead of standing here crying?"

The man frowned and nodded. He pushed his shoulders back and stood tall.

"What's your name?" Byrd asked.

"Hutchins. Hans Hutchins," the young man said, followed by a long sniff. "I'm an archaeologist."

"And you were taken captive on this island?"

Hutchins nodded.

"I need to find the Professor... Professor Wall," Hutchins said. "But it's too dangerous. There are too many of them, and they're hardened criminals. I don't even know where they have taken him."

"Well, that's something you can discuss with the authorities," Byrd said, already distancing herself from the situation. "I'm having a small problem with these thugs myself," Byrd said. "Scratch that—these are big, life-changing problems. I'm definitely not here to find your friend."

"The authorities won't do anything," Hutchins said, his squeaky tone hinting that he found the suggestion idiotic. "We bribed them to let us dig on this island. If a couple of academics can stump up the cash to get them to turn a blind eye, how much influence do you think a criminal gang can buy?"

Byrd stood silent for a moment, recalling her conversation with the police officer the night before, and the scratchy voice on the phone. "I'm afraid you're probably right," she conceded. "Then, you need to get off this island and get help from...somewhere."

"How?" Hutchins asked.

"Great question. I can tell you have an inquisitive mind." Byrd thought for a moment. "How did you get here in the first place?"

"We paid someone to ferry us over here with our truck. There's a dock somewhere, but I have no idea where it is." Hutchins looked left and right as though there might be a sign he'd missed until this point.

"Okay. None of that gave me any inspiration," Byrd said.

"Please help me." Hutchins looked up at Byrd like a puppy hoping it was time to go out for a walk. "I have to look for my colleague... for my friend. He may be alive or dead; I don't know where he is."

"I'm sorry, kid, but a rescue operation is not my priority," Byrd said, holding a finger to her lips. "I need to find out what's going on here and clear my name. I've got too much riding on this to launch into a hare-brained rescue."

"Clear your name?"

"Yeah. I'm in enough trouble as it is." Byrd looked in the direction of her island, thinking of bodies that washed ashore.

"Then let's find my friend," Hutchins said, hope lacing his voice. "He could help us."

"Repeat: Not my priority. Sorry, kid."

"But we might have the chance to save his life," Hutchins whimpered. "We can't just leave him to die."

"People die every day," Byrd said, placing her hands on her hips. "And there's nothing we can do."

"No, you're wrong!" Hutchins' voice dropped into full pleading mode. "We *can* do something. And this is important. You wouldn't just be helping me, and you wouldn't just be helping my friend. You'd be helping the entire human race."

"Now you're gettin' hysterical," Byrd said, struggling to keep a straight face. "This is just some local hoodlums—probably gun-running or drugs. Except for a few back-alley drug addicts up in Miami, this won't bother anyone."

"No... you don't understand." Hutchins took a sudden step forward.

Afraid he was going to hug her again, Byrd stepped back.

"What we discovered... it's extremely valuable. Or, at least, it would lead us to something extremely valuable. And, in the wrong hands, that plant could change the world forever."

"Wait a second," Byrd said, pulling the scrap of paper from her pocket. "Does this have anything to do with white snakeroot?"

She held the paper up in front of Hutchins, whose eyes widened.

"It most certainly does," he said, taking the paper and turning it over in his hands. "I think they might be experimenting on people to find a lost plant. Some poor person is being held in the same place I was. I should have saved them, but I ran." Hutchins hung his head, looking at his filthy boots.

"And what place is that?"

"A cell. Torture chamber. A lab, maybe. A bad place." He looked around again. "It's not far from here."

Byrd took the paper back from Hutchins and slid it into her pocket again. She closed her eyes and took a deep breath, silently cursing her luck.

"It sounded like a young woman who was screaming," Hutchins said quietly. "Are you really going to leave her to die?"

"Leave no man behind," Byrd said, opening her eyes and locking them onto Hutchins'. "I'm sure that goes for young women and young academics covered in mango juice, too. You got yourself a partner, kid."

## 23

**Isla de la Vida Eterna, Caribbean Sea.**

"You know I'm going to have to cancel my flight program for this," Byrd said, catching Hutchins' eye. "It'll cost me around forty thousand dollars, but you're going to cover that, right?"

Hutchins looked more terrified than he had when he mentioned the torture chamber.

"Don't sweat it, Hutchins. Just joking. Now, let's go find some danger," she added, much to her new companion's obvious relief.

"I'm not sure I like this paradise island," Byrd muttered as she swatted aside a giant green leaf, clearing a path through the tangled vegetation.

"Me neither," Hutchins replied. "Great mangos. Shame about the hospitality. By the way, I'm sorry, ma'am, but I haven't asked your name?"

"Nora... Sierra Byrd."

"Nora Sierra Byrd?" Hutchins said.

"Just Sierra Byrd. Nora makes me sound like I belong in a retirement village."

*The Shadow of the Sunstone*

"Got it."

"How close are we to the building?" Byrd asked, pushing aside a spiky-looking bush for Hutchins to shuffle past. The buzzing of a million insects now sounded like a malfunctioning power plant.

"Maybe another ten minutes," Hutchins said, waiting for Byrd to join him and move the next bush aside. "We should probably keep our voices down."

"Agreed," Byrd said, looking the slim man up and down. "Just one quick question. How's your right hook?"

"My what?" Hutchins said, sweeping away an insect and missing.

"Your hook," Byrd mimed the movement with her fist. "What about your left cross? Ever been in a fight?"

"I can punch, I think," Hutchins said, looking at his balled fist then testing out his right hook on a palm frond. "But until this morning, that was simply theoretical." The large, green palm swung back, slapping Hutchins in the face.

"Next time, duck," Byrd said, trying not to laugh.

"Good advice." Hutchins nodded solemnly. "Can you fight, Nor–Ms. Byrd?"

"I can defend myself, but I prefer to rely on wit."

Byrd continued to scan left and right as she pushed through another fern. A caterpillar the size and shape of Field Marshal Kitchener's moustache wriggled away into the gloom.

"Yes, agreed," Hutchins said, ducking laboriously beneath a branch. "Where I'm from, brains always trumps brawn."

"That's what worries me," Byrd said quietly, an eyebrow raised.

"What's that?" Hutchins said, pausing.

"I said, where are we going?" Byrd replied.

"Not sure. I was just following you," Hutchins looked around as though someone else might step through the foliage and offer him directions.

"You're the one who's been to this building before, Hutchins!" Byrd hissed, stopping in her tracks.

"Right. I'm pretty sure we——"

The sound of an anguished wail cut through the forest.

Byrd turned to face the sound as a finger of ice worked its way up her spine.

"I hate to say it, but that sounded human," Byrd said, eyeing Hutchins. The young man nodded, his face tight with concern.

Byrd pushed her hand up the length of her forehead, using the sweat collected on her palm to slick back her voluminous hair. After throwing Hutchins a reassuring glance, she shoved her way on through a curtain of vines that hung between massive trees, bringing a squat concrete structure into view. She signaled for Hutchins to move silently in beside her.

Hutchins struggled valiantly through the hostile flora, adding yet more weird stains to his shirt, then awkwardly lowered himself to the ground.

Another devastating howl cut through the air. Byrd glanced at Hutchins, who met her eyes with a panicked sideways look. Hutchins opened his mouth to speak, but Byrd quickly pressed a finger to her lips.

Byrd studied the wall of the building ahead, then carefully surveyed the surrounding area. The howl came again, louder this time. Hutchins visibly shuddered.

Leaning close to Hutchins' ear to speak, Byrd said, "We need to get in close and see what we're dealing with. Stay in my footsteps, slow and deliberate."

Hutchins nodded vigorously, his Adam's apple bobbing.

Byrd reached into her boot and pulled out her compact tactical knife, flipping it open. She offered it to Hutchins, who stared at it as though she'd handed him a live scorpion.

"You take this. I don't intend to kill anyone else today," she whispered. "I find more than three bodies brings bad karma."

Hutchins took the blade in a shaking hand.

"If I get into trouble, you come running with that," Byrd said, pointing at the blade. "That end is for the bad guys, and the other end is for you."

"Got it," Hutchins replied solemnly. "Sharp end for the bad guys." He held up the knife with all the confidence of a child attempting to eat with chopsticks for the first time.

"It's a bit like citing sources in your papers," Byrd said, not quite sure where the comparison was going. "Stick it in, move on, and hope no one will ever look."

"Ahh, I see," Hutchins said, nodding more confidently now.

"After me," Byrd said, shuffling as close to the building as possible before she would have to break cover. She paused behind the final bush and checked their surroundings for movement. Although there was clearly someone inside the decaying single-story structure, the outside was unmanned, for now at least.

"I'm going in first," Byrd said, not even turning to look at Hutchins, who she figured would have uncertainty smeared across his face as obviously as the soil. "You're backup. I get in trouble, charge at them with that." Byrd pointed at the knife, which Hutchins held in an extended arm, pointed at the ground. "It'll be no help to you down there," Byrd added.

"My mom said you should always carry knives with the blade facing downward," Hutchins said, his tone serious.

"What did your mom say about starting fights with criminals?"

"It's funny, she never mentioned that," Hutchins replied.

"Well, mom's the word," Byrd said, and gave Hutchins a wink. She then turned and stalked off toward the structure. She emerged from the undergrowth and paced across the grassy open ground.

The building looked as though it had once been some kind of storage facility but had now been reclaimed by nature. Thick vines strangled the exterior walls like hungry pythons, probing between cracks in the crumbling concrete. One small window remained partially intact, though several glass shards jutted from the frame like teeth. The others were entirely gone, with jungle plants spilling outward through the openings as if the building itself was sprouting vegetation.

Byrd headed directly for the entrance. She followed a narrow path that cut across the grass. With a deep breath to steel her nerves, she raised her hand and knocked on the door.

Someone thumped around inside with erratic movements. Just as Byrd considered knocking again, the door creaked open. A massive figure filled the doorway: a man with huge, plate-like hands and a thick, square head topped with a military-style crew cut. His bare, rounded shoulders glistened with sweat, and his once-white vest bore stains in a rainbow of colors. The expression on his face was one of a dog owner who was about to give his mutt a beating.

"Good mornin', neighbor," Byrd said, flashing her best neighborly smile. The man stepped forward, his jaw jutting out and his lip curled.

## The Shadow of the Sunstone

"What you want?" he growled, his voice rumbling like a tractor engine.

"I want to know what you're doing in there, and why that person keeps howling."

The man fixed Byrd with a stare somewhere between confusion and malevolence. His eyes narrowed, bloodshot veins spreading from the corners like spiderwebs.

"Look, I'm not here to judge y'all," Byrd said. "I just know that come nighttime, I'm not getting a wink of sleep with all this racket."

Within the building, something crashed to the floor, followed by a muffled groan.

The brute's nostrils flared as he sucked in a breath. It looked as though he couldn't quite decide how to react to Byrd's arrival.

A breeze wafted through the open door, dragging with it a smell like death itself had been left out in the sun.

"Well?" Byrd said, crinkling her nose against the scent. "You see, screaming is certainly the sort of noise that's going to attract—"

Byrd was still halfway through speaking when the monster's mental calculations—spinning like a roulette wheel—clearly landed on the idea of violence.

## 24

**Isla de la Vida Eterna, Caribbean Sea.**

The man charged, dropping his shoulders and coming at Byrd like a fully laden freight train.

Byrd pivoted, twisting her body just enough for the charging man to miss her by inches. As his momentum carried him past, she grabbed his vest with both hands, using his own weight against him. With a sharp yank and twist, she directed his barreling mass toward a nearby tree.

The attacker spun, smashing into the trunk with an impact that caused him to grunt from the depths of his huge body. He staggered, momentarily dazed.

"Well, that's the last time I try to help a neighbor out," Byrd said, settling into a fighting stance with her fists raised.

The man turned, shook his head like a bull clearing cobwebs, then roared. This time, he was more cautious, circling Byrd with his massive fists clenched.

Whilst Byrd had practiced the fighting stance many times, this felt very different from the gym. As though growing tired of the stand-off, the man lunged. His hand swung, but his size reduced his speed, and Byrd saw the shot coming.

Byrd pivoted smoothly to the side to parry the blow. The giant fist sailed past her face, close enough that she felt the disturbed air brush her cheek. She countered, using his open guard to deliver a pair of swift, hard jabs to his ribs.

The brute barely registered the hit, his hefty size now an advantage in absorbing blows. He spun and lashed out again. Byrd ducked beneath the strike—a wild haymaker that would have taken her head off if it had connected.

"For a hardened criminal," she taunted, dancing back out of his reach, "you're awfully slow."

The guy swung in close, but Byrd ducked the juggernaut fist. She sent an uppercut in response, clattering into his chin with the bone-cracking thump. The brute's fists dropped momentarily, and he shook his head. He looked down at Byrd as though seeing her for the first time. He raised his fists and lunged forward again.

"Didn't see that one coming, did ya?" Byrd said, sidestepping as he lined up another wild swing. She bobbed up to the right of the man's guard and crashed another fist into his jaw. This time, the strike snapped the man's head back. He staggered, clearly disoriented. The big man steadied himself, placing his feet shoulder-width apart once again. He swung out, this time making a grab for Byrd's arm.

Just a touch of complacency at the man's lack of speed caused Byrd to miscalculate her defensive strike, not realizing what he was doing until his fingers closed around her bicep. She pivoted, stiffened her palm, and delivered a fierce open-palm strike, digging the heel of her hand in under his chin.

The man grunted, but didn't budge.

Shocked by his resilience, Byrd paused for a moment too

long. She didn't see the fist coming until it smashed into her temple, colors exploding behind her eyes. As she struggled to regain her balance, a heavy right hand plunged into her ribcage so hard she thought vital organs might explode inside of her.

Wheezing, she leaned back. Though in shock, she managed to ball her fist and draw back her arm. She swung the shot, pivoting just before connecting—the corkscrew motion of the wrist drawing more muscles into the shot and adding extra impact. The punch landed on the thug's jaw with a crack like fireworks on the Fourth of July. He released his grip, unwittingly allowing Byrd to deliver a left hook to the other side.

Byrd stepped backward, putting some distance between them when the man's meaty hands reached toward her, heading for her throat. With her mind still cloudy from the blow, her reflexes let her down. The thug covered ground and got his hands around her.

She clamped her hands around his, trying to pry them away from her flesh. But his hands remained as firm as bricks in a wall, and the beast growled from the depths of his being as he exerted more deadly pressure.

She drew on her experience to stay calm, trying to divert her attention away from the crushing weight around her neck while thinking of a way to escape the man's clutches instead. But the pressure demanded attention. Byrd's vision blurred, and her oxygen-starved brain filled with fog.

"You hear that?" Byrd managed to croak. She flicked her eyes toward the jungle. "That's my backup on the way."

Clearly getting the message, Hutchins moved in the undergrowth, rustling vegetation. The movement wasn't much, but it was enough to attract the brute's attention for the half-second Byrd needed. She dug a knee into his thigh, and he released his grip just enough to give her options. She put both hands on his chest and shoved with everything she had. He stumbled back, and she slipped free.

With a grunt of effort, she dropped to a crouch and swept her leg in a wide arc, connecting solidly with the assailant's ankles. His balance already compromised, the man toppled like a felled tree.

The impact when he hit the ground shook the earth beneath Byrd's feet. Before he could recover, Byrd pounced. She drove her elbow down hard, catching him precisely at the junction of his neck and jaw—a pressure point that required minimal force for maximum effect.

The brute's eyes rolled back, his massive body going slack.

Byrd straightened up and pulled a deep breath.

"I'm definitely not as nimble on the old feet as I used to be," she said, rubbing a hand across her wrist. "I'll have to work on that. Good work, Hutchins—thanks," she added, turning her attention to where she expected to see him emerging from the jungle.

"Er... thanks. For what?" Hutchins replied from somewhere in the undergrowth. "I was just trying to move further into my hiding place."

Byrd looked at the jungle and saw Hutchins barely hidden by a bush, both shoulders and a leg sticking out.

"Unbelievable," Byrd said, shaking her head. "At what point would you actually have come to help? When that guy ripped my head from my body?"

"I... but you said..." Hutchins stuttered an answer.

"Don't worry about it," Byrd told him, brushing herself down and stepping toward the building. "Let's check this place out before it's too late to help anyone." She tried to shake her head again, but the pounding of her brain made her think better of it.

Hutchins emerged from his cover, and Byrd held her finger to her lips. She pushed the door open slowly and carefully. After listening for movement and hearing none, she led the way into a small room at the front of the building. The room looked as though it served as a makeshift office. Opposite the door, a rotten desk had been pushed up against exposed cinder blocks. Two chairs that looked like they'd been taken out of a dumpster sat either side. The filing cabinet in the corner had long ago turned into some kind of small-scale rust farm.

Two doors, side by side, led to back rooms off the small office. With no one in the office and seemingly no other guards in the back rooms dishing out misery, Byrd led the way further into the building. She stepped toward one of the two doors at the back of the room, then gave it a push. The door creaked open loudly. Byrd shook her head in frustration, and Hutchins nodded in recognition.

"What is this place?" Byrd said, eyeing the hooks on the wall and the broken glass across the floor. Beside her, Hutchins noticeably tensed up, hunching his shoulders.

She stopped in her tracks and froze when her attention turned to a long, rickety table—the kind an injured athlete might find in an underfunded sports clinic. In the shadows, a dark lump lay on the table. Byrd took a step closer and saw a motionless woman wearing only a medical gown. Once probably white, the gown was now filthy and stained. The woman's arms, legs, and matted brown hair hung limply over the edges of the table. Byrd inhaled a strange, pungent scent reminiscent of rotting leaves.

"Oh my gosh," Hutchins said, his voice panicked and his

breath coming out fast as he too turned to look at the woman.

"Hutchins," Byrd said, spinning around and eyeing the man. "This is no time for panic. Panic is like a virus that kills in seconds; I learned that at ten thousand feet. See if you can find a bottle of water," she said, thinking quickly. "We're going to need more than that, but it's a start."

Hutchins nodded and shuffled gratefully out of the room.

Byrd stepped forward, eyeing a large plastic tub under the table. The tub appeared to have once contained a thick purple liquid, with some of the pulp still clinging to the sides.

Glancing at the woman, Byrd saw that her eyes were half open, though she appeared to be unconscious. Fearing the worst, Byrd grasped the woman's wrist. She felt for a pulse. It was weak, but it was there.

"She's alive, thank God," Byrd said. She looked closely at the woman's head, searching for signs of injury. Finding none, she assumed that the woman's state of unconsciousness was due to whatever substance had been in that container.

"If this is what that symphyotrichum puniceum does, I definitely don't want any," she said, remembering what had been written on the paper she'd swiped from the thug on the beach.

"Got some water," Hutchins said, hurrying back into the room with a pair of large bottles the guard had obviously ignored.

"Great," Byrd said, stroking the woman's matted hair and then rolling her onto her side. "I've got a feeling we're going to need that real soon." Byrd's voice dropped into a whisper as she spoke to the poor woman. "I'm sorry."

Then, she stuck two fingers into the woman's mouth and down her throat, grimacing the whole time. The purple poison came spraying out, covering the walls.

Hutchins shrieked and tried to cover his face.

The woman retched for several seconds. She stared at Byrd with wide, wild eyes, then abruptly fell back into unconsciousness.

"She's very weak," Byrd said, holding out her hand for the water. First, she held the woman's head up and poured a little into her mouth, then she used a glug of the water to clean the goo off her hands.

"I'm not sure moving her is such a great idea," Hutchins whispered.

"You're right," Byrd said, "but I don't see that we have a choice." She nodded toward the door. "Mr. Nice Guy won't be out for long, and who's to know what friends he's got hanging around."

Sierra Byrd placed one hand under the woman's filthy hair and another under her knees. She gently lifted the woman and placed the limp form over her shoulder. She then made her way quickly toward the door.

Hutchins picked up the container and followed, his breathing audible with each shaky breath.

## 25

**Isla de la Vida Eterna, Caribbean Sea.**

Emerging from the building, Byrd rounded the structure and headed in the opposite direction from the way they'd come.

"You got lucky," she said to the unconscious guard, noticing his chest still rising and falling. She stepped over his comatose figure and headed toward the forest. She carried the woman across her shoulders in a fireman's lift, the extra weight already burning her muscles.

"Wait a second. We came from that way, I think," Hutchins said, running a few steps to catch up with Byrd.

Despite the woman's added weight, Byrd's assured stride put her well ahead of the academic.

"You wanna go back that way, be my guest," Byrd said, locating the narrow path quickly and striding into the forest. "All that's back there is a burning plane and something nasty the tide washed in."

"What? What did the tide wash in?" Hutchins said, still hurrying to keep up.

"Look," Byrd said, stopping in her tracks and spinning around to throw the academic a look. "You asked me to help you, and I'm helping you. Now get in front and help *me*. This path is too narrow for me to carry her without bashing into every leaf and spike the forest has to offer."

Hutchins stomped around her and started pushing the undergrowth aside. On a couple of occasions, he looked as though he was about to moan, but Byrd silenced him with a look that could melt the tungsten blades of a turbofan engine.

Hutchins yanked aside a particularly large fern, then froze.

"What's wrong?" Byrd said, her shoulders now burning from the weight.

Hutchins pointed at something a few feet from the path, currently out of Byrd's eyeline.

"We need to keep moving," Byrd said, shoving her way forward. "It's alright for you. You're not carrying—" Byrd stopped talking when she saw what Hutchins was looking at, and she froze too.

On the floor of the jungle, poking out from beneath the large leaves of a banana plant, lay four legs. Two side by side, like two bodies in a morgue.

Hutchins pulled the hanging leaves aside, revealing the bodies of a man and woman, both apparently in their late thirties. They both had light brown hair, tinged yellow by hours spent in the sun. Byrd's gaze shifted up across the bodies, and she realized how healthy they looked—except for the bullet holes in each forehead.

"There's no sign of experimentation," Hutchins replied, looking left and right as he scanned the ground around the bodies.

"Most likely, they were just in the wrong place at the

wrong time," Byrd said. "I came across a yacht down at the beach. It looked to me like someone tried to shelter out the storm here."

Hutchins swallowed, although it looked as though he was having a hard time of it.

"I'd say they ended up beaching their boat and came ashore looking for help. The rest is obvious," Byrd continued.

"They found out what was going on," Hutchins said, pointing at the bodies. "And those men wouldn't let them leave in case they reported it."

Byrd nodded while shifting the unconscious woman across her shoulders, attempting to reduce the pain. "Kneel down and check for a pulse—two fingers just next to the big vein. We need to make sure they're beyond help."

"I... I'm not sure..." Hutchins said, his eyes doing a full rotation of their surroundings as though checking for someone else to volunteer in his place.

"Fine, you just take this lady, and I'll do it," Byrd said, making to pass him the woman.

"Okay, fine," Hutchins said, kneeling quickly. He touched the female victim and then the male. His grim expression told the story long before he said the words. "They're gone."

"Left to rot, just like the poor souls who washed up on my beach," Byrd said, shaking her head. "I'm going to deal with whoever did this—personally."

"What should we do?" Hutchins asked.

"Right now, we need to get out of here. I don't know about you, but I like my head without bullets in it."

Byrd started off again down the path, the woman pressing on her shoulders like a huge sand timer, pressing her harder into the earth with each passing second.

"You can be damn callous sometimes, you know that?" Hutchins said, running after her.

"Yeah. I do," Byrd said, pausing and turning back to Hutchins.

"Then why do it?"

"Because life is callous. And blissful ignorance isn't my thing." She indicated the direction of their movement with her head. "But most importantly, if we don't get off this island soon, there'll be many more victims, starting with us."

Without a reply, Hutchins pushed in front of Byrd and once again started clearing the path. After a minute or two, the forest became less dense, allowing the two to walk more easily.

Hutchins removed the container he'd picked up back at the makeshift lab, pulled off the top, and stuck his index finger inside. He scraped out some of the pulp and held it in a beam of sunlight to get a better look.

"You think there's some purple in there?" he asked, turning around and wielding the finger toward Byrd.

"Looks pretty purple to me."

"Damn. They're closer than I thought," Hutchins said, wiping his finger on a thick leaf as they passed. "They know what they're looking for."

"Normally I wouldn't care, each to their own and all that, but since you're the only conscious person here, I'd really love it if you made sense," Byrd said.

Hutchins huffed out a breath, pulled aside another plant, and then turned to look at Byrd. "Alright, so the people who took the professor from this island must be the same people who are experimenting here," he said, sighing heavily. "And the experimentations are appalling for the subjects. The man who captured me told me that 'First, there will be great pain, then there will be great joy.' Many plants used by indigenous folk healers and shamans carry such a dichotomy." Hutchins looked around at the vegetation surrounding them. "It's like Ayahuasca," he continued. "The plant that's used as a recreational drug."

"Give me a single malt any day," Byrd said.

"Extreme sickness usually follows extreme enlightenment and psychological healing," Hutchins explained. "You know, the astral plane?"

"Does it have wings?" Byrd said, and Hutchins shook his head. "Then it's safe to say I've never heard of it," Byrd added.

"Okay, but this is the plant of the gods we're talking about. It looks as though they're testing whatever they find on people like her." Hutchins pointed at the unconscious woman.

"Human lab rats," Byrd said.

"Exactly. Some of the subjects may even be force-fed white snakeroot, a plant so toxic to humans that the suffering is unimaginable. Linium is its antidote. Witnessing those positive effects would be a way to prove that they've found the right plant."

"What kind of sick person would do something like this?" Byrd said, turning sideways to move between a pair of trees.

"The guard who first held me mentioned a 'mentor'—a man named Sallas," Hutchins replied. "A man who 'everyone works for.'"

"Weird. Sounds like maybe... a cult."

"Yeah," Hutchins agreed. He thought for a moment as tropical birds honked like ships' horns overhead. "Someone has to be bankrolling this. Someone with money; someone prominent. If it's the guy I think it is, Lucian Sallas, he's the younger brother of Ewart Sallas––a decorated scientist and winner of the Kavli Prize.

"And why are they experimenting?" Byrd said. "What are they looking for?"

"The plant. Linium. Lost for two centuries." Hutchins locked eyes with Byrd, and she felt the young academic was beginning to trust her. "One of the most powerful, health-giving plants ever to have existed. Some people believe it could bring eternal life. That's simply not possible...but it's not too far from the truth. It could also bring a vast amount of wealth to whoever rediscovers it."

"Why don't you just tell this Sallas guy where it is? Avoid any more experimentation?" Byrd asked between heavy breaths. As she plodded on, she heard the sound of waves crashing against rocks, growing louder with each step.

"Because I don't know where it is. I just know that such a plant exists. First, we need to find the Sunstone. And anyway, even if we could tell Sallas where to look, it might stop this particular trial, but it won't stop him being cruel and destructive. It will just provide enablement and wealth for whatever he's got planned next. We need to find the plant before he does. We need to show the world, and his followers, that he's a fraud."

"How are we going to do that?" Byrd said.

Hutchins leaned in close to Byrd and said, "The Sunstone is believed to be the only source of instructions on how to use the plant. It may also help us to find the plant itself."

Byrd nodded her understanding, then asked, "How much do you know about the Sunstone?"

"A little. I was being educated on it when... things got weird."

"Educated by whom?"

"Professor Wall," Hutchins said, a sheen of sadness crossing his eyes. "Finding him would be more expedient than blindly trying to find the Sunstone. In many ways, the man and the relic are very similar. They are both a pathway to knowledge."

"Okay. I'm in," Byrd said, taking a deep breath. "The people who washed up on my island, and those we saw lying in the jungle back there, deserve justice. The best way to do that is to bring this whole operation to an end. After we get this poor girl to a hospital, let's find your friend. Then your plant."

"Sounds good to me," Hutchins agreed, smiling warmly. "The only small problem is... we're stuck on this island."

"Not for long," Byrd said, nodding toward the path ahead.

The pair took another few steps forward, bringing the sea into view. Bobbing gently on the waves, tied to a concrete jetty, was the de Havilland seaplane Byrd had seen from the air. "Time for a little plane-jacking," she said.

# 26

**Mexican desert, north of Cabo San Lucas.**

Professor Wall woke before opening his eyes. Someone's gentle, rhythmic breathing came from very close by. For a moment—just a fleeting moment—he thought it was his wife. He imagined they were back home, and tried to shuffle his limbs awake so he could head downstairs to make her coffee.

Registering the dryness in his throat, as though someone had poured a fistful of gravel into his mouth, his eyes snapped open. Instead of his wife's curly gray hair, he found himself staring at long, straight, almost perfect hair. *Almost* perfect, but lacking the aging perfection of his wife's silvery white curls.

He looked around and recognized The White Room—so The Mentor had called it. The space was indeed completely white, save for a large and vividly green plant standing in the corner. The ceramic tiles on the floor had clearly been well scrubbed and polished. The place was pristine—hell masquerading as heaven.

"A symbol of deceit," he whispered, looking at the girl lying next to him. "Like Cleopatra, history's most famous femme fatale."

With aching muscles and creaking joints, Wall dragged himself out of the bed.

Suddenly, Briony rolled over and met his gaze with wide, hazel eyes. She broke the stare and looked down at her fully clothed body. She met Wall's gaze again and smiled weakly.

"Thank you for being a gentleman," she said. "For not even trying."

Wall nodded, remembering the night before. He had stood in the center of the room, fully clothed, not knowing what on earth to do with himself. Mercifully, Briony had taken things into her own hands by simply pulling back the bedsheets, lying down, and immediately going to sleep.

"Of course," Wall said. "I'm old enough to be your—"

Tears welled up in the young woman's eyes before the professor could even finish his sentence.

"When did you last see him?" he asked quietly.

"Seven months ago."

Wall's body tightened. "What is this place?"

"I'm so thirsty. Could you please get me some water?" Briony asked, clearly steering the conversation back to more comfortable ground.

Wall nodded and paced across to the door. Half expecting it to be locked, he tried the handle. The door swung open, revealing blazing sunshine beyond. Wall paced through as a young man with blond hair fashioned into a top knot sauntered past.

"He's borrowed his physique from Doryphoros," Wall muttered, referencing the perfect proportions and balanced musculature that Polykleitos had rendered in marble around 440 BCE.

From somewhere inside the compound, the sound of a hammer on metal rang out repeatedly. Wall turned toward the sound, suspecting someone with far more enthusiasm than talent was once again trying to turn twisted metal into art. A young woman wearing a floral sarong drifted through his vision.

"Everyone here is so beautiful," Wall muttered to himself, his voice croaking through his parched lips.

"You're right," came a familiar deep, smooth voice from behind.

Wall spun around, his heart in his throat. The Mentor, Sallas, paced from another building—a white, round hut beside the place where Wall had spent the night.

Two young women followed The Mentor out. One slipped away, but the other clung onto the man's arm. Wall recognized her floral headband and freckled face, having seen her from his cage during The Mentor's speech. The shrieking woman.

Tammy looked up at Wall with a wry smile on her face, like she was amused by how out of his depth he was.

"Many of the people here are very physically perfect. And you were lucky enough to lie with one of them," The Mentor said and nodded toward the door through which Wall had exited the White Room.

"What?" Wall barked, appalled by the smirk playing across the other man's face.

"I hope you enjoyed your evening with Briony. Not many men are fortunate enough to be with a woman like that. Especially not at your age." Sallas pointed at Wall's scrawny legs.

"I didn't touch her," Wall hissed, his tone vicious. "She slept immediately. And... and I wouldn't have touched her. She's young enough—"

"Of course, you would deny it. You are married. The instinct to deny is as strong as the instinct to do the deed in the first place." Sallas' smug smile tainted his handsome face.

"I am telling you, I did not do anything."

"Telling me or telling yourself?"

Wall paused. The heat pressed down upon him, just as oppressive as his strange environment. The sun and his captor grilled him simultaneously.

"I'm sorry," Wall said, clearing his throat, "but do you know where I might be able to get some water?"

"Such politeness," The Mentor replied, smirking again. "I wonder if that's a trait that could be bred into future generations. It's not one I had considered."

"Clarity of thought and directness of communication are also excellent traits," Wall said confidently, despite the dryness in his throat.

The Mentor's eyes narrowed, a muscle twitching in his face like he was a dog about to snarl. Wall briefly enjoyed seeing the smug man's annoyance at being outwitted.

"Follow me," Sallas said, turning and striding around the back of the White Rooms. Tammy skipped away, while Sallas led Wall across a barren stretch of sand and between two buildings made from dark wood. They reached a narrow path where yellow palo verde trees cast welcome shade, and the surroundings became more like an English country garden than a harsh desert. Wall cast aside memories of home.

Walking further, Wall saw pink and orange sword lilies lining the stone path. The fresh scent of watered plants and the gurgle of a fountain drifted through the air.

The Mentor led Wall up to the fountain and pointed at one of the chairs that surrounded it.

Registering the gesture as an instruction, Wall slumped into one of the chairs. He looked around and noted how different this area was from the rest of the compound. It had obviously been cultivated as a private area for the cult leader.

"I have a gift for you in my Gloriette," the younger man said, crossing to a small wooden shed.

"That's the least glorious Gloriette I've ever seen," Wall muttered to himself.

"Welcome to my personal sanctuary," The Mentor said, returning with two bottles of water, frosted and dripping.

Wall grabbed the bottle delightfully, his fingers already enjoying the cold exterior.

"It must be a long time since you've had such refreshment," The Mentor said, nodding toward the bottle.

"Yes, many hours, I can't..." Wall's voice trailed off as he snapped open the lid. He lifted the bottle to his lips and then froze. He looked up and saw the other man watching him closely. Wall had seen the look before—a scientist with a test subject.

"Briony... she needs water as well," Wall stuttered.

"She'll be serviced, don't worry about that," The mentor said, sounding frustrated. "I take care of the good ones."

Wall lifted the bottle to his lips again and then glanced at the unopened bottle in the Mentor's hand.

"I thought you were thirsty?" The Mentor asked.

The tinkling of the fountain and the cold touch of the bottle tormented Wall's thirst. "Of course I'm thirsty," he said, watching a bead of condensation run down the bottle.

"Then drink," The Mentor said, shrugging playfully.

Wall couldn't figure out the man's gestures. It was as though he went from contented to frustrated and back again in the blink of an eye.

"I... I'm just..." Wall's throat longed for the water, but something didn't sit right. He thought about how unfocused Briony had been the night before—if the same chemical was in the water, Wall certainly didn't want any.

"I understand," The Mentor said as though they were old friends. "You don't trust me. That's to be... expected." The ice returned to his voice. "But I can assure you, the bottle you see before you is the only refreshment you're going to get." The Mentor pointed a stiff finger at the bottle in Wall's hand.

Wall lifted the bottle an inch and then lowered it two. He longed to take a sip, but while his body cried out for him to drink, his head told him not to.

"I'm not going to waste my time demonstrating to you where our refreshments came from," The Mentor said, his lip curling into a snarl. "And I'm not offering you a guided tour of the catering facilities—you might be from England, but you're certainly not royalty."

Wall's gaze shifted from the bottle in his hand to that in The Mentor's.

"Oh, I see," the younger man said, now talking to Wall like he was an annoying younger brother. "You think that these two sealed and identical bottles are somehow different?"

Wall opened his mouth to speak, but the dryness in his throat reduced his voice to a groan.

"I will go so far as leaning over and changing bottles with you," The Mentor said, his tone suggesting that the gesture was probably the most charitable thing one human had done for another since the dawn of time. "Would that make you feel better?"

Wall's gaze shifted from one bottle to the other, then back again.

"But then again, did I know you might be suspicious and want to swap?" The Mentor asked as he leaned toward Wall, holding out the bottle. "Had I prepared for such a request? Is the problematic bottle in my hand or yours? Or both, or none?"

"Look––" Wall croaked before his voice gave up on him. Heat radiated up from the earth, baking his bare feet.

"Or...," The Mentor hissed, his voice rising in pitch, "have I just generously handed a bottle of water to a sad old man who begged me for one, taking up time in my busy day when I didn't need to? Is the sad old man turning the very boring situation into a problem in his head?"

Wall didn't reply. The fountain gurgled.

The Mentor brushed a hand over the stubble that ran in two perfectly symmetrical strips up to his cheekbones.

"Just drink the damn water, or not, I don't care," The Mentor hissed, pulling his bottle away and slumping into a chair.

Wall stared at his liquid temptress. His only thoughts were of the raging, awful thirst, and the heat and sweat that continued to make it worse. Unable to resist any longer, Wall lifted the bottle to his lips and drank. The ice-cold liquid replenished and delighted him. But only for a second.

## 27

It took Wall almost no time to realize he had been tricked. The bottle contained far more than pure water. He closed his fist around the plastic as the first wave of sensation crashed across him.

He dropped the bottle to the ground like a poisoned fruit. The liquid glugged out across the floor.

Wall looked across at the Mentor and saw, instead of one person, three people staring back at him. The look of a curious scientist returned to The Mentor's eyes as he watched Wall closely.

Wall opened his mouth to speak, but no sound came out. An invisible force pushed down on him, pinning him to the chair.

"What you are experiencing is entirely natural," The Mentor said, his voice distant and discordant. "What you have imbibed has been plucked from the earth in its purest form. How could anything so natural be damaging? Just enjoy the ride."

"Enjoy...? I can't...I don't..."

"That is one of the most interesting things about plants

with strong physical and psychological effects," The Mentor said, his voice swirling around inside Wall's head. "You know, some of the most potent may not have even been discovered yet. Or they have been discovered by ancient civilizations before being lost again."

Wall clamped his eyes shut, willing the sensation to pass. It came on stronger still, tilting his surroundings like a ship in a storm.

"Imagine the treasures that are most likely right there, growing naturally around the world."

Wall's head lolled to one side, as though it was now too heavy for his spine to hold.

"The way I see it, life is one big experiment," The Mentor said, talking like a proud parent. To Wall, his voice sounded as though it was underwater. "Some experiments are small—trying a new drink or taking a new partner for the evening."

Wall thought he saw the other man winking but couldn't be sure. He tried to speak, to stop the tirade of self-obsessed nonsense spouting from The Mentor's mouth, but he couldn't get any words out. He thought about stuffing his fingers in his ears but feared that if he let go of the chair, he might slide off and bounce across the floor.

"In this place, we like to experiment," The Mentor continued. "But the experiments we perform here are far more important than you'll find in most universities. We are doing this for the benefit of humankind."

"Stop. I want it to stop," Wall groaned, his head now lolling so far forward that his chin almost touched his chest.

"Imbibing substances like this provides a window into another world," The Mentor continued, ignoring the pleas and clearly enjoying having a captive audience. "We are visiting the world that lives deep in our souls. What we do here offers a new perspective, both on ourselves and the whole human condition."

Wall forced himself upright and noticed that the curling branches of the trees appeared like wings sprouting from The Mentor's back. But this man was no angel; he was a demon in hippy clothing.

"The power of plants, Professor Wall. I believe you are a seeker yourself?" The Mentor said, his head splitting into three and moving in a kaleidoscopic dance in Wall's vision.

"Why...why would I seek...this," Wall croaked, each word a crushing effort. "This...I feel terrible. Confused."

"Not the psychedelics, Professor. The healing." The Mentor's voice now sounded like it was coming from directly above Wall's head. "You seek the plant that brings eternal life."

The leaves around Wall vibrated in and out, as though they were breathing.

"There... there's no such thing... you idiot," Wall spat, lucidity returning for a moment.

The Mentor suddenly rushed at Wall, covering the distance in two steps. In his confused state, Wall hadn't even seen him coming. He felt hands grab his cheeks, and then a face loomed large in front of his eyes, blocking his entire view.

"Say that again, and see what happens," The Mentor growled.

Wall said nothing as he looked up at the other man's face through narrowed eyes. The skin appeared to bulge and flow, as though Wall could see each and every biological process happening beneath the surface. Blood vessels pulsed visibly, expanding and contracting with each heartbeat. Cell division appeared as tiny ripples across the cheeks. The man's pores looked like vast craters, secreting oils that glistened in Wall's hyper-enhanced vision.

"My friend," Wall said calmly, placing his hand across one of The Mentor's forearms. "There is no such thing... as eternal life." He lost focus as the trees around him reeled into intricate geometric patterns, branches weaving themselves into impossible mathematical structures. Colors intensified—the greens becoming emerald fire, the sky a violent blue that hurt to look at.

"If there is no eternal life," Wall managed to add, "then there is no plant that can provide it."

"Longer life. A healthier life. Stronger. You know what I mean," The Mentor hissed, looking down at Wall's hand and then quickly whipping his own arm away. "You know the plant I am talking about."

Wall thought carefully about his next words. Thinking seemed easier for the time being.

"The only things I seek are truth and clarity," Wall said, his voice sounding distant even to himself.

"Like a God, almost, aren't you?" The Mentor nodded, his head bobbing up and down as though disconnected from his body. "Well, here's a truth for you. Those of us who built this place intend to live long and magnificent lives, and to breed happy and magnificent children. The plant will help us with the first part of that, and maybe even with the second part. We have to find it."

The Mentor moved his face even closer to Wall's, their noses almost touching.

"There are two ways of doing that," The Mentor continued. "The first is to add your knowledge to our knowledge. To build on what is written in ancient texts and to find the sacred stone, which will lead us to the plant."

"The sacred what?" Wall replied.

"The second option is trial and error," The Mentor said, his lip twitching. "We need volunteers. These people are brave, but they will suffer. Depending on which plant they try, they may suffer quite terribly."

"I... I don't..." Wall felt lucidity slipping away again, replaced by a dream that had been recorded on corrupted tape.

"White snakeroot, for example," The Mentor continued. "A substance to which our sacred plant is an antidote. If our antidote works, then we have found our fabled plant. Dreadful symptoms, but it's part of the process." The Mentor stepped back. Wall slumped forward, almost folding in two.

"You need..." Wall slurred.

"What do I need?" The Mentor said, urgency lacing his voice. He grabbed Wall by the chin and lifted his face.

"You need therapy," Wall said.

The Mentor drew back his hand and slapped Wall hard. Pain exploded through Wall's face, and angry, red stars danced throughout his vision.

"I will benefit from your academic research, Professor," The Mentor growled. "And with your help, the volunteers can discontinue their service. The suffering can end."

"Volunteers?" Wall muttered. "Why... why would anyone––"

"Do you see anyone trying to escape?" The Mentor asked. "We have thirty-seven happy people here. Actually, now thirty-eight. The tiniest one of them is growing inside Briony."

# 28

**Isla de la Vida Eterna, Caribbean Sea.**

Byrd hurried down the jetty toward the de Havilland Canada DHC-6 Twin Otter seaplane, her shoulders now burning from the weight of her unconscious passenger. Reaching the plane, she laid the woman gently on the pier and then leaned out and pulled on the lever to open the cabin door. The door seemed to sigh as it opened, emitting a sound like the relief Byrd felt that they weren't going to have to break in or overpower anyone.

"Come and help me," she called to Hutchins as she scrambled into the plane. "We need to get her inside."

Hutchins cautiously shuffled the woman to the edge of the jetty, and together they lifted her inside. Byrd placed her in one of the rear seats and did up the belt.

"Getting the thing in the air won't be so easy," Byrd said, moving to the flight deck. "It's great the cabin door was open, but if we can't take off, it doesn't help us at all."

"How do you even start a plane that's not yours?"

Hutchins asked, looking at the controls and dials like a child picking up a book for the first time.

"Great question, kid. First, you hope the key is in the ignition. But today is really not our lucky day—as you might have noticed." Byrd pointed to the empty ignition socket.

"Funnily enough, I thought the same thing," Hutchins said.

"If the key isn't in the ignition, there's one option left..." Byrd pointed at the propeller through the windshield. "All we need to do is sever the p-leads. That'll disable the ignition shutoff and let me hot-start the engine by spinning the prop. Messy, risky, but it might just work."

"Sounds sim— Wait a second, you've got to start the prop by—"

"Spinning it by hand. Yeah," Byrd interjected, stepping toward the door.

"You could lose your arm doing something like that. Then how would I—" Hutchins said, stopping himself as Byrd shot him a glare.

"It's basically the same as turning a key in the ignition," Byrd explained, "but it messes your engine up a hell of a lot more in the long term. I'll try not to lose an arm and mess up your well-thought-out travel plans." She dropped onto the float, rocking the plane from side to side.

"If you're sure," Hutchins said, looking out at the horizon.

"Give me my knife back," Byrd said, extending her arm back inside the cabin.

With the knife back in her possession, Byrd moved toward the front of the plane and pulled open the hatch to access the engine. She wiped sweat from her eyes, then leaned in, breathing in familiar scents of oil and warm metal.

"Hold on!" Hutchins said from the cabin door.

"What is it? This is a pretty crucial moment," Byrd replied, leaning inside the hatch.

"I can hear something. It's..."

"Great to know your ears still work, but care to be a tiny little bit more speci—" Then Byrd heard it too. "That's an engine," she said, standing tall. "And it's—"

"Coming this way," Hutchins added. He cupped a hand over his eyes and searched the sea. "Quick, cut the G-strings or whatever it was you needed to do."

"P-leads," Byrd replied. "G-Strings is something completely different you'll learn about when you leave high school." Byrd glanced up at Hutchins before leaning back into the engine bay.

"It's coming!" Hutchins roared, the plane now rocking with the motion of his looking from side to side.

"Alright. I'm going as quick as I can!" Byrd said. Gripping the knife in her teeth, she pulled the leads' wiring loom toward her. She separated the wires and found those she needed. Triple-checking she had the right ones, she sliced the leads with the blade.

"Done," she said, emerging back into fresh air. The noise from the nearby engine drifted loudly across the sea now, getting closer with every second.

"Great. Let's go!" Hutchins said.

"Hold this." Byrd held out the knife for Hutchins to take. After he accepted the blade, she flashed him a smile that said, *You might need that.*

"Now the part that might result in me losing an arm," Byrd said, moving to manually spin the propeller.

"It's them; I know it is!" Hutchins said, his teeth clenched. "Please hurry!"

Byrd grabbed the propeller and prepared to haul it into

motion. She counted down, running the quick forward-and-reverse motion through her mind.

"It's a Jet Ski," Hutchins said, his voice slightly calmer than before. "A Jet Ski just came around the headland over there."

Byrd cast a look over her shoulder and saw the Jet Ski cutting through the sea, a flag of blonde hair flowing behind it.

"I'll be damned," Byrd said, scrambling up onto the jetty. "It looks as though our luck is about to change." She waved at the Jet Ski, and the engine noise cut. The craft arced through the sea, coming directly for them.

"Need a ride?!" Candi said, pulling in close to the jetty.

Byrd put her finger to her lips, but she couldn't help beaming.

Candi pulled up smoothly alongside the jetty.

"I'd love a ride, girl, but I've got passengers," Byrd said, throwing her student a genuine smile. "And one of them needs to get to the hospital in Chetumal. I don't think a Jet Ski will cut it."

Candi scrunched her nose up, bunching up light freckles and tanned skin. The young blonde then turned to Hans Hutchins, and Byrd watched their eyes meet. The gaze lingered for several seconds as Byrd saw smiles flicker on both faces.

"Erm... I hate to interrupt," Byrd said, "but can I ask what in the name of the Almighty you're doing here, miss?!"

"I saw you fly over here, like, hours ago," Candi said. "Then I saw smoke, and I feared the worst. I tried to come earlier, but Tom talked me out of it."

"Well, thank you for coming now. You're right; we are having a little troub—"

The air split with a savage crack as a bullet tore past

Byrd's ear, slamming into the jetty and sending splinters into the air. A moment later, the thunder of the gunshot rolled across the water.

"Get down!" Byrd yelled, crashing front-first onto the pier.

Hutchins and Candi slammed down beside her, their stomachs pressed to the wood.

"I'm glad you're here, girl, but your Jet Ski attracted unwanted attention," Byrd said through gritted teeth.

"Who's shooting at us?!" Candi said, quiet but urgent, her fingers interlocked on the top of her head. "I thought this island was supposed to be—"

"Bad people," Byrd interrupted. "And right now, they're stopping me from getting my passenger to a hospital. Hot-starting a plane under fire ain't easy."

Byrd saw Hutchins glance at Candi, admiration glazing his eyes like honey. Suddenly, the young academic sprang to his feet and immediately broke into a sprint. He ran hard along the jetty toward the tree line.

"Hey!" Hutchins yelled out in the direction of the gunfire. "Over here!"

"What on Earth is he doing?!" Candi said.

"What on Earth have you done to *him*?!" Byrd replied. "That pretty face of yours has turned him into someone else!"

Hutchins ran along the edge of the beach, keeping under the shade of trees that overhung the sand. Byrd felt all of her muscles tense as she watched the young man sprint along the beach. Gunshots boomed again, and bullets kicked up plumes of sand a few feet behind Hutchins.

"He's incredible," Candi said, watching the young academic go. "Is he special forces or something?"

"You have no idea," Byrd said out the corner of her

mouth. Not letting the distraction go to waste, she ran for the propeller.

Candi rolled from the jetty and swung her leg over the Jet Ski.

"You get to the hospital," Candi shouted. "I'll take care of our hero." She fired up the engine and set off in an arc toward the beach, white spray kicking up all around her.

Byrd clamped a hand around a blade of the propeller and pulled it hard. The blades blurred as they spun, and the engine came to life.

"Our hero," Byrd said, rolling her eyes before sliding into the pilot's seat. Then, she smiled. "I guess I'd have to say he is."

# 29

**Isla de la Vida Eterna, Caribbean Sea.**

Hans Hutchins charged down the beach, pumped full of adrenaline like a racehorse on stimulants. He'd never felt such energy in his life. His legs moved with surprising strength, each stride more powerful than he thought possible.

Behind him, bullets tore into the shoreline, kicking up violent geysers of sand and spray. The sharp crack of gunfire should have terrified him, but in his adrenaline-soaked delirium, each shot barely registered. He swung to the left and then the right again, zigzagging across the beach with all the coordination of a newborn giraffe.

Still running at full pelt, he risked a backward glance. A man, similar looking to all the nasty brutes he'd seen since Wall's kidnap, ran out of the jungle. Hutchins pushed his shoulders back, stiffened his fingers like an Olympic sprinter, and ran like he'd never run before.

As he lurched left and right, gunfire strafed past him,

smashing into a palm tree and sending chunks of bark spiraling into the forest.

Hearing an engine, Hutchins turned and saw the Jet Ski cutting through the surf behind him. The beautiful blonde woman at the controls waved him across. In all his life, Hutchins didn't think he'd seen something quite that gorgeous. He pictured ancient Valkyries coming to carry fallen warriors to Valhalla—though in his case, hopefully avoiding the "fallen" part.

Candi whipped the Jet Ski around for Hutchins to climb onto the back. He stomped into the water and jumped on, covered in sand and sweat.

"Chetumal please, driver," Hutchins said, pulling himself onto the seat behind Candi. "And don't screw me on the fare."

Candi let out a delightful laugh and hit the throttle, bouncing the Jet Ski over the surf and toward the open ocean.

"I would never dream of it," she said, raising her voice over the howling engine. "I'm Candi, by the way. Our introduction was sort of interrupted."

"Hans. Hans Hutchins. Pleased to meet you," Hutchins said, the first grin of the last several hours lighting his face.

"Come and get us now!" Hutchins bellowed, turning to see a bare-chested man with the physique of a world champion boxer. He looked like all the others, with swirling tattoos covering his torso. The thug raised the pistol and squeezed off two shots, although he was now too far away for accuracy, and the bullets plopped into the surf. The man unclipped what looked like a radio from his belt and spoke into it before turning away and striding down the beach.

"It seems you've made an impression," Candi shouted over the howling engine. Now that they were in the open water, the Jet Ski cut a sharp line across the surface, which was as flat as polished glass.

"Well, I like to try, even though we've only just met," Hutchins said, casting a look over his shoulder at their V-shaped wake rolling out behind them.

"Whatever you did to those guys, it's wound them up," Candi said, clearly not hearing Hutchins' reply.

"Ah, yes, of course, sure," Hutchins said, nodding vigorously, though he was unsure what she'd said. They rounded the headland and sped in the direction of the mainland.

"We've got about three miles to cruise for cover!" Candi shouted through the spray, noise, and fuel fumes. "Shouldn't take long in these conditions."

"No, I'm not Tom Cruise's brother, although people have commented on our likeness." Hutchins ran his fingers through his hair.

"You see the coastline right ahead?" Candi said, pointing toward the hazy outline of land barely visible on the horizon. Buildings and docks gradually materialized from the haze.

"Yes, I suppose I am quite widely read!" Hutchins enthused, completely oblivious but beaming with academic pride.

Candi pointed frantically to the right, where the blocky shapes of several boats were becoming visible. "That channel looks clear!"

"You saw me on the panel last year?" Hutchins replied, following her finger but missing her point entirely. "That was only a small thing, on Mesoamerican burial practices. My real contribution was the excavation at Tikal, where we uncovered a previously unknown temple complex. The hieroglyphic inscriptions suggested a completely different dynastic lineage than previously thought!"

Candi glanced over her shoulder, then her body stiffened.

"There's a boat! A boat!" she screamed, turning back and accelerating.

"A moat? Most temples didn't have—"

"Get your damn head down!" Candi screamed.

Bullets strafed into the water on both sides of the Jet Ski, followed by more booming gunfire. Hutchins turned around and saw, for the first time, a speedboat powering away from the island in pursuit.

"There's... there's a boat!" Hutchins screamed, pointing frantically.

"I know!" Candi shouted.

Hutchins saw two figures in the speedboat, one at the controls, the other clutching an assault rifle.

"Get ready to swerve," Hutchins bellowed. "Now!"

This time, Candi got the message loud and clear. She flicked her wrist, sending the Jet Ski barreling to the right.

Hutchins clamped his feet hard against the hull, fighting with the momentum to keep his balance.

"Yes! Faster!" Hutchins said, now leading forward too. Pressing their bodies together made talking possible.

"It's maxed out!" she yelled back. "I can't!"

"Keep turning, that'll stop them shooting ahead of us," Hutchins said, enjoying the feel of her flowing hair on his face.

"How do you know all this?" Candi said. "Has this sort of thing happened to you before?"

"Just something I picked up on the way to Mexico," Hutchins said, pleased that the statement wasn't technically a lie—he remembered it from the action film he'd watched on the plane.

"If it makes you feel safer, hug me all you want!" she shouted.

"Not hugging, protecting!"

"Oh! Well, protect me all you want!"

The sound of the speedboat's powerful engine rumbled across the water as it powered closer.

"That'll do seventy knots in calm water," Candi said, glancing behind them. "We'll max at forty-five, maybe fifty if we're lucky."

"How do you know—"

"I know boats!" Candi said, glancing back at Hutchins.

Hutchins broke the stare and looked at the rapidly approaching speedboat. A man with mirrored sunglasses worked the controls, while the bare-chested guy aimed the assault rifle and fired.

"Swerve!" Hutchins shouted.

Candi jerked the handlebars, sending them into a sharp banking turn that nearly threw Hutchins from his perch. Bullets sliced through the water just off their port side, kicking up a thin spout before skipping across the surface.

The sharp snap of another bullet cut through the engine noise—closer this time. Hutchins ducked instinctively, crushing his eyes shut as though not seeing the danger might somehow ward it off.

"He won't keep missing!" Hutchins yelled. "Swerve, zig-zig, anything!"

Candi pulled one swerve and then slammed straight into another, drenching them both with spray.

Hutchins gritted his teeth and clung on tight, straining every muscle to maintain balance. His stomach dipped violently as the Jet Ski bounced off its own wake.

The crack of another bullet made Hutchins duck, and he squeezed his eyes closed even tighter.

"We're sitting ducks!" he shouted. "There's no escape!"

"There, look," Candi yelled, pointing at other boats in a marina close to the shore. "We can use the other boats for cover. They won't dare take shots with the Coast Guard around."

"You sure about that?" Hutchins asked, opening his eyes a touch to assess the scene.

"I can't say for—" A strafe of gunfire cut Candi's sentence in half, and bullets sliced the water to the starboard.

Hutchins glanced back at the speedboat. "They'll catch us before then!" he said, turning away before he could lock eyes with either of the assailants.

"I'll ride in arcs," Candi said, tilting slightly as she coursed a long, curving arc through the water. "Every time they do the same, wave resistance will slow them down."

Hutchins glanced up and saw the mainland come into sharper focus. The wind rushed past him like the hand of Mother Nature trying to rip him from the vessel.

He dared not look back again, but the noise of the speedboat engine grew louder with every second.

"There's the marina," Candi said, pointing to one of the shapes that now came into clear focus. "We'll be safe there. I hope."

Hutchins squinted and saw the forest of masts and antennas ubiquitous to marinas and harbors.

"Safety seems a long way away right now," Hutchins shouted over the wind.

Candi jerked the handlebars to the left, carving another bow shape through the water. Hutchins clung on as the Jet Ski's nose lifted, slicing over a wave before slamming back down, drenching them both with more salty seawater.

Behind, the pursuing boat closed the gap, its twin

engines roaring like angry beasts. The sleek craft was now barely thirty feet away. Hutchins caught a glimpse of the gunman taking aim.

Candi spotted it too and immediately veered toward a cluster of fishing boats anchored in the bay. She threaded the Jet Ski between two weathered hulls, forcing their pursuers to throttle down. The speedboat's driver cursed audibly as he cut the engines, momentum carrying them dangerously close to a net-draped trawler.

"Hold tight!" Candi shouted, weaving through the floating obstacle course.

A small tourist catamaran appeared ahead, and passengers pointed excitedly at the high-speed chase. Candi cut directly across its wake, using the choppy water to mask their path. The Jet Ski bounced violently over the disturbed surface, nearly sending Hutchins airborne.

The speedboat reappeared in pursuit, but now the advantage was Candi's. She zigzagged between moored yachts and day-cruisers, using each vessel as cover. Each time the gunman almost had a shot, another boat would slide between them.

The pursuers disappeared as Candi weaved between a group of yachts sitting at anchor. She swung in past a hulking trawler with a peeling green hull and nets dangling over the side. Suddenly, the speedboat roared in from the side, closer than before. Bullets slammed into the water just inches from Hutchins' legs.

Candi swung inside the marina, with the speedboat looming terrifyingly close behind. Tourists and boaters turned to face the approaching noise. A dockhand abandoned his hose and dived for cover as a security guard reached for his radio.

Gunshots split the air, the bullets tearing into the side of a small fishing boat, splintering fiberglass and sending a plume of dust into the air. The fisherman aboard dove belly-first onto his deck.

Candi ducked at the sound of more gunfire, but the sudden movement caused her to lose balance. She slipped halfway off the Jet Ski, and she plunged into the water on her side.

"Candi!" Hutchins grabbed her arm just before she sank under the surface. He held on to her with one hand while clinging to the Jet Ski handle with the other. Her weight tilted the Jet Ski almost into a roll, her leg drifting toward the churning propeller of a nearby boat.

"Hold on!" Hutchins bellowed. Gritting his teeth, he tightened his grip on her arm and pulled, growling with the effort. He yanked her back onto the Jet Ski, and she slid onto the rear, coughing and sputtering.

"You okay?" he asked breathlessly, shuffling forward to take the controls.

"Still breathing," she choked out between gasps.

Hutchins gripped the controls. "You're riding shotgun now," he said. "I've never done this before, but we don't have a choice."

He twisted the throttle, and the Jet Ski surged forward. The craft wobbled violently, nearly tipping over.

"Relax! Keep it straight!" Candi steadied him by placing her hands on his sides.

"That's what I'm trying to do!" Hutchins snapped, sweat and seawater dripping down his face.

Bullets punched through the side of a small sailboat just five meters to the right. The family aboard screamed, ducking for cover as the thugs closed the gap.

Scanning the marina, Hutchins saw a row of brightly

colored paddle boats lined up near the dock, bobbing gently in the water.

"Hang on," he shouted to Candi, veering sharply toward the paddle boats.

"What are you doing?!" she shouted back, her voice shrill.

"Getting creative!"

Hutchins steered the Jet Ski straight at the row of paddle boats. His knuckles turned white as he gripped the handlebars, mentally calculating trajectories with the questionable precision of an academic suddenly thrust into a high-speed chase.

At the last possible second, he cranked the handlebars hard to the left. The Jet Ski leaned violently, nearly tipping as it cut a tight arc through the water. They shot through the narrow gap between two paddle boats with inches to spare.

The maneuver sent them rocketing back into open water, spray exploding behind them like a watery afterburner.

Close behind, the speedboat—too large, too fast, too committed to its course—had no time to correct. The man at the controls spun the wheel—but it was too little, too late.

The speedboat slammed into the line of paddle boats at full throttle. The collision unleashed a cacophony of destruction—fiberglass splintering, metal twisting, engines screaming in mechanical agony. The speedboat's bow launched upward from the impact, while its stern drove deep into the water.

As the bow came back down heavily, both criminals catapulted forward like human missiles, their bodies cutting through the air in slow-motion horror. The shooter lost his grip on the weapon, the gun tumbling end over end before disappearing with a splash.

The attackers crashed into the water with twin explosions of white spray, their momentum carrying them skipping across the surface like human stones before they disappeared beneath the churning foam. The men surfaced moments later, heads turning toward their shattered speedboat wedged firmly in the wreckage.

Hutchins guided the Jet Ski toward the marina dock, where a large crowd now watched the commotion. He killed the engine as they pulled up, and the Jet Ski drifted gently to a stop. He jumped off, helping Candi onto the dock.

"That was insane," Candi said, turning to look up at him.

Hutchins nodded, swallowing hard as the adrenaline began to fade. "Yeah? Wait until you hear about the rest of my week."

# 30

**In the air above Isla de la Vida Eterna, Caribbean Sea.**

Sierra Byrd banked the de Havilland seaplane gently to the east, subconsciously making minor adjustments to the yoke. Through the windscreen, the Caribbean stretched before her like a vast turquoise canvas, its surface rippled by trade winds that crafted dazzling patterns of light. Scattered islands dotted the blue expanse—including her own—each rimmed with white sand beaches and dense tropical foliage. For a moment, the view reminded her why she had chosen this particular piece of paradise for her flight school.

The seaplane's radial engine thrummed steadily, vibrating through the airframe. Despite the non-traditional method of starting the engine and the hurried takeoff under fire, the plane was performing well. These machines really were the workhorses of the region. Often patched, repainted, and rebuilt more times than she cared to count, they were reliable when it mattered. Byrd wondered how many unfortunate souls had been ferried around by criminals in this particular plane, and guessed that Hutchin's academic colleague might have been one of them.

A soft moan from behind made her tense. In the rear seats, secured with only the seatbelt, sat the young woman she'd rescued from the island—still drifting in and out of consciousness. Whatever those criminals had forced into her body was powerful stuff.

After takeoff, Byrd had been in contact with the coast guard for permission to land, and for an ambulance to be on standby. Although involving the coast guard was a risk, landing a seaplane carrying an unconscious woman at a Mexican port without proper clearance would be problematic to say the least.

Byrd allowed herself a moment to breathe. Halfway through that moment, a sudden bang from the rear of the plane sent heavy vibrations through the airframe. The plane lurched to port, causing the loose equipment in the rear compartment to shift and clatter. Byrd's knuckles whitened as she gripped the yoke, wrestling the aircraft back to level flight.

Then, the woman emitted an ear-splitting, panicked scream that cut through the drone of the aircraft. Holding the controls steady, Byrd turned and glanced at the terror-stricken woman strapped into her seat. The woman glared at Byrd with eyes so wide they seemed to be popping out of her head, and her fingers crept up her cheeks like claws clasping her skin.

"Stay calm!" Byrd shouted over the engine noise and the rattling airframe. "You're safe!"

"You!" the woman yelled. "You took me from my yacht on that awful island!" Her head twisted left and right, eyes darting around as though nothing made sense. Her hands flailed wildly, first pointing accusingly at Byrd, then clutching at the seat beneath her as the plane hit a pocket of turbulence.

Watching the poor woman's erratic movements, Byrd realized that to this victim of experimentation, everything was probably devoid of sense. The confusion in her eyes shifted between fear and anger as she tried to orient herself in the unfamiliar aircraft.

"My two friends were shot right in front of me. I was dragged into that jungle and... I don't remember." The woman's voice cracked as she spoke, one hand now pressed against her temple where a bruise was forming. Her other arm hugged her midsection protectively. She attempted to sit up straighter but winced and fell back against the seat.

"I'm taking you *away* from that awful island. I am taking you to a hospital!" Byrd said, softening her tone. "Ma'am, please listen to me. The only people I encountered on that island were men with tattoos. I am sure you encountered them too. Do I really look like any of them?"

The woman stopped rocking. She shook her head slowly.

"Good. What's your name, ma'am?" Byrd asked.

"Kasey," the woman said quietly.

"Okay, thank you, Kasey. I need you to help me so that we can help others. Is there anything you remember from when you were held captive? Anything you saw or heard? Anything at all."

Kasey said nothing for a while. Then, softly, she said, "I heard them talking. About how they get their... Guinea pigs."

"And what did they say?" Byrd asked.

"One of them said to the other, 'this is better than wasting our time at the goddamn Green Frog Cafe.'"

"Anything else?"

"The other replied, 'Yeah, but the women are a lot hotter in Cancu—'" The woman suddenly stopped talking, and a stream of purple liquid gushed from her mouth.

"I think she said 'Cancun'," Byrd muttered calmly to herself over the noise of the engine and the gurgling. Given what the poor woman had been forced to imbibe, Byrd was not surprised that her body was rejecting it in such a dramatic way. At least, Byrd thought, it wasn't her plane that was now covered in vomit.

"This mission will be long and unclean in many ways," Byrd said to herself, starting their descent toward Chetumal. "I hate to say it, Kasey, but you're probably one of the lucky ones."

MEXICAN DESERT, north of Cabo San Lucas

THE WATER from the fountain made a gentle tinkling sound, each droplet falling in a graceful arc like an Olympic diver before vanishing into the pool below. Sallas sat beside it, stretched out on a cushioned lounge chair, a glass of gin and tonic resting in his hand. The warm breeze, scented faintly with desert blooms, brushed over his skin.

He raised the glass to his lips, ice clinking softly. Just as he was about to take a sip, a scream echoed across the compound, raw, panicked, and full of agony that curled the spine.

Sallas froze, the rim of the glass brushing his lower lip.

Another scream followed. Then a low, distant moan.

Sallas sighed.

Then, he heard someone approaching, their footsteps crunching on gravel. He didn't turn until the noise broke the illusion of peace completely.

The Ogre lumbered into view, sweat shining on his forehead. In his arms was the limp body of a blond-haired boy—the kid looked to be sixteen at the oldest. The boy's head lolled, his limbs hanging slack. Tammy came trailing behind, her face pale and stricken.

"He passed out," The Ogre said. "Choked on his own vomit. Pulse is weak. He's not doing so good."

"What he means," Tammy said, her voice shaky, "is that the boy is on the verge of death. We need to call for air evacuation to a hospital."

Sallas slowly turned to her, narrowing his eyes. "I thought you understood what we're trying to achieve here, Tammy."

Tammy turned her eyes toward the ground.

The Ogre laid the boy down on the gravel. Sallas knelt on one knee beside him, studying the boy's ashen face and damp forehead.

"Please," Tammy whispered.

"Shh," Sallas spat, without looking at her. "Let me think."

After a long moment, he stood, took a long drink from his glass, and exhaled.

"Can I find someone with a phone? Call a doctor?" Tammy asked.

Sallas fixed her with a stern gaze. "No. He doesn't need a doctor." He glanced once more at the pitiful boy. "A bonfire will do just fine."

# 31

**Chetumal, east coast of Mexico. The following day.**

With Kasey handed over to the medics at the marina and a sizable tip given to keep Byrd's name and description out of all official records, Byrd checked into a less-than-adequate hotel. There, she managed to grab a few hours of less-than-adequate sleep.

When dawn lazily arrived, streaming into the room through and around the curtains, she got up, dressed, and headed out. For a couple of hours, she walked the strangely quiet backstreets of Chetumal, heading toward what counted as its downtown area. All the while, she resisted the temptation to get back in the plane and leave this mysterious mess of crime and chaos behind. Whilst the prospect of heading back to her island and the Dakota Skytrain was tempting, she knew it wouldn't be long before trouble came knocking again. She had to clear this mess up. Right now, the best course of action was to wait until Kasey was conscious and then try to talk to her.

Kasey had mentioned that people were being taken from

a cafe in Cancun, or more likely a bar with "cafe" in its name. Victims were probably snatched from bars when intoxicated and their guard was down. Perhaps they were then taken to the same place Professor Wall was being held.

Whether the hospital would allow someone in to talk to the girl was one issue. Whether the girl would even *want* to talk was another. But since Byrd and her team—as she reluctantly thought of them—had no other information that might help them find Professor Wall or the Sunstone, this was their best option.

As an hour or more passed, the small city came to life. Neighbors called out to each other, kids played in the morning sunlight, and storefront shutters scraped open.

Byrd headed along the Malecón de Chetumal, a wide promenade along the bay at the mouth of the Hondo River, toward the town center. Palm trees swayed gently, and the water glistened like molten mercury—a sight that always brought her a moment of peace, even amid the turmoil.

She came to a section of the promenade lined with cafes and small restaurants. She glanced down at her watch—a Breitling Navitimer. It was just after nine, she was reliably informed by the iconic watch admired by generations of military and ex-military pilots.

"Time for a little sharpener," Byrd said, glancing at one of the cafes. A morning tipple was one more little tradition that service personnel were fond of, and she hadn't indulged in a while. Given that Kasey would need the rest of the day to recover, Byrd considered this her day of leave.

She stopped at the first cafe she came to and pulled up a lightweight metal chair next to a matching table on the leafy terrace. She smiled at the handsome young waiter who approached.

"*Una cerveza, y asegúrate de que esté bien fría,*" Byrd said to the broad-shouldered young waiter, holding up one finger to emphasize her order. The Spanish rolled off her tongue deceptively quickly, hiding the fact that it was pretty much the only phrase she knew.

The waiter returned with the beer. Byrd smiled in thanks and met the young man's gaze. She let the eye contact linger until he looked away bashfully. As sunlight twinkled in the brown glass of the bottle, she lifted it to her lips and took a slow swig. The liquid was crisp and refreshing, like coolant to an overheating engine after a long haul at high altitude. It spread through her system, cooling the tension that had built up over the last twenty-four hours.

Turning her thoughts from one hunky young man to a decidedly un-hunky young man, Byrd took out her phone to check that Hutchins was safe and well. She called Candi.

"Hey, Byr—ma'am," Candi said, her tone as chipper as usual.

"If you got that boy out of trouble, you can call me whatever you like. How is he?" Byrd said, flashing a wry smile at the thought of the pair of them.

"I think he's okay," Candi said. "He looks and smiles at me a lot, but he's not saying much."

"Where did you stay last night?" Byrd tried to hide the curiosity in her voice.

"Hotel."

"The devil is in the detail," Byrd said, taking another sip of ice-cold beer. "Separate rooms?"

"What do you think?"

"Come on, Candi," Byrd said. "I need some juicy gossip to pass the time."

"I have plenty of gossip for you, just not that kind. Much more exciting."

"Juice me up!" Byrd said as she caught sight of her waiter

at the other side of the terrace and gave him a wink. This time, he smiled back.

"Are you drunk?" Candi asked.

"Not yet," Byrd confirmed. "Maybe soon."

"Great! Where?"

Byrd flipped over the coaster on the table and gave Candi the name of the bar and a description of the location.

"We'll be there ASAP," Candi said. "Order us a beer."

"Roger that," Byrd said, hanging up and dropping her phone to the table. She slumped back into the chair and let her gaze rest on the rugged Mexican guy testing the engine of his Ducati motorbike in the cafe parking lot.

The sleek machine gleamed in the sunlight—candy-apple red with matte black accents and chrome exhaust pipes that curved like liquid metal. Each time the guy revved the throttle, the Ducati responded with a deep growl. As he bent over to check the tires, muscles shifting visibly beneath his thin cotton shirt, Byrd caught herself leaning forward to get a closer look. The sight of him at work managed to pass the time for another full beer.

"You didn't order us beers yet?" Hutchins' voice snapped her from her daydream. He approached the table, followed by Candi.

Byrd glanced at her watch. "You have military timing, but it's a shame about your posture."

Candi beamed a smile, subconsciously eliciting one from Byrd in return.

"No bother, I'll get the beers on the way back from the bathroom," Candi said, striding inside.

Hutchins turned and watched the young woman go, his gaze lingering on the spot she'd been in long after she'd disappeared.

The look made Byrd smile, as she remembered, hazily at

best, the last time she had felt that way about another person. Her memories drifted back to that night in Bangkok —or was it Manila?— the details had faded, but the memory of the feeling remained.

"You, stop right there! Do not move!"

The sharp command cut through the cafe's morning chatter. Byrd turned to see a uniformed police officer striding purposefully toward Hutchins.

The bony man appeared to be in his early forties, with gray streaks in his greasy black hair. He had smooth, tight skin and small, dark eyes. The uniform he wore hung slightly loose at the shoulders but strained across his midsection, suggesting it wasn't tailored for his frame. Perhaps it wasn't even his.

"Is there a law against having fun in the morning, officer?" Byrd asked as casually as she could. She subtly pushed the chair back from the table a little in case a quick getaway should be called for. The officer completely ignored the question, his stare locked on Hutchins.

"Name?" the officer said, reaching out and clamping a hand onto Hutchins' shoulder. "Confirm your name, Professor," the officer said.

Hutchins' face cycled rapidly through confusion, fear, and the particular expression of someone desperately trying to remember if they'd done something wrong.

Byrd shook her head as subtly as possible, indicating that Hutchins should stay quiet.

"Professor?" Hutchins questioned, shifting his gaze to the officer.

Several people, in the cafe and on the street, had their eyes glued to the scene.

"Where's your partner?" Byrd asked. "I thought it was some kind of rule that you guys worked in pairs."

"I ask the questions," the man snapped, his dark eyes boring into Byrd.

"On this occasion, I'm asking some too," Byrd said, standing slowly. "This young man works for me. So, you'll need to tell me what this is about."

For a moment, the officer said nothing. Then, "Airplane?"

Byrd paused. "Err—that doesn't really mean anything."

"You come by airplane!" the man spat. Something about his scratchy, gramophone voice sounded familiar.

"Yes, I did." As the guy clearly knew something about her already, there was no point playing dumb.

"Come with me," the officer instructed Hutchins, turning away from Byrd.

"To where?" Hutchins said.

"Come with me. Just talking."

Byrd noticed the guy twitching his shoulders nervously under his uniform.

"You come!" the officer growled, low and dog-like. "Just talking. You don't come, big problem."

# 32

"You come, now!" the officer barked. He clamped a hand around Hutchins' forearm and pulled, dragging him toward the exit.

"No, wait! Wait!" Hutchins pleaded, his feet sliding across the tiles as the officer dragged him with surprising speed.

The growl of the Ducati cut through the conflict, drawing Byrd's attention. Acting on instinct, she darted toward the officer, knocking the table into the air. Beer and glass exploded like fireworks. She barged into the policeman with her shoulder, sending him sprawling back into another table where a young couple leapt to their feet and yelled their complaints. Byrd clamped her fingers around Hutchins' wrist and dragged him into a run. The pair charged across the terrace, swinging around another table and then hurdling a low railing.

Byrd landed on the seat of the Ducati while the broad-shouldered biker was still checking underneath. He peered up, his mouth falling open to reveal a flash of gold dental work. Hutchins thumped down onto the seat behind Byrd.

"I'll bring it back, I promise," she shouted at the biker, adding in a wink for good measure. "Some time!" Then she revved the engine, feeling it rumble with a throaty growl that vibrated through her entire body. She kicked the bike into first gear and tore away from the cafe, leaving a streak of rubber and the rightful owner's curses hanging in the air.

She pulled onto the wide coast road, which was now packed with several lanes of traffic. The morning sun glinted off windshields as Byrd twisted the throttle and veered toward the outer edge of the road.

Two elaborately dressed middle-aged women with huge, shiny shopping bags blocked the narrow gap between jammed cars and the sidewalk. Their matching wide-brimmed hats bobbed as they gestured animatedly to each other, oblivious to the approaching motorcycle.

The wail of a siren cut through the morning air as the officer leapt into his car and gave chase.

Byrd gritted her teeth and gripped the handles. "Pretend they're pigeons," she said to herself, aiming for the pedestrians. "They'll scatter."

The two women remained engrossed in conversation, oblivious to danger. Even as Byrd's engine roared louder, they continued gesturing enthusiastically, shopping bags swinging.

"MOVE!" Byrd yelled, the Ducati's front wheel now just yards away from the women's feet.

The two women saw the approaching bike at the last moment, their lips falling open in horror. Snapping out of their shock, they jumped to safety, shopping bags flying in all directions.

Surrounded by exhaust fumes, shimmering heat, and the sound of sirens, Byrd picked up speed. She skirted the sidewalk, her tires between two yellow lines, inches from cars on one side and pedestrians on the other. Heads turned as Byrd picked up even more pace. Behind her, the police cruiser's siren wailed louder.

"If you're gonna arrest me," Byrd muttered, "at least arrest me for something real."

"He knew about us!" Hutchins said, shouting over the howl of rushing sea air, the bike's engine, and the approaching sirens. "How?!"

"I don't know!" Byrd said. "But the number of possible informants is very limited."

"Surely it can't be Candi?!" Hutchins shouted.

"Be quiet! Head down!" Byrd yelled, scanning the area for a way off the main road. She swung toward an intersection where traffic lights controlled Chetumal's busiest junction. Digital numbers counted down the seconds until the lights changed as tourists and locals alike crowded the corners.

"What are you doing!" Hutchins shouted, his nails digging into Byrd's sides. His voice pitched higher with each word, cracking on the final syllable.

"This is our best chance," Byrd said. "Just ignore the lights." She figured that the intersection would be clear for just a moment during the light change—that limited space where one direction stopped and the other hadn't yet begun to move.

"Are you sur—" Hutchins said, his voice dropping out as they shot out into the intersection and into the path of the already accelerating traffic.

The Ducati's tires chirped against the sun-baked asphalt as Byrd leaned into the turn. A taxi driver slammed his brakes, horn blaring. A delivery truck swerved, its cargo shifting with a metallic crash. Time seemed to compress and stretch simultaneously as they threaded through the maze of vehicles, missing a bus mirror by inches.

As Byrd entered the intersection, the patrol car's sirens screamed louder, the sound bouncing off the tightly packed buildings of Chetumal's bustling streets. She stole a glance in the rearview mirror and saw the officer following her into the intersection. The black-and-white police cruiser—an older model BMW with faded decals—weaved through the traffic. She dipped her shoulder and turned onto a hill road that wound away from the ocean.

There were fewer vehicles in her way now, but the steep incline taxed the Ducati despite its powerful engine. Hutchins' additional weight didn't help matters.

The glare of the sun created a haze on the wide road as it wound around the contours of the hill lined with red dirt, garbage, and small shrubs.

"We need some more power," Byrd said, her fingers dancing across the digital console to switch the bike from 'Urban' to 'Sport' mode. The Ducati responded instantly, its character transforming as electronic limiters disengaged. A vast reserve of power surged through the machine like the first moments of a rocket launch.

The bike shot forward with newfound aggression, front wheel lifting slightly as Byrd twisted the throttle. The police cruiser accelerated behind, but the strength of the Ducati's engine flooded Byrd with a strength of her own. The strong breeze swept over her skin, and the asphalt swept by in a blur under her wheels. This thing was now flying. She couldn't help but smile.

The corner up ahead looked sharp and long, a serpentine curve carved into the mountainside with nothing but a flimsy guardrail separating the road from a sheer drop.

"Be careful!" Hutchins cried out, digging deeper still.

"Not so brave when the blonde's not here, are you?!" Byrd yelled back.

"Just make sure I see her face again!" Hutchins shouted.

"Lean into the turn, but not too hard. Got it? Not too hard!" Byrd yelled, turning back toward him slightly.

"Got it!"

The power of the engine suddenly seemed untamable as Byrd approached the wall. The Ducati screamed beneath her, a mechanical beast fighting against its rider's commands. Just up ahead, the road curved around until it slipped out of sight. Byrd hit the bend and turned the bike away from the towering wall of rock covered with netting. The corner seemed to go on and on, the g-force taking hold of her jowls. "Not too hard, Hutchins, okay. Hold on!"

She felt his weight shift—too much, too quickly.

Suddenly, there was no weight at all. The bike lurched upright, unbalanced by the sudden change.

"No!"

Byrd heard the thud. She turned her head and saw Hutchins skidding along the asphalt. The patrol car hit the brakes, stopping just a few feet from where Hutchins lay on his back.

Byrd took a moment to consider her options. Figuring she would be more use if she had her freedom, she reluctantly turned away and picked up speed. She felt like she was deserting her own child.

## 33

**Mexican desert, north of Cabo San Lucas.**

Professor Wall had not had a hangover for thirty years. This felt like the worst of his life. Beyond the grogginess, headache, and general malaise, there was something more disturbing. He could still taste the earthy tang of the drug that had effectively poisoned him—the substance The Mentor had proudly claimed was merely a natural compound that enabled people to take an insightful trip inside their subconscious.

But Wall had no need for such a psychological trip or its revelations. He already knew exactly where his mental state was. He was in a state of severe anxiety and misery. *This man could kill me*, he thought, staring up at a dirty ceiling with cobwebs in each corner. *I need to get out. Now.*

He rolled his head to one side to take in more of his surroundings. He seemed to be in an old barn that had been set up with a few bunk beds. The bunkhouse certainly didn't have any bucolic charm and felt more like a military barracks than an idyllic rural setting.

Wall could not see every part of the barn, but he felt like he was alone. Suddenly, wet, phlegmy coughing from a far corner of the structure told him that was not the case. The coughing continued, bringing Wall's attention to his own chest, which––now he thought about it––felt worryingly tight.

*Am I tied down?* he wondered. He wiggled his legs around and held his hands up in front of his face. He could move freely, though he had no idea if the barn door would be locked. In reality, it wouldn't make a big difference either way. He had been free to walk out of the White Room, but The Mentor had been on his shoulder as soon as he had stepped outside.

Even if the weird hippy freak wasn't around this time, one of his beautiful, terrifying followers would soon alert him. Those sun-kissed, perfectly symmetrical zombies popped up everywhere around the compound. They seemed to have nothing to do except wander about, look attractive, and discuss how this existence was better than the real world.

Wall climbed down from his bunk, making it squeak and shake, and planted his bare feet on the dusty floor. The coughing coming from the far end of the bunkhouse was too loud and pain-filled to be ignored. He shuffled his way barefoot toward the sound, passing empty bunk beds. He was the only one who had been given a mattress. "I guess our great leader thinks these luxuries will make me talk," he muttered.

When he got to the far end of the bunkhouse, he saw a hemp blanket with a heaving form underneath it.

"Are... are you okay?" Wall asked. The coughing and heaving stopped, but there was no reply. "Do you need medical attention?"

"I've had too much of that already," came a voice, barking out before descending into more fits of coughing. Wall thought the voice was female, but it was difficult to tell.

"I'll get help," the professor offered.

"No!" As arms flailed, the blanket came flying through the air, revealing a young woman with a shocking appearance. Though matted red hair obscured part of her face, the left side appeared to be drooping. Her left eye and the corner of her mouth sagged noticeably lower than the features on her right side. Wall couldn't tell if this resulted from a stroke, experimental drug abuse, or a birth defect.

Wall caught the blanket, keeping hold of it so that the woman couldn't cover her face again.

"What is happening here?" he asked.

"I don't want to talk about it."

"They're experimenting on people, right?" Wall asked, undeterred.

"Some people," the woman said quietly. "Please, could I have my blanket back?"

Wall stepped closer and passed back the blanket, saying, "I just want to talk a little bit, okay?"

The woman sat up, covering her legs with her blanket and hugging her knees. She fixed her eyes on Wall as if to say, "Go on, then, talk." Despite her otherwise unusual appearance, her eyes were bright, kind, and intelligent.

"How did you end up here?" Wall asked.

"I was hanging out in Cancun. The beach and the bars. Lots of attractive people kept coming up and talking to me. Hot guys, the kind who never gave me attention back home. I thought it was a travel thing. They told me about a place where people can live a better life. Be happy, healthy, and live longer."

"That's not going very well, is it."

"It is for some people. For some, it's completely true. But we are separated. They call us Providers and Receivers. I am a Provider, and they keep us hidden. That's why you have probably only seen healthy people walking around freely here."

"You're right, I have," Wall said, "What are you providing?"

"My body. To be tested. Not willingly, of course. The Receivers, I dunno, I guess they will receive the benefits of whatever is eventually found from the testing."

"Long life. That is the benefit," Wall said. "A very long life. I have seen the attractive people walking around here. The Receivers, as you call them. I guess they think they deserve to live longer and to produce superior future generations."

"So you're a Provider, then?" the woman asked while swiping matted hair away from her forehead. Wall watched her as she took a moment to cast her eyes around his features—the deep wrinkles, the wiry beard, and the white hair.

"I guess I am. I think at first, the leader...The Mentor... whatever that creepy prophet is called, wanted me to help fast-track his way to the secret of long life. But I wasn't too keen on helping with that." There was a second of silence. Then, Wall asked, "What's your name?"

"Lucy. Lucy Green. But that doesn't really matter." Lucy's gaze dropped downwards, like hope crashing to the ground.

"Why not?"

Lucy clammed up, remaining quiet for a moment as her bottom lip gently pushed up her top one. "Because I'm almost finished," she said, finally.

"No, no, you're not, and you're far from finished. There must be a way out of here."

"If you get out, please tell my mom and dad I love them. They're in Belle Haven, Virginia. Everyone knows the Greens."

"You can tell them yourself," Wall said firmly. "We're getting out together."

"I don't know if—"

"We're getting out *together*. Then we'll alert the world to this place's evils and free everyone else too." Wall's stomach twisted with guilt for those he couldn't immediately rescue—especially Briony. He clung to the hope that her closeness with The Mentor might keep her safe. Lucy, trembling before him, needed immediate help. Briony still radiated health.

Lucy didn't say anything, and Wall hoped he could take that as agreement. "It won't be easy," she said after a time. "But if you can get me out, I can help you. He told me the location of one of his mansions on a private island. Even if he abandons this place, there may be evidence there."

"He did? Where is it?"

"It's—" Lucy stopped talking as she descended into a fit of hacking, heaving coughs, the noise echoing off the wooden structure.

Professor Wall rubbed her back to comfort her while looking around nervously, hoping the noise would stop quickly. "Let's get out of here first," he whispered. "Give me the details later."

Lucy nodded and pulled herself together while Wall thought for a second. "Do you always stay here? In this... barn?" he asked. "Or do they move you around?"

"I'm always here. When they're not... working on me," Lucy said.

"Okay. I guess I will be brought back here too." Wall looked around again. "After I have done what I'm gonna do."

"What are you going to do?" Lucy asked, meeting his gaze.

"I'm not exactly sure yet. But after I've done it, I promise you we'll be far away from here."

Wall saw Lucy smile for the first time. There was hope for her yet.

## 34

**Chetumal, east coast of Mexico.**

The slamming of the cell door reverberated through Hutchins' flesh. The sound felt so visceral, so real, that he thought he must have experienced this before. But he had never been in police custody at any point during his life until he went searching for a fabled plant in Mexico. As he lay on a thin mat on the hard floor, he realized why the clanging door had affected him so deeply. Everyone knew they might someday be unfairly arrested—a nightmare that could become reality. For Hans Hutchins, today was that day.

The worst part of captivity became immediately clear to him: being completely at somebody else's mercy. Having no control over your situation and no idea when it might end.

Hutchins surveyed his surroundings. A large slab of wood on legs stood in one corner, and he couldn't tell if it was meant to be a bed or a bench. In the opposite corner sat a bucket whose purpose was unfortunately obvious.

The cuffs had been removed, but that mostly added to

the sense that he had no say in his own movements. Even with his hands free, there was nothing to use them for except to rub the deep cuts and grazes he had acquired after falling from the bike. With the bike cornering so close to the ground, he'd only fallen a few inches, though the speed of the Ducati meant he'd suffered heavy bruising. The stinging and throbbing was far less troubling than the fear of captivity.

Something clattered outside in the corridor—an officer going about their business, probably. The noise got louder as though the officer was moving toward Hutchins' cell. Hutchins struggled upright, listening intently to the noise. Then, the noise drifted away again as the person moved in the opposite direction.

Silence. Minutes passed like hours. As time ticked by, Hutchins began to sink into a dark psychological hole. He thought of home. His parents. Would he even be allowed basic rights? A phone call?

He snapped back to the present when he heard a forceful movement at the door. An officer shoved the metal monstrosity open, sending it clanging against the wall, and marched into the cell. He grasped Hutchins under the armpit, dragged him up, and led him out. They shuffled down the corridor, passing a couple of haunted faces poking through cell bars, and into what was clearly an interrogation room.

The room contained a simple wooden desk and folding chairs on either side: two on the far side and one on the nearest. The officer shoved Hutchins down into the nearest chair and clamped the cuffs on his wrists once again. The pain cut through his flesh, which was still raw from his various injuries.

The officer turned and closed the door behind him, once

again leaving Hutchins alone. Sometime later—probably ten minutes, although Hutchins couldn't be sure—the door swung open, and two different people stepped into the room. Seeing the thin man who had dragged him here, Hutchins shuddered.

The Thin Man had lifeless eyes—black centers surrounded by yellow irises with bloodshot streaks. He looked as though he'd never existed outside of dark interrogation rooms with single spotlights, just like this one. His boring crew cut suggested life's aesthetic beauty meant nothing to him.

The woman to his right was buxom and almost homely. Her presence made the whole situation much worse. A rose in a hospital. Hutchins knew that any hope of feminine kindness would be a false hope, and one look at the woman's face confirmed the suspicion. The lips were full, but the smile was thin.

Both officers pulled their chairs closer to Hutchins, the legs scraping along the floor. Across the small table, the man spoke first. "*Hablas español?*"

Hutchins shook his head. He did, in fact, speak a little Spanish, but he certainly wasn't going to let that become apparent. Being interrogated in his native language would be bad enough. The male interrogator then looked to his colleague, who addressed Hutchins in heavily accented English.

"Do you know why you are here?" she asked.

Hutchins shook his head again. The woman locked eyes with him. "I think you know," she said coldly.

"I'm sorry. I really don—"

"Yes! YOU DO!" the man interjected loudly. He raised his fist, and Hutchins flinched.

"You have been accused of kidnapping," the woman told

him. "It's very serious. You are not helping yourself by remaining silent. It is like an admission of guilt."

"I would like to talk to a representative from my embassy," Hutchins said as calmly as he could.

"They cannot help you to get out of here," the woman said, just as calmly. "They can only ensure you are not being mistreated. Are you being mistreated?"

"A lawyer. I need a lawyer also."

The Thin Man placed his fists on the table, clenched tight, as if showing Hutchins he was ready to fight. The woman continued, "It could take many days. This is not a town full of lawyers."

"I have contacts," Hutchins insisted. "Not here, but people at the embassy will help me. I agree that it may take time. But I will need a lawyer."

The woman made an awkward attempt at a smile, then said, "If you can explain simply, you can be free much sooner."

Hutchins tried to stop his foot from tapping under the table, but he barely felt connected to his limbs.

"If you are talking about what happened on the island, then the explanation is very simple," Hutchins told her. "I was *rescuing* a victim of kidnapping."

"Then why did the victim say you were the kidnapper?" she asked. "You and the pilot woman."

"I have no idea. Maybe because she was drugged and out of her mind."

"She has recovered now," the female interrogator said, interlocking her fingers as she placed her hands on the table. "Her story has not changed."

"Then I don't know what to tell you. I have told you the truth."

The stiflingly hot interrogation room smelled like a

public toilet. Hutchins feared this was because people brought here often relieved themselves involuntarily. The man suddenly stood, jabbing his finger toward Hutchins. "You! It was you!"

The woman waited until her colleague sat down again, then said, "I do not believe you either. Maybe you do need a lawyer. It will take many days. Your court date will take many months, and your prison sentence will last for many, many years. If only you had helped us, you could have walked free."

The interrogators stood and left without another word. As Hutchins shuffled back to his cell, escorted by a younger officer, tears stung behind his eyes. When the door closed behind him, he felt emptier than ever before. He feared that situations like this were a lottery. Even if he could prove he was telling the truth, it would be after months or maybe even years of pre-trial detention. This was just a local station, and he would likely soon be moved to a remand center or even a regular prison where gang members and violent offenders ran the show.

He placed his head against the wall. Right now, he hated himself more than the interrogators. They were just doing their job, but he was a stupid kid who had pretended to be brave—out of his depth and making terrible decisions.

## 35

**Mexican desert, north of Cabo San Lucas.**

Professor Wall walked the length of the bunkhouse. He reached the worm-eaten door and turned the handle. The door swung open easily.

The cogs in his brain started whirring. He realized he was allowed to roam freely only because the compound itself was one giant cage. He stepped out and looked around, narrowing his eyes to force his clouded vision as far as possible. Beyond the high wire-mesh fence surrounding the compound, barren desert stretched in all directions. Only a few shrubs and rocks broke up the dusty, sandy expanse.

Wall hadn't seen much transportation around the compound; in fact, he couldn't recall seeing any four-wheeled vehicles at all. Just one or two low-cc motorcycles that might not be super-quick but would easily catch up to some poor, exhausted soul trying to escape on foot. Plenty of the people strolling around this place seemed more than happy to be there. The others were being mercilessly experimented on and would be no physical match for the desert in their weakened state.

All of these considerations added to Wall's uncertainty, but he knew he wasn't going to sit around and wait to see what substance they put into his body next.

He paced across the compound and passed a typically young, tanned, and attractive guy. The man looked at Wall in the way someone might contemplate a stray cat on the street.

"Excuse me," Wall said, stopping the man in his tracks.

The dark hairs in the center of the man's bare chest glistened with sweat, like fairy lights decorating his perfect pecs.

"What's up?" the man said languidly.

"Have you seen The Mentor? I'm looking for him."

The man frowned hard as if thinking, *Why would royalty wish to speak to a stray cat?* Nevertheless, he slowly raised his arm and pointed in the direction of the White Rooms, where Wall had come across The Mentor previously.

Wall thanked the man and ambled toward the structure. As he neared, he painted a fake smile across his face. Rounding a corner, he almost walked right into the man he was looking for. The Mentor raised an eyebrow as if requiring an explanation for Wall's smile.

"Are you busy right now...sir? I would like to talk to you," Wall said.

"Shaping the future is an endless task," The Mentor replied. "I am always busy. But if you finally have something useful to tell me, I can make time."

"I can see that there are... two kinds of people here," Wall said. "I want to be on the right side. I want to help."

The Mentor nodded, then turned and walked toward the

garden where things had gotten very weird for Wall. The professor followed with trepidation.

When they arrived, The Mentor held out a palm, gesturing for Wall to sit beside the cascading fountain. Its fresh scent brought Wall a momentary and contradictory sense of peace. The younger man sank into a chair nearby.

Wall cleared his throat and then locked eyes with The Mentor.

"So, my friend. You seek the Sunstone," Wall said, trying to keep his voice level.

"You're right. I do." The Mentor's eyes widened. "But what I really seek is the information it provides. The rituals that bring long life."

"And the plant that is imbibed as part of that ritual," Wall replied.

"The plant. Yes. That is at the center of everything we are trying to achieve. What can you tell me about it?" The Mentor said, leaning forward.

Wall looked up at the clear blue sky and wiped the sweat from his brow. "Wow. It is even hotter than usual today. Do you have any beers?"

"Okay," The Mentor said, his hopeful expression collapsing into one of confusion. "I see how this works." He paced around the fountain and into the structure he had laughably called his *Gloriette*. He clattered around inside before re-emerging with two ice-cold beers in frosted glass bottles. He snapped off the lids, took a small sip from both, smiled knowingly, then handed one to Wall.

Wall accepted the bottle and took a sip. The crisp liquid ran down his throat, instantly chilling his body.

"The name of the plant? Or its location?" The Mentor asked again as Wall ran his thumb along the bottle's smooth glass, collecting condensation along the way.

"Sinthium," Wall said calmly. "That's the plant you seek."

"And do you know where to find it? Or how to use it?" The Mentor shuffled in the opposite chair, leaning forward in interest.

"Only the Sunstone will tell you that. And even then, you will almost certainly need expert knowledge to decipher what exactly the stone is telling you," Wall said. The Mentor nodded again. He opened his mouth to speak, but Wall interrupted him. "—Yes, I do have that expertise."

"I knew you were the right man for the job," The Mentor said, raising both eyebrows. "I'll help share your knowledge with the world. We'll create success together."

"I hope so," Wall replied. "And promise me my wife won't have to worry about our retirement savings anymore?"

"I promise," The Mentor said with something approaching warmth.

Wall didn't have to ask for the next beer. He didn't even have to hint at it. It was simply brought to him with a smile.

"Are you not going to join me in another cold beverage?" Wall asked, noticing The Mentor had not brought a beer for himself. "Surely you're not going to make me drink alone?"

Several of The Mentor's facial muscles twitched very slightly, which Wall guessed—and hoped—meant the man was not enjoying losing control of the situation. Regardless of how he felt about it, The Mentor turned and went back inside his little Gloriette.

Wall took the opportunity to survey his surroundings. Through the greenery, twisted metal structures rose skyward—pretentious "art" installations that failed to capture his interest. What did catch his eye lay a little further away, near the rusting mesh of the compound fence.

Sleek, shiny black metal gleamed in the sunlight,

partially hidden under a tarp. Wall's pulse quickened as he peered through the leaves. A motorcycle—not one of the puny scooters he'd seen puttering around the compound, but something substantial. Even partially obscured, the machine's powerful frame and robust tires suggested serious off-road capability.

He quickly averted his gaze, not wanting to draw attention to his discovery. A potential escape vehicle, sitting there like an invitation to freedom.

When The Mentor reemerged, the two men locked eyes, and Wall knew he had been caught looking at the bike.

"Beautiful machine," Wall said casually, pretending he'd seen more of the bike than he had.

"Royal Enfield Himalayan," The Mentor informed uninterestedly.

"Mind if I take a look? Hear the engine turn?" Wall said. "Classic machines like that are a passion of mine."

Those muscles twitched again. But the man agreed. The Mentor stood, reached inside the Gloriette, and grabbed an electronic key fob from just inside the door. He then showed Wall to the bike. The Mentor swiftly pulled back the tarp, flapping it in the air with a flourish of evident frustration at the time being wasted.

"She's an angel," Wall said, hoping that was the sort of thing people said about bikes. "Do you mind if I hear the roar?"

"The what?"

"The engine."

Rolling his eyes, The Mentor started up the engine. The machine growled to life, its deep rumble reverberating like distant thunder. The sound rose to a sharp snarl as The Mentor briefly twisted the throttle.

Wall watched carefully to see how it was done.

"Magnificent," Wall said before turning back toward the chairs. The Mentor cut the engine and slung the key fob inside the Gloriette again before taking a seat.

"People may tell you that the plant you seek does not exist," Wall said, watching The Mentor's eyes widen and sparkle once more. "That is a myth. Do not believe them. Some may even be seeking it themselves. I can assure you that it is real, and it is powerful. Cheers to that!" Wall took a long swig of his beer and eyeballed The Mentor's bottle until the younger man drank also.

"But I have to ask: why do you seek it?" Wall said. "Of course, it will bring fame even beyond academic circles. In a world increasingly obsessed with wellness, it would be like announcing that you discovered antibiotics. But is fame all that motivates you?"

"I think you have answered your own question. It will deliver not only health but happiness to millions of people," The Mentor said.

"There's more to it than that. I know there is. Why do you have to base yourself in the desert, away from the world?" Wall asked.

The Mentor fell silent for a moment, and Wall could see that he was uncomfortable from the way he rocked back and forth very slightly. The young man looked edgy.

"You may think there are people who do not want to be here. But really, they all do," The Mentor said. "They were looking for something. If they couldn't make their own life work, why not contribute to a better world for others?"

The famous phrase *'Some people improve the world by leaving it'* came to Wall's mind, though he strongly felt that idea applied more to The Mentor than the people he subjected to testing.

"I am willing to help you," Wall said calmly, "and I won't

make you explain all of your motives. But, please, do tell me one more thing. What is your real name?"

"Sallas. Lucian Sallas."

"Thank you, Mr. Sallas. It's better if we know each other well. We are going on a long journey, and I suggest we start tomorrow. Please, do not bring any companions. If you have any... special friends... you would like to see before we go, perhaps you should visit them tonight."

The Mentor gave a knowing smile and nodded at Wall. "Tomorrow, Professor."

Sallas' celebratory raising of his bottle was interrupted by a distant howl of agony, a sound becoming too familiar to Wall.

"Seven o'clock," said the professor, who planned to rise much earlier. His attempted escape was so close he could taste it.

## 36

**Chetumal, east coast of Mexico.**

In the dead of night, the cell door creaked open. Hutchins awoke from his uneasy sleep as footsteps shuffled across the cell toward him. A firm hand clamped around his arm. He tried to jerk away, but the strong grip held him still. He feared resisting might make his situation worse.

Blinking away the remnants of sleep, he focused his eyes and could just make out the form of the wiry man who had interrogated him earlier. The man glared at Hutchins as he yanked him from the bed. The interrogator put his crooked finger to his pale, lifeless lips.

Hutchins did as he was told and did not make a sound. He still held out a tiny kernel of hope that law enforcement officials here might figure out that this was all one huge misunderstanding. The interrogator pushed him out of the cell, along the corridor, and into another interrogation room.

Hutchins rubbed his eyes and looked around. The interrogation room looked exactly like the one he had been in not long before, but when the corridor and the surroundings were so dark, it was difficult to know for sure. He sat with his cuffed hands on the small desk in front of him. The Thin Man stood at the opposite side of the desk. He leaned across the desk, like a viper ready to strike for its prey.

"Where's your colleague?" Hutchins asked, his voice quavering. "The lady."

The Thin Man did not respond, his bloodshot eyes fixed on Hutchins. "Just confess," he growled after several torturous moments.

Hutchins opened his mouth, but no words came out.

"Confess," The Thin Man said again.

Hutchins once again remained silent.

The officer stared for what felt like a geological age, then walked calmly around the desk and stood beside Hutchins. The officer was now so close that the young academic could smell stale sweat and tobacco. The interrogator leaned forward, his mouth just an inch from Hutchins' ear.

"Confess. Tell me what you did. You and the woman. Confess now, and your sentence will be shorter."

"There's... there's nothing to confess," Hutchins said, shaking his head. He suddenly wondered why he was being interrogated in the middle of the night. Because the interrogation was off-book? Sleep deprivation?

"If you die here," — The Thin Man glanced at Hutchins' heart as he said the word 'die'—your government will find out. Eventually. There will be trouble. We don't want that."

"You're right. We don't." Hutchins nodded.

"But if you are injured here," The Thin Man continued, "no trouble would come. It could be anything. An accident. Self-harm. Who would know? Who would care?"

Hutchins tried to speak, but his tongue felt like a dead lizard inside his dry mouth. He tried hard not to shake. He dug his fingernails hard into his palms, fighting to salvage some bravery from somewhere deep inside.

"Why were you on the island?" the man asked. "Who sent you?"

"It's... it's all a misunderstanding," Hutchins said, his voice just a squeak.

"No, it is not."

"If I rescued someone from a fire," Hutchins said, feeling increasingly delirious, "would you say I started the fire?"

"Shut up."

Hutchins did. For a moment. Then, "Sir, if I..."

"Shut up," the officer spat. "This is not America. I will keep you here until you confess. Sleep will disappear, then food, then water. I will make sure you stay out of the way."

"Out of the way? Of what?" Hutchins said, looking up at the man. "Why are you interrogating me in the middle of the night? This is not correct protocol."

"You're right," The Thin Man said. "It is not. What are you going to do about it?" Dreadful silence followed. The man leaned forward again. "Where is the plant?"

Shock and realization hit at the same time. With a brief burst of hatred and determination, Hutchins shook his head firmly. "Never."

The Thin Man whipped a dark object from his pocket and lunged forward. Everything went black. Hutchins quickly realized that a hood had been placed over his head. He heard the high-pitched zipping sound of tape being torn from a roll. The man wrapped tape tightly around the hood at the location of Hutchins' ears, muting all sound. The same thing happened where his mouth and nose touched the hood, blocking oxygen almost completely.

Fear rose like an icy flood in his stomach, his chest, his throat. He focused on breathing, just getting a gasp of air each time. At any moment, he expected to feel pain in some part of his body. A blade digging into him, a fist striking him, or hands around his neck, crushing his windpipe.

No pain came, nor did any sound. After a long time, Hutchins assumed that the man must have left the room. But the silence, the darkness—in some ways, these things were worse than pain.

Time passed, thoughts hammering his brain like Barbarians at the gates. Finally, a hand gripped his head, tearing the tape free. The person ripped the hood away.

The Thin Man stood there, his scent even stronger than before. He placed a glass of water in front of Hutchins. Hutchins reached for it, his throat screaming for hydration. Just as he was about to grasp it, the officer slapped it away. Water splattered onto Hutchins' face, and the glass shattered against the wall.

The Thin Man grabbed Hutchins by the collar and shoved his face up close.

"Give me something," the man hissed. "My boss needs answers. Help me, and I'll help you. Ignore me, and I will hurt you. I will make you beg me to stop. If you don't know where the plant is, tell him where the missing piece is."

"What... what missing piece?" Hutchins stammered.

"The ancient document. You know what he wants."

"I really—"

The Thin Man slapped Hutchins across the face, causing him to bite a chunk out of his tongue. While his head still spun, another slap landed on the same spot, doubling the pain. The crack from the blow echoed in the small room, and the iron taste of blood filled Hutchins' mouth.

"I can do anything to you!" The Thin Man squealed, enraged. "Anything! Nobody cares about you!"

Hutchins trembled uncontrollably. He hung his head, drooping almost to the table. "National Museum of History, Mexico City. Hidden in the basement archives," he whispered.

The Thin Man walked quickly out of the room, leaving Hutchins convulsing with tears.

## 37

**Mexican desert, north of Cabo San Lucas.**

The 'Gloriette' was stuffed full of heavy, oppressive heat. A single lantern swung from the low ceiling, lighting airborne dust particles. The scent of incense hung thick, mingling with the background odor of sweat and dirt. Outside, the desert wind whispered against the walls.

The Mentor leaned back in his chair, his long fingers tapping rhythmically against the armrest. Across from him, in the dusty armchair chair where Lucy had previously sat trembling, The Ogre hunched over, his bulk filling the cramped space.

The Ogre coughed. Again. A harsh, wet sound that echoed in the stillness. He wiped a meaty hand across his mouth and glared at the burning incense stick set in a crude clay holder beside the table leg. The stick's thin trail of smoke curled toward the low ceiling.

"Shut up," The Mentor snapped. "I'm trying to think."

The Ogre's eyes widened, but he said nothing. He shifted in his seat, the old chair groaning beneath his weight. His gaze flicked to the incense again, his lip curling in anger at the smoke that made him cough. Noticing it, The Mentor leaned down and used one of the incense sticks to light two more next to his feet.

"I have new information," The Mentor said, his tone softening. He leaned forward, interlocking his fingers. "My contact in the Mexican police did his job. It turns out scrawny academics are easy to intimidate."

The Ogre smiled, deepening the grooves in his rubbery face. "You know where the plant is?"

"Not yet. But I soon will. The weakling academic handed us a huge clue. The professor is becoming more amenable, too."

"It'll make you rich," the big man said, his voice rough from the smoke.

"I'm already rich. This isn't about money. It's about legacy. Fame. Recognition. When people think of great discoveries—Fleming and penicillin, Jenner and vaccinations—they'll think of me. I'll be more famous than any wellness guru selling snake oil on the Internet. I'll be a mega-celebrity."

The Ogre snorted, then coughed again, muttering a curse under his breath. His massive shoulders heaved as he loudly tried to clear his throat. "Your family might even accept you again," he said finally.

The Mentor stiffened. "Your family might never hear from *you* again. Never welcome you back into whatever cave they live in. Careful with your words, my friend."

The Ogre nodded. "I... I just meant, you would be respected."

"About time," The Mentor said quietly.

"But not if anyone tells the world what you did here," The Ogre added.

"Exactly," The Mentor said. He felt a tingling around the follicles on his hairy arms. "That's what I want to talk about. Let's make sure they never can."

The Ogre's eyes narrowed, light from the lantern reflecting in the dark pupils. "You're really going to…?"

The Mentor interrupted him. "The experimentation phase is over. Thanks to the new information, we have other options, and there are too many loose ends. Those crazy gangsters I employed to guard the island are conducting ad hoc experiments, thinking it will impress me. One woman escaped from there already. Let's start covering our tracks."

The Mentor turned to look at the shelf in the corner of the hut, where bundles of dried white snakeroot sat tied with twine. The poisonous herb had been meticulously harvested for their cruel experiments, initially meant to test the supposed antidote properties of the miracle plant. The dried leaves and roots looked innocuous in the dim light, but The Mentor knew their potential for destruction.

"Prepare it," Sallas ordered. "Grind it down and brew it into a drinkable form. Enough for everyone."

The Ogre blinked. "Everyone? You mean the sick ones? The… the ones we brought in to test?"

"*Everyone*," The Mentor repeated. "The healthy ones too. They were meant to be proof of the plant's effectiveness, but they have seen too much."

The Ogre's gaze darted toward the door, and for a fleeting second, The Mentor wondered if the man would walk out, refuse the order. He almost smiled at the thought of The Ogre fearing he too may be forced to drink.

"Everyone except you and me," The Mentor said calmly. "And the professor. We may still need him."

The large, spherical shoulders seemed to relax, but only a little. "And your favorite girl?" The Ogre asked.

The Mentor thought for a moment. He did not like the conflict in his head. "Prepare enough for her. I'll see how happy she makes me tonight."

"Why would they drink?" the big man asked. "Am I supposed to force it down their throats one by one?"

"Tell them it's what we have been seeking. Make it purple somehow—the only concrete information we ever had about the plant. Tell them this is the fruit of their labors, and they will soon start out on the path to a healthful life."

"This is..." The Ogre paused, his jaw rolling. "...you're getting paranoid, Sallas."

"I know," The Mentor said simply. "Paranoia is what's keeping us alive. If even one of them escapes, talks to the wrong person, this all falls apart. Everything I've worked for —everything we've done—gone."

The Ogre grunted, looking away. For a long moment, the only sound was the whistling of desert wind through cracks in the wood. The Mentor's fingers tapped against the armrest.

"How long?" he asked finally. "To prepare enough for that many people?"

The Ogre scratched at his stubble and did not speak.

The Mentor leaned forward, his gaze boring into the man's eyes. "How long?" he asked again. He felt tense, and he did not like it. The silence allowed room for doubt.

"Give me twenty-four hours," The Ogre said at last. "It's delicate work, and I'll have to do it alone if you don't want anyone else involved."

The Mentor leaned back, satisfied. "Good. Don't forget to mix in some purple with it; make it look authentic. God knows there are enough random purple plants around here to use."

The incense burned low now, its smoke thinning as the sticks turned to ash. The Ogre coughed one more time, his massive frame shifting as he rose to his feet. He lumbered awkwardly toward the door as though he carried the weight of the decision physically. He stopped and looked intently at The Mentor. "Mass suicide?" he asked. "Is that the story?"

"Exactly. The work of a cult leader who lured me here too. I tried to stop it."

"And who should I say was the 'leader'?"

"Anyone. They will all be dead. Just point at a corpse."

Without saying another word, The Ogre departed. As the door creaked open and then shut behind him, The Mentor remained seated. His gaze drifted to the shelf where the white snakeroot lay.

He stood and walked to the shelf, where he ran his fingertips over the thin, hairy stems. From somewhere across the compound, through the gaps between the window frames, he heard someone laughing. The light, delicate laugh of a young woman. He ran a hand through his hair, his thoughts turning darker.

He glanced back to where the last faint spiral of smoke rose from the incense.

"Twenty-four hours," he murmured to himself, the words carrying both a promise and a warning. The Mentor closed his eyes briefly, steadying himself. He shook his head, his eyes squeezing closed even more tightly.

"Killing your own unborn child," he said quietly. "This is a new low even for you, Sallas."

# 38

**Mexican desert, north of Cabo San Lucas.**

Professor Wall stared at the bunkhouse ceiling, listening to the sounds of the desert. He blinked several times, but it made no difference in the almost total darkness. He was unsure whether he had slept or not, uncertain whether the images flashing through his mind had been thoughts or dreams.

He listened with heightened hearing to any scrape or shuffle that could be a small creature, or someone loitering outside, ready to apprehend him. He would have to take his chances.

Moving slowly and carefully, he slipped down from the bed. Reaching back up to where he had been sleeping, he ran his hands along the ragged mattress, searching for the biggest of the many holes in its surface. He stuck his finger into the hole and pulled the fabric back as far as he could. He searched blindly for the errant spring that had been digging into his back. Finding the spring, he twisted and bent the metal. With his teeth gritted, he worked away until, finally, the coil popped free.

He slipped the spring into his pocket and paced across to Lucy, sleeping in the far corner. Reaching out in the low light, he gently shook her awake. Her eyes shot wide, two pale orbs in the darkness. She gasped as though preparing to scream.

"It's me," Wall reassured her. "We need to go."

As Wall had feared, Lucy shook her head. Clearly, her time in the compound, and the drugs, had stripped the fight from her.

"You must come with me," Wall whispered, his mouth just an inch from the woman's ear. "We're getting out of here. You need to go home, and I need to find my friend Hutchins. We need to tell the world about this evil place."

As softly as he could, Wall clasped his hand around the girl's upper arm and lifted her out of bed. She rubbed her eyes and swept tangled knots of hair from her face. Wall helped her to her feet and then led her, shuffling step-by-step, toward the door.

Reaching the door, Wall grasped the handle. He shoved down, the latch clicking as it disengaged. The sound was little more than a tick, but to Wall, it sounded like the clattering of heavy machinery. With sweat greasing his palms in the warm desert night, he gently opened the door just a few inches and peered through. Fortunately, it didn't look as though anyone was guarding the building. Surrounded by the barren desert, with its endless sand, rocks, and spiky shrubs, they were as good as trapped. Captives were given the impression of freedom by moving around the complex while being unable to leave safely.

"Where are we going?" Lucy whispered, peering out at the moonlit compound.

"The Mentor's 'Gloriette'—his shed," Wall said, pointing in the direction of the verdant area that The Mentor seemed to keep for himself.

"What? Are you crazy?" Lucy scrunched her face as though Wall had suggested a casual trip to Mars.

"Trust me," Wall added, touching Lucy's forearm. "We can do this."

Wall turned, opened the door another few inches, and then slipped through. He took three steps away from the building, then paused. The sound of shuffling drifted from a nearby building.

Wall ducked and pinned himself to the side of the bunkhouse, narrowing his eyes to see in the low light. A figure moved slowly, almost drunkenly, through the moonlight. The figure took another few steps, and Wall saw that it was a young woman, stumbling and groaning. It was impossible to tell if she was drunk, high, or crazed, either as the result of something she had consumed voluntarily or as a result of coercion. Either way, she stood in his path, blocking the route.

Wall took Lucy by the wrist and slipped behind the bunkhouse. He put his finger to his lips as the pair stood rigid against the wall. Wall leaned slowly to the side and peered around the corner. The woman swayed and stumbled, now laughing at some internal joke.

"Move on, for pity's sake," Wall whispered to himself.

The drunken woman covered her face with her forearm and leaned against a wall, apparently taking a moment to gather herself. She hissed and wheezed as though the whole experience had suddenly become far too much for her to cope with. Looking directly at the floor, with her arm covering her eyes, she wouldn't see much.

In another situation, Wall would have liked to help her, but now she was in the way. He turned to Lucy and tipped his head in the direction they needed to go. Time to move.

He stepped out, leading Lucy by the hand and pacing past the intoxicated woman as quickly and quietly as possible. Wall led the way across the quiet compound toward the area with the fountain. He paced through the greenery, pausing beside one of the trees to check for movement. Seeing none, he pushed on, deeper into The Mentor's domain.

"I really hope that guy took my advice and found someone to snuggle with tonight," Wall said under his breath.

"What?" Lucy asked just as quietly.

"Nothing. I just hope he's not here."

Wall led Lucy on through the trees and flowers that stood in stark contrast to the harsh desert compound and the evil taking place inside it.

"Please wait here a moment," Wall said when they arrived next to the fountain. "I need to go into his shed. His *Gloriette*."

Lucy nodded, then crouched down behind a cactus with arms long enough to stick out like they were shielding her.

Wall listened for movement, glanced behind him, then, in a stoop, stalked toward the Gloriette. He crossed the ground slowly, expecting at any moment to hear the sound of rushing feet or a raised voice. To his delight, none came. He got to the Gloriette and reached for the door handle. Closing his eyes, he took a deep breath. The professor pushed down on the handle, but nothing moved. He tried again, more forcefully. Again, nothing. He hissed a curse at the locked door.

He threw his head backward and looked toward the stars, clear and bright in the desert sky. Silently, he told himself not to blame fate, the divine, or anyone or anything. He was responsible for what happened over the next few minutes.

Narrowing his eyes, Wall peered in through the grimy window. With the help of light from the moon, he could just make out the glimmer of the metal rim along the motorcycle's key fob.

Wall looked over both shoulders one more time, then, gritting his teeth, he punched through the glass. A stinging pain shot through his hand and up his arm. He clamped a hand over his mouth, muting his howl of pain into a low growl.

Composing himself, Wall reached through the jagged hole and grabbed the key fob. Working carefully to avoid cutting himself, he pulled the small device through the gap. He closed his fist over the key and then darted back to where Lucy was waiting. Lucy rose from her position as Wall approached. He nodded and led the way to the motorcycle.

Wall gently slid the tarp to the floor and pointed at the saddle. "Climb on," he whispered. "I'll just be a second."

Wall pulled the bed spring from his pocket and then crossed to the fence. He slid the spring through a gap in the chain-link and then bent the spring into a hook. With the heavy night already making him sweat, he pulled, the exertion adding to the moisture dripping down his back.

A lack of food had left the professor seriously low on energy, but, somehow, he found the strength to work away at the hole and stretch the mesh. As he had hoped, the wire was old and weak, and with each strong tug, he was able to stretch the wire and extend the size of the hole by a few inches. The metal of the spring dug into his flesh, adding to the cuts caused by the broken glass.

He thought about his wife and her smiling face. He thought about Lucy's parents when they eventually laid eyes on her after so long. He pulled again. Finally, the hole was big enough. If the two of them ducked down low on the bike, they could slip beneath the wire.

Wall returned to the Royal Enfield and threw his leg over the seat, his body now buzzing with adrenaline and anticipation. Beyond the hole, the shadowy horizon beckoned him toward freedom.

"Please," he said softly to the bike, "get me out of here. Get me home."

Lucy's arms curled softly around his waist as he kicked up the stand.

Copying what The Mentor had done earlier, Wall put his thumb on the button required to start the engine.

"Hey!" boomed a raised voice from behind him, followed by footsteps. Wall recognized the voice as The Ogre's and felt like his heart had stopped. Forcing himself to act despite the fear, he hit the button and twisted the throttle. The powerful machine leapt from its position like a caged animal, and Wall picked up speed immediately.

"Duck!" Wall yelled as they sped toward the fence, kicking up a cloud of sand. Wall and Lucy ducked at the same time, and the motorcycle charged for their portal to freedom. As the tires churned up more dust, the hole Wall had made loomed larger. Wall worked the throttle again while straining every muscle to maintain balance on the powerful machine.

Lucy clung to him, her fingers digging into the flesh

under his ribcage. With the hole and freedom now just feet away, Wall ducked lower as the warm desert wind rushed over him.

"Faster!" Lucy screamed. "Please get us out!" Then, she howled, "No!"

A heavy hand landed on Wall's shoulder. His body tipped backward, yanked off the saddle with brutal force. He flew through the air and crashed to the ground, the impact knocking the wind from his lungs. The hard ground ripped skin from his body as he skidded across the dirt. He bounced once, twice, then rolled to a stop on his back. Through blurred vision, he recognized the monstrous face looming above him.

He pulled his legs and feet up over his stomach to protect himself from the creature. He scanned his surroundings, searching for Lucy. The motorcycle lay flat on the ground, a few feet from the gap in the fence. Lucy lay on her back beside the machine.

"Get up! Drive!" Wall yelled just as a huge hand closed around the throat. Wall kicked out at the beast of a man, striking him in the stomach, but it was like kicking an oak tree. He kicked again, harder. The Ogre growled but did not budge.

The sound of the motorbike rose again, cutting through the grunts of the struggle.

Wall squinted through the darkness and saw the bike standing back on two wheels with Lucy standing beside it. The Ogre's head twisted sharply as the big man turned to look too.

"Hey!" The Ogre shouted as Lucy threw her leg over the powerful machine.

The beast let out an anguished howl and pinned Wall to the ground by the throat. Clearly knowing it was too late to stop Lucy, The Ogre took out the anger of his failure on Wall's windpipe. The professor could not look up to see Lucy speeding away. But he did not need to. Beneath the rough hand, he smiled. She was out.

But he most certainly was not.

## 39

**Chetumal, east coast of Mexico. The next day.**

Hans Hutchins awoke on the hard floor of his cell. Immediately upon waking, he wanted to cry again but forced himself not to.

"You may be a prisoner, but you're not a child," he told himself quietly. He took a deep breath and composed himself.

"Visitor," a guard said, throwing open the door.

"My lawyer?"

Without replying, the guard walked over to Hutchins and helped him up—much to Hutchins' surprise. They moved through to the station lobby where Hutchins had originally been booked and relieved of his belongings. Sierra Byrd stood with a handsome older gentleman at the counter.

"Ready to go?" Byrd said, her gaze meeting Hutchins.

Joy flooded through Hans Hutchins and bolstered the last bit of strength he had left.

"How... how..." he stuttered, staggering forward.

"My friend Tom here." Byrd pointed a thumb at her companion. "He's better connected than I thought."

The suave man offered his hand, and Hutchins gladly accepted.

"I have connections. Luckily for you," Tom said, giving Hutchins a smooth-operator wink.

Hutchins couldn't contain his smile as an officer handed his belongings back to him. "Thank you for a wonderful stay," Hutchins said. The rotund officer flashed him a look that said, *Don't push your luck.*

Hutchins stepped out with Byrd and Tom into the brilliant sunshine, and his smile widened further when he saw Candi. The blonde stood waiting for him, bathed in sunlight, grinning like a proud parent picking their child up from school.

"Are you okay?!" she asked, rushing forward.

"Not really. But that's not important right now," Hutchins said. "We've got work to do."

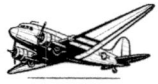

CANCUN, Mexico

THE COMPETING thuds of three different bass drums welcomed Byrd and her offbeat ensemble to the never-ending party that was Cancun. Bright sunlight reflected off the white sands of the beach, where turquoise waves lapped the shoreline, and palm trees rippled their leaves like the arms of salsa dancers. Jet Skis bounced across the water, causing Hutchins and Candi to share a grin. Byrd noticed the moment and made a mental note to get the full story as soon as possible.

Despite it being only late afternoon, the bars that dotted the promenade were filling up, their outdoor tables shaded by towering, gleaming white hotel blocks.

"Should we ask someone where the Green Frog Cafe is?" Hutchins asked the group.

"Well, I was planning on heading for that bar with a giant green frog standing over the entrance," Byrd replied with a wink as she pointed down the street. "Come on," she added, taking the lead. Hutchins and Candi followed, along with Tom, who looked immaculate in his white-linen shorts and lilac short-sleeved shirt.

The quartet ducked inside and emerged into a space of cluttered, kitschy decor. Frog-themed trinkets dominated every surface—from ceramic frogs playing tiny instruments on shelves to Kermit puppets dangling from light fixtures. Frog-shaped tankards lined the bar, while vintage amphibian advertisements plastered the walls.

A group of four gym-toned young men stood around the central pool table, their white muscle vests leaving their sculpted deltoids on full display under the garish neon lights.

"This place reminds me of a remote roadhouse along Route 66," Byrd said to Tom, raising her voice over the thumping beat of 1980s hair metal music. "As if the owner had gone frog-crazy."

They bought drinks and found a table beneath an enormous poster of a frog riding a speedboat. Byrd's eyes lingered on the poster for much longer than its entertainment value warranted. This was certainly the sort of place where people came for quirky vibes, cheap drinks, and a good time. A good time without any of the constraints of normal life, such as avoiding conversation with strangers.

"Why would anyone come to a place like this?" Hutchins yelled at Byrd across the table, competing with a Bon Jovi key change coming from the many speakers.

"Isn't it obvious?" Byrd replied loudly. "Young men come to make eyes at young women. It's happening in every town across the entire Western Hemisphere, from Cancun to London."

The music suddenly stopped. "But all the men in here look ridiculous!" Hutchins said loudly before he could stop himself. Several heads turned in his direction before the next song started.

Byrd leaned in toward the center of the table, and her three companions followed suit.

"The poor girl Hutchins and I picked up from the island said she heard her captors talking about this place," Byrd said at a volume that allowed the music to disguise her words to anyone beyond the table. "Possibly a place to pick up victims who think it's just a bit of flirting. Be on the lookout for that kind of activity."

Hutchins nodded, then looked at Candi with a furrowed brow.

"Tom, did any of your contacts in the Mexican police say anything about this place?" Byrd asked, turning to look at the man next to her.

"I'm afraid not," Tom said, sipping at his Scotch. "But I'll see if I can get someone arrested for this music."

Byrd smiled but quickly got serious again. "But if you have someone in the force you can trust, someone higher up, could you put out a few feelers?"

"You shouldn't overestimate my influence within the

Mexican police," Tom replied, casting his eyes around the bar. "I pulled some strings with an old friend, but I can't keep doing it. And I honestly have no idea who is corrupt and who is not."

"Understood," Byrd replied, swirling the bourbon in her glass. "It's a meat market for sure," she said, looking around. Her gaze rested on the only guy in the whole place who wasn't making eyes at people, yet was the most alluring of the lot. The olive-skinned gentleman in the corner with his deep brown eyes buried in a book. Perfect diagonal lines at the top of his stubble highlighted pronounced cheekbones, and his linen shirt rested easily on broad shoulders. Long, dark hair was tied up behind his head.

"Have you undressed him yet?" Tom asked with a mischievous smile. "In your mind, I mean."

"We came here to look and learn, didn't we?" Byrd replied.

"And what have you learned?"

"I've learned that the red-blooded Southern girl in me ain't dead yet," Byrd said, just about resisting the urge to wink at Tom.

Byrd expected, even hoped, to see a touch of resentment on Tom's face, but she saw something completely different. With his Rock Hudson eyes, he looked like he wanted to prove that youthful beauty was no match for experience.

"Let's just be on the lookout for anyone trying to pick up women," Byrd told the group, getting back to business. "It could be innocent, or it could be our honey trap." She took a sip as she glanced over at Hutchins, who gazed adoringly at Candi. The young blonde raised her iced beer glass and clinked against Hutchins'.

Looking back at Tom, Byrd saw him mouth the words "honey trap?" with a smile.

Byrd smiled back as a cacophony of shouts and cheers erupted from the young men around the pool table.

"If they react like that to winning a game, they're not gonna trap anybody," Byrd said, watching the guys exchange high-fives. "Ah, dammit," she added, realizing that looking in their direction was not a good idea when she got a smile and a raised eyebrow in return.

Byrd looked away, remembering that no female should ever do anything as cavalier as look in the direction of a young stallion in a situation such as this, for risk of giving the wrong impression.

One of the men, with a chiseled jaw and a crew cut, suddenly paced toward Byrd, clearly not getting the message. Byrd allowed every drop of emotion to drain from her face, leaving her looking as if she had recently died. The only indication that she was still alive was a very slow shake of the head that she directed at her suitor.

"Hey, lady!" the young stud said, standing just six inches from Byrd and towering over her. "What's a sophisticated gal like you doing in a place like this?" His top lip curled at one side like a grinning Elvis.

Slowly, Byrd got to her feet. She put her face right in front of the young man's and locked eyes with him. "I have some pain I need to inflict," she said calmly, "and I'm looking for volunteers."

The Elvis smile fell from the face, replaced by a frown. The man opened his mouth to speak, then clearly thought better of it. As he turned to walk away, Byrd added, "Make sure you keep that body healthy."

Turning back to the table, Byrd couldn't tell if the look on Tom's face was one of fear, admiration, or lust. "I'll get us another drink," she said, already walking away.

Approaching the bar, Byrd noticed the server, a bubbly

brunette, sharing a joke with the guy she was finishing up serving.

"What would you like?" the girl asked when it was Byrd's turn to order. The accent was Southern US and not dissimilar to Byrd's own.

"I'd like a real man who knows how to treat a woman. But if that's too much to ask, I'll just take an Eagle Rare, neat."

"I meet a hundred guys a night, and I can't find a guy who makes me feel all that," the server said, letting out a full-bellied laugh.

"Plenty of fish in the sea, girl. Problem is, too many of them act like fish, gawping and going round in circles. Make the Eagle Rare a double. Another Scotch, and two Modelo for my friends."

"I hope those meatheads weren't giving you any trouble?" the girl said, preparing the drinks.

"Not at all. I know exactly what I'm dealing with when it comes to guys like that." Then she added more quietly, almost to herself, "Although I can't say the same about everyone in here."

"What's that?" the young bartender asked.

"What's the deal with the suave guy in the corner there?" Byrd asked. "Catwalk Jesus reading his book."

"Good question. He's an interesting one. Just sort of sits there until girls fall in love with him from across the bar. Then he takes them home without doin' hardly anythin'."

"Wow," Byrd replied, stealing another look at the guy. "There's gonna be a problem when some of these girls show up here at the same time."

"You'd think," the bartender said, "but none of them ever seem to come back."

"Really?"

"Yeah. It's weird," the young woman said.

"Sure is," Byrd replied, looking the girl in the eye. "I'd stay away from him if I were you."

"Don't worry. I don't get intimate with the customers. Usually!"

Byrd smiled as she paid for the drinks, but the smile soon faded.

"This place feels like Spring Break got even creepier than it usually is," Byrd said to herself, returning to the table.

While Byrd took a slow sip of her second drink, Catwalk Jesus stood and made his way out of the bar.

"See you again soon," he said to the server in a slow, baritone voice. His tone suggested that would be something for her to look forward to. The server smiled at him, then looked at Byrd across the room and rolled her eyes.

"I guess we need to come back here soon too, then," Byrd said, watching the guy go.

"Why?" Tom asked over the top of his glass.

"Because he's the one we gotta watch." She nodded toward the door.

"We should follow him right now," Hutchins suggested. "He could take someone any time. Not only here."

"Where did you learn your spycraft, kid?" Tom asked. "College? How do four of us follow one guy without him noticing?"

"Where did you learn your manners, pops?" Hutchins snapped back, then added, "So what's your big idea?"

"Okay, okay," Byrd interjected. "Looks like the booze is talking. Clearly, one-and-a-half drinks was too much for us all. Let's get out of here. We're getting close, but we need a plan. A good one."

# 40

"This is definitely better for private talk," Byrd said, stepping out on the gleaming white balcony of their newly rented apartment. She dropped four sodas to the table, slid three across to the others, and took one herself. "And these will keep the little grey cells sharp," she said, snapping the top. She took a swig and grimaced; a beer or whiskey would have been much better, but she needed the others to stay as sharp as possible.

"Diabetes in a can, if I've ever tasted it," she said, looking up at the label. She took a seat at the table and glanced at the others.

Traffic grumbled down the boulevard beneath them, coughing out exhaust fumes that drifted up to the balcony on the warm breeze. But neither the fumes nor the occasional screech from drunken passersby detracted from the view of the vivid blue ocean, green palm trees, and white sand.

"Okay. Here's what we've got so far," Byrd said, her gaze completing a full circle of her compadres around the table. "We're pretty sure the smooth operator from the bar is there

*The Shadow of the Sunstone*

to pick up women, maybe even men too, and then convince them to go someplace with him."

"Wouldn't catch me goin' anywhere with that creep," Candi said, a frown clouding her face. Hutchins grinned at her, clearly pleased to hear this.

"That's good to hear, girl. You're clearly more switched on than most," Byrd continued. "The question is, how do we find out where that place is? We could follow him, but we only get one shot at that. And as Tom pointed out, we are by no means experts in the art of tracking and surveillance."

"As I see it, the only other option is for one of us to go with him voluntarily," Tom interjected. "That's the only way to find out where these people are being processed or held."

"That means at least one of us ends up captive, though," Hutchins said, looking around in panic. "Probably end up being experimented on... and... and..."

"What else do you suggest?" Tom piped up, leaning forward toward Hutchins. "It's your friend we're all trying to rescue. Did you expect it to be easy?"

"I'm not really sure why you're here, to be honest," Hutchins said, his eyes locking on Tom as though he was to blame for the whole sorry mess.

Tom's chair scraped along the balcony tiles as he suddenly shoved it back and stood. "Well, clearly, I have the life experience to be able to point out the most basic problems," he retorted. "How about start with that?"

"Alright, gentlemen," Byrd interjected, placing a hand on Tom's arm to bring him down. "Let's start simple. We'll hire a car. Maybe park up outside the Green Frog."

"Won't that look suspicious?" Candi asked, taking a sip of the soda before grimacing.

"We'll have to keep moving. Drive round the block every half hour," Byrd said.

"It's a busy street too," Hutchins added. "And it's easier to tail someone in a car than on foot, especially when there are four of us."

"The kid's an expert now, right?" Tom said, earning himself a scornful glance from Byrd.

"I'll organize the car," Hutchins said, standing and leaning slightly toward Tom before leaving the balcony quickly.

"I'll come with you," Candi announced, panning her beaming smile around the group, although it didn't look quite as genuine as before.

"Go ahead, darl'," Byrd said.

"Thanks!" Candi said, striding inside.

Byrd heard the apartment door click back into position and then leaned back in her chair. Some kind of muscle car rumbled down the boulevard several stories below, a bassline thumping on top of its howling engine.

"To a new dawn," Tom said, raising his glass to Byrd.

"If it's a new dawn, I want to go back to bed," Byrd said, shaking her head. She met Tom's gaze and noticed a glint in his eye. Finally, she raised her own glass out of politeness and then took a sip. "This stuff really is awful," she said, pushing the drink away from her.

"Now that the kids are gone, how about a proper drink?" Tom asked, once again catching her eye. He pulled two Laphroaig miniatures from his shorts pocket. "There's a depth to this single malt that tastes like the soul of the land."

*I suppose you think that just because you got my friend Hutchins out of jail, I owe you one*, Byrd thought. "Are you trying to get me drunk, Tom? We're supposed to be sharp and alert here, and your poetic talk is making my head spin enough as it is."

"Just trying to take the edge off the stress, that's all," Tom said, stroking one of the miniature bottles with his thumb.

"Give me a minute. I'll need some water with it." Sierra Byrd stepped off the balcony and into the cool darkness of the apartment. She moved barefoot across the tiles toward the kitchen, past the large granite island, and opened the refrigerator. As she was pouring herself a glass of water, she heard movement behind her. She turned to see Tom standing dead still, his eyes deep and mysterious.

"Actually, how about we enjoy a drink inside?" Tom said as his lips tightened into a coy smile. "A little privacy?"

Byrd felt her skin tingling all over, but she wasn't sure if it was excitement or apprehension.

"I think I'd prefer a stroll on the beach or someth—" She stopped and looked into those deep eyes. "Ah, heck," she said. "Let's have a drink."

"Wonderful," Tom said. "How about a gin and tonic before we get into the Scotch—something light and refreshing?" He stepped over to the drinks cabinet and pulled open the glass door.

"Sounds good to me," Byrd replied. "I think I saw some lime in the fridge. Perks of renting a high-end apartment. Thanks again for this, Tom. The favors just keep on coming."

Byrd opened the fridge and took out the bright, healthy-looking lime, then pulled a sharp knife from the drawer. As she prepared the chopping board, she sensed Tom stepping up behind her, close enough that she could smell the sea air on his skin.

Slowly, he reached around her and moved his hand toward the chopping board. The knuckle on his index finger gently brushed her skin as he wrapped his fingers around the handle of the knife.

"Allow me," he said softly, stepping in to cut the lime. Byrd felt like her stomach was vibrating, butterflies drunk on gin tonic.

As ice plunged into the drinks, making a satisfying fizz, Tom took one step back, locked eyes with Byrd again, and proposed a toast.

"To you," he said. "To your flight school. And, of course, to your Skytrain. I hope one day, you look at me like you look at your C-47."

"To my loyal students," Byrd said, ignoring the flirting. For now. "Please accept my apologies that the first week hasn't exactly gone... smoothly. I'll make it up to you."

"Will you now?" Tom said as he took a slow sip. He raised one eyebrow before adding, "I'll look forward to that."

"Easy there, pilot," Byrd said, resting a hand on the granite counter. "I mean, I dunno, I'll cook for you or something."

"Are you a good cook, Sierra Byrd?" Tom asked.

"I love me a little Southern cooking. I like preparing it almost as much as I like eating it. I'll bet you didn't eat many grits up there on Wall Street, did you, Tom?"

Byrd watched as the suave man cast his eyes around individual features of her face, remaining silent for a moment. "You're right about that," he said finally, seemingly without too much interest in the conversation. "More like Michelin-starred restaurants around Manhattan."

"No Michelin-starred grits?" Byrd replied, tailing off as she noticed Tom slowly edging toward her. "How about another slice of lime?" she asked, eyeing the knife on the board.

Tom didn't reply. He stood tall and walked toward her, striding now. Suddenly, he lunged. Byrd dropped her shoulder like a football player evading a tackle and slid to her right. Tom half-stumbled, then straightened up.

"Whoa! What's going on there, Tommy boy? Was that supposed to be a kiss?!"

Tom said nothing. He just stared.

"You made your move a little too soon, I'm afraid," Byrd quipped, running a hand across her curls to make sure nothing had fallen out of place. "Sorry to dodge you n'all, but this is neither the time nor the place."

"Yes," Tom said quietly. "A kiss. Or my attempt at a kiss. Apologies."

"Don't mention it," Byrd said casually, frowning and smiling at the same time. She felt like her legs were turning to liquid. His eyes looked almost murderous with lust.

As casually as she could, Byrd stepped over to the chopping board and picked up the knife, twirling it once in her fingers before making a show of slicing some lime. *Not the first time in my life I've had to leave a man in no doubt that he should back off*, she thought.

Tom slowly wiped a hand across his forehead, then tugged at his collar to let some air in. "I'm sorry," he said, only making eye contact with Byrd for a second. "I need a bit of fresh air. And privacy. Would you excuse me?"

The not-so-smooth operator walked over to the balcony door and stepped outside before closing the door, shutting out the noise of the street and the rolling ocean. Byrd watched as Tom leaned against the balcony railings. He pulled his phone from his pocket and put it to his ear. He had his back to her, so she couldn't tell if he was speaking to anyone, but it seemed like he was only listening.

"You're handsome, and—more importantly—you're useful," Byrd said quietly to herself. "But you're starting to give me the creeps."

Mexican desert, north of Cabo San Lucas

Lucian Sallas sank into his heavy wooden chair beside his tinkling fountain. He drew a long, slow breath and then pulled out his phone. His thumb hovered over the screen, which displayed his father's private number.

"What's the damn point," he said quietly, hitting the back button. "You hate me anyway."

He scrolled and dialed a different number, ready to leave a voice message. He knew the person at the other end would not pick up and risk an impromptu conversation on such a sensitive topic.

"Fine work at the jail," he said in a low voice. "We got the information we needed, and you got him out of there before any lawyers came sniffing around. Now, we need to clean up. My location is no longer secure—someone got out. I'll clean things up here, then we can follow our new lead."

The Mentor paused and scanned the area. Satisfied that he was alone with only insects for company, he continued. "You take care of people on the outside. I don't care how you'll do it, but do it somewhere remote, away from eyes. Take out everyone except the beautiful blonde you sent a photo of. I've made plans to keep her for myself."

## 41

**Cancun, Mexico.**

"Nice car; it suits you," Candi said, climbing out of the Chevrolet Silverado in the parking lot.

"You think?" Hutchins replied, sliding out of the driver's seat and slamming the truck's door. *A thousand bucks for the smallest scratch, remember!* he chided himself, wincing.

"Definitely," Candi said, her gaze sweeping from the car's sleek lines and up to Hutchins.

"Maybe I'll get one myself, when... urm... well that's the thing... archaeology doesn't pay all that great," Hutchins said, a blush sweeping across his face.

"That doesn't matter," Candi said as the pair started across the lot, which was now bathed in the soft light of the sun's last rays. "Money doesn't impress me. The way you stood up to Tom earlier, now that was impressive."

"Yeah?" Hutchins said, questioning. "Yeah!" he said again, more certain this time. "What's that guy even doing here? It's weird how he got me out of jail only to berate and belittle me."

Candi grasped Hutchins' hand, and his anger instantly morphed into an entirely different feeling. His heart fluttered, and he felt as though he'd just been injected with something that was probably illegal.

Candi led them along the promenade in the direction of the Green Frog Cafe, passing groups of Ivy League types carrying trays of beer to the beach. Young men and women stumbled around like they were on the deck of a ship, clutching their bottles tightly to save them from crashing to the ground.

Cars rumbled past, their engines competing to be the loudest on the strip.

"Let me go on that side," Hutchins said, shuffling around Candi to be on the road side.

"What, just in case any drivers lose control?" Candi said, meeting his gaze.

"You never know,' Hutchins said, puffing his chest out a little. "It's a dangerous world out here, anything could—"

"Hey!" Candi hissed, elbowing Hutchins in the ribs. "Look, isn't that..."

"What? Where? I don't..." Hutchins looked frantically from side to side.

"The best-looking guy in the Bible," Candi said, pointing at a figure hurrying across the street. "Catwalk Jesus, as Byrd called him. Good looks, bad news."

"You're right," Hutchins said, trying and failing to play it cool. The pair watched as the smooth hippy from the Green Frog crossed the street, his head swaying to and fro on his lean, muscle-toned frame. He cut a line toward a white sports car waiting at the side of the road.

"That's a Mastretta MXT," Candi said, pointing at the vehicle.

As the man reached for the handle, the wheels began to

roll. He jumped into the vehicle and closed the door with a bang. The engine growled to life, and the car started to cut through the traffic. The Mastretta accelerated, weaving between slower vehicles and cutting across lanes. Pedestrians backed away as the car approached like a precision-guided missile locked in on a target.

"Is it me," Hutchins said to Candi, his voice tightening, "or is that car getting pretty loud and close?" His hand found hers and squeezed.

"Everyone drives erratically around here," Candi said, her eyes remaining fixed on the approaching vehicle. "Play it cool. They have no idea who we are."

The engine's pitch changed as it downshifted. The vehicle crossed another lane, swinging around. With a thud, the car mounted the curb, scattering tourists like bowling pins. A woman screamed and yanked her child back from the sidewalk's edge.

"We need to move!" Hutchins said, dragging Candi away.

The sports car slalomed through the crowd, somehow finding gaps and closing the distance with frightening speed. People scrambled to get out of the way, and drinks sprayed on the pavement.

"Move, move!" Hutchins yelled. Through the windshield, he saw two pairs of eyes fixed on Candi. "They're gonna ram us!"

Hutchins tried to pull Candi toward the beach, but they ran straight into a horde of tourists standing around a kiosk bar. Bodies pressed against them from all sides, blocking their escape.

"Get out of the way!" Hutchins shouted, his voice drowned by the crowd's confusion and the roaring engine behind them.

As the Mastretta closed in, the crowd finally registered

the danger. Panic erupted in the low light of dusk. A man in a Hawaiian shirt stumbled backward, crashing into a table of drinks. Glass shattered, and a child screamed in terror. The crowd surged in various directions—a chaotic mass of flailing limbs.

"This way!" Candi screamed, pointing Hutchins toward a gap in the crowd.

They lunged for the opening, but the Mastretta suddenly swerved, fishtailing across the sidewalk in a violent skid that sent more pedestrians diving for cover.

Tires smoked against pavement as the vehicle screeched to a halt, blocking their escape route. Before Hutchins or Candi could react, the passenger door shot outward, banging into Hutchins' knees. Cartilage crunched, and his legs buckled beneath him. He hit the sidewalk, palms scraping against the concrete. Through blurred vision, he saw a muscular arm shoot out from the car and grab Candi by the hair.

"Hans!" she screamed, grabbing the wrist that held her. She kicked and thrashed, landing a solid elbow to her attacker's chest. The man grunted but maintained his grip. Her elbow connected with the hippy's jaw next—but another pair of hands emerged from the car's interior, grabbing her flailing arms.

Hutchins scrambled to his feet. He lunged toward Candi, fingers outstretched to grab her, just as she disappeared into the car and the door slammed shut.

The tires spun, leaving twin strips of burned rubber as the car lurched back onto the road.

"No, no, no!" Hutchins cried, gasping for air. He turned and sprinted back toward the Chevy. Each footfall sent daggers of pain up his leg, but adrenaline pushed him forward.

"Out of my way!" he bellowed, shouldering past shell-shocked tourists frozen in the aftermath. Sweat trickled down his face as he rounded the corner, scanning frantically for his rental. For one heart-stopping moment, he couldn't spot it among the sea of vehicles.

There—Hutchins fumbled with the keys, his hands trembling so badly he dropped them onto the asphalt. He cursed, scooped them up, and unlocked the car. He jumped inside, yanked the door closed, and fired up the engine. The Chevy roared to life, but in his ears, it sounded painfully inadequate compared to the Mastretta's high-performance growl.

"Come on, come on," he muttered. The tires squealed as he backed out, nearly clipping a passing moped. He thrust the gearshift into drive and floored the accelerator.

Hutchins swerved onto the strip, cutting off a taxi whose driver jabbed on the horn. Hutchins ignored it, desperately searching for the white sports car among the traffic ahead. The Mastretta was nowhere in sight.

"No," he whispered, panic rising in his throat. "I can't lose them."

He pushed the Chevy harder, swinging through traffic. The steering wheel shuddered, and doubt crept in with each passing second. Then, through a gap in the traffic, he caught a flash of white disappearing around a corner ahead. Relief flooded through him for an instant before dread returned. Even if he could keep them in sight, the Chevy would struggle to match the sports car's speed and handling. It was like chasing a greyhound with a bull mastiff.

"You can do this," he told himself, both hands gripping the steering wheel as he followed the Mastretta. With the car now in sight, Hutchins dragged his phone out of his pocket and called Byrd.

"Come on answer, damn it!" he groaned as the phone buzzed.

The driver of the Mastretta expertly navigated a bottleneck of traffic toward the end of the strip, the white sports car slicing through gaps barely wider than its chassis. Its taillights flashed red as it dodged between a lumbering tour bus and a delivery truck, then accelerated away. Hutchins shoved his foot down on the accelerator, the Silverado's engine roaring in protest.

"What's up?" came Byrd's voice as Hutchins swerved around the truck.

Hutchins explained quickly while trying to keep the Mastretta in his sights.

"Come on, you beast," he muttered, fighting the steering wheel.

"What?" Byrd replied.

"Not you, the car."

"What direction are you going?" Byrd said, her voice surprisingly calm.

"Out of town, that's for sure," Hutchins said as he powered into a residential district. The streets narrowed, hemmed in by parked cars on both sides. Yellow taxis idled at corners, their drivers chatting in clusters.

"Get back!" Hutchins shouted, leaning on the horn as a group of teenagers stepped off the curb. They jumped back, shouting obscenities as the Silverado thundered past. Through it all, he kept the Mastretta's taillights in view.

Up ahead, the sports car accelerated onto a wide, straight road. Hutchins followed, relief washing over him as the Silverado finally had room to build up speed.

"Okay, keep on them," Byrd said. "I'll get a map."

"Wait a sec, Aeroporto five km," Hutchins said, reading a sign as it flashed past. "They're taking her to the airport."

The Mastretta's taillights grew smaller as the sports car pulled away on the open road.

"Gotcha," Byrd replied. "Don't lose them and stay on the line."

Hutchins floored the accelerator again, feeling the truck reach its limits as the needle pushed past a hundred. The steering wheel vibrated violently in his hands, the entire chassis seeming to float above the asphalt at this speed.

A sharp curve appeared ahead. The Mastretta took it with grace, barely slowing. Hutchins gripped the wheel tighter and braced himself, the Silverado's tires squealing as he fought to keep the truck on the road. The backend fishtailed, nearly sending him into the guardrail before he regained control.

When he looked up, the sports car's taillights were even farther ahead, twin red dots shrinking into the darkness.

The Mastretta zipped between two semis, getting away. A motorcycle zipped in front of Hutchins, slowing his speed. He took a risk and veered onto the shoulder to get around the bike, his tires kicking up gravel as he sped alongside traffic. The world outside blurred—greenery, road signs, the occasional startled face of a driver yelling at him from behind a window as he flew past.

Suddenly, the Mastretta slowed, its brake lights flashing red through a cloud of dust. Hutchins eased off the accelerator, squinting through the windshield.

The Mastretta pulled onto a narrower road that ran alongside a chain-link fence. The car pulled up to an access gate and stopped.

"They're going into the airport right now," Hutchins shouted into the phone. He slowed and then pulled in behind a clump of trees, still a few hundred feet from the car.

"Restricted area, it says on the sign."

Hutchins slowed, following at a distance. He pulled to the side of the road and rolled to a stop. Ahead, the Mastretta approached the chain-link gate flanked by a small guard booth. The driver's window lowered. One guard approached while the other circled to the passenger side, his hand resting on his sidearm. Hutchins couldn't hear the exchange, but he saw the guard nod and step back. The barrier arm lifted.

The Mastretta accelerated through the checkpoint and approached a small jet sitting on the runway.

"What's happening?" Byrd replied.

'They're going inside the airport, but they have armed guards and barriers. I could ram them?" Hutchins said, hearing the doubt in his own voice.

"Don't do that," Byrd replied. "You'll be back in jail."

"Then I've lost them," Hutchins moaned, slumping in his seat and running a hand through his hair.

"Can you see what plane they're heading for?" Byrd said, her voice cutting through Hutchins' panic.

Hutchins scrambled out of the truck and walked quickly, approaching the chain-link. The Mastretta pulled alongside the sleek, private twin-engine plane, its turbine blades already spinning lazily.

"Yes, it's a small one, private, I think," Hutchins said. "But I don't know anything about planes. It could be a—"

"There's a number on the tail," Byrd said.

Hutchins watched the men drag Candi from the car and bundle her into the aircraft.

"No, no, no!" Hutchins shouted.

The door closed, and the aircraft's engines roared immediately. Hutchins sprinted and reached the fence. He skidded to a stop, panting, his hands on his knees. He clung to the chain-link, watching helplessly as the plane began to taxi.

"Hutchins, listen to me," Byrd's voice cut down the line. "Number on the tail. This is important."

Then he saw it—painted in bold black letters on the tail. N7349.

"Got the number," he breathed.

"Good work," Byrd replied. "Now get back here. We need to move fast."

## 42

**Cancun, Mexico.**

"What in the name of the Almighty do you think you're playing at, getting into a high-speed chase without help?" Byrd asked, approaching Hutchins on the bustling main strip and eyeing his sweat-streaked face and clothes.

"I was trying to rescue her. There was no time..."

"Okay, okay. You did your best, kid," Byrd said. "The tail number is something to work with."

"Then we need to get to our plane," Hutchins said, breathless, his eyes flitting between Byrd and Tom, who remained silent.

"Hold on a minute, Hans," Byrd said. "Which direction did they take off in?"

"I think northwest."

"You think?" Byrd asked. "Your ladyfriend is counting on you."

"Northwest," Hutchins said firmly.

"That means they're heading inland. Chasing them in a seaplane is like trying to chase a boat in a car. But I'll get us another plane. I'm pretty sure I can get a land-configured version of the same aircraft. Sit tight."

"How? What are you gonna do?" Hutchins asked, shifting his weight from foot to foot with nervous energy.

"Whatever it takes."

Byrd led her remaining two compadres down the still-buzzing strip, where many businesses serving tourists remained open.

"People will buy anything when they're drunk. Look," Byrd said in a low voice. She led them up to a small shop with posters of planes and aerial Caribbean vistas on the walls and windows. Inside, an older American gentleman with a desperate combover sat behind the desk.

"Please wait outside," Byrd told Tom and Hutchins. "I don't want you to hear this..."

Inside the air-conditioned shop, a young couple, also American, sat on the other side of the desk from the man with the combover. The woman's head flopped onto the young guy's shoulders, almost knocking him off balance and out of his chair.

"Only a few hours 'til dawn," Combover explained. "We can get you guys up in the air for the best part of the day. Pilot will be good and rested, but you guys don't need to be."

Somehow, the couple managed to hold a pen steady enough to sign up, then handed over a bundle of notes. They rose unsteadily, smiled, and stumbled back out into the night. Byrd took their place at the table.

"Would you like to see the sea from the air?" the man asked.

"Sure would," Byrd replied, leaning forward across the table.

"Great!" Combover said, rubbing his hands together.

"But I'll be flying the plane myself," Byrd said, steepling her fingers.

The man closed his lips together like a toad after eating an especially delicious bug.

"I'm afraid we don't offer that service, ma'am," he said, sweeping a hand through the strands of hair. "Just sightseeing fli––"

"Afraid? You should be afraid," Byrd said, leaning even further forward. "Was that drunk young couple able to fully understand the insurance documents and incident waivers you just made them sign?" She drove a finger into the table to illustrate her point. "Will they understand the safety instructions when they're still hammered?"

"Ma'am. This is Mexico," Combover said, his voice lowered. "Nobody really cares about that kinda––"

"So you never plan to work in the States again? Never plan to go home?" Byrd locked him in with her steely eyes. "Never plan to be part of the respected community of American aviators who prioritize their passengers at all times?"

"Ma'am. Renting a plane from us will cost a lot." Combover shifted his weight, eliciting a squeaky protest from the chair. "Do you realize how much––"

"Not a problem. Got me a great pension from the Air Force."

The man sat up straight. He stiffened his fingers and moved his hand toward his forehead to salute.

"I wouldn't draw attention to that part of yourself," Byrd advised, glancing at what remained of his hair. She pulled a brochure across the desk and opened it up. "Now... Ah, yes, perfect. A Twin Otter DHC-6 turboprop short takeoff. Land-configured. Prepare the plane, sir."

## 43

**Just outside of Cancun. The following day.**

Dawn radiated a delicate pink when Byrd, Hutchins, and Tom stood beside their new plane on the short runway just inland from Cancun's main strip.

"Any message yet?" Hutchins asked, anxiety adding a slight tremor to his voice.

"No," Byrd replied flatly. "Not yet. I have sent the details to everyone I know who is still working in air traffic control. Actually, everyone I *trust* who is still working in air traffic control. That narrowed the list considerably."

Hutchins ran his hand through his hair three times in quick succession. "I hope they reply soon," he said breathlessly as his fringe flopped back down across his forehead.

"I'll get the plane ready," Byrd said. "We know they're heading inland. At least we have a vague path to follow."

As Hutchins paced around in a full circle, Byrd climbed into the cockpit.

She settled into the pilot's seat and checked the instrument panel. She clicked on the master switch, bringing the instruments to life with a series of soft beeps. Flipping a few more switches, she muttered under her breath, "Fuel pump... on. Throttle... set for start. Mixture... full rich." She leaned forward to check the fuel gauges, tapping each one with her fingernail. The needles bounced slightly before settling just above half-full.

"Should be enough," she mumbled, calculating the distance in her head.

She glanced out through the window and saw Hutchins pacing nervously. Tom said something to the younger man and got a fiery look in return.

"These boys are like cats in heat," she said, climbing to her feet and beckoning them inside.

"We good to go?" Hutchins called out, impatience plain in his voice.

"Ready as we'll ever be," Byrd replied. "Not got all day to just stand there."

Hutchins stomped on board, the Twin Otter DHC-6 rocking slightly under his weight. He threw himself into one of the seats and buckled up. Tom followed more deliberately, dropping casually into a seat. Byrd secured the door and moved to the cockpit.

"Starting engines," she announced, narrating the procedure—it was an old habit from the Air Force she knew she'd never drop. She pressed the starter, and the propellers began to turn lazily before picking up speed. Once the engines were running stable, she radioed the tower and received clearance. The Twin Otter rolled toward the runway threshold.

"Hold tight," she called back. "This bird jumps."

She advanced both throttles smoothly to takeoff power. The engines roared in response, the propellers becoming invisible discs as they clawed at the air. The

Twin Otter surged forward, pushing them back in their seats.

The airspeed indicator climbed rapidly: 40 knots... 50 knots... 60 knots. After just a few hundred feet of runway, Byrd pulled back on the yoke. The Twin Otter responded, nose lifting toward the sky. The main wheels broke contact with the runway, followed quickly by the tail wheel.

At barely 65 knots, they were airborne—a testament to the short takeoff and landing capabilities that made the Twin Otter legendary. Byrd held the aircraft in a steep climb, the engines working hard.

Below, Cancun's shoreline receded, the turquoise waters giving way to the dense, lush carpet of the Yucatán.

"Anything yet?" Hutchins asked, his voice coming through the comms system. "Please, Byrd. Anything?"

"Not yet, kid," Byrd replied, scrolling through her phone, which was mounted on the instrument panel. She tapped the FlightAware app and entered the tail number again—nothing.

"When everyone else lets you down, rely on a drunk," Byrd said, firing off a message to Bourdell.

Three minutes later, a smile crossed her face. "Cabo San Lucas. The Cancun of the Pacific," she announced after reading Bourdell's info.

"Cabo makes sense," Tom said as Byrd looked down at the shadowy landscape. In the moonlight, the boundaries of farmland stretched out in a patchwork of boxes as far as she could see. "Another perfect place to pick up carefree boys and girls looking for adventure," Tom added.

"The professor, my friend, wasn't looking for adventure," Hutchins replied. "Certainly not that kind, anyway. And he wasn't carefree; I can assure you of that."

"Yes, but he got in the way, didn't he," Tom said coldly.

"Whatever they're up to, he got too close to it. So now he's probably being held in the same place."

"I don't mean to be rude, but what exactly do you know about it?" Hutchins snapped.

Listening to the conversation over her headset, Byrd rolled her eyes.

"I know one thing," Tom said. "When people say, 'I don't mean to be rude,' they're usually about to say something rude."

"Gentlemen," Byrd interjected. "Are your seatbelts fastened? We may be about to hit some turbulence."

"Turbulence?" Hutchins said. "It's completely still outside."

"It doesn't take much to shake a plane like this," Byrd replied. "Especially when you're pushing it...hard." Byrd raised her voice over the increasing noise of the engine.

"Why are you pushing it too hard?" Hutchins asked.

"I didn't say 'too hard'; I said 'hard.' The other plane is a long way ahead. I need to push the limits."

"What limits?" Hutchins asked. Even through crackling headsets, the apprehension was clear in his voice.

"We'll need to go a little over the recommended speed," Byrd said, glancing through the canopy at the tip of a wing bouncing up and down. "Cross a few flight paths. Nothing major."

"That's pretty major if there's another aircraft in the flight path!" Hutchins squealed, his voice distorted through the headset.

"Do you want to rescue our friends or not?" Byrd said, raising a questioning eyebrow, even though Hutchins couldn't see from his seat. "I can assure you, Hans. My risks are calculated. The risks you take on the ground will be much higher."

"Maybe we should just contact the authorities," Hutchins said quietly. "What can we really do alone?"

"What, and get one or more of us arrested again, just for trying to help?" Tom hissed.

"I gotta agree, kid," Byrd said. "The Mexican justice system is pretty slow-moving. Especially when you're in a jail cell."

"You've got one choice," Tom said firmly. "You go into the lion's den, then you fight your way out again, bringing your friends with you. You're young and strong. Well... young."

Hutchins grumbled something unintelligible.

"Your friend's an old man who needs your help," Tom continued. "Your girlfriend's a ditz who was stupid enough to get herself kidnapped. She needs your help too."

"Don't call her that," Hutchins growled, and Byrd heard uneasy shuffling over the comms.

"Okay. The girl who rejected you is a ditz."

This time, Hutchins didn't reply. An uneasy silence settled across the cabin as Byrd pushed the plane across Mexico.

Byrd looked out over the vast distance beneath the aircraft. Seeing that they were finally crossing the desert close to Cabo San Lucas, she began the descent.

In the gentle morning light, the expanse of orange was almost pristine, save for the odd patch of rocks, cacti, or other vegetation that tried to cling on for life.

"And what have we got there?" Byrd said, spotting a perfect rectangle on the ground to the plane's port side.

"What?" Hutchins said, his interest piqued.

"Hold on, I'll bring us around for a better look." Byrd tilted the wings, creating a better angle for them all to see the structure.

"See that," she said, looking down at the ground. "It looks like some kind of compound."

"You're right," Hutchins replied. "Is that a wire fence around it? Looks almost military. Like an army base."

"Not an army base," Byrd countered. "A military installation would have better infrastructure. There's not even a paved road out there. Looks like just a dirt track."

"Could that be where people are being held?" Hutchins asked.

"Could be," Byrd replied. "And if it is, that's not an easy place for a rescue. They'll see us coming from miles away."

"So we're back to square one," Tom said, grumbling through the comms. "Contact the authorities and wait a month for them to sign off the paperwork."

"We just need to think about our options," Byrd said. "We need to question whether we're lion tamers going into the lion's den, or just chunks of meat that get thrown in never to come out again. But I'll tell you this for certain. However we do this, I don't plan to let Candi's kidnappers live."

A subtle shift in weight sent a tremor through the airframe. The Twin Otter rocked slightly on its axis; the movement so distinct in the small aircraft that Byrd felt it immediately. Her pilot's instincts registered the imbalance before her mind consciously understood its cause.

The fuselage creaked as footsteps approached behind her. Byrd spun around and saw Tom standing in the doorway. His frame filled the opening, swaying slightly with the aircraft's motion. The cabin lights caught his eyes—the cold, calculating gaze, utterly devoid of the charm Byrd had witnessed earlier.

"What are you doing? Take a seat," she said. "We're coming into land soon."

Tom didn't reply as his fingers curled into fists. A vein pulsed at his temple. He leaped forward with sudden, explosive energy. The Twin Otter's sensitive balance shifted awkwardly with his movement.

"Tom! Sit down!" Hutchins shouted. His voice got lost in the roar of the engines.

As Byrd turned to face Tom again, his hand clamped around her throat with shocking force. His fingers dug into the soft tissue beneath her jaw. The sudden attack jolted her hand on the controls, and the plane dipped to the right. Warning alarms blared, and the artificial horizon tilted on the instrument panel.

## 44

Byrd kept one hand on the controls, desperately fighting to level the aircraft as black spots danced at the edges of her vision. With her free hand, she clawed at Tom's wrist, her nails digging deep enough to draw blood. Her attacker didn't flinch. His grip only tightened, crushing her windpipe.

His face loomed closer, eyes wide and manic. The plane continued its sideways slide, the altimeter unwinding with terrifying speed. Through the cockpit window, the ground tilted into view—a harsh desert landscape rushing up to meet them. Sun-scorched plains swirled in a dizzying blend of browns and reds, growing larger with each passing second.

"We're going to crash!" Hutchins yelled, his voice cracking with panic. The aircraft pitched violently as it caught a pocket of turbulence. Warning alarms shrieked—multiple systems screaming for attention as the Twin Otter spiralled out of control.

"You think you're so clever," Tom snarled, his spittle

flecking Byrd's cheek. "You should have gotten out of Mexico while you had the chance."

Byrd tried to stand, leveraging her weight against the control panel, but Tom's body slammed her back into the seat. His thumbs pressed deeper into her throat, crushing her larynx. The cockpit spun around her—instruments, controls, and the rapidly approaching ground all blurring together as oxygen deprivation took hold.

Her lungs burned with desperation. The edges of her vision darkened further, consciousness slipping away. The aircraft shuddered, metal groaning under stresses it wasn't designed to withstand.

The altimeter's needle spun downward—eight thousand feet. The plane was in free fall. Seven thousand. Red warning lights illuminated Tom's wild eyes and the tight skin that stretched over his strained grimace. Six thousand feet.

Byrd kicked out hard with her heel, striking Tom in the shin. He growled, but then squeezed even harder. She fought against the black smog in her head as a deadly impact with the ground grew closer still. She kicked again. Harder this time.

Tom flinched and yelled out in pain, then turned his head and looked down at his leg, loosening his grip slightly.

Byrd focused on his eyeball. She stiffened her index finger and jabbed it toward the pupil. It plunged into the soft fibrous tissue, and Tom howled in shock. He removed his hand from Byrd's neck and grasped his face.

An arm snaked around Tom's neck from behind as Hutchins recovered from his shock. His face was contorted with determination as he attempted to drag Tom back with all the strength he could muster.

"Pull up," Hutchins shouted, his voice strained as Tom thrashed violently against him.

Byrd gasped precious oxygen back into her lungs, her vision clearing in painful bursts. She turned back to the controls. The altimeter continued its relentless countdown —three thousand feet and falling fast.

Behind her, the men crashed against the cockpit wall. Tom drove his elbow back into Hutchins' ribs with a crack. Hutchins cried out but held on, his face reddening with effort as they spun just inches from the aircraft controls, then tumbled across the cockpit toward the cabin.

Byrd lunged for the yoke. The control column vibrated violently in her hands, fighting her attempts to pull the nose up. The relentless warning lights flashed across every instrument—hydraulics failing, engines overheating, structural integrity compromised.

The desert floor filled the entire windshield now, individual rocks and scrub brush visible with terrifying clarity. The Twin Otter's shadow raced across the ground below them, growing larger as they plummeted.

Byrd threw her entire body weight into the movement. The muscles in her arms burned as she fought against physics itself, willing the aircraft to respond. "She wants to fly, let her fly!" Byrd told herself, remembering Bourdell's sage advice all those years ago. She eased up on the controls but kept them steady. For one heart-stopping moment, nothing happened.

Then, almost nonchalantly, the nose lifted. The g-forces pinned Byrd to her seat as she pulled the aircraft out of its death dive, the fuselage groaning in protest. Her vision narrowed to a tunnel as blood drained from her head, the horizon finally reappearing in the upper portion of the windshield.

Behind her, the violent struggle continued. A spray of blood spattered across the instrument panel as Tom landed a vicious blow to Hutchins' face. But somehow, against all odds, the plane continued its agonizing climb away from certain destruction.

Byrd turned to see Hutchins sliding along the cabin floor, with Tom still standing firmly on his feet. The older man turned toward the cockpit again.

"Are you crazy?!" Byrd yelled. "Do you want us all to die?"

"If I have to die for my leader, I will," he replied, pacing toward Byrd again.

"Well, you're out of luck."

Byrd ensured the plane was flying straight, then stood, her muscles coiled like springs. This time, she was ready for him. Tom's eyes flickered between her and the instrument panel, calculating his next move. In the momentary stillness, the only sounds were the drone of the engines and Hutchins' labored breathing from the cabin floor.

"You can't stop what's coming," Tom snarled, blood trickling from the corner of his mouth.

He exploded into motion, lunging toward Byrd just like he had in the apartment kitchen. She pivoted, preparing to counter, but realized his true target too late. Tom feinted past her with unexpected agility, his fingers closing around the yoke before she could intercept him.

"No!" she shouted as Tom shoved the controls forward with brutal force.

The Twin Otter responded instantly, its nose pitching down at a sickening angle. The horizon disappeared, replaced by the rushing desert floor. The altimeter spun backward as they entered a near-vertical dive, the airspeed indicator climbing past the red warning line into territory the aircraft was never designed to survive.

Byrd launched herself at the controls, her hands finding whatever space remained on the yoke. The muscles in her forearms burned as she pulled back against his strength, their contest of wills translated directly into the aircraft's trajectory.

"Let go!" she hissed through clenched teeth, her face inches from his.

"Never," he spat back, eyes wide with fanatical determination.

With their strength matched and their battle locked in stalemate, the plane maintained its death plunge toward the ground. Light and dust zipped past the canopy in a blinding storm.

The airframe shuddered as the desert floor rushed up to meet them. Warning systems screamed in a cacophony of electronic panic.

Byrd gritted her teeth, planting her feet against the control panel for leverage and pulling on the yoke with everything she had. Veins bulged at her temples, sweat streaming down her face as she fought for their lives. The Twin Otter continued its relentless dive—down... down... down...

The entire cockpit shook as if caught in an earthquake. An overhead panel broke free, swinging wildly on exposed wires. Outside, the ground loomed ever closer, individual rocks and cacti now distinguishable. From somewhere behind Byrd, Hutchins let out a guttural scream of terror.

"You're all going to die with me!" Tom shouted, his face stretched in a grotesque rictus of triumph.

Tom stared straight at the ground below. He appeared to have no fear of death.

"Ready to depart?" he shouted over the noise of the screaming engine.

"You know what," Byrd said, loosening her grip. "I'm ready. I'm out of things to live for."

"Then we'll die together. So romantic," Tom shouted, a sinister grin spreading across his face.

"Let's get intimate, shall we?" Byrd whipped back her head and then threw it forward, bouffant first. Her forehead collided with Tom's temple with a crack like a starter pistol, and he tumbled off the pilot's seat. "I might hate the world," Byrd finished. "But I hate you more."

Taking the pilot's seat, she righted the plane quickly, but the threat from Tom remained. Hutchins stepped between the seats and pointed a gun between the older man's eyes.

Byrd knew immediately that he had taken a flare gun from the plane's emergency kit. Whether Tom also knew that, she had no idea. Either way, the thing would do some damage from that range.

"Playtime is over," Hutchins said calmly. "Hands on head, there's a good boy."

Clearly still in shock from the headbutt and eyeing the gun closely, Tom slowly put his hands on the top of his head and interlocked his fingers.

"Excellent," Hutchins said, still calm. "Using some of your life experience wisely there."

Byrd allowed herself a little smile. Up ahead, she saw the straight lines of a runway calling the plane home.

## 45

**Mexican desert, north of Cabo San Lucas.**

The Ogre grabbed Professor Wall by the collar, hoisted him upward with terrifying ease, and flung him like a garbage collector tossing a heavy bag into a truck. Wall sailed through the air, suspended in a moment of terrifying clarity where he could pinpoint the exact jagged rock waiting to break his fall. He covered his face with both hands, instinctively protecting his eyes and skull. When he crashed down, the sharp stone jutted into his unprotected abdomen. The impact forced a hollow grunt from his lips as air exploded from his lungs. With a groan, he rolled onto his back, only to find himself in the undignified position of an upturned tortoise—legs waving helplessly in the air as pain radiated through his body.

The Ogre towered over him, blocking out the sun that was already fierce, even early in the morning. The big man held a roll of wire that looked like it could be used, ironically, to fix holes in the perimeter fence. The Ogre twisted the wire into a loop and bound it around Wall's wrists and then his ankles. The beast twisted the wire until it cut into the professor's skin, then turned to walk away.

Wall looked at his surroundings, trying to keep as still as he possibly could to ease the pain.

A tall wooden fence enclosed the open-air pen, which was around the size of a small urban backyard. It looked like a place that had once been used to keep livestock—only the species in captivity had clearly changed. Through small gaps in the fence, Wall saw that activity in the compound seemed more hurried than usual. People packed things up and took down sculptures in a frenzy.

Wall thought about fighting or running, although with the Ogre nearby, he didn't stand a chance. The professor tried to lift his legs to see the wire that bound him, but his limbs flopped back down onto the dirt. He didn't have the energy to plot, let alone run. He thought about his wife, hoping the mental picture of her face would bring him strength, but it only brought him more desperation.

He glanced up at the sun, which was already baking his skin.

"You can't leave me out here," he croaked, barely loud enough for anyone to hear. "I'll die."

"Yes," replied The Ogre, turning back to look at the professor. "You will."

"Please," Wall whimpered.

The Ogre stomped back across the rough ground, bent over, and pushed his face up close to Wall's.

"Would you like some medication?" the big man asked, grinning. "Something for the pain? We are like doctors here. We have plenty of medication."

Wall shook his head hopelessly, then closed his eyes. Unconscious delirium claimed him instantly. In his fevered state, he imagined he had wandered into an abandoned factory during an expedition. He'd climbed into an old furnace to examine it, only for factory workers to return unexpectedly and ignite it with him still inside. Real and imagined heat closed in around him as darkness took hold.

His skin burned because of the choices he had made—because he had sought too much. Although in a semi-delirious state from the heat, dehydration, and blows to the head, he figured that the dream was a metaphor for reality. He had placed academic immortality over all else—even his wife, even the children they'd never had.

As the morning wore on without shelter, the headache and nausea intensified. Wall's heart thumped inside his chest, pounding as if desperate to escape and seek shelter. He recognized these symptoms all too well—and knew their deadly conclusion. He had witnessed this exact progression during an expedition in Africa, when his party leader had recklessly approved a daytime trek across semi-desert terrain. Young Brice, so fit and healthy in the early morning, brimming with enthusiasm and a promising career ahead of him, had succumbed to the merciless sun by early afternoon. His life was extinguished in mere hours.

While the professor recalled this painful memory, a rich, sweet scent suddenly reached him. He forced open his dry eyelids. A figure moved toward him, appearing only as a silhouette against the blinding sun. As the face came into focus, Wall recognized The Mentor—his tanned skin seemingly impervious to the harsh sunlight and his distinctive floral cologne announcing his presence. The Mentor knelt beside Wall, holding a bottle of water with condensation beading on its surface. With unexpected gentleness, he pressed the bottle to Wall's parched lips and helped him drink.

The younger man helped the professor sit up and lean

against the fence before standing over him at an angle that blocked out the sun. This time, the liquid brought no strange effects, only relief. But the look in The Mentor's eyes did not sync with the kindness he showed.

The Mentor pointed at Wall accusingly. In Wall's disturbed vision, the finger split into two and then blurred into a wavering smudge. The professor squinted desperately, struggling to regain normal sight. The Mentor's voice reached him as if underwater—distorted and muffled by the heatstroke that had seized control of Wall's faculties. Despite his compromised state, Wall could still make out The Mentor's words—much to his profound regret.

"Very soon, everybody here will be dead," The Mentor said, his tone casual. "Bodies will be strewn around in the open air, legs and arms spread out across the dirt. From the air, it will look like a work of art. And the reason they will be dead?" The long finger loomed closer. "You."

"No," the professor croaked. "*You*."

The finger swept from side to side. "Wrong," The Mentor hissed. "You are responsible for this. You helped that pointless lump of matter to escape, and now she will alert the American authorities."

"I thought you wanted to provide eternal life?" Wall said.

"Of course, you will be dead much sooner," The Mentor continued, ignoring the question. "The heat will take you first. The water I just provided to you will be the last you ever have. I simply wanted you to be lucid enough to understand what I am now telling you."

"I will be gone," the professor said. "So be it. Good."

"It's not 'good', though, is it?" The Mentor said, nodding with finality. "You have a wife waiting for you. Family. Friends. Just like all the other people here. Is it good for them?" He paused, and Wall heard the sound of movement drift from outside the pen. "Is it good that all of this has to be brought to an end because of you? You will be responsible for mass suicide. Soon, this place will fall silent. After the screams of pain, of course."

Even in his delirious state, Wall pieced together a clear understanding of The Mentor's scheme. He planned to tell his devoted followers that he had discovered the magical plant they had been desperately seeking. He would then instruct them to drink it.

"It's not suicide when people drink your poison without knowing it will kill them," Wall replied. "That's murder, at your hands."

Voices called to each other beyond the fence, followers ignorant of their coming fate.

"The deaths weren't necessary except for your interference," The Mentor said. "Everyone—most people here could have lived long, rewarding lives. Even you." The younger man glanced at the sun as it grew hazier in the shimmering sky. "I'm going to let you watch what you could have had. My big, ugly friend needs a break. I'll stay with you. You'll be like a pet in the corner, watching mommy and daddy."

"You sound like you've drunk one of your potions already," Wall replied with as much acidity as he could muster.

"No. I will be the only one not drinking it," The Mentor said, smiling. "In a few hours, I will be far away from this place. I have *discoveries* to make, Professor."

## 46

**Cabo San Lucas Airport.**

Byrd swung the de Havilland onto the apron, aligning it perfectly with the painted guidelines. She pulled the condition levers to cutoff, and the propellers spun down with a decreasing whine until they locked into position. The sudden silence after hours of engine noise felt almost physical.

"Avionics off," she said, flipping switches across the panel. "Battery master off."

The instrument lights dimmed and went dark as Byrd completed the shutdown checklist, methodically securing the aircraft.

"We're here," she said, removing her headset and hanging it on its hook. "We don't have long before Air Traffic Control starts asking questions."

She paced into the cabin and took the flare gun from Hutchins. Although the pair had taken a seat for landing, the gun hadn't wavered from Tom the entire time. Byrd leaned forward and placed the snub-nosed barrel firmly against Tom's temple. She looked deep into Tom's eyes, saying nothing at all.

"Do you have any military background, Tom?" Byrd asked, finally. The man opened his mouth to speak, but Byrd interrupted him. "Actually, no need to answer that. I already know the answer."

She continued to stare, once again allowing silence to do the talking.

"You would be amazed by the stories that eyes can tell. I have seen teenagers' eyes that tell the deep and tumultuous history of Afghanistan over two hundred years," Byrd continued.

Tom shifted his gaze to the floor, clearly desperate to break the intense moment.

Byrd paused until he met her gaze once again.

"Their eyes speak of troubles they never witnessed and never even read about. Knowledge of hardship is passed down through DNA. Their own troubled lives built on top."

Tom looked away again. This time, Byrd lifted his chin and held firm.

"*Your* eyes tell me that you are weak and afraid," she said coldly. "You correctly believe that you have lost control of this situation. What's happening at the compound?"

Tom opened his mouth again, but Byrd stopped him. "No. Do not even think about lying. Your clothes are smart, but you are not. The truth. Now."

"They... they are trying to build a better life—"

"—The truth. Now," Byrd interjected.

"They—"

"A better life for who?" Byrd said, putting pressure on the gun and pushing Tom into the seat. "The people they are experimenting on?"

"I don't agree with what they're doing." Tom hung

his head. "I don't know. Somehow, I got involved. A friend told me I would fit right in. Paid me compliments."

"You're easily led. I can tell. Give me your phone."

Tom hesitated for a second. Byrd raised an eyebrow. He shuffled the phone from his pocket and handed it to Byrd, who slipped it away.

"Hutchins, a word," Byrd said, pointing to the cabin door. "I'm watching you, and I'm a good shot," she told Tom as she and Hutchins shuffled to the door and stepped out onto the tarmac. Byrd locked Tom inside and stashed the gun away.

The airport buzzed with activity, especially on the apron designated for private planes. Passengers wearing garish, loose-fitting shirts and designer shades stumbled across the baking concrete, clearly still drunk as they disembarked. Meanwhile, handlers led sniffer dogs around the aircraft, searching for narcotics that might be secretly transferred between planes.

"Are you okay?" Hutchins said, leaning in close to Byrd. He wiped a bead of sweat from the tip of his nose.

"Feeling no pain," Byrd lied, stroking her throbbing neck. "I think he tried to attack me back at the apartment, you know, but thought better of it. Maybe he wanted to take us all out in one go."

Hutchins tightened his lips and furrowed his brow. "Deceitful piece of—"

"—Easy there, kid," Byrd interrupted. "He's subdued now."

"Yeah, but what are we gonna do with him?" Hutchins said.

"We *should* just hand him over to the authorities," she said, "but who knows which of them he's in league with.

And he may still be of use to us if he knows the setup at the compound."

"We can't hold a gun to his head the whole time," Hutchins said.

"He's been broken," Byrd replied. "His will is weak, and he has lost courage. And right now, we've got a damsel in distress to rescue," she added with a wink.

"Yes, we do," Hutchins said, turning his attention to the action around them.

A group of college-aged men in matching neon tank tops lurched from a sleek Gulfstream, their laughter too loud as they passed a flask between them. One tripped on the stairs, caught himself, then raised both arms in triumphant celebration as his friends cheered.

"How easy is it to spot a tail number?" Hutchins asked. "These private planes all look too similar."

"Usually pretty easy. They should be in large numbers on...well, the tail," Byrd said.

Hutchins took a few strides back and forth, trying to get a better view of the tails on various aircraft around the apron.

"Even if you spot it," Byrd said, "don't get your hopes up that she's still on the plane, kid. Who knows if they took another flight or went through the airport and traveled overland."

"We should get to the compound," Hutchins replied. "That's our best chance."

"Right. So let's get going."

"Wait. I dunno," Hutchins said, glancing between different aircraft. "I just have a feeling. A feeling she's here somewhere."

"I thought you guys just developed the hots for each other," Byrd said with a smile. "Not telepathy."

"What if the man who took her waited until the airport got busier?" Hutchins asked, way too edgy to smile back. "He's going to have to move her somehow without anyone noticing a commotion. Now is the perfect time. In the dead of night, there are fewer people for security to pick on."

A drunk brunette, barely able to stand, lurched against her shirtless companion as they crossed the tarmac in designer shades and minimal clothing. They stumbled directly into the path of two security guards, colliding with enough force to send the woman's sunglasses skittering across the concrete. The guards exchanged knowing glances, perfectly illustrating Hutchins' point.

"Okay, I get it," Byrd said, burning a glare into the drunks. "And you're right—he's going to have to move her somehow without getting spotted."

"In that case, it makes more sense just to put her on another aircraft, right?" Hutchins said.

"Right. Smuggling made easy."

"Wait!" Hutchins suddenly yelled, then quickly lowered his voice.

"You spotted the tail?" Byrd asked.

"No. I spotted the guy!"

"Really? Where?"

"There, stepping out of that plane," Hutchins said, pointing his finger but keeping it low, close to his stomach. "Catwalk Jesus. The suave hippy. Remember?"

"Sure do." Byrd squinted through the heat haze as she assessed the man standing around thirty meters away. "You're right. That is the guy."

"What's that he's wheeling?" Hutchins asked in a low voice.

"Instrument case. But I'm gonna guess it doesn't contain instruments. It is the perfect size for—"

Hutchins set off before Byrd could finish her sentence. Byrd's hand shot out, fingers clamping around his forearm and stopping him in mid-stride.

"Wait," she hissed, holding him firmly in place. "We can't just go and tackle him. You start a fight, and we'll end up sharing a cell."

"What do you suggest?" Hutchins said, spinning around to shoot Byrd a red-hot glare.

"Moss Phlox," Byrd said, looking at a row of pink flowers growing along the edge of the apron.

"What! Have you lost your mind?" Hutchins said, his voice ramping up like a jet engine during takeoff. "Candi is in danger, and you're looking at flowers?"

"Flowers that also smell a lot like cannabis when you release the spores."

"Really?" Hutchins said, his gaze panning between Byrd and the man with the instrument case.

"See the handler with the two dogs over there?" Byrd said, nodding in the direction. "Go and tell him you heard the guy with the instrument case talking about drugs."

"We don't know who has been paid off around here," Hutchins replied. "Same problem we always have."

"The men in uniform might have been paid off, but the dogs haven't. That's who we need."

"A distraction," Hutchins acknowledged, nodding his head slightly. "And what are you gonna do?"

"Trust me."

## 47

Byrd waited for Hutchins to saunter toward the dog handler, tracking his progress from the corner of her eye. The moment he engaged the handler in conversation, drawing the guard's attention away, she made her move.

She darted across the apron to the grassy bank that bordered the terminal building. She crouched down and plucked several flowers, gathering them into a tight bundle. Concealing the flowers behind her back, she straightened up, adopting the casual confidence of someone who belonged exactly where she was.

"Excuse me, sir?" Byrd called out, closing the distance to Catwalk Jesus with an easy, unhurried gait.

Catwalk Jesus turned toward the sound, his handsome face hardening into a suspicious glare.

Before he could react further, Byrd flashed her most disarming smile and slammed her free hand down hard on the instrument case. The sharp crack did its work, attracting his attention.

"Get your hands off my case, how dare—"

"What kind of instrument do you play?" Byrd said. "I'm a

musician myself." With his attention fixed on the case, Byrd side-stepped and slipped the flowers into the back pocket of his loose-fitting jeans.

"I'm sorry to bother you. I just thought you might be playing at the Cabo Festival on the beach this weekend," Byrd said, putting more work into the smile. "It's great to meet fellow musicians, ain't it?"

"The Cabo wha—"

The chorus of barking struck up louder than an orchestra. The two German Shepherds charged across the tarmac, followed by the shouted commands of their handlers.

Catwalk Jesus spun toward the sound, his face transforming from annoyance to horror as he spotted the animals barrelling toward him. He tried to sidestep, but the dogs were too fast. They bundled into him with the force of linebackers, their combined weight knocking him off his feet.

He tumbled backward, arms windmilling as he crashed to the ground. The dogs jumped on him, their trained noses following the scent. One shepherd pinned his shoulder with a massive paw while the other circled frantically, barking.

Byrd darted forward and kicked the instrument case with the inside of her foot, sending it skittering across the tarmac. The case spun and rolled along the length of the plane. At the other end of the aircraft, Hutchins stepped out and stopped the case.

Byrd turned to walk away.

"Stay where you are, ma'am," one of the officers said in perfect English, clearly having been trained to deal with unruly foreigners. "This may be a crime scene. No one leaves."

"What? I'm with the guy who tipped you off in the first place," Byrd said, wheeling on the officer.

"You may be, but nothing is as it seems in Cabo, ma'am."

The officer took a step forward, his intention clear. "Need your ID, now."

"Look. This is ridiculous. We were trying to help you people."

The officer's eyes hardened, his patience drifting away on the warm breeze. He called the dogs to heel, allowing Catwalk Jesus to climb to his feet.

"No one leaves until we do a full search of the area," the officer in charge said, his gaze shifting from Byrd to the young man.

"You know who I am," the biblical figure said, dusting himself down. "This is going to cause issues for you all."

The two men exchanged glances, then both turned on Byrd.

"Okay, enough," the officer in charge said. He unclipped a pair of handcuffs from his belt and stepped toward Byrd.

*Well, that didn't go to plan*, Byrd thought, watching the men close in. *Time for plan B.* She curled her hands into fists and touched them together in front of her in a show of compliance. The officer in charge moved closer, the cuffs now hovering over Byrd's wrists.

Byrd waited until the cuffs were just an inch away, then thrust her arms up into the air. The cuffs flew from the man's hands and spun in a wide arc. The momentum of the strike carried the officer's fist toward his own chin. He smacked himself so hard in the jaw that his head snapped backward. As the cuffs fell, Byrd snatched them out of the air. She clipped one around the officer's wrist and the other around the metal bar on the portable stairs.

The unconscious officer slumped down, the dog whimpering and sniffing around its fallen comrade.

Byrd turned her attention to Catwalk Jesus. The man raised his hands to fight, but Byrd caught a glimmer of doubt in his eyes. "You know," she said softly, "you're pretty cute."

"What?" The man frowned, confused.

Byrd stepped toward him, lips curling into a smile.

"Yeah, you are. You're physically perfect, did you know that?" She stepped again and stood directly in front of him. Then, she pouted seductively.

As the man continued frowning—yet failing to suppress a proud smile—Byrd launched a right hook. Her fist crunched into his nose with a devastating crack. His head twisted ninety degrees. His legs wobbled briefly, then collapsed beneath him, sending him crumpling to the ground.

"You *were* perfect. Past tense," she added, flexing her fingers.

Byrd crouched down and rummaged through the man's pockets. She found a phone with a 'Surfer Girl' emblazoned case in one pocket and a small key in the other. She took both items and darted around the nose of the plane.

"Sorry about that," Byrd said, striding up to Hutchins. "Another problem with the law." Byrd instinctively rubbed her knuckles.

"I can't get the damn box open," Hutchins said, hopping from toe to toe, his fingers working frantically at the latch.

"I think I've got just the thing," Byrd said, grabbing the box. "But first, we need to get out of sight. Got a moody security guy I don't want to see again." She hefted the case and wheeled it behind their de Havilland, her eyes scanning the tarmac for any sign of approaching authorities.

"What guy?" Hutchins said, rushing after her. "I thought—"

"I think this is what we need," Byrd interrupted, holding

the key. She thrust it into the lock and twisted. The mechanism clicked, and she pulled open the lid with a swift jerk.

Candi exploded from the box like a compressed spring. She pushed her arms out in front of her, fingers curved into claws as she launched herself at what she clearly presumed were her captors. Her face was a mask of fury and desperation, eyes wide with fight-or-flight intensity.

"Get away from me!" she screamed, swinging blindly.

Byrd ducked to the side, the blow whistling past her ear. Hutchins wasn't quite as quick, catching a glancing hit to his shoulder as he stumbled backward.

"Candi! It's us!" he shouted, raising his hands in a placating gesture while continuing to backpedal from her assault.

Candi froze mid-swing, clearly processing what her eyes were seeing. Recognition dawned slowly across her face, confusion giving way to disbelief, then to overwhelming joy.

"Hutchins!" she gasped, her voice cracking. "Byrd!"

"In the flesh, sweetheart," Byrd said with a crooked smile.

Candi's battle stance melted away. She launched herself forward again, but this time into Hutchins' arms, nearly knocking him off his feet. She clung to him fiercely, a small yelp of excitement escaping her lips.

"Honey, are you okay?" Byrd said when the pair pulled apart.

"I am now," Candi replied, taking a deep breath. The young blonde grinned, giving Byrd a hug.

"How are you *still* smiling?!" Byrd said. "You really are something. Now you need shelter, water, and possibly medical treatment."

Byrd and Hutchins gently helped Candi to get steady on her feet.

"Honestly, I'm fine," Candi replied, clamping a hand on Hutchins' shoulder.

"Then we need your help," Hutchins added. "We have to get to a compound...that you would probably have ended up at if we hadn't—"

Candi suddenly stumbled, and Byrd and Hutchins caught her just in time.

"Okay. You're clearly not fine," Byrd said.

"Honestly, I'm just a little battered and bruised," Candi protested. "Which plane is yours?"

"That one," Hutchins said, pointing at the de Havilland before Byrd could suggest Candi should go in the other direction, toward the medical station in the terminal.

"Grab the medical kit under the nearest seat to the cockpit," Byrd called to Candi as she and Hutchins approached the plane. "At least find some damn painkillers to swallow!"

## 48

**Mexican desert, north of Cabo San Lucas.**

The sun clawed at Professor Wall, shredding and burning skin layer by layer. He lay his cheek on the hard, sand-dusted ground and covered his eyes with his hand. Hearing something move, he peered between his fingers.

At the far side of his pen, just a few feet away, The Ogre pushed a couple of white plastic chairs, a parasol, and a camping table into position, apparently for some kind of strange display conceived by The Mentor's twisted mind. It was clearly a performance designed to tease and torment.

As the afternoon light softened, the professor saw a figure entering the small enclosure to join The Mentor. Briony dropped into a chair at the table.

The Ogre laid a white tablecloth across the camping table and placed at its center a vase with a single red rose. Briony glanced up at the monster, her facial expression rigid and impassive. Wall recognized the same stoned expression —or whatever the word was for the state that she was in— she had worn the first time Wall had met her in the tent.

The Ogre left, and The Mentor sat opposite Briony. The young woman's gaze shifted to The Mentor, her face still expressionless. Even through the haze of his own decaying vision and waning consciousness, Wall saw her eyes half-close. Her skin glowed, and her pronounced and perfect facial bone structure caught the light enchantingly. A youthful perfection that didn't make it to her jaded eyes.

The Mentor reached down to an ice bucket at his feet and pulled out a magnum of champagne.

"Magnum," Wall said quietly, using the action to distract himself from his agony. "A word the Ancient Romans used for 'large'. What pointless knowledge I have."

The Mentor popped the bottle in one slick move and then poured the champagne into two crystal glasses. Light gleamed through the cut crystal, incongruous in the desolate compound.

Wall gasped at the thought of the cool liquid as it fizzed in the glasses.

The Mentor passed a glass to Briony, who accepted it reluctantly.

"Here's to the new dawn," The Mentor said, raising his glass. He paused, then asked, "Do you believe in God?"

"Good luck with that one," Wall muttered to himself.

Briony stared into the Mentor's eyes as though she didn't understand what he had said.

"Fate?" The Mentor said, as though prompting a conversation.

"If you want her to talk to you, you should probably stop feeding her your potions," Wall groaned.

"It's lucky you're beautiful," The Mentor told Briony, taking a long drink of his champagne and then tipping his companion's glass toward her mouth. "Because you're boring as hell."

Suddenly, Briony glanced in Wall's direction.

"Hey! Don't look at him." The Mentor clicked his fingers in front of Briony's face. "Don't worry about him. I'll take care of him; he's important to my mission."

Briony drew a phone from her pocket, crossed her long legs, and looked down at the screen.

"Put that away," The Mentor demanded, grabbing her wrist. "You shouldn't even have such a thing in this place. You're one of the privileged few, but privileges can be lost."

Briony huffed but did what she was told. She took a long drink and then slowly slid her glass across the table.

"Whether you believe in God or fate, there must be something that dictates destiny," The Mentor said, refilling the glass. "It's not talent, and it's not hard work. Luck. Maybe that's what it is. My older brother. Ewart. My–––." The man stopped and took a deep, angry breath. "–––why has he succeeded? A world-famous scientist. Loved by the family. The magazines. He can't even wash himself. Looks like he got dressed in the dark. And yet–––"

The Mentor glanced over at Wall as though suddenly remembering he was there.

Wall saw the movement and closed his eyes, not wanting The Mentor to see him watching.

After a moment with nothing but the sound of buzzing insects and distant chatter, The Mentor said softly to Briony, "I love you. More than any of the others. Soon, I will show you my mansion. We'll marry in the Great Room amid the portraits of my ancestors who guard the vaults."

More silence followed between the two. The sounds of people packing up drifted across the compound.

"Did you hear me?" The Mentor suddenly barked, banging on the table. "I told you that I love you!"

Wall opened his eyes to slits as Briony leaned forward.

"And I hate you. We all do," she whispered, her words drifting across the slight breeze.

The Mentor bolted to his feet. He stepped forward, towering over Briony. He grasped the girl around the chin, forcing her to meet his gaze.

"You look thirsty," he hissed. "Let me get you something more nutritious." He turned and walked away, pulling out a phone and holding it to his ear. "Everyone. Soon," he said.

## 49

**Cabo San Lucas Airport.**

Standing on the apron beside the de Havilland Twin Otter, Sierra Byrd sucked the scent of jet fuel and warm, sweet air into her lungs. She always felt great when she was near a runway, and right now, she also reveled in the fact that she hadn't let Tom get the better of her, physically or mentally. "One more who tried and failed," she said with a slight smile.

Through the shimmer of the heat haze, she scanned the area for an aircraft to help them on the next leg of their mission. The de Havilland was running low on fuel, and she had a strong sense that a chopper would be more useful from here on out. Most people wouldn't simply scan an airfield in search of an aircraft to commandeer and take away, but Sierra Byrd did a lot of things most people wouldn't do.

Over in a far corner of the airfield, a bunch of helicopters glistened in the sun. The markings on their sides suggested they were all private craft. Byrd went and brought

Tom from the aircraft, nodding to Hutchins to let him know he could remain inside with Candi.

Tom's broad shoulders now sagged, and his eyes fell downward.

"Tom!" Byrd snapped sharply. He turned to face her. "See those helicopters over there?" she pointed at the craft.

Tom slowly turned his head, then turned back to Byrd and nodded.

"Good," Byrd said. "Go get us one of them. Tell the owners we'll need it for a day, maybe two. We'll probably return it safely, of course. Second thoughts, leave out the 'probably' part."

Tom's brow scrunched, moving closer to his upturned lip. The once-sophisticated gentleman looked like a child who thought he'd been scolded unfairly but couldn't quite explain why.

"I guess they will require payment," Tom mumbled.

"Sure will. A big payment."

Tom paused and then asked, "How much are you willing to offer?"

"Me? Zero."

"But..."

Byrd faced Tom square-on. With her eyelids half closed, Byrd intentionally gave the impression that she may lose consciousness if it took the man any longer to get the point.

"You're a man with access to wealth, Tom. Figure it out."

Tom shook his head sullenly. Byrd tapped her index finger three times on her Breitling Navitimer.

"And what if they have any other prerequisites?" Tom said quietly.

"Any *what*? Tom, time is a-wasting, and you just wasted even more of it with that stupidly long word. If they have any more conditions, figure it out. And remember, I'll be watching your every step."

Tom narrowed his eyes in an expression that seemed to say, *I'll deal with you later.*

Byrd returned it with a smile that said, *I'm looking forward to it.*

Tom walked away, and Byrd turned to see Hutchins stepping down from the plane.

"Where's he going?" Hutchins asked, a tremor in his voice.

"To get us a chopper," Byrd said. "Don't worry. He'll come back."

"But do you think he'll come back with a helicopter?" Hutchins asked after a second.

"Yeah," Byrd replied. "Otherwise, he'll be jumping out of our plane over the desert."

"But we don't have parachutes on boa— oh, got it!"

It wasn't long before Tom beckoned them to a luxurious Leonardo AW109.

"It looks like the boy's done good," Byrd said, leading Hutchins and Candi across the tarmac as the real owners walked away, frowning and looking confused, but smiling and clearly pleased with their unexpected windfall.

"I knew Tom was a charmer," Byrd said to Hutchins, surveying the controls in the cockpit as he hovered over her shoulder. "It's all fake, of course, but they don't know that." She shuffled into a comfortable position in the pilot seat and swept through various options on the digital touchscreen. "Autopilot with four-axis stabilization, synthetic terrain overlay, full navigation. Don't people actually fly anymore?"

She glanced back into the cabin, where Candi had the flare gun trained on Tom's head as a reminder that he was under control. "Get belted up," she told Hutchins, "and keep an eye on that guy."

Byrd pressed the engine start button, and the whine of the starter motor filled the cockpit, gradually increasing in pitch until the engine caught with a distinctive low rumble. She watched the temperature and RPM gauges rise steadily, ensuring they stayed within normal parameters.

"I think we'll go without clearance," she said, glancing over at the position of the fallen security guard. "Don't wanna be rude, but sometimes you just gotta fly."

Both turbines now humming with power, she eased up on the collective while keeping her feet light on the anti-torque pedals.

The AW109 shuddered slightly, then lifted smoothly from the tarmac. Byrd kept it in a steady hover a few feet above the ground, checking that all systems were functioning properly before committing to full flight. Satisfied, she pitched forward and accelerated into the clear Mexican sky.

"Hey, Tom. You've been to this place before, right?" Byrd said over the comms as they powered back across the desert.

"Yes," came the quiet reply.

"Okay. You're gonna help me now. Any insincere answers, and Candi might get a little twitchy." Byrd adjusted the cyclic stick as a crosswind buffeted the helicopter, causing it to drift slightly to the right. "So, where are they likely to keep captives? Do they have imprisonment facilities there?"

The Leonardo responded immediately to her correction, banking gently back on course. She scanned the instrument panel, noting the altitude and heading indicators while waiting for Tom's response.

"Actually, there are a lot of captives there," Tom said.

"Maybe half the people there are captive. Of course, that's not supposed to be acknowledged. But that's what they are."

"And where are they kept?" Byrd asked.

"Kind of big barns, really. The kind of place you might keep livestock," Tom said.

"That sounds charming," Byrd replied, her sarcasm crackling across the comms. She glanced down at the desert stretching below them, its barren expanse occasionally broken by rock formations and clusters of scrubby vegetation. "What a place to be imprisoned; you wouldn't even need walls. No wonder you chose that place to hang out. So that's where we might expect the professor to be?"

"I'm gonna say he might be treated differently," Hutchins interjected. "Most people there are probably being experimented on. Wall was taken for his expertise. He'll likely get better treatment."

"That's assuming he's cooperating," Byrd said. "Giving them what they want. Is he the kind of person who would cooperate just like that?"

"Erm..." Hutchins mumbled.

"I'll take that as a no," Byrd added. "So, he's the kind of person who might cause trouble? Maybe even attempt to escape?"

"Definitely more likely than cooperating."

"Okay. So, Tom," Byrd said. "Where are they likely to keep someone like that? A troublemaker?"

"I don't know."

Byrd's muscles tensed. "Tom, have you ever jumped out of a plane?"

"Er.... no."

Byrd looked at the airspeed indicator. "Would you like to try today?"

"No," Tom said, his voice shaky. "Do we... do we even have parachutes?"

"We do not," Byrd said.

Byrd heard Tom sighing through his headset while Hutchins let out a laugh.

"Your guess is as good as mine," Tom said, frustration crackling in his voice. "If they are not only keeping him captive but punishing him as well, they will want to make things uncomfortable for him. They can do that by keeping him outside."

"Good stuff, Tom," Byrd said. "Anything else?"

"They won't want to leave him in an exposed area where someone will have to sit out in the heat with him," Tom continued. "I suspect they will put him in some kind of small pen attached to a building. A pig pen next to a barn, which they have a few of there. Something like that."

"Great thinking, Tom," Byrd said, for once with minimal sarcasm.

"Do I have to do any more thinking for you?" Tom grumbled. "You both have brains, don't you?"

"We do," Byrd confirmed. "But thankfully, we don't need them when we have one as big as yours to use. You can stop talking now."

## 50

**Mexican desert, north of Cabo San Lucas.**

Wall watched through the fence as the camp's occupants shuffled into a circle. Many held hands with the person next to them, looking at the ground in quiet meditation. Most of them were young, under twenty-five, he estimated. But they were a mix of Sallas' devoted followers and the victims who unwillingly served their cause. Perfect specimens beside people whose bodies had been damaged by torment. Many of these victims had been hidden from view until now.

The Ogre moved around the circle, placing a drink in front of each person. The cobbled-together collection of plastic cups, champagne flutes, and coffee mugs contained a murky purple liquid.

Although Wall knew he would soon succumb to heat stroke or dehydration, he felt pity for those about to drink the white snakeroot, disguised as purple linium. Their death would be slow and agonizing.

The Ogre completed his macabre task and stepped onto a makeshift stage. Created from wooden crates, the stage was complete with a lectern and microphone. The giant man lumbered across to the microphone and surveyed the scene. He slid a piece of paper from his jacket and flattened it out on the lectern.

"Our leader and mentor could not be with us today," The Ogre read, his voice booming through a distorted loudspeaker. "That is because he has been out into the world to do what he promised. It has been *found*!"

The crowd applauded, some enthusiastic and smiling, others more reticent as they eyed the purple goo in front of them.

"Our leader is at the center of a great discovery," The Ogre continued, his eyes on the lectern. "And the world wants his attention. You are part of this success." He glanced up, as though checking that his audience was still there. "Now we must drink and prove to the world that the discovery is safe. We must prove this is the savior humanity has been seeking." Although clearly reading The Mentor's words, The Ogre's voice had none of his enthusiasm. "In just a few days, you will see the benefits of this miracle plant. Clearer skin. Brighter eyes. Greater beauty. Abun—Abun—" The Ogre paused. "Abundant health."

Heads turned, and a murmur ran through the group. The Ogre raised a hand for silence.

"Now," he announced, coughing, "we drink together." He raised a ceramic cup in a toast. Around the circle, the people obeyed, lifting their drinks.

"Wait!" someone shouted.

Heads turned in unison toward the source of the voice. Briony rose to her feet, her phone held high in the air. She stepped into the centre of the circle.

"No one in the outside world is talking about this discovery," she declared. She swept her gaze around the circle, making deliberate eye contact with those who seemed most hesitant. "It is a lie. She turned, ensuring everyone could see both her face and the phone's screen. "It's all a lie. Every promise, every claim of miraculous healing—none of it is real." She paused, letting the weight of her words settle over the group. "Sallas is a fraud."

Gasps erupted. Some people pushed their cups away. Others gazed into theirs, doubt creeping across their faces.

"Sit down!" The Ogre boomed.

"If you drink," Briony screamed, "you will die!"

"Liar!" another voice cut through the air.

Wall turned to face the voice and recognized Tammy, climbing to her feet.

"He would never betray us," Tammy shouted, pointing accusingly at Briony. "If any of you believe he would, why are you even here?"

"Drink. Now!" The Ogre commanded. "Or he will hear of it!"

Tammy picked up her cup, tipped back her head, and downed the purple sludge. Some followed her lead.

"Don't drink it!" Briony snatched up her cup and swung her arm outward, flinging the purple liquid on the sand. "It will kill you all!"

From his place of confinement, Wall dragged himself closer to the fence, ignoring the pain that shot through his bound wrists and ankles. His parched lips cracked as he tried to call out a warning.

The Ogre abandoned the microphone and stormed toward Briony, crates shaking under his heavy feet before he marched across the sand. Before anyone could intervene, he seized her by the hair and yanked her head back with savage force. Briony clawed at his grip with her nails, but The Ogre didn't flinch.

Across the circle, Tammy doubled over. Her body convulsed as she fell to her knees, hands splayed in the dirt for support. A violent retching sound escaped her throat before the purple liquid came rushing back up, mixed with bile and blood. Others who had drunk began to clutch their stomachs, faces contorting with the first waves of pain.

The Ogre held Briony like a doll. She twisted and fought against his grip, but each movement only seemed to increase her pain as her hair pulled taut from her scalp.

"You will drink," he growled. "Show the others!"

Briony thrashed, her legs kicking up dust, her hands still clawing helplessly at The Ogre's arms. The group's attention flickered between the scene unfolding and the trembling Tammy.

"Stop!" a voice cried out. One of the younger men, bare-chested and lithe, stepped forward. "You can't force her. This isn't right."

The Ogre's gaze snapped to the young man, his eyes narrowing. "You dare question our leader?"

The young man faltered and stopped in his tracks, his courage evidently waning under the weight of The Ogre's glare. Before he could respond, another figure stepped up beside him. It was an older woman, her frail body marked by scratches caused by struggles and needles—evidence of the experiments she'd endured in the name of the leader's vision. Wall frowned, surprised to see an older person, but realized that test subjects did not necessarily need to be young and supposedly beautiful. They had been hidden until now.

"He's right," the older woman said, her voice shaking but resolute. "This isn't salvation. It's murder."

A murmur spread through the group like wildfire. Those

who had already drunk the purple liquid writhed uncomfortably. Some shoved their fingers into their own mouths.

The healthier, stronger members moved protectively closer to The Ogre, their faith still unshaken. But the weaker ones—those who had endured too much, lost too much—rose, their eyes blazing with defiance.

The Ogre snarled and yanked Briony upright, forcing her face close to his. "Do you see what you've done?"

Briony spat in his face. The Ogre roared and shoved her backward, sending her sprawling to the dirt.

"If you will not drink willingly," he bellowed, "I will make you drink!"

Several of his loyalists surged forward, grabbing Briony and pinning her down by her arms and legs in the sand. She kicked and screamed, her voice hoarse as she cried out with panic that had replaced her graceful beauty.

"No! Stop—this is murder!" The older woman's voice carried through the noise. Her words ignited the powder keg of fear and doubt.

People leapt to their feet, then at each other. A young man with tattoos covering his arms lunged at one of The Ogre's loyal followers, tackling him to the ground in a cloud of dust.

Three women who had refused to drink scrambled backward, desperately searching for anything to defend themselves. One grabbed a splintered wooden plank from a nearby crate, wielding it like a baseball bat. Another found a jagged rock, its edge sharp enough to draw blood.

"Traitors!" shouted a muscular man with a shaved head, pointing accusingly at those who had thrown away their cups. He charged forward, only to be met by a makeshift barrier of bodies as five of the doubters linked arms to block his path.

On the outskirts of what had been the circle, two women clawed at each other's faces, one defending The Mentor's honor, the other a doubter fighting for survival.

Those who had already consumed the poison staggered in circles, some retching violently, others clutching their stomachs as the toxins began their deadly work. Their weakened state made them easy targets in the frenzy, and several were trampled beneath the feet of the fighting mob.

In the middle of the chaos, The Ogre clamped his thumb and forefinger over Briony's nose. As she opened her mouth to gasp for air, The Ogre snatched up a cup and poured the contents into her throat. He put his hand under her jaw and squeezed her mouth closed. Briony spluttered and gurgled, twisting her shoulders left and right.

Clearly satisfied that she'd swallowed the concoction, The Ogre released his grip. Briony rolled onto her stomach on the rough ground and shoved her fingers into her mouth. She retched, but no liquid came forth.

The Ogre turned and barreled off into the pandemonium, looking for his next victim.

Wall watched as Briony staggered to her feet and assessed the scene. Nearby, two men forced a young woman —barely older than a teenager—to drink from a plastic coffee cup. The woman's screams became muffled as they pinched her nose and poured the purple liquid down her throat.

Nearby, the older woman fought hard, wielding a jagged piece of wood like a sword. She struck out at one attacker close to his eye as another approached her from behind and drove his elbow into her back, sending her crashing to the ground. Blood seeped from a wound on her temple, but she still tried to rise again.

Briony went to assist her, unaware of a thin but

muscular man approaching from behind, brandishing a loop of rope.

"Briony! Turn around!" Wall shouted, summoning all the strength he had.

Briony turned just in time. She ducked, and the rope swung wide, causing the assailant to stumble with the momentum of his lunge. While the guy was off balance, Briony clocked him with a sweet right hook to the jaw, and Wall heard the crunch even through the noise of the madness.

The Ogre climbed back onto the stage and tried to call the place to order. Even using the microphone, his words became lost in the din.

Briony charged for the stage, snatching up a heavy wooden crate on the way.

"You can do it, Briony," Wall muttered to himself, watching the action unfold.

With a surge of strength, Briony swung the crate as hard as she could into The Ogre's legs. The strike knocked him off balance. He stumbled and toppled heavily onto the ground below.

"Yes!" Wall said, clenching a fist in celebration.

Briony grabbed a nearby plank and charged for The Ogre before he could climb to his feet. She held the plank above her head like a club, then swung it down and smacked the big man in the chest.

The Ogre roared in pain, pushing himself up off the ground. Before he could fully rise, another woman emerged from the chaos, brandishing a metal pole.

Together, both women rained blows on The Ogre's head and body, forcing him to stay down.

Briony delivered the final strike, swinging her heavy plank into the side of the big man's head with such force that the wood cracked and splintered. The giant of a man lay motionless, his breath shallow. Briony's hands trembled as she dropped the plank.

"Yes!" Wall shouted again as the fight slipped from The Ogre's giant body.

Around Briony, the tide of the fight began to turn. Those who doubted The Mentor—though weaker and fewer in number—fought with a desperation powered by pure desire for survival.

The loyalists, evidently losing morale after seeing The Ogre toppled, became overwhelmed, succumbing to blows and falling to their knees. "Tie them up and put them in there, out of the sun," Briony instructed her makeshift army, pointing at a small structure behind the stage. Although it wouldn't be comfortable, it was out of the fierce heat. "No one's dying today."

Then, as Wall watched, the poison made itself known again. More people fell to their knees in the baking sun.

Briony doubled over, clutching her stomach as the toxins did their devilish work. "Get to the White Rooms," she shouted to the other doubters. "Lock yourselves inside away from the heat...and the enemy."

## 51

**Mexico City.**

The National Museum of History in Mexico City neared its closing hour. Visitors' footsteps echoed less frequently as people shuffled toward the exits, their murmured conversations fading into silence. Golden light from the setting sun streamed through high arched windows, glinting off polished marble floors and protective glass cases. Inside these displays, pre-Columbian jade masks glowed green, their intricate carvings catching the light.

Striding through the quietening gallery, Sallas allowed himself a moment to smirk at the irony of his situation. Scholars had spent years poring over these ancient relics, while he would simply take exactly what he needed without any of their painstaking labor. He glanced left and right, assessing the few remaining visitors. To maintain his cover, he paused at several glass display cases, feigning interest in their contents.

Sallas caught a glimpse of himself in the reflection of the

glass. He wore a sharp black jacket over a white shirt, with its top two buttons deliberately undone.

"Is it almost time, boss?" said the gaunt man stepping alongside. The man was Sallas's opposite in many ways. A nondescript gray shirt hung off his wiry frame like a scarecrow's rags, almost matching his dirt-colored face.

"It is," Sallas said, turning away from the display. He glanced at The Thin Man. Beyond his scruffy exterior, this man was clearly a competent interrogator. He had put the young academic—Hans Hutchins—through psychological torture in the Chetumal jail, which had allowed Sallas to uncover this museum as the place he needed to search.

"For now, we keep moving," Sallas commanded, striding through the gallery.

The Thin Man nodded, his lips curling into a skeletal grin.

Sallas paused to study another display, while his attention was actually focused on a museum worker tidying pamphlets on an information desk near the elevators. The young woman organized the various leaflets with a speed that suggested she did the task every day. Once the counter was clear, she turned and strode away.

"She's our way in," Sallas said, watching the woman's every movement. "This way."

He set off after the young woman, maintaining a casual pace that wouldn't draw attention. As she stepped into an elevator at the far end of the hall, he quickened his stride. He slipped through the narrowing gap just as the doors began to close, forcing them to open again. The Thin Man slid in behind.

"Wait. You shouldn't—" the young woman started, her eyes widening with surprise. Her hand instinctively moved toward the control panel.

Before she could reach it, Sallas pushed her against the elevator wall, one hand clamping firmly over her mouth while the other pinned her wrist.

"Don't scream," he whispered. "We need your help with something, that's all." He glanced down and read the name from her lanyard. "Good evening, Maria. I'm going to remove my hand now, and you're not going to shout, are you?"

Maria shook her head as the doors slid shut.

Sallas removed his hand and took half a step backward. Cornered in the elevator, Maria wasn't going anywhere.

"Take us to the archives," Sallas said, pointing at the control panel. "We're here on business."

"I'm not supposed to—"

"Do not argue with me," Sallas spat, grabbing the lanyard.

Maria began to tremble.

"Archives, now," Sallas said.

With a shaking hand, Maria lifted the badge to the elevator's screen. A soft beep sounded, and the panel lit up with a new set of options. She selected one of the lower floors, and the elevator descended. The doors reopened, revealing a large and dimly lit space. Rows of metal shelving units stood end to end, stretching up toward the ceiling where cobwebs shrouded light fixtures like mist.

"Get out," Sallas said, pointing Maria toward the door and giving her a little shove in the back to remind her of his authority.

Sallas eyed the stacks of folders and frayed papers lining the shelves. They strode past several large tables stacked with dusty boxes, scrolls, and artifacts.

"Take a seat," Sallas instructed, dragging a chair from beneath a desk.

Maria did what she was told, taking short, sharp breaths mixed in with whimpers.

The Thin Man produced a length of cord and quickly bound her to the chair. Clearly suspecting she might scream as her eyes glistened with tears, The Thin Man clamped a hand over her mouth.

"Listen carefully," Sallas said, reveling in the control. "We're looking for a specific artifact—a torn piece of parchment, Mayan hieroglyphs. Where can we find it?"

Maria shook her head violently, tears streaming down her cheeks.

Sallas reached out and slapped The Thin Man's hand away, then clamped his hand around Maria's throat, not squeezing but with enough pressure to make her gasp.

"Don't play games with me," he warned. "I am not a patient man. Where is it?"

Maria nodded that she was ready to speak, and Sallas removed his hand. "Mr. Flores," she whispered, her voice barely audible. "The chief archivist. His office is... at the end of the room."

"Good," Sallas said, straightening up. He gestured to The Thin Man, who tied a piece of cloth around the young woman's mouth, muting her sobs.

"You never know, you may even survive this," Sallas said, placing a hand gently on her cheek.

Sallas turned and led them across the archive, their footsteps echoing softly. They moved between metal shelving units filled with centuries of Mexican history, catalogued and stored.

As they approached the far end of the room, a small office encased in glass walls came into view. Inside, an elderly man with a shock of white hair sat hunched over his desk.

Sallas knocked on the glass, and the archivist looked up, startled. The old man stood from his desk and crossed the office with the help of his cane. The door creaked open.

"Mr. Flores, I assume," Sallas said.

"Yes, but you should not be here. This area is not open to the public."

"We're looking for something specific," Sallas said, his tone polite. "A parchment with Mayan glyphs. It forms half of a complete document."

"I'm afraid that's not possible—"

"You'd be doing us a great favor," Sallas interrupted, wearing a smile.

Flores frowned, clutching his cane. "I'm sorry, but access to the archives is restricted. Now, as I've already said, this area is not—"

"I think you misunderstand me," Sallas said, his tone hardening. "I am not asking."

"This area is not open to the public. Get out!" The old man hobbled back toward his desk.

Fearing the man might be walking toward a hidden panic button, Sallas surged forward. He exploded into the office and pushed the man into a stack of books. The old man recovered and raised his cane with surprising speed. The Thin Man lunged forward, catching the cane and tossing it aside.

"Now, now," Sallas said, shaking his head. "Let's not make this unpleasant."

"I—I won't help you," Flores said, his voice faltering. "I'd rather die."

"Sure, all options are on the table," Sallas hissed.

"We have your colleague," The Thin Man said and leaned in. "Maria. Young, lots of life to live. Let's make sure you're not responsible for spilling her blood."

Flores blinked several times as the fight physically drained from his body along with the color from his face. He stumbled, then steadied himself against the desk.

"Take us to the parchment," Sallas said, pointing toward the door. "And we will be out of your way in mere minutes."

Flores led the two men through the archive. Reaching a row of doors, he produced a ring of keys from his pocket and opened one of the doors. He snapped on the light and moved to a locked storage cabinet at the back of the room. With shaking hands, he unlocked the cabinet and pulled open a drawer. He paused as he laid eyes on something wrapped in layers of protective cloth.

"Now," Sallas barked. "Quickly."

Flores peeled back the cloth to reveal an aged piece of parchment covered in intricate glyphs.

The archivist reached for a pair of white gloves, carefully lifting the artifact. Sallas snatched it from his grasp. The old man protested, but Sallas shoved him backward, sending him sprawling to the floor.

"Pathetic," The Thin Man sneered.

Sallas examined the parchment briefly before tucking it into his jacket. He turned back to Flores, who coughed and clutched his chest.

"Someone will find you in the morning," Sallas said coldly. "If anyone cares enough about you to check."

He then whipped the keys out of the old man's hand, stepped out of the room, and locked the archivist inside.

As Sallas and The Thin Man made their way out, they passed Maria, still tied to the wooden chair, her eyes red and swollen. Sallas paused, leaning close enough for her to hear his whisper. "Archaeology is one of my hobbies," he said. "Torture is another." He strode toward the elevator and then paused and glanced back at the woman. "Keep what happened here to yourself, and tell the old man to do the same. Have a comfortable night."

## 52

**Mexican desert, north of Cabo San Lucas.**

Wall's eyes snapped open as consciousness returned with shocking force. Every organ in his body screamed in protest—his kidneys throbbing, his liver aching, his stomach twisted into knots—each taking turns to announce their rebellion against the extreme dehydration. His tongue fused to the roof of his mouth like dried cement. Blisters formed on his skin where the desert floor radiated heat like the coals of a barbecue grill. One horrifying certainty crystallized in his mind: this barren patch of Mexican desert would be his final resting place.

An eerie quiet hung across the compound—the sound of chaos had long dissipated. Distant groans and the agony of sickness now floated through the fence. Wall's stomach lurched and heaved. Nausea crashed over him in waves. Each wave pulled him closer to the dark undertow of unconsciousness. Wall fought to keep his eyes open, knowing that if he surrendered to darkness now, he would never surface again.

"I have given in," he croaked, his voice just a hiss of air. "I am weak. I have given in."

A tiny sliver of shadow ran along the bottom of the fence, and with the last trickle of strength inside of him, he rolled over and pushed himself against the wood. He licked his cracked and bleeding lips, but his tongue held no moisture. His head pounded like helicopter blades as his life ebbed away.

"THERE IT IS," Byrd said as the compound came into view beneath the Leonardo AW109 chopper. The blocky shape of the perimeter fence stood out against the vast undulations of the desert.

"What's the plan?" Hutchins asked, his voice crackling through the comms system.

"I'll be honest, I haven't got one," Byrd said, slowing their approach. "Sometimes, that's when I do my best work. We'll do one flyover, see if we can get a visual. Remember, we're looking for a small enclosure, open air. He's likely to be exposed."

"Got it."

"Good boy," Byrd said. "Pretty soon, you may have to do things you've never done before—to save your professor friend. I know you're up to it. Candi, still got that gun to our friend's head?"

"I sure do," Candi said. "Tom's not going anywhere."

"She's doing a great job," Hutchins added proudly.

"Good to hear our guest is secure," Byrd said, dipping the Leonardo's nose and expanding her view of the compound below. The setting sun bathed everything in an eerie red-orange glow, like the horizon during a forest fire. She glanced between the canopy and the screen displaying feed from the chopper's exterior cameras. She searched for any sign of movement, but the compound appeared eerily still.

"Can't see anything," Hutchins said.

"Keep lookin'," Byrd replied. "Hope we find him soon. This bird's makin' enough racket to wake the dead. Every gun-totin' maniac from miles around will come runnin'."

"And we don't even know if he has the strength to climb up," Hutchins said.

"Don't make me laugh," Byrd replied. "No one's climbing a rope dangling from a chopper without the correct equipment. This ain't the movies. Fortunately, whoever we borrowed this bird from had the foresight to fit a winch." Byrd tapped a button, and the door slid open, letting warm desert air into the cabin. She worked another control and let out a few feet of rope. "Hutchins, carefully pull in that rope and tie a loop in the end. With any luck, Wall can slide that under his arms, and we can haul him up without him having to hold on."

"*If* we spot him," Hutchins said. "And *if* he has the strength."

"He'll have it," Byrd said firmly. "We all will."

Byrd felt movement in the craft as Hutchins followed her instructions.

"Done," Hutchins said. "I can see the wooden buildings like we saw before. Barns, maybe," he said, peering out through the open door.

"Any small, enclosed areas out in the open?" Byrd asked.

"Not yet. Wait. Maybe. I can't see details."

Byrd heard shuffling and feared Hutchins had moved closer to the door.

"Stay away from the door unless it's totally necessary," Byrd yelled. "One jolt and you're out." Then she added to herself, "You're getting braver, kid, but more reckless too."

She glanced at the screen and tapped through the options. The Leonardo had two external cameras and one internal.

"With passengers like mine, having eyes on the cabin is never a bad thing," Byrd said to herself, flicking back to the nose-mounted camera. The image reappeared, and she saw the small compound Hutchins had mentioned.

"The fence there," Byrd said, her eyes darting between the instrument panel and the compound below. She adjusted the collective slightly, maintaining a steady hover while keeping the fence line in view. "Could anyone be sheltering beside it? It's the only place giving any shade, so it's possible."

"They would have to be pretty thin," Hutchins called back, his voice competing with the rotor wash.

"Your professor friend is thin, right?" Byrd asked. She made a minor correction as a gust of wind buffeted the chopper.

"Sure is. Probably even more now—wait!" Hutchins yelled. "I think I see it! A foot!"

"Is that someone sheltering beside the fence?" Byrd asked and eased down on the collective, bringing them twenty feet lower for a better view.

"Yes! I can just about make out their foot," Hutchins confirmed.

Byrd maneuvered the chopper closer to the enclosure. She brought them into a precise hover directly above the position.

"Okay. This is it, Hutchins. One chance." Sweat beaded on Byrd's forehead as she maintained the delicate hover. "You tied the rope?"

"Yes, ma'am."

"Good man." She adjusted the cyclic, compensating for another gust pushing against their portside. "Don't go down there with it. He'll get the idea." She hit the winch control, and the rope unspooled, dropping toward the compound below.

"Understood. Oh my God, I think it's him!" Hutchins yelled.

"Good. Shout and tell him to get into the loop—it should act like a harness. As soon as he's in, I'll reel him up."

"Yes, ma'am."

"And stop calling me ma'am!" Byrd hissed. "That's a waste of oxygen."

"Yes... Nora."

"And definitely don't call me Nora!"

"I can see him. But he's not moving," Hutchins said, falling silent for a moment. "Oh God, someone's coming. A huge monster of a man is running right this way."

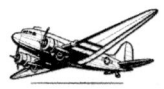

THE THUDDING BEGAN as a faint rhythm inside Wall's skull—his failing heart, he assumed, counting down its final beats. But the sound swelled and sharpened, growing impossibly loud for something internal. He opened his eyelids as the vibration rattled his bones.

A crash echoed across the compound from a small shed in which The Ogre had been subdued. A whole side of the structure fell away, and the beast charged out. Clearly recovered and enraged from his unconsciousness, he sprinted across to Wall's enclosure.

"Where's the damn key," The Ogre bellowed, looking at the padlock and chain that sealed Wall inside.

The professor looked up at the brute, then jerked toward another sound—a mechanical, rhythmic thudding, coming from above.

"You left one behind, you know. And now he's going to burn!" The Ogre yelled in the direction of the White Rooms. He sprinted back to the shed and returned with a fuel canister. He yanked off the lid and splashed the contents around the fence.

The sharp, chemical stench of gasoline jolted Wall's senses. He rolled over with a groan, forcing his eyes to focus on a blur of movement nearby.

The Ogre dug a silver Zippo from his pocket, rolled it into action, and dropped it into the fuel.

Wall gasped as flames leapt up at the fence. The orange tongues climbed hungrily up the dry wood, spreading rapidly along the perimeter. The fire accelerated with terrifying speed, the heat rushing toward Wall like an approaching train.

The professor pressed his palms against the dirt, desperate to push himself upright, but his arms trembled violently and then gave out completely.

The roar of the flames surrounded him, combined with —was it—the thud of helicopter blades somewhere overhead. He rolled over and saw The Ogre shoving at two burning fence posts with a length of wood. The big man was clearly trying to break into the enclosure and finish the job.

Wall squeezed his eyes closed. Pain wracked his body.

A shadow moved out across the enclosure, blocking out

the setting sun. At first, Wall thought his vision was failing until he looked up and saw the outline of a chopper hovering above him.

Wall craned his neck and looked up, squinting at the aircraft.

Behind him, wood splintered as the Ogre finally smashed his way into the enclosure. Oblivious to the heat, the brute shoved his way through the flames.

"I'm hallucinating," Wall said to himself, looking back up at the chopper. With a jolt of adrenaline, he saw a figure leaning from the open doorway, waving frantically. His eyes strained into focus, colors from the sun and flames dancing across his hazy vision. Then, like a bolt of electricity moving through him, he recognized the figure.

"Hutchins!" Wall shouted with a sudden, short burst of strength.

A rope snaked down through the air.

"My boy, you've come for me," Wall croaked.

Now inside the enclosure, The Ogre closed in on Wall, the fuel canister still in his hands. He came closer, raising the canister in the air.

## 53

"I'm going down there!" Hutchins told Byrd. "He can't move!"

"That's madness," Byrd insisted. "You'd be taking on a raging fire and the biggest guy I ever saw—some kind of ogre. Tell him to climb into the loop. It's faster and safer."

"Not if he's in a coma, it isn't!"

Byrd punched the mixing unit in front of her, taking out her frustration at the chaos unfolding.

"Goddammit! Okay, but we need to take out the big man first. You still got that switchblade, Hutchins?"

"Sure do."

"And how's your aim?" Byrd asked.

"Average. But my luck is high as a rocket right now."

Somehow, Byrd just knew Hutchins would be looking at Candi when he said that.

"Okay, big shot," Byrd said. "I'll get you in close. Hold on to something."

Byrd pulled on the cyclic control and rolled the aircraft smoothly to the right, redirecting the lift vector to initiate a banking turn. As she circled around the line of dancing flames, she waited for the moment when the chopper would be closest to the ground.

"Hutchins. Now!"

Byrd eyed the screen and saw Hutchins take aim, his fingers tight around the handle. The metal glinted as he extended his arm. For a guy who'd never thrown a knife before, his stance wasn't bad—legs slightly apart, shoulders squared, eyes locked on target.

"Steady," Byrd whispered to herself, adjusting the hover.

The chopper dipped suddenly in a crosswind. Hutchins wavered, nearly losing his balance against the fuselage. The thug below looked up, his massive face contorting as he spotted them through the swirling dust.

"Now or never," Byrd muttered into her headset.

Before she could offer any more advice, the young academic swung his arm forward like a slingshot. The blade shot through the air, shining in the last rays of sunlight. It cut a path through the swirling sand, the aim straight and true.

Byrd tracked its trajectory, unconsciously holding her breath. She switched to the external camera view and zoomed in.

The thug remained on his feet for a long moment. Then, miraculously, the knife sliced into his leg, embedding itself up to the hilt. The giant's expression shifted from rage to confusion. He threw back his head in a silent roar, then crumpled to his knees, reaching for the blade.

"Well, I'll be damned," Byrd breathed. "You actually hit him."

"I hit him!" Hutchins said, sounding as amazed as Byrd.

"Indeed you did," Byrd replied. "The neck would have been better, but that was a good shot. It buys us time."

"I was aiming for the neck," Hutchins said, pulling off his headset and grasping the rope. "I'm going down."

The Leonardo rocked gently as Hutchins swung out through the door.

"Without a harness, that's insane," Byrd said—a few moments too late. "I've created a monster," she muttered, shaking her head at the previously meek academic's recklessness. She turned her attention back to the screen to check on his descent.

"Let me help," Tom shouted from his seat at the back of the cabin. "I'll help to pull them in."

"Negative," Byrd replied. "You're not going anywhere, come hell or high water. Candi, keep that gun trained on our guest."

"Will do!" Candi said, as cheerfully as ever.

Holding the chopper as still as she could, Byrd looked at the screen. Hutchins's boots appeared on the feed as he lowered himself toward the compound. Although he wasn't moving with the speed Byrd had seen in the military, he shuffled toward the ground with a determination that made her smile.

"You can do it, kid," she said quietly, a warm shot of pride flowing through her.

Hutchins closed the distance, foot by foot.

Byrd adjusted the camera, panning across the compound. The big guy was still down, but stirring—one hand clutching his bleeding leg, the other pushing against the ground to rise.

"Hostile back in play," Byrd said, forgetting Hutchins had taken off his headset. "Dammit."

On the screen, Hutchins touched down, stumbling as his boots hit the uneven ground. He dropped into a crouch and shielded his eyes from the helicopter's downdraft. He quickly assessed Wall's condition—checking for a pulse first, then injuries.

Wall lay motionless, his clothes stained with dirt and what looked like blood. His sallow face and sunken cheeks made him look like a frail bag of bones.

Hutchins tried lifting Wall but faltered, clearly struggling with the awkward weight. Byrd silently noted that even a skinny guy becomes a challenging deadweight when unconscious. Hutchins readjusted, kneeling to hoist Wall over his shoulder in a fireman's carry. This time he managed it, securing one arm around Wall's legs while reaching for the rope with his free hand.

Hutchins gritted his teeth and then attempted to haul them both up the rope. His arm trembled under the combined strain.

"You'll never lift him like that," Byrd groaned. "Use the loop harness, like I told you,"

Then, Byrd saw what she had feared. A few feet behind Hutchins, the big man slowly dragged himself to his feet. He looked at Hutchins and then down at the hilt of the knife still sticking out of his leg.

"Hostile incoming!" Byrd shouted, unsure whether Hutchins could hear her.

The brute took an unsteady step forward, clearly suffering from blood loss. His massive hand wrapped around the knife handle, and with a guttural roar, he yanked it free. Dark blood squirted out from the wound, but rage seemed to override his pain.

Hutchins, clearly sensing movement behind him, glanced back. His eyes widened at the sight of the approaching giant. With newfound urgency, he gripped the rope again. This time, instead of trying to climb it, he looped it beneath his arms, then around Wall's torso, using the crude tandem harness instead.

"That's my boy," Byrd muttered, watching him secure the knots with shaking hands. "Hold tight!" she said as she started the mechanism to pull them in.

As the two men rose into the air, the Ogre lunged forward and grabbed out, narrowly missing Hutchins' ankle. The brute stumbled, his injured leg buckling beneath him.

"Candi!" Byrd called over her shoulder. "Keep Tom covered, but if you can, get to the cabin door! They'll need to be pulled inside."

Hutchins kicked out at the brute's reaching hand, connecting with the man's wrist. The giant growled but retained his balance and launched at Hutchins again.

This time, Byrd was ready; she pulled back on the controls, raising the chopper and dragging Hutchins and Wall further from the ground.

"Pressure, not movement," Byrd told herself, turning her attention to maintaining the best hover she could. She had to avoid sudden movements or overcorrection that would make the aircraft tip or roll.

She glanced at the screen and saw Hutchins and Wall closing in on the door. Candi waited, ready to drag them inside.

Byrd switched back to the exterior feed and saw The Ogre yet again hauling himself to his feet.

"Why don't people know when to give up?" Byrd said, watching the oaf stumble forward and reach up into the air. For a few moments, Byrd questioned what he was reaching for. Then, she saw the tail end of the rope still dangling free. She gripped the controls, considering pulling them higher into the air but not wanting to do anything that might dislodge Hutchins and Wall.

"Should have pulled the whole rope up with you, Hutchins!" Byrd hissed. "Should have pulled the rope up."

The Ogre wrapped a meaty hand around the bottom of the rope. Byrd felt the new weight as the creature hauled himself up with surprising speed, using his massive upper body strength to compensate for his injured leg.

"They're here, cut the winch!" Candi yelled as Hutchins and Wall appeared at the cabin door.

Byrd cut the winch and then looked at the cabin camera. Candi leaned precariously out of the open door, her hair whipping wildly in the rotor wash.

"No harness or anything," Byrd said, watching the woman work. "Incredible."

"I've got you!" Candi shouted over the deafening noise of the helicopter blades.

Hutchins, his face contorted with exhaustion, pushed Wall first into the cabin. The older man's head lolled to the side, and he didn't appear to be conscious.

Candi grabbed Wall under the arms and pulled him in. For a moment, the skinny scientist caught on something, then with a final heave, Candi dragged him into the cabin and up onto a seat. She buckled him in, then returned to the door.

"Now you!" she yelled to Hutchins, extending her hand.

Hutchins gripped her wrist, his arm trembling with the effort. He planted one foot against the helicopter's skid and pushed himself upward. Then, he froze.

Although Byrd couldn't see the issue, she knew it instinctively.

"What's happening?" Byrd called out, eyes darting

between her controls and the side mirror, where she could just make out the struggle.

"It's him!" Candi screamed, her grip on Hutchins' wrist tightening. "He's got Hutchins' leg!"

The helicopter lurched sideways as the weight distribution shifted. A series of warning lights flashed across Byrd's console. She fought to stabilize the aircraft, every muscle tensed.

Hutchins twisted violently, using his free leg to stomp down on the giant's fingers. The Ogre let out a guttural roar but maintained his grip, those massive fingers like iron bands around Hutchins' ankle. With his other hand, the brute reached higher, getting a better grip on Hutchins.

"He's pulling me down!" Hutchins shouted, his voice cracking with panic.

Candi braced one foot against the cabin wall and pulled on Hutchins' arm with both hands, her face flushing with effort. Inch by excruciating inch, she dragged him further inside while The Ogre maintained his iron grip on Hutchins' ankle.

The giant's head appeared at the door, his bloodied face a mask of rage. One massive shoulder heaved into Byrd's view as he pulled himself up further, using Hutchins as leverage.

"Let go of him!" Candi screamed.

The helicopter lurched again as The Ogre dragged himself higher.

Candi released one hand from Hutchins—still gripping him tightly with the other—and grabbed a small fire extinguisher mounted on the wall near her head.

"Hold on," she shouted, wrenching the extinguisher from its bracket.

The Ogre pulled himself further into the doorway, his fingers digging into Hutchins' flesh.

Candi swung the extinguisher in a wide arc and brought it down onto The Ogre's exposed hand. The giant howled in pain and anger, his hold on Hutchins momentarily loosening. Candi struck again, this time targeting the fingers where they gripped the edge of the doorway.

"Let! Him! Go!" Each word was punctuated by another blow of the extinguisher.

Blood sprayed across the cabin floor as two of The Ogre's fingers released the doorjamb. Releasing Hutchins, the monster swung his other hand across and grabbed the door in a different position, now just trying to stay airborne. Hutchins scrambled into the cabin.

"Byrd!" Hutchins shouted. "Do something!"

"Strap in!" Byrd said.

Hutchins and Candi threw themselves into the nearby seats, clipping themselves in.

Byrd swung the controls, and the helicopter banked hard, the sudden motion causing everyone inside to slide. The Ogre, half-in and half-out of the doorway, lost his balance. His massive body slid sideways, but he clung on. With murderous intent written across his face, he tried to haul himself into the cabin.

Byrd tilted the chopper a little more, barrelling it to almost thirty degrees. She heard Hutchins and Candi scream, clearly terrified even though they were strapped in. Glancing at The Ogre again, Sierra Byrd saw the big man grimacing as he clung on desperately. Then, he slipped. The interior feed no longer showed his grotesque face.

The sudden absence of his weight caused the helicopter to lurch upward. Warning alarms blared through Byrd's headset as she fought to stabilize the aircraft. Through it all, she kept her eyes on the exterior camera feed. The Ogre's massive body tumbled, limbs flailing against the empty sky. His mouth opened in what must have been a scream, but it was lost to the roar of the rotors and the howling desert wind.

"Watch your step there, sir," Byrd murmured under her breath, allowing herself the smallest smile of grim satisfaction.

## 54

**Mexican desert, north of Cabo San Lucas.**

"How's the professor looking?" Byrd asked as the fence of the compound disappeared from view. "If you need to tend to him, Hutchins, you can unbuckle yourself now."

"Yes, ma'am."

"Move him as little as possible, but try to get some water between his lips," Byrd said, fingers dancing across the console as she punched in their new route. "Even just a small amount will help with the dehydration. And check that medical kit—there should be a standard field assessment kit in there."

The silence from the cabin stretched uncomfortably long. Byrd adjusted her headset, thinking perhaps the connection had failed.

"Hutchins? You copy?"

Another beat of silence, then Hutchins' voice came through, barely above a whisper.

"I... I don't know if he's alive." His voice cracked on the last word. "I can't find a pulse."

Byrd's hands tightened on the controls. Through the cabin monitor, she saw Wall's ashen face, his head lolling against the headrest. The sight of his slack features turned something cold inside her chest. Too many missions had ended this way, and she hated the memory of every single one.

"No pulse?" Byrd's voice sharpened.

"I—I don't know. I'm pressing but—I can't tell if that's—" Hutchins fumbled with the words, panic edging into his voice.

"Okay. Keep calm." Byrd scanned her instrument panel, mind racing through options for how to get to a hospital more quickly. "Check his neck, not his wrist. Press firmly under his jawline."

She weighed her choices. Her military combat medic training could help, but that would mean leaving the controls. Helicopter autopilot systems weren't like those in fixed-wings—they couldn't just cruise along safely while she stepped away. One wrong air current or mechanical hiccup, and they'd all be in trouble.

Her fingers hovered over the autopilot switch. Wall needed help now, but risking everyone on board wasn't an option.

"Try again," she commanded, pulling back from the autopilot. "Two fingers, carotid artery, press—"

"Ma'am." Tom's voice cut in, unexpectedly soft and deferential. "If you would allow me. I have basic medical training. I can help."

"If you would allow me?" Byrd repeated back at Tom. "That depends on if you're gonna try and kill the guy, doesn't it?"

"And then what?" Tom replied, his tone meek. "You'd just throw me out over some remote part of the desert."

"Now, that's not a bad idea," Byrd said, making her tone as threatening as possible. She paused and shook her head. "Okay," she said finally. "But if he dies, you're next."

Byrd tapped the monitor and zoomed in to watch closely as Tom unclipped his harness and moved toward Wall.

"I need a better visual," she muttered, adjusting the contrast.

Tom's broad shoulders blocked most of the view as he hunched over the unconscious professor.

"Move to your left," she ordered through the headset, not trusting the guy an inch. "I can't see what you're doing."

Tom shifted slightly, but not enough. His hands moved in quick motions that set off alarm bells in Byrd's mind. She couldn't shake the feeling that he was performing for the camera, not for Wall's benefit.

"Explain everything you're doing," Byrd said. "Don't miss a single thing."

"He's got a pulse. It's faint, but he's alive," Tom said.

Hutchins gasped with relief. Candi shuffled closer, the gun still levelled at Tom.

"I'm now going to try and get an indication of systolic blood pressure by checking the lower thumb and the pulse at the wrist at the same time." Tom's hands moved into that position.

Everyone watched in silence for a few seconds.

"Okay, blood pressure is very low. We need to cool him down for the heatstroke, and he needs sugar to raise his blood pressure. Is the air con at its fullest?"

"Already did it," Byrd confirmed. "Soon as he boarded."

"Okay. How else can we cool him?" Tom asked.

"There's a fridge at the back, probably has a small freezer section with ice," Byrd said. "Then check the coffee station for packs of sugar." She shook her head. She would never allow something so frivolous aboard her aircraft.

"Yep, got it," Hutchins said, pacing back through the cabin.

"Good. Coat one of the smallest ice cubes with sugar," Byrd instructed, "then try to get it into his mouth. It will melt before any risk of choking. Put the other ice cubes around his collar."

"Roger that," Hutchins replied.

Silence filled the cabin as they got to work.

Byrd took a moment to assess their position and speed.

"He's shuffling in his seat. I think it's working," Tom said. "Movement is good to see."

"It is good," Byrd agreed. "Give him one more round of ice, then get back to your seats. It's an hour to the hospital in Cabo San Lucas, so try to get some rest. After that, who knows what's going to happen."

"I can certainly get on board with that," Tom replied.

"Alright, Tom," Byrd said, watching Tom stride back to his seat. "And...well done."

Byrd looked out at the desert beneath them, its simplicity and expanse providing a moment of calm. Silver moonlight spotlighted the contours of undulating sand and rocky outcrops. Above it all, the giant, star-filled sky stretched out to infinity but somehow still felt like home.

"Now this would be a great place to bring the Skytrain," she said to herself, looking from the sky to the sand. "Definitely overdue some 'me' time," Byrd muttered, shaking her head. "Been way too long."

*And how long is too long for me to be around other people?* she wondered silently. Then, with a small smile, she thought, *In truth, I would have to say about three minutes...*

She cast a glance down at the monitor. Tom had

slumped into the seat right at the back. Hutchins and Candi were settled behind Wall, looking tranquil for the first time in what seemed like weeks.

"Don't get too comfortable, girl," Byrd said quietly after seeing that Candi had the flare gun resting in her lap, her eyes half closed. "He might have helped us, but—" She muttered the words to herself, but her hand hovered over the mic on her headset as she opened her mouth to send out the same warning to Candi.

A metallic clatter jolted her as something crashed to the cabin floor. Then, heavy footsteps pounded behind her, vibrating through the helicopter's frame.

She glanced down at the monitor in time to see a chaotic blur of movement in the cabin behind her.

"Get away from him!" Hutchins shouted, his voice cracking with panic.

The camera focused, showing an image of Hutchins shoving himself between Tom and the unconscious Wall, arms thrust outward like a human barricade.

"Get out my way," Tom snarled, trying to push Hutchins aside.

Hutchins shoved Tom back, spinning him around to face the camera. The camera caught his face—no longer calm and helpful, but determined and hard as ice.

"What's going on back there?" Byrd asked.

"You piece of—you're trying to kill him!" Hutchins bellowed, grabbing Tom by the shoulders.

"I'm just checking on him!" Tom said, taking a step backward, which looked to Byrd like attack preparation.

"You were trying to put your hand over his mouth and nose," Hutchins yelled, pointing at Wall. "He can't defend himself."

"Hutchins, Candi, sit him down and strap him to the chair," Byrd said. "If you need to hurt him, do it."

"No, you won't," Tom said, dropping into a fighting stance with his fists raised. He swung an overhand right. Hutchins raised his left forearm and blocked it, then Candi stepped forward to join the fray.

"Fight dirty, Hans," Byrd said.

"Candi, stay back," Hutchins told her. "I've got this. Protect Wall."

Hutchins lunged at Tom with both arms raised, half-punching, half-grappling—his lack of fighting experience on full display.

Tom took one step forward with his left foot as he swung a huge right uppercut. The shot got through Hutchins' guard, smashing him in the chin and snapping his head back. Hutchins staggered backward, then collapsed to the floor.

Byrd put her hand to her headset and flicked a switch, cutting Tom out of the conversation.

"Hutchins," she said. "Go for the eyes or between the legs. You're not a trained fighter, so fight dirty."

Hutchins didn't reply. Byrd looked at the screen and saw Hutchins' headset lying on the floor.

The younger man clambered to his feet. Crimson blood ran in a long, wide streak from his nose. Tom rushed forward, ready to unleash another attack.

Before Tom could get there, Candi stepped forward and put her body between the two men.

"Stop!" she yelled in the older man's face.

"Step aside!" Tom said, attempting to shove her away.

"Tom, you don't need to do this!" the young woman said, more calmly. "You know you're better than this!"

Byrd looked on with rapidly growing confusion as the young woman stepped closer to Tom and stretched out her arms, a smile on her face. As Tom dropped his guard, Candi wrapped him up in a huge hug.

Sierra Byrd gasped as the pair stood there for a long moment, locked in an embrace.

"What the..." Hutchins started. "She can't be...surely?"

"Oh, she can," Byrd said bitterly. "Anyone can do anything. I should have remembered what I already knew—trust is a fool's game." The devastation on Hutchins' face was clear, even through the screen.

Just as Byrd finished speaking, Candi stepped back from her hug. Tom stared at her intently. His hateful expression softened, then melted altogether. His head tilted to the left before rocking forward heavily, his chin landing on his chest. He flopped sideways onto the nearest seat, his eyes closed.

"What's.... what's going on?" Hutchins said, looking from Candi then to Tom as though they'd each grown another head.

Candi, now grinning even wider, held up a small syringe.

"What on Earth have you got there?!" Byrd asked.

"Sedative," Candi replied. "That medical kit is well-stocked. I slipped something out of it when no one was looking. Figured I might have to start protecting myself a little more."

Byrd grinned, partly at the young woman's audacity and partly at the shocked, wide-eyed expression on Hutchins' face.

"That... that should keep him out of trouble," Hutchins said, his gaze resting on Candi.

"Yeah. I think it's a strong one," Candi said. "He'll be unconscious or dazed for a good while."

"Great work, darlin'," Byrd said. "You just saved the professor's life all over again."

## 55

**Hotel suite close to Cabo San Lucas.**

"I'm not sure about this," Hutchins said, glancing around the plush suite as he made his way across the smooth floor tiles and past Byrd, heading across the living room toward the open patio bathed in moonlight. "Do we really have time for this kind of luxury?"

"Ten minutes' relaxation, Hans," Byrd said. "Clear your head. Then, fill it again with everything you've got on the Sunstone, online, or in the depths of your memory. We're out of here again in a few hours."

The suite felt like beachfront heaven after everything they had been through over the past few days. The soft coastal tones and thick wood ceiling beams had a wonderfully calming effect, and the headboard on the wide bed that called to Byrd from the adjacent bedroom had the appearance of interlocked pieces of driftwood. She longed to flop down onto the mattress and sleep for a week, but an hour would have to do.

She turned her gaze toward the doors to the patio,

leading to the private pool with direct swim-up access to the terrace. Hutchins walked out, dipped in, and front-crawled to the far side of the pool. As he rested with his forearms on the smooth tiles, Byrd couldn't help but notice how, despite the time he had spent outdoors taking on feats of courage and strength, he still looked skinny and ghostly white. The slight tan on his face only served to highlight just how pale the rest of his unclothed torso was, like a bottle of milk on a doorstep. But Hutchins clearly couldn't care less. He smiled while he allowed the balmy night air to dry him.

Then, quickly, his smile turned to a rounded mouth fallen open in shock. His peaceful eyes grew wide. Candi padded out from her room wearing a floral bikini that revealed her toned, healthful body. She stood at the side of the pool with hands on hips, looking like she was doing a photo shoot for a swimwear brochure.

She slipped into the water beside Hutchins, her golden-blonde hair spreading out across its surface. She bobbed in the water, moving closer to him. Close enough to give him a playful poke in the upper arm.

Byrd turned away, walked over to the drinks cabinet, and poured herself a bourbon. She dropped into the smooth leather armchair, its scent mixing with the notes of leather fragrances in the whiskey. She took a sip, and the warmth of the liquor felt like someone lovingly drawing a warm blanket over her heart and tucking it in.

"Relaxation is the fuel of productivity," Byrd told herself quietly.

After a few blissful minutes had passed, Byrd's gaze returned longingly to the bottle as she considered a refill.

"Got one of those for me?" Candi asked, stepping into the room with a raised eyebrow. She paced across the living room, trailing in a little pool of water as she wrapped a towel around herself.

"Sure!" Byrd replied, returning to the cabinet and readying another drink.

Hutchins came in and took a seat too, a white-linen shirt covering his equally white torso. He'd left a couple of buttons open at the top, clearly working on that poolside look. Byrd handed him a glass, and Hutchins swirled the deep-brown liquid around like a connoisseur.

"Okay," Byrd said, glancing between her two young friends. "Tom is with the authorities—a risk we have to take unless we plan to haul him around like luggage. Wall can't tell us exactly what's happening at that compound until he recovers, but I'm pretty sure he'll want us to find that relic of yours, Hutchins. So let's get ahead of the game. Where do we start?"

"I don't know what information Wall gave the cult leader, if any," Hutchins said, "but they could be getting close to the Sunstone regardless. Because..." His voice trailed off, and he suddenly focused on an invisible point on the wall.

"Because?" Byrd asked, leaning forward with her glass cupped in both hands.

"Because I gave away the location of the second marker under interrogation," Hutchins said, taking a long drink and staring into the glass.

Byrd gripped her glass tighter but held her tongue. "It happens, kid. You're doing great. Where is the second piece of the parchment?"

"The archives of the National Museum of History in Mexico City. But it may have been taken already."

"Did the professor give you any information while we transported him in the chopper?" Byrd asked.

Hutchins shook his head. "He was mumbling, but I couldn't make out any words. We need to talk to him as soon as we can. Without him, we're going into this half-blind."

"Going where?" Candi said.

Hutchins held his glass up in front of him and then said with an intrepid tone: "In search of the Sunstone."

*If she doesn't do it tonight, buddy, she never will*, Byrd thought, grinning but keeping her thoughts to herself. Instead, she said out loud, "So, Hutchins, what's in that head of yours?"

"A canyon. A demon rock," Hutchins said. "Somewhere in Mexico. We'll have to find it without the second piece of parchment."

Byrd picked up a tablet computer that belonged to the suite and threw it across the room, landing it perfectly in Hutchins' lap.

"I'm giving you an hour to research every geological feature in Mexico," she said. "Better get started."

Byrd walked over to the music system and put on some Ritchie Valens.

"This should help us focus," she said, tapping her foot on the cool tiles.

"What is this noise?" Candi said, scrunching up her nose. "It's kinda... screechy."

"Girl, you don't know nothing," Byrd said, her bouffant bobbing to the beat. "This is the history of your country right here in a song."

Clearly knowing better than to argue, Candi smiled, and the group got down to sipping bourbon and tapping on tablet screens.

"Have you found the Sunstone yet, Hans?" Byrd said after two tracks had played out.

"I'm afraid not," Hutchins replied without looking up.

"So, what have you found?" Byrd asked, walking across to peer over his shoulder. "We need to move fast, Hans. You've seen what Sallas is capable of. Don't let him get his hands on that thing first."

"I know," Hutchins said, jabbing at the screen. "There's nothing here I haven't come across before. A lot of conjecture but nothing set in...well...stone."

"Such as?" Byrd asked, tapping her foot to the beat of her restlessness.

"A canyon. There's always mention of a canyon. The idea comes from ancient Mayan hieroglyphics."

"Well, I don't know much about hieroglyphics," Byrd said. "In fact, one more bourbon, and I won't even be able to say it. So I'll stick to what I do best and refresh my mind about flying in canyons, 'cause I'm guessing you'd prefer to avoid a long trek when time is short. Meanwhile, I'll leave the archaeological research to you two. Sound good?"

"Sounds good!" Candi replied.

Hutchins didn't respond, instead gazing unblinking at the screen.

Another two songs played, and by the time "Come On, Let's Go" started up, Byrd couldn't agree more with Ritchie Valens.

"Wait!" Hutchins shouted. "This looks promising." He read from the screen. "'A Quintana Roo native and archaeologist with extensive local knowledge has identified what he believes is a long-lost plant that ancient civilizations called the key to eternal life. Marcello Rodrigo—"

"You know the guy?" Byrd asked.

"—Rodrigo disappeared around a year ago," Hutchins continued, his voice dropping lower. "Wall had been in contact with him, then he just dropped off the map. We were concerned he might have been—"

A shadow flickered across the terrace. Byrd's instincts prickled.

"Hans," she interrupted, setting her glass down with deliberate care. "Did you lock the patio door?"

Hutchins glanced toward the moonlit terrace, frowning. "I thought I—"

The window exploded inward with a deafening crack. Glass erupted across the room like crystal shrapnel. Hutchins threw himself sideways, bourbon arcing through the air as his glass shattered against the tiles.

Candi froze, and a terrified gasp escaped her lips. The curtains billowed inward like ghostly arms, framing two silhouettes poised on the sill.

The figures launched themselves through the opening, landing on the glass-strewn floor. The men strode forward, sinewy muscles rippling beneath the swirling tattoos on their bare chests. One of them carried a jagged knife, the other a length of chain.

"Get down!" Byrd barked, dropping out of sight. "Now!"

## 56

The first man lunged at Byrd, his knife slashing through the air. She spun and grabbed a nearby dining chair, swinging it at the assailant. The blade bit into the wood, sending a shower of splinters across the room. Byrd stepped and swung the chair again, this time hard enough to catch the assailant across the jaw. He staggered back, dazed but not down.

Hutchins scrambled to his feet, turned his head left and right in search of a weapon, and grabbed a stool from beside the kitchen counter. The attacker stepped toward him, swinging the chain so hard it whistled through the air.

Hutchins raised the stool, using it as a makeshift shield.

The chain-wielder circled, edging Hutchins into the corner. With shocking speed, the attacker flicked his wrist, sending the chain's end arrowing toward Hutchins' face. Hutchins jerked the stool upward—metal met wood with a fearsome crack.

The attacker whirled the chain in a figure-eight pattern, then struck from below.

Hutchins pivoted, nearly losing his balance. The chain

wrapped around one leg of the stool, and the attacker yanked hard. Hutchins clung on desperately, straining against the other man's strength.

The attacker let go, sending Hutchins stumbling backward and crashing into a side table. He remained on his feet —just. With Hutchins off balance, the assailant struck, lashing the chain toward the throat.

Hutchins ducked just in time, the metal whipping past his head.

Candi rushed in to help, but the chain-wielder saw her coming. He pivoted smoothly, driving his elbow into her jaw. Candi cried out in pain, drawing Byrd's attention away from her own attacker.

Seeing Candi stunned and vulnerable, the knife-wielder turned away from Byrd, recognizing the easier target. He lunged toward Candi, knife held high in a balled fist, the blade catching the light from the chandelier above.

Candi saw him coming, her eyes widening with terror. She raised both forearms above her head in a clumsy X-formation. The knife arced down like a blacksmith's hammer, the blade glinting just inches away from her flesh.

In one fluid movement, Byrd stooped down and swept a strewn liquor bottle up off the floor. She hurled it toward the knifeman's head as the blade closed in on Candi's neck. The bottle sailed through the air and crashed into the side of the attacker's head, knocking him to the floor. As the man hit the hard tiles in an unconscious heap, the bottle bounced away and landed, miraculously, still in one piece.

"Someone is looking down on us," Byrd said, eying golden liquid still sloshing around inside the bottle.

Clearly realizing he was now alone, the man with the chain reached out with his dirty hand and got a solid grip on Hutchins' stool. He yanked the stool away and swung it against the wall, where it broke into pieces. Backtracking quickly in panic, the young academic lost his footing and stumbled to the ground.

Candi rushed forward, trying to help, but walked right into the attacker's grip. With ruthless reflexes, the man grabbed her from behind, wrapped the chain around her throat, and pulled it tight.

"Stop, or she dies!" he snarled, his voice deep and accented. "I will kill her, I swear."

Byrd froze, her mind racing through tactical options. The man pulled harder on the chain, baring yellow teeth as he dug the chunky metal links into Candi's flesh. Veins bulged on Candi's forehead, and her neck glowed a deep red, but her eyes remained fierce, defiant.

"Stop your searching!" the assailant shouted, spittle flying. "Everything you seek belongs to *him!*"

Candi clawed at the chain, fingernails breaking as she fought for leverage. Though she couldn't speak, she locked eyes with Byrd. A fire burned in the young woman's eyes, showing that she wasn't even close to giving up.

Candi shifted her weight, dropping slightly to change the pressure points. In the same motion, she stomped backward with her heel, driving it into her captor's shin. The assailant flinched, earning her a slight reduction in pressure on the chain. She then drove an elbow backward, striking him in the chest. The chain loosened just a tiny bit, allowing Candi to gasp a precious breath.

"You little—" the man growled, tightening his grip again.

Byrd shifted her weight to her back foot and was about to charge when she saw Hutchins move. Out of the attacker's eyeline, he stepped toward the whisky bottle. Reaching the bottle, he rolled, and in one swift and slick move, he twisted off the cap, sprang upward, and slung the liquor in the chain-wielder's face. The man growled and covered his eyes.

Candi twisted to one side, then jammed her hands between the metal links and her throat. She dropped her weight, bending her knees and driving her body downward instead of pulling away. The shift in direction threw the attacker off balance; he tried to pull the chain in again, but not quickly enough. She dropped to the floor and rolled away from the assassin.

The chain-wielder roared with anger, wiped his eyes, then charged at Hutchins for another swing.

Byrd saw the attack and moved fast, her eyes locking on a gleaming object displayed on a marble-topped pedestal. She seized a weighty bronze sculpture of the Greek goddess Athena and swung it toward the assailant.

The sculpture sailed across the room and struck the attacker square in the chest, its outstretched spear making first impact. The man let out a pained grunt as he tumbled backward over the glass coffee table. The sound of his head cracking against the travertine tiles rang out like a gunshot, while the bronze goddess rolled to a stop beside him, her eternal expression of serene strength unmarred by violence.

"Rather fitting," Hutchins muttered, taking a cautious step forward. "Athena is the protector of heroes."

"I'll let her know," Byrd said, assessing the chaos while casting her mind to the young woman she knew by the name of Athena. "But right now, you two need to protect yourselves. Get out of here."

"But..." Hutchins started. "Why... what are you?"

"I need to have a conversation with our guests." Byrd snapped. "No arguments. Move!"

"No," Hutchins said, standing up and meeting Byrd's gaze. She looked at the young academic and saw a determination in his eyes that was a million miles from the fear she'd seen back on the island. "We're in this together; we stay together."

Byrd drew a deep breath and considered pulling rank.

"We don't know if they've got friends waiting outside," Candi said, pointing at the window.

Byrd let the breath go in a huff. "Fine, but what's about to happen might get nasty. Don't say you haven't been warned. Hutchins, grab some cables out of the back of the TV and tie that guy up." She pointed at the man who had wielded the knife. "Good and tight now."

"Gotcha," Hutchins said, crossing to the suite's entertainment center and pulling out a few cables from the rear.

"I need to have a conversation with the man in charge." Byrd stalked over to the man who had wielded the chain, now lying on his back in the puddle of single malt.

"How do you know he's the one in charge?" Candi said.

"Call it instinct," Byrd said, kneeling next to the prone figure. His bare chest rose and fell beneath a tattoo of what looked like a serpent coiled around a dagger. "I saw the other guy glancing at him for instructions. Time for a rude awakening."

Byrd crossed to the kitchen and filled a ceramic bowl with scalding water from the dispenser. Steam rose as she tested it with the tip of her finger, wincing slightly at the heat. Candi watched her with a mixture of fascination and horror as she returned to the prone figure, the bowl held steady in her hands.

"Go and help Hutchins tie that guy up," Byrd said to Candi, nodding at the other assailant.

Byrd tilted the bowl carefully, pouring a thin stream of steaming water directly onto the man's face, targeting the bridge of his nose where it would run into his eyes and mouth simultaneously.

The effect was instantaneous. The man's body convulsed as if hit by electricity. His eyes shot open—bloodshot and wild with panic—and his mouth gaped in a primal scream.

He thrashed violently, gurgling as he tried to speak. His hands flew to his face, clawing frantically as if battling invisible flames.

"That was just to wake you up," Byrd said, pressing her knee firmly against his sternum. "The next one will go somewhere much more sensitive." She nodded toward the kitchen.

The man's eyes darted around the room, assessing, calculating his odds. Through gritted teeth, still panting from the shock and pain, he glared up at Byrd, defiance hardening his features.

Byrd smiled back, though she knew the expression had not reached her cold eyes.

"Where's the artifact?" Byrd demanded, pushing down on the man's chest. "From the museum."

The man groaned, his lips moving sluggishly. "What?" His accent thickened deliberately, playing dumb.

"Where is it?" Byrd pressed harder.

The man spat to the side, a mixture of saliva and blood spattering on the tile. "I don't know what you talk about," he said, his voice steadying. "Wrong guy, señorita. I'm just... hired muscles."

Byrd slammed her fist into his stomach, causing him to wheeze and then cough. "You're the one giving orders. I saw it. You *do* know." She leaned closer. "Where is his sanctuary? His hiding place?"

The man's face hardened into an expressionless mask. "Kill me if you want. I'm a dead man if I talk."

With one knee on the tiles to keep her steady, Byrd moved her other foot up toward the man's face, stopping on his windpipe. She pushed down, channeling all of her weight onto his throat. The man's eyes bulged, hands clawing weakly at her ankle.

"Your employers don't have to know," she whispered. "But I guarantee you'll wish for death before I'm done here."

The man's resolve wavered, fear flickering across his face as his oxygen depleted. Byrd eased the pressure slightly—just enough to let him speak but not recover.

"His mansion," the man finally croaked, hatred burning in his eyes. "On the island."

"Which island?" Byrd pushed down again as a reminder that she held all the cards.

The man's face contorted with internal conflict—fear of Byrd warring with fear of his employer. A network of veins bulged at his temples, pulsing visibly beneath his close-cropped hair. He blinked rapidly, his pupils dilating with each labored breath.

"I swear I don't know the name," he gasped, his voice rasping. "He don't tell us nothing. We get texts. Burner phones. Different drivers each time." He coughed, and a thin spray of spittle flecked his stubble. "I know it's near the Cayman Islands. There are many! That's all I know, I swear to God." His right hand twitched toward his chest as if reaching for a crucifix that wasn't there.

A sharp buzz cut through the tense atmosphere. Byrd whipped around, half expecting to see the first attacker back on his feet, knife in hand. Instead, she saw Hutchins' cell phone vibrating across the marble tiles, skittering through the wreckage that used to be the coffee table.

Hutchins rushed across the room and stooped to retrieve

his phone. He thumbed a button, then squinted at the screen.

"It's Wall," he said, looking up at Byrd and then Candi, his expression brightening. "He's awake. We can go and see him now." Relief softened the tight lines around his mouth.

"Lucky, we're done here," Byrd said. She pivoted and delivered a precise kick to the thug's neck. His eyes rolled back, sending him back into oblivion without so much as a grunt. "Let's go. I'm driving."

## 57

**Armação dos Búzios Hospital. Early the next day.**

When Hutchins entered the hospital room and laid eyes on Professor Wall, he drew a sharp breath. The sight of the rake-thin professor, a tiny strip of skin and bones engulfed by the huge bed, sent a shock through Hutchins that started in his feet and traveled upwards until it gripped his throat. Hidden behind a mess of medical equipment, Professor Wall had so many wires and drips attached to him that it was hard to make out his features at all.

Hutchins approached slowly. When he was close enough to finally get a look at Wall's face, he saw the professor looking serene and comfortable with his eyes closed and his cheek resting gently on the pure white pillow. The deep lines that crossed Wall's gray skin seemed many more in number than when Hutchins had last seen his colleague.

So much knowledge rested behind the professor's closed eyes, lying dormant while he was hooked up to his machines. Slowly, Hutchins reached out to touch the professor's wizened hand lying limp on the bed. Then, he stopped in his tracks.

"Lives are at risk," Hutchins said quietly. "I'm so sorry, Wall, but I need your help."

Hutchins felt a hand on each shoulder as Byrd and Candi stepped up behind him.

As Hutchins took another step closer to the bed, the professor's eyes shot open, staring wildly. The machines' beeping increased in intensity.

Then, Wall's gaze softened in recognition. His lips moved into a faint ghost of a smile, and tears formed in his eyes. The professor shuffled, trying to sit up and hug his younger companion.

"Don't move," Hutchins said, gently placing a hand on the older man's shoulder.

"Am I... am I okay?" Wall said, his voice just a croaky whisper.

"You're alive," Hutchins said, grinning broadly. "How do you feel?"

"I feel like I'm on the verge of death," Wall said. "But I've felt like that for twenty years..."

Hutchins let out a loud belly laugh, and the professor managed a small chuckle himself.

"And who are your friends here?" Wall said, his eyes focusing on Byrd and then Candi.

"This is Nor— Sierra Byrd," Hutchins said, "and this is Cand—"

Before Hutchins could finish, the door crashed open, making all three visitors jump. A young nurse with tightly braided hair strode into the room.

Hutchins tensed, preparing to face a reprimand for exceeding the visitor limit. He quickly arranged his features into what he hoped was an apologetic expression, only to be disarmed by the nurse's face breaking into a radiant smile.

"Mr. Steadman!" the nurse said. "We hoped you would open those eyes today. When I heard laughter, I knew it must be a good sign."

Hutchins threw Byrd a glance and a smile, appreciating the false name.

The nurse placed a fresh flask of water on the table beside Wall and checked his vitals. Apparently satisfied, she turned to Hutchins. "No excitement, okay? And no bad news. Promise me?"

"I...erm...prom..." Hutchins stuttered, but the nurse had already turned on her heel and left the room, pulling the door closed behind her.

"Professor," Hutchins said urgently. "What's happening at that compound? Are they still experimenting on people?"

Wall frowned, and then his eyes widened.

"We need to find the plant before Sallas does," Hutchins continued. "We need to expose him as the fraud—"

"You need to expose him as a murderer," the Professor said, a tone of steel returning to his voice. "That man has poisoned countless people. More than thirty, I think."

"Poisoned? With what?" Byrd said, gasping along with the others.

"White snakeroot." Wall paused, then coughed. Hutchins helped him take a sip from the glass of water. "The substance that linium is an antidote to. It was stocked to test linium's authenticity if and when it was found."

"But linium hasn't been found," Hutchins said, replacing the glass. "Which means they're dying?"

"Exactly. They're dying a slow and agonizing death as we speak," Wall said, closing his eyes tightly for a second as if the thought caused him physical pain. "We need to find that plant, kid. Have you made any progress on the canyon? We can pinpoint the exact cave, next to the demon rock, but only if we know what canyon it's in."

Hutchins hung his head. "No, I haven't. In fact—"

"In fact what?" Wall asked, the wrinkles on his brow bunching together.

"I gave away the location of the second piece of parchment under interrogation," Hutchins continued while looking at the floor. Silence filled the room for a few moments, broken only by the beeping medical monitors.

"So," the professor said quietly, "Sallas may have the parchment already?"

"He almost certainly has," Hutchins replied, just as quietly. "He may even know where the Sunstone is."

"He doesn't yet." Byrd's voice cut through the tension. "The parchment is in his mansion on a private island."

"So we have time," Wall said, his bushy white eyebrows raising in the center and giving him an owlish look.

"Yes, but not much," Byrd replied. "Sallas will need a plane and a pilot who can fly that canyon successfully, both of which are not easy to find."

"So, where is the mansion?" Candi asked, turning to Byrd.

"The thug didn't know," Byrd said, leaning against the wall. "But with Sallas being such a public figure, I thought we could find that online."

"Give me two minutes," Candi said, pulling a tablet computer from her backpack. Her fingers flew across the screen as she ran a search. She frowned at the results. "Nothing direct. Every promising link redirects to a 404 error." She tapped again, pulling up cached versions only to find them scrubbed. "Someone's been systematically purging his digital footprint."

"Four-oh-four errors and digital footprints," Wall muttered, shaking his head with a bemused smile. "In my day, we called that 'missing' and 'covering your tracks.' You young people talk like Martians."

"Roger that," Byrd replied.

"Professor, you wrote the book on ancient communication systems. Literally," Hutchins said.

"Precisely my point," Wall replied, levelling a finger at his friend. "Cuneiform tablets and Sumerian pictographs make sense—"

"To you at least," Hutchins said.

"You don't get four-whatever errors with ancient stone tablets," Wall said.

"I'd love to hear your thoughts on blockchain technology sometime," Candi said.

"Merciful heavens, child, haven't I suffered enough?" Wall gestured weakly at his various medical attachments, but his eyes twinkled with humor.

"You're the bravest professor I ever met," Candi said.

"Could we run a deep crawl through the Wayback Machine archives and cross-reference with maritime property registries in the Caribbean?" Hutchins asked.

Byrd rolled her eyes. Wall caught the gesture, and the two exchanged smiles.

"Just stop and listen to an old man for a second," Wall said, raising a finger for silence. "There's no need for your wayback doo dah. I know someone who has the info."

"Who?" Byrd asked, taking a step forward.

Wall cleared his throat, then coughed again. "Lucy Green. Resident of Belle Haven, Virginia," he said, recovering his voice. "Call her, contact her. Get the name of the island."

"See if the family registered their landline with

Whitepages," Byrd said, glancing at Candi. "Or am I better fetching the physical phone book?"

"Got it." Candi read the number out to Byrd, who typed it into her phone, then stepped outside to make the call.

"Professor, do you remember the name Marcello Rodrigo?" Hutchins said, stepping closer.

"Of course. A fine academic."

"It seems he may have been close to finding the Sunstone before he was impeded," Hutchins explained.

"You're right, boy!" Wall said, stroking his beard with his skeletal hand. "I remember him calling me one night, rambling about a cave filled with rubble. He was going to explore it the next day, but he cut the call short. Seemed very edgy. I never heard from him again."

"Might that have been the cave containing the Sunstone?" Hutchins asked.

"Very possibly. In which case…"

Hutchins' lips tightened, and his eyes narrowed. "In which case, the Sunstone is buried behind rubble?"

"It may be," Wall said sadly, his gaze dropping to his wizened hands trembling slightly against the hospital sheet.

Candi stepped forward, moving closer to Hutchins. She slipped her hand around his forearm, fingers wrapping with surprising strength for someone so slender. The contact sent electricity racing through Hutchins' body and gave him the strength to catch the professor's eye in a determined stare.

"There must be a way," Hutchins said. "And we're going to find it."

Sitting up straight in his bed, Professor Wall interlocked his fingers and rested them under his nose. "How much rubble can be in a cave?" he said finally. "It can only have fallen from within."

"Still too much to move with our bare hands, surely!" Hutchins replied.

"Then you need a little help," Wall said.

"A little help from...?

The professor's eyes twinkled. "...from dynamite."

"Okay," Hutchins said, nodding. "If that's what it takes. But you can't just buy dynamite in the supermarket!"

"No. But in certain parts of Mexico, you can buy anything. Don't forget what I always told you, kid." Wall pointed at Hutchins, then Candi. "Prepare for every eventuality. I strongly advise buying weapons while you're there, too."

Hutchins tensed at the thought, then lifted his head and nodded once. "We've come this far. Now we're going to finish this." He felt Candi's hand grip him a little more firmly.

The door swung open with enough force to rattle a nearby vase, and Byrd strode back into the room, phone clutched tight in her hand. "Professor Wall, sir. I have Lucy Green on the line." She lowered her voice, glancing at the hallway. "But she's refusing to speak with anyone but you. Says she won't trust a stranger claiming to work with you."

"Sensible young lady," Wall said.

Byrd crossed to the bed and passed the phone to Wall.

"Lucy?" Wall said, his accent as distinctive as any identification. Suddenly, his eyes welled with tears that spilled down his wrinkled cheeks. "You're safe? That's so wonderful!" His voice cracked with emotion. "Yes, it is me!"

Hutchins exchanged glances with Candi and Byrd, smiling at the color returning to Wall's ashen face. The professor nodded several times, his lips moving silently as he absorbed information. After a few anxious minutes, Wall ended the call. He clutched the phone to his chest for a moment before extending it back to Byrd.

"Well? Did she know?" Hutchins said, inching forward.

"I see this experience has done nothing for your patience," Wall said, glancing up at the younger man.

"Sallas' mansion is on Herd Island," Wall said. "Lucy says it's the only one there, so very easy to find. The vault, however, is a little more challenging."

Candi pulled up a map and quickly found the island.

"When—" he coughed, then corrected himself, "—*if* you get inside the mansion, look for what they call the Great Room." His gaze darted from face to face, making sure they understood the significance. "Portraits of his ancestors guard the vaults. They're the key somehow."

"Portraits guarding vaults? What does that mean?" Byrd said, pulling a small notebook and pen from her pocket and jotting the information down.

"I'm sorry," Wall said, his brief surge of energy already fading. His eyelids drooped despite his efforts to keep them open. "I didn't hear more than that." He reached out, surprising them all by grabbing Byrd's wrist. "Please do everything you can. There are good people being held in that compound." His voice dropped to a hoarse whisper. "And one of them is carrying a baby."

## 58

**Chetumal, Mexico.**

Despite the morning heat, Hutchins shuddered as he led Candi deeper into the gang-controlled area of Chetumal. He pulled Candi in closer to him, steering her away from a bullet-pocked wall where yellow police tape fluttered in the breeze. Three buildings down, the charred skeleton of what had once been a restaurant stood like a missing tooth in a dead man's mouth.

"It's quiet," Candi whispered, her voice barely above a breath. Her fingers dug into Hutchins' forearm, nails leaving half-moon impressions in his clammy skin. No children playing, no radios blaring music, no sounds of cooking or conversation drifting from the buildings. Even the birds seemed to have abandoned this part of town.

"Yeah," Hutchins whispered back. "But I wouldn't say peaceful." He glanced up at one of the low-rise concrete buildings. With metal grates over their entrances, the structures looked like prison cells that stretched on for blocks, rising up a steep incline.

Hutchins pulled them to a stop as something moved in the shadows. They stepped in behind an overflowing dumpster as a lone dog prowled across the streets. The mutt stopped and sniffed at the base of a gang-tag-covered wall. Hutchins looked at the wall, the red and black spray paint depicting skulls with snakes writhing through eye sockets.

"Are you sure this is a good idea?" Candi asked quietly.

"I'm sure it's *not* a good idea," Hutchins replied, swallowing what felt like a fistful of sand. "But what choice do we have? Byrd has to search the mansion, and reaching the island requires a plane. So we're on guns and dynamite."

Candi nodded, leaning into Hutchins as she held onto his arm.

Hutchins took a slow, quiet breath, then led the way further up the hill.

"They call places like this *cinturón de miséria*—belt of misery," he said, gesturing toward the sprawling maze of concrete structures that clung to the hillside like a tumor. Laundry hung from balconies on frayed lines, and satellite dishes—many broken or rusted—sprouted from rooftops. "Most people want to get out of here, but we're heading right in."

"Because this is where the weapons are," Candi said.

"Right. But there's no one on the street to even ask about how black-market transactions go down. It feels like this place has been deserted."

The sound of shuffling drifted from an alleyway on the right.

Hutchins froze and then backstepped. A square-shouldered teenager sprinted across the street. He darted into a building opposite as though evading a threat. A younger boy, maybe twelve years old, followed a second later. He also disappeared into the same one-story building, and the sound of laughter followed.

"Let's follow them," Hutchins whispered, relieved that the boys seemed to be playing a game. He stepped across the cobbles, slipped down an alleyway, and moved to the side of the building. The window had no glass, and Hutchins pinned himself to the wall beside it. Heat radiated from the concrete, and a trickle of sweat ran down his neck.

"Hey, come out. We wanna talk to you," Hutchins called out, surprising himself with the confidence in his tone. Something moved in the shadows, but no one replied. "You boys like money or not?"

The older boy stuck his head around the window frame. He scowled, eying Hutchins like an exhibit in a museum that had suddenly started moving of its own accord.

Hutchins' stomach tightened in fear as he realized how much the boy reminded him of the attackers at the suite.

The boy's gaze shifted to Candi, his frown softening somewhat. The younger boy appeared, grinning and showing brown-yellow teeth. The two boys climbed out of the window and approached.

"I have an offer for you," Hutchins said, beckoning the boys closer. "Do you know anyone who has weapons? We need pistols and explosives."

The two boys looked at each other and smiled, then nodded in unison.

"Do you know anyone around here who *doesn't* have weapons?" Candi asked.

The boys shook their heads.

"Thought so," Candi added.

"Good," Hutchins said. "If you can get us some explosives, fast, we'll pay well. Hand grenades would do, but it would have to be a bunch. Sticks of dynamite, even better."

"Money first," the younger boy said. The other kid nodded.

"Half," Hutchins insisted.

The young kids looked at each other again and then nodded.

Hutchins rummaged in his pocket and removed two hundred dollars. The glint in the younger boy's eyes told Hutchins he was overpaying. The older kid snatched the money from Hutchins' grasp and quickly darted off.

"Have we just made a two-hundred-dollar donation for nothing?" Hutchins said, watching the boys disappear into the shadows.

"Maybe," Candi said. "Let's hope not." They exchanged wary glances, then crouched in the narrow side street, leaning against the cracked wall of an abandoned home. They sat in silence for a few moments, taking deep, quiet breaths to steady their nerves. From somewhere in the distance, the sound of barking dogs carried across the breeze.

"What's the point trying to get weapons to defend ourselves when we're probably gonna be killed by the people selling them to us?" Candi said.

"Good question," Hutchins said, tightening his lips into a wry smile. He glanced to the side, realizing how close he and Candi were. Dirt streaked her face, but her eyes sparkled with healthy radiance. Hutchins' gaze fell down to her lips as they curled into a coy smirk. Already shaky from trying to acquire weapons, Hutchins now had to stop himself from visibly jittering.

Looking into Candi's eyes once again, he held up his index finger and gently moved a strand of hair away from her face, allowing his finger to linger for just a second on her skin. He smelled the sweet scent of her sweat, just like the first time he had met her.

"Can... can I kiss you," Hutchins said, his voice little more than a hiss of air.

Candi remained still and silent. Then, she shook her head slowly.

"It's just not right, Hans," she replied, her brow tightening and her eyes glazing over with sadness. "I'll explain later."

"Okay. But why—"

The patter of footsteps cut him off.

"Mister! I have! I have!" The boys appeared again, rounding the corner at full pelt. The older one held a brown leather backpack.

"Money, money," the older kid said urgently, his eyes darting up and down the side street. Hutchins handed over the rest of the cash and grabbed the bag. "Get out of here," the boy instructed.

"Gladly," Hutchins replied. He flipped the bag open, his fingers trembling as he peeled back a corner of one of the wrapped packages. The kids sprinted out of the alleyway and disappeared again.

"Looks like different parts of weapons and explosives to be put together later," Hutchins whispered, quickly zipping the bag shut. The contents shifted with a metallic clank. "We're gonna need Byrd's help on this one. I don't want to blow myself up trying."

"Let's get out of here. Now," Candi said, scanning their surroundings.

They edged out of the side street, Hutchins clutching the backpack against his chest like it might detonate if jostled. Every window, every doorway now seemed to hold the potential threats of the gang, adding to the anxiety that came from carrying highly illegal items.

They hurried down the hill, their pace quickening until they were nearly jogging, Hutchins gripping the backpack full of explosives to stop it bouncing around. He almost slipped on the uneven surface as sweat dripped into his eyes. Candi moved more gracefully beside him, but her breathing came in shallow gasps that matched his own.

Finally, they approached the edge of the slum, where the buildings began to look less neglected, and the presence of passing cars suggested a return to civilization.

Hutchins grabbed Candi's arm, ready to sprint the final distance to safety, when the crack of a gunshot split the air.

## 59

The sound of the gunshot reverberated between the buildings, amplified by the narrow street. A chunk of concrete exploded from the wall, peppering Hutchins' face with dust. Glancing up at the site of the impact, Hutchins reckoned the shot was probably a warning—and probably the last.

Candi and Hutchins froze, sharing a glance. They turned slowly. Hutchins lowered the backpack, now dangling precariously from his fingertips.

A stocky guy with a black muscle vest over the standard-issue swirling tattoos marched toward them. He held a gun casually, in the manner most people hold their phone. He slowed and then raised the weapon, a smile playing over his lips.

"There will be no more warning shots," Hutchins said quietly. "Get ready to ru—"

"Go!" Candi shouted, spinning around and breaking into a sprint. They charged down the hill, heading for the safety of the main road. Two more shots zipped past, sailing high over their heads.

"Head down!" Hutchins yelled, and Candi hunched down while continuing to sprint, her footsteps slapping against the cobbles.

Another bullet whistled by and punched through a rusted metal sign, the impact ringing like a distorted bell. Hutchins gasped for air, his lungs burning with each breath. Risking a glance back, he saw their pursuer round the corner, the man's bulk slowing him down on the narrow street.

"We're almost there," Hutchins said, "he's falling behind."

Hutchins turned back to face their direction of travel when a huge figure leaped from one of the low-rise buildings. He landed, blocking the lane just a few steps ahead of Candi and Hutchins. His bare chest was covered in the same swirling tattoos. The brute looked at Candi, then locked on Hutchins, zoning in on his target.

"We paid the money," Candi said, her voice wavering. "What do they want?"

"These aren't just gang members," Hutchins said, sliding to a stop. "Look at those tattoos. These men are from the same group as those working for Sallas."

Hutchins took a step backward, then glanced at the man behind them. The man slowed to a casual walk—clearly knowing the game was up for his prey.

Hutchins eyed the buildings on both sides, then returned his gaze to the man in front of them. The brute pulled out a knife, the blade glinting. With a subtle nod to the man behind, the attacker approached.

"We'll have to go up," Hutchins yelled, gripping Candi by the hand. He charged to the side of the street and clambered up onto a cracked window ledge. Reaching up, he clamped a hand around the top of the open shutter, then pulled himself up onto the roof. He lay on his stomach and dragged Candi up behind him as two bullets pinged off the rusted shutter.

"This way," Hutchins said, climbing to his feet and then sprinting across the rooftops. The buildings extended in rows, lining the narrow lanes of the district.

Hutchins led the way across the first roof, his shoes slipping on loose gravel and dust. He reached a low concrete parapet and scrambled up, hauling himself onto the next roof—a few feet higher than the first.

"Come on!" he called back, extending his hand to help Candi up the small ledge.

They sprinted across the second rooftop, weaving around a rusting TV aerial and an air-conditioning unit with its insides missing.

Hutchins stumbled on a pipe. He lurched forward, feet skidding across the gritty surface. He careened toward the edge of the roof, looking down at the drop to the street below. His momentum carried him forward, feet sliding, panic surging.

Candi spun and lunged, grabbing him by the upper arm. Her fingers dug into his bicep and yanked him backward. He found his footing and barreled back across the roof and onto the next building.

"They're coming!" Candi said. The hard clang of metal announced the first man scaling the wall. The man's head appeared above the precipice, followed by the gun.

"There's a gap, get ready to jump," Hutchins said, spotting a small space between the buildings just ahead. Instead of slowing, he grabbed Candi's arm and dug in, accelerating hard. They leapt, sailing through the air.

Hutchins glanced down and saw a dog pacing back and

forth in the gloom of a tiny yard below. The beast looked up and growled, teeth flashing in a foam-slicked snarl.

Hutchins landed on the opposite roof with a grunt. Glancing over his shoulder, he saw Candi strike the edge of the roof and slide slowly down toward the aggressive animal.

Hutchins backstepped and grabbed Candi's wrist. The dog's howls built into a deafening rage as the beast scaled up the wall just beneath Candi's ankles, its claws extended. Gritting his teeth, Hutchins dragged Candi up. He hooked a hand under her armpit and dragged her to her feet.

Two more shots announced that their attackers were closing in. Hutchins turned and saw the attacker sling the weapon away in rage, and the gun bounced off the roof tiles.

"He's out of bullets," Hutchins said, watching the men closing the gap second by second.

"No doubt they can kill with their bare hands," Candi snapped back. "Move!"

They ran across the next roof, ducking under a washing line and then stepping around a rusty water tank.

Candi suddenly skidded to a halt and looked to their left. She glanced over her shoulder, then looked down into a small yard beneath them.

"We can't keep running," she said. Without waiting for Hutchins' reply, she dropped into a crouch.

"But we'll be trapped down there," Hutchins said, looking around nervously.

"Not for long," Candi said, jumping from the roof and landing neatly in the center of the yard. "Come on!"

Hutchins hesitated, then followed her lead. He dropped off the roof, landing with a jarring thud that sent pain shooting up his ankles before he fell onto his shoulder and rolled twice. Dust billowed around him as he scrambled to his feet, blinking through the haze.

The filthy yard enclosed them on all sides. Along one wall, a single faded child's shirt hung from a clothesline. In another corner, mosquitoes buzzed around disused household gear: white goods, a TV with a cracked screen, and an armchair with the lining bursting from it like it had been shot. The scattered aerosol cans had likely been used to crudely graffiti the back wall of the small home, which was a mess of scrawled words.

"Stay here," Candi said, pointing to the ground at her feet.

"What?!" Hutchins said, looking from Candi to where their attackers would appear at any moment. "You know that saying about ducks in a barrel."

Candi stalked up to a door at the rear of a small wooden shed. She tried the handle. When it wouldn't open, she placed her shoulder against it. The weak lock and rotten wood took little more than a strong shove to open.

Footsteps thundered across the rooftop, then the men appeared. Noticing Hutchins, the lead man stopped and raised a hand to get his comrade's attention.

"Where the girl?" the man barked, his eyes doing a full circuit of the yard.

"She ran that way," Hutchins said, pointing further down the building.

The man's eyes narrowed for a beat, calculating his next move. He stepped up to the precipice and jumped down into the yard, landing with surprising grace. He glanced up at his partner and jerked his chin. The other man stepped forward and dropped into the yard behind him.

Hutchins groaned, the men clearly seeing through his ploy to send one of them off down the rooftops.

Hutchins stepped backward until his spine pressed against the wall. Small pieces of debris skittered from under his feet as he pushed back. The attacker advanced, his shoulders rolling with each step, muscles flexing beneath the tattooed patterns Hutchins had grown to hate. The knife in his right hand caught the sunlight, sending a flash of light across Hutchins' face.

"The Mentor no longer has use for you," the man hissed, spraying spittle and the stench of tobacco. "Or her."

"Wait, please—" Hutchins said.

The attacker lunged forward, shoving Hutchins hard against the wall with a forearm across his chest. The painful impact knocked the air from his lungs. Stars danced at the edges of his vision. The brute lifted the blade toward his throat.

Hutchins attempted to raise his hands to slap away the knife, but his arms hung uselessly at his sides, and he understood the meaning of being frozen with fear.

Then, over the brute's shoulder, Hutchins saw Candi step from the doorway. In her hands, she hefted a length of rusted iron rebar. She closed in, raising the bar above her head. She swung, the iron arcing down with all the force she could muster. The bar connected with the side of the knifeman's head. The knife clattered to the dirt, his body crumpling after it a moment later.

The second man stooped and scooped the knife up off the floor as Candi turned and swung at him with the iron bar. The criminal raised his forearm, blocking the blow as he stood up straight. Candi lost her grip, and the rebar went skidding across the yard. The young woman hesitated, and the attacker took his chance, grabbing a fistful of her hair and yanking her head back.

Hutchins stepped forward but suddenly stopped in his

tracks. He looked down and saw a hand around his beltline and the enraged face of the first attacker, blood spilling between bared teeth as he pushed up off the floor on one knee. As Hutchins tried to wrestle free, the man holding Candi raised his blade to her face. The knife touched the skin just beneath Candi's eye. "You have seen too much," the man told her quietly.

Hutchins watched as her right hand felt around the waist area of her attacker, sliding over his denim jeans. "Do it," Hutchins growled. "It's life or death." But instead of sliding around to the front to fight dirty, Candi slipped her hand inside the thug's jeans pocket. When she pulled her hand out again, she held a shiny silver object that looked like a Zippo lighter. She rolled her thumb and flicked her wrist.

The flame stayed on as the lighter glided through the air and across the yard. It landed among the aerosol cans that had been abandoned by some wannabe graffiti artist. A second passed. Then, noise and light filled the air. The explosion sent paint, metal, and plastic into the sky.

With the attackers' attention diverted just for a moment, Hutchins dug a heel into the shin of the man holding him, and Candi dug a knee in somewhere even more painful. The sound of the agonized howl competed with a new explosion. Avoiding the flying shrapnel, Hutchins headed for the gate, picking up his backpack with one hand as he ran. He yanked the gate open, allowing Candi to run through.

They darted out into the street and sprinted, feet pounding as they made for the center of the city. This time, they didn't look back.

## 60

**In the air close to Herd Island, Caribbean Sea.**

"You sober, Bourdell?" Byrd asked, turning to look at her old friend sitting in the co-pilot seat of the Leonard AW609 as they glided at three thousand feet above the Caribbean Sea.

"Actually, I've been off the booze recently," Bourdell said, flicking Byrd a grin as he monitored the GPS.

"Really? For how long?" Byrd replied with a raised eyebrow.

"The whole time I was in the air."

Byrd smiled and shook her head as she smoothly worked the controls, maintaining a course toward Herd Island.

"I can't thank you enough for bringing me a plane down here at short notice," she said, her eyes scanning the horizon for the first visual of their destination while simultaneously monitoring the weather radar showing the approaching storm front.

"Don't mention it," Bourdell replied in his easy Alabama

drawl. "I'll mention it next time I need something from you." The laugh turned into a phlegm-filled cough.

"Damn fine aircraft, too," Byrd said.

"Sure is. This Leonard AW609's a beast—brand new on the market. Compact little tilt rotor can cruise like a fixed-wing but still hover and land like a chopper. Cuts down runway dependence, and you can get in and out of places you've got no business being in."

"A thing of beauty," Byrd said softly.

"Sounds like you're in love," Bourdell replied, smirking.

Byrd grinned. "Wouldn't be the first time I fell for something that could fly. Seeing as I am so smitten with it, maybe you could tell me where you got it."

"Maybe I could," Bourdell replied, staring straight ahead.

"Well, spit it out!"

Bourdell lovingly stroked the dashboard. "Let's just say Florida Keys is a place that attracts a lot of aircraft owners, a lot of drinkers, and a lot of people who enjoy backroom gambling but ain't no good at it. Once the money goes, they start wagering their possessions."

Byrd nodded knowingly. "Okay, you're right," she said. "Maybe I shouldn't have asked. Let's focus on the mission."

She checked the weather radar display, which showed an expanding mass of angry red and yellow blotches creeping toward their position from the southeast. She adjusted the trim controls to compensate for the increasingly gusty crosswinds buffeting the aircraft.

"Yes, the mission," Bourdell said with a rare tone of seriousness. "You really gonna fast-rope down onto that island? You know it's extremely risky even from a tilt rotor."

"No choice. Something bad is going on, Bourdell. Real bad. There's a bunch of kids been poisoned in a weird desert compound north of Cabo San Lucas." She banked the aircraft slightly to port to avoid the leading edge of the weather system. "They're dying. We got a matter of hours to find the antidote."

"I saw that place on satellite imagery when I was tracking that plane you gave me the tail number for. Thought that compound looked pretty out of place when I spotted it." Bourdell stared out at the vast expanse of the Caribbean as if looking for answers. "Is the place heavily guarded?" he asked. "Why not just whip them all out of there?"

"There are more than thirty of them," Byrd explained. "This plane carries ten max, and we certainly don't have nothin' bigger."

"You fixed up your C-47, no?"

"She's not ready for the sky yet," Byrd said, hearing the regret in her own voice.

"*Más desafortunado*," Bourdell replied. *Most unfortunate.*

"And anyway, no one is getting out of that place alive without the antidote. We need a compact aircraft that can get us where we need to go."

Byrd looked out across the waves and saw the outline of the island, the tree line forming a dome. As she eyed her destination, a brooding cloud passed over the sun. Rain started hammering against the windshield, and crosswinds soon buffeted the craft.

"We're approaching," Byrd said.

"So is the storm," Bourdell said ominously, glancing out at the gathering clouds. "You sure this is a good idea?"

"It's almost certainly not a good idea, but as I say, choice is a luxury I don't have." Byrd slipped out of the pilot's seat, and Bourdell took the controls.

"Careful out there," he added.

"Always."

Byrd moved to the center of the plane. She reached for the handle and swung open the AW609's side door—hinged like a helicopter's, and wide enough for fast exits. Warm air tinged with the scent of rain blasted her in the face. She blinked against the gust. The wind snapped at her flight suit as if trying to tug her off balance.

Standing close to the doorway, she adjusted her gear, tightening the straps across her chest, double-checking the clip on her harness, and securing the small earpiece with its in-built microphone.

She took one step forward and looked out as the sky churned with black and gray clouds, like dirt kicked up by heavy machinery. Below, the private island loomed—a tangled sprawl of dense jungle wrapped by a pale slash of beach, the mansion just a dark suggestion behind the treetops. The trees thrashed in the storm, their branches clawing at the air like wild hands trying to slap away intruders descending from above.

"See you on the flip side, Bourdell," Byrd yelled over the crackle of her earpiece.

"I'll be waitin' for ya'," Bourdell replied, pulling back on the throttle to reduce their forward airspeed while simultaneously adjusting the nacelle tilt angle. The twin proprotors—massive three-bladed propellers mounted on wingtip nacelles—pivoted from their forward-facing position to point skyward.

"Holding steady," Bourdell said, his voice coming through the comms system.

"You call this steady?" Byrd replied as the aircraft pitched and yawed. Rain hammered in through the open door like gravel from a tire skid.

"It's the best I can do; now get outta here," Bourdell replied.

Lightning flashed nearby, momentarily illuminating the roiling sea below and the dark mass of the island.

Byrd gripped the rope tightly, secured her harness, and swung out into the void. She descended quickly, her legs braced and her gloved hands controlling her speed in smooth movements. Fast-roping wasn't new to her—years of training made it second nature—but the whipping wind added extra danger.

Heavy gusts battered her, pushing her from side to side. The sound of the angering ocean, the tilt rotor's blades, and the swirling wind roared in her ears.

"Methodical, rhythmical, foot by foot," she said to herself. One step and one slide after the next, she steadily made progress toward the thick foliage.

The wind surged again, and a violent gust caught Byrd mid-descent like a falling leaf. The sudden shift sent her swinging wildly, the momentum of the plane dragging her sideways. Her grip burned against the rope as she struggled to regain control, but the force of the gale had her now, tossing her around at will.

She slipped down the rope faster than planned, the trees now looming beneath her feet. Trying to regain composure, she plunged into the jungle, and sharp branches immediately dug into her skin.

Through the rain-slicked darkness, she caught a glimpse of something below—thick, gnarled bark rushing toward her. Byrd twisted her body midair, tucking her chin down and bringing her legs up. Her boots struck the trunk hard, sending a shock through her knees, but she'd managed to avoid a skull-cracking impact. She absorbed the force, pushing off with every ounce of strength she had. The kick sent her spinning, and she braced for impact from any other tree around her. Tightening all of her muscles, she brought the spin to a halt.

Breath steady, mind focused, she recentered herself, gripping tighter and slowing her descent in increments as the scent of wet leaves and other vegetation filled her nostrils. Her heart slammed against her ribs, but she kept her movements controlled and methodical. Once again, she ran one hand and then the other over the smooth ridges of the sturdy rope.

Finally, her boots hit the jungle floor with a muffled thud. She crouched low, unclipping her harness and pulling the rope free.

"Touchdown confirmed," Byrd said through the comms, glancing up at the AW609.

"Copy that," Bourdell replied. The engines shifted pitch as he increased power, the whine climbing to a higher register.

Byrd watched the aircraft bank away, circling the island. For a moment, the craft's dark silhouette was visible against the stormy sky, then it disappeared into the clouds, leaving her alone with the jungle and the distant lights of Sallas' mansion.

Byrd turned and threaded her way toward the imposing building. The dense jungle was dark as night in the storm, and the thick underbrush clung to her boots as she moved, low and silent.

A bolt of lightning seared the sky, illuminating the looming mansion. Byrd took in all she could in the brief flash—the colonial façade, the stucco walls streaked with moss, and the wide, arched windows. Just one room in that place looked to be bigger than the entire floor space of some of the apartments Byrd had occupied in her time.

Emerging from the jungle and scanning left and right, she darted to the perimeter fence. Taking sharp, silent breaths, she skirted the chain-link fence. She reached the edge of the tree line and froze. Ahead lay the main gate, guarded by a solitary man pacing from side to side.

His figure was dark against the glow of an overhead light, and the rifle slung across his back gleamed in the rain. Pulling a small pair of binoculars from her pocket, Byrd scanned her surroundings quickly, spotting a glasshouse nestled along the edge of the jungle—a separate structure with faintly glowing lights inside. An orangery, she realized.

Byrd eyed the ground for a rock of the right size, then picked up a smooth, wet stone around the size of a baseball. She quickly took aim, then threw. The rock sailed through the misty air and struck the glass with a shocking crash, shattering a pane into thousands of shards. The guard's head snapped toward the direction of the noise, and he took off to investigate.

Byrd dashed forward. She got a toe onto the bottom rung of the wrought-iron gate and pushed up, using curves in the ornate iron as footholds. She threw her leg over the top of the gate and dropped down on the other side, landing in a crouch. The heavy rain and darkness from the storm gave her cover as she darted across the lawn. She reached the building and pressed herself against the side of the mansion. She took a deep breath as she prepared to plunge right into the heart of Sallas' private life.

## 61

Byrd moved fast, skirting the nearest side of the mansion, her boots sinking slightly into the rain-softened ground. She darted between several sculpted bushes, keeping to the shadows as much as possible. Floodlights cast their beams across the lawns, illuminating the rain that fell in sheets. Tucking in close to the wall, Byrd slipped around the back of the grand house. The storm made such a racket that she didn't need to worry about her sound, only keeping out of sight. Reaching the rear of the building, she peered around the corner.

The back side of the estate was less manicured than the front, with dirt-streaked stone and moss creeping up the walls. Only two floodlights illuminated the ground here, their effectiveness reduced by the rain. She crept across to a small door at the side of the house and knelt close to a cluster of cigarette butts lying in a soggy heap.

"Must be the servants' entrance," Byrd said quietly to herself, turning her attention to the door.

She pressed on, checking each window as she passed, but found nothing open. She reached the next corner and peered around. The mansion's perimeter appeared sealed tight—every window latched from within, heavy wooden shutters drawn against the storm.

She stepped in close to a window that was almost obscured by vines. Switching on her tiny penlight, she checked the glass for alarm systems. Nearly invisible in the darkness, she saw thin copper wire embedded in the window frames, running to small magnetic contact points on the frame and the glass.

"Standard model," she whispered, reaching inside her jacket and pulling out a compact electronics kit. "Give me a challenge, please."

Using a narrow glass cutter, she scored a perfect circle near the window's edge. As the cutter completed its work, she applied gentle suction to the glass disk and carefully removed it. She reached through the hole and placed a probe across one of the magnetic sensors, then flipped up the handle. Pulling open the window, she paused, listening for an alarm.

Confident no one was coming her way, Byrd hoisted herself and dropped silently to a crouch inside the grand home. She scanned and saw that she had dropped into what looked like a dining room. A bulky wooden table sat in the center of the room, and portraits lined the walls.

Byrd pulled the window closed, leaving only the small circular hole and wet footprints as evidence she'd ever been there.

She took ten seconds to slow her breathing, then padded to the door and let herself through. The corridor, which looked as though it ran through the entire building, was silent and deserted. Small lights mounted on the walls cast the scene in a dull red glow—fortunately, just enough to see by.

Chandeliers hung from high ceilings, gilded mirrors lined walls decorated with intricate floral patterns, and the faint scent of aged wood and wax lingered in the air. It felt like stepping into a European palace complete with the musty scent of passing centuries.

Byrd pushed on, heading toward the heart of the building. If the Great Room existed, that's where it would be. She paused at every corner, ears straining for the sound of footsteps. Carefully, she peered around and saw a set of velvet-upholstered double doors, much larger than the others.

As though advertising the importance of what lay beyond, a guard stood watch outside the double doors. He was young and slim, with a holstered weapon at his hip. The guard paced restlessly back and forth, his movements a mixture of boredom and anxiety.

Byrd watched the man, timing her move. The moment he turned away, she sprang from her hiding place. Three silent strides closed the distance between them. In one motion, she extracted the pistol from his holster while clamping the other hand over his mouth. The guard's body went rigid with shock, his startled cry nothing more than a muffled vibration against her palm.

"Open the door," Byrd growled, pressing the gun's muzzle to his temple. "And don't even think about turning around."

The guard did as he was told, and Byrd pushed him inside. She took a moment to assess the room. Priceless ceramics in glass cases glowed under spotlights. Enormous portraits of ancestors dominated the walls, their solemn faces illuminated by the warm glow of wall sconces.

"I'm not here for the full tour, just show me the vault," Byrd said.

The guard went to turn his head, and Byrd whipped him with the pistol, opening a gash on his cheek.

"I told you not to turn around," she said, moving in close and regaining control. "If you want to see your loved ones again, show me the vault."

The guard stood stationary, clearly weighing up the risk of Byrd's threats and Sallas' wrath. Sweat beaded on his forehead despite the air-conditioned chill of the Great Room. Almost imperceptibly, the young man's gaze shifted toward a particularly large portrait hanging on the far wall. The painting depicted an elderly man with a long handlebar mustache and a complexion so sallow that it reminded Byrd of the time Bourdell attempted to make Alabama white barbecue sauce from scratch. The congealed mixture of mayonnaise, vinegar, and horseradish turned the color of a three-day-old bruise.

"It's behind old fungus face there, yes?" Byrd said. "Nod once now, and you can tell Sallas that I already knew."

The guard nodded, squeezing his eyes closed as he did it.

"Good boy. Now we're onto level two... tell me the code."

"I don't... know code," the guard said. "I swear—"

Byrd twisted his arm behind his back, eliciting a sharp cry. "Code. Now."

"I don't know, miss!" the guard squealed. "Please! I open the door for you, but code I don't know!"

"Okay, quiet!" Byrd hissed. Her eyes darted around the room. Looking up, she spotted a mounted camera facing the portrait.

"Where does the feed for that camera go?"

The guard gestured toward a side door.

Byrd dragged him toward it, finding a small guard room with monitors showing various angles of the mansion. She forced him into the chair and spat, "Find me footage of someone opening that vault."

The guard fumbled with the controls, rewinding through hours of sped-up footage. Finally, he found a grainy clip of a toned young man with long hair swinging open the portrait and entering a code.

"Sallas," Byrd said under her breath.

Her sharp eyes caught the sequence of numbers just before the vault opened.

"Rewind that," Byrd said, pointing at the screen. "Zoom in and play in slow motion."

The guard did what he was told, zooming in on the keypad.

Byrd picked out the numbers one by one as they were pressed.

"Perfect," she said, grabbing the guard by the collar and dragging him back out to the Great Room. She swung the portrait from the wall, revealing the vault hidden behind it. Punching in the code, she stepped back as the small door swung open.

The open door revealed not just a safe, but an entire walk-in vault concealed behind the wall. Byrd shoved the guard inside and then stepped in behind him. Motion-activated lights flickered on, illuminating a climate-controlled room roughly the size of a small bedroom.

"You greedy—" Byrd said, not finishing the sentence, as what she saw literally took her breath away.

On the wall directly facing her hung an unmistakable masterpiece—Rembrandt's *The Storm on the Sea of Galilee,* the artist's only seascape, stolen from the Isabella Stewart Gardner Museum in 1990 and never recovered. Until now. The painting's dramatic contrast between light and dark seemed almost alive in the vault's carefully calibrated lighting.

Adjacent to it hung Raphael's *Portrait of a Young Man*, looted by the Nazis during World War II from Poland and considered one of the most valuable paintings ever to vanish. The elegant Renaissance masterpiece, widely believed to be Raphael's self-portrait, had been missing since 1945 when it disappeared from a castle in Kraków.

Byrd shook her head and turned away from the stolen treasures worth hundreds of millions. Right now, she couldn't afford distractions, although she knew her friend Eden Black would love to know about this find.

"Get in the corner," she said to the guard. "Hands on your head, fingers locked."

When the guard was positioned where Byrd could still see him in her peripheral vision, she crossed to the drawers and started searching. Starting with the top row, she slid each drawer open and flicked through the contents. The first section contained various documents—property deeds, offshore account information, blackmail material that would have ruined countless powerful people.

The middle section contained jewels arranged on black velvet trays—diamonds, rubies, and emeralds. Beneath that, a row of gold bars stacked on a shelf, each stamped with a serial number and a symbol Byrd recognized—a triangle with an eye in the center. She snapped a photograph with her phone and then moved on. The next shelf contained neatly bundled stacks of currencies from around the world —euros, pesos, yen, and dollars.

"Where is it?" she whispered, frustration mounting. Maybe this really was a wild goose chase.

She eyed the final compartment, right at the bottom of the safe. After a deep breath, she pulled open the drawer.

Inside this final compartment lay the most valuable items in Sallas' collection—artifacts that predated modern wealth. A small golden idol with jeweled eyes sat beside a dagger with a wavy blade and inscriptions on the hilt. And there, nestled in a custom-fitted foam cutout, was what she had come for—a piece of parchment, its edges yellowed and crumbling with age. The faded ink showed symbols that matched Hutchins' description exactly.

"Gotcha," Byrd murmured, carefully lifting the ancient document and securing it in her waterproof inner pocket.

She stood, her gaze returning to the Rembrandt. For a brief moment, she considered the possibility of recovering both—but the painting was too large, too fragile to transport in the storm.

"Another time," she promised silently, slipping back toward the vault door.

"Not a word to anyone," she said to the guard, then slammed the door, sealing him inside.

## 62

Byrd moved swiftly back through the mansion and out the way she'd arrived. She dropped through the window and paced back to the gate. She peered through the gate and noticed the guard had returned. Speed now beating stealth, she scrambled up the gate and threw her legs across the top. She waited for the guard to pass directly beneath her position and then jumped, swinging the gun she'd relieved from the other man. The barrel cracked down on the back of the guard's head, sending him to the floor.

"En route to exfil," Byrd shouted, tapping the mic in her ear. "ETA, five minutes."

"Roger that," came Bourdell's reply, his voice as smooth as a late-night radio host. "Don't hang about. The weather really ain't playing nice."

"Tell me about it," Byrd said, sliding back into the jungle.

Sheets of rain slashed through the canopy like shrapnel, turning the forest floor into a treacherous network of muddy sinkholes and concealed roots. Lightning cracked overhead in jagged forks, momentarily casting the dense vegetation in harsh relief before plunging everything back into a darkness that made daytime seem like midnight.

Byrd pushed on, weaving her way through the jungle, placing each boot carefully to avoid the sinkholes and roots that seemed to span the entire forest floor. She ducked under a low-hanging branch and then slipped into a small clearing. Another fork of lightning seared across the sky, momentarily illuminating her surroundings.

In the flash, she saw something that had no place in the forest. The man stood as though waiting for her to come to him. Tall and broad-shouldered, he wore a white linen shirt now plastered to his chest by the rain, hinting at a toned frame beneath. His long, dark hair was slick with moisture. After seeing the CCTV footage in the mansion, she knew this had to be Sallas.

"Sierra Byrd. The thorn in my side," Sallas said, cradling his shotgun with the loving grip of a new father. Rain streamed across his face, catching in his dark stubble and dripping from his chin. "I gave you the opportunity to sell up and move on, to get out while you had the chance—"

"I don't do business with psychopaths," Byrd replied, taking a tiny backstep and assessing her options. She held her weapon down by her hip, but avoided provoking him by raising it. His rifle was closer to firing position than her gun was.

Sallas tilted his head back to the sky and barked out a laugh.

A new sound emerged through the cacophony of the storm—faint at first, then increasingly distinct. The rhythmic thrum-thrum-thrum of propeller blades slicing through moisture-filled air.

"I would have paid you well. You could have set up your

little flight school somewhere... anywhere else and lived a peaceful life," Sallas continued.

"Maybe you didn't hear me," Byrd said, shouting over the storm. "I don't do business with—"

"Oh, I heard you," Sallas interrupted. "But you misunderstand me. It's the system that is psychopathic. The globalists, with their cliques and clubs. Ugly little men who think they're smart but only get a second glance from a woman once they're rich. The future, and the people in it, will be beautiful."

He stood with his feet wide apart and his shoulders back as rain washed over him like a cleansing from the gods.

"Now that I see you, Sierra Byrd, I can see that you are beautiful yourself. But, sadly, you will not be part of the future." He pumped the shotgun's action, the mechanical noise cutting through the forest. His form was perfect—elbows tucked, stance balanced, ready to shoot.

Another bolt of lightning split the sky, giving Byrd the view of two more armed men standing either side of Sallas. They took a step forward, silent as shadows. Their tactical gear marked them as professionals, not cheap hired muscle from among Mexico's gangs.

Clearly noticing Byrd's realization that the odds were stacked against her, Sallas grinned.

"She's got something that belongs to me." Sallas nodded toward Byrd. "Find it and then kill her. The parchment must not be damaged."

"Looks like you've got some company down there," Bourdell's voice came through the comms system. His cheerful tone sounded strangely at odds with the deadly situation. The tilt rotor's sound intensified overhead. "Tap once, and I'll send in the welcoming committee."

Byrd reached for her ear and tapped the comms system once, sending the signal to Bourdell.

"Copy that. Fire in the hole," Bourdell replied, his tone shifting from cheerful to focused in an instant.

The boom of rocket fire erupted from the mist overhead, the staccato thunder drowning out even the storm for several deafening seconds.

Tracer rounds sliced through the rain in burning orange streaks, striking a tree at the edge of the clearing. Wood splintered and sparked as the projectiles tore into the trunk. On impact, several rounds ignited, designed specifically for creating incendiary diversions rather than casualties.

The tree burst into flames. Despite the downpour, the sudden inferno cast the entire clearing in a hellish orange glow, throwing wild shadows across the jungle floor.

"I see you fitted a few little additions to your aircraft, Bourdell," Byrd said quietly as her sharp eyes scanned the unfolding scene.

Amid flames and smoke, Sallas and his men leapt for cover. The men cowered behind a fallen tree trunk, and Sallas darted into the forest, light on his feet.

Taking the chance, Byrd jumped backward and rolled behind a fallen log. After assessing her route, she scrambled to her feet and sprinted, moving perpendicular to the burning tree. The jungle closed around her as she ran, her boots finding purchase on the slick ground through muscle memory and training.

"Target moving northeast!" one of the men shouted, evidently already on their feet and giving chase.

Byrd zigzagged through the dense undergrowth. She ducked under hanging vines, leaped over exposed roots, and pushed through wall after wall of dripping vegetation.

"I've got you on thermal," Bourdell's voice came through

her earpiece. "Extraction point Charlie is three hundred meters ahead. You've got a one-minute lead on your new friends."

Behind her, gunshots rang out. Bullets splintered bark, shredded leaves, and thwacked sodden soil with dull thuds. She pushed through a bush, vines whipping against her face, and ran out onto a rocky outcrop. She took another few paces and then slid to a stop. In the darkness beneath her, the frothing sea lashed the base of a cliff.

"Your directions are out!" Byrd shouted into the comms, her voice fighting against the storm's fury. "I can't go—"

She stopped talking as she recognized a dark shape moving around beneath her. The Leonardo rose through the darkness like a great metal falcon, its silhouette materializing against the churning sea. Rain streamed from its hull in silver ribbons, illuminated by the aircraft's running lights. The craft pulled level with the clifftop, allowing Byrd to see Bourdell directly through the windshield.

Bourdell flicked a salute, deftly swung the craft ninety degrees, then drifted toward the cliff edge.

"Your ride, madam," Bourdell said, humor now lacing his voice.

The aircraft hovered just feet from the rocky ledge, stabilizing despite gusts that would have sent lesser machines spinning away.

Byrd tensed her muscles, gauging the narrow gap between cliff and cabin door. Three feet of empty space separated her from safety—three feet of nothing but a perilous drop beneath.

The crack of a rifle shot pierced the air, distinct even above the storm and rotors. The bullet struck the aircraft's side with a metallic ping, punching right through the fuselage. A second round followed immediately, then a third.

"I hate to rush you, but we really should go," Bourdell said, his voice hardening.

The Leonardo wavered, battling another crosswind.

Byrd took three steps back and then sprinted for the aircraft. She covered the distance to the clifftop in two huge paces and leaped. For a heart-stopping moment, she was suspended in empty space, nothing below her but a stormy abyss and the distant crash of waves against rocks. Her hands reached out, fingers splayed, straining for the edge of the doorway.

Shots ricocheted off the cliff face, sending stone fragments flying. Another struck the doorframe with a shower of sparks.

Byrd's outstretched fingers caught the edge of the doorway, her momentum carrying her forward. For an instant, her lower body dangled precariously over the drop. She pulled up, dragging herself inside, and tumbled onto the metal deck.

More bullets pinged against the fuselage, some piercing, others bouncing off.

"Secure," Byrd said, grabbing hold of a rail.

Bourdell wasted no time, banking hard to starboard and dipping the nose in a combat evasion pattern. G-forces pressed Byrd against the cabin wall as the aircraft dropped like a stone, then railed out and across the sea.

Byrd secured herself in one of the jump seats, chest heaving as she caught her breath. Her soaked clothing left puddles on the metal floor.

"Well, that looked like fun," Bourdell said, glancing over his shoulder.

"I'm glad you were entertained," Byrd replied. She sat up, looking out of the window as the island disappeared into the distance. "Something tells me that isn't the last we'll see of that slimy b—."

"Save your energy, Byrd," Bourdell said. "Anger is a waste of it."

"Yeah? Then I'm amazed I have the energy to wake up every day."

# 63

**Sumero Canyon.**

Now that the morning storm had passed, the afternoon brought a clear view of the Sumero Canyon stretching wide, its terrain seemingly untouched from an aerial viewpoint. The place had a primeval feel, as if winged monsters could sweep across the open space in the radiant light. Brown-green vegetation clung on in parts, and in others, reddish rock was laid bare.

"These valleys, mountains," Bourdell said, seated beside Byrd in the cockpit as she guided the plane through clear blue skies and down toward the fabled canyon. "Reminds me a little of Afgh—"

Byrd turned her head sharply to look at him, cutting him off. "Plenty of places look like this, Bourdell. No need to take your mind back there."

Sierra Byrd pulled the mic on her headset closer to her mouth. "Hans, Candi, you all good back there? Thanks to you, we have everything we need—weapons, dynamite, and a big dose of geeky knowledge rattling around in Hutchins' brain."

"Yes, ma'am!" they replied in unison.

"What plane are we in here, Byrd?" Hutchins asked through his headset.

"A Pilatus PC-24. My good friend Bourdell here procured it for me."

"Seeing as my Leonardo now has bullet holes in it, I'm glad I had a friend fly a backup plane down here for me," Bourdell mumbled, seemingly distracted in the co-pilot's seat as he ran his finger over details of the flight deck, landing on the Synthetic Vision System that presented a 3D display of surrounding terrain.

"This plane's aerial dexterity is unparalleled," Byrd said.

"And in English that means?" Candi asked.

"Unlike a chopper, it can cover long distances," Byrd explained, "and it can land and take off on just a flattish strip of grass or gravel, which may be all we get."

"This Pilatus PC-24 is one of my all-time favorites," Bourdell said, tapping his foot restlessly. "Pretty small; I'm surprised we fitted your bouffant in it, Byrd. But a wonderful plane, nonetheless."

"The Royal Flying Doctor Service of Australia uses them," Byrd continued, "due to their ability to land on tiny, unpaved runways. Or, in our case, no runway at all." She then turned to Bourdell and asked, "Any tips for flying in a canyon, buddy?"

"Huh?" came the distracted reply. Bourdell looked to be deep in thought again.

"Bourdell, you sure you're okay?" Byrd once again noticed the slight trembling in her old friend's hand as he rested it on the dashboard.

"Yeah, 'course," Bourdell said. "But you got decades of experience too, Byrd. Tell me about canyon flying."

"Sure will. Flying in the center of a canyon should be avoided," Byrd started. "Turbulence is created when air flows down the lee side and up the windward, and shear can cause abrupt changes to headwind or tailwind. Additionally, flying to one side allows more room for the plane to turn widely if needed. The steeper side is preferable to choose as it provides more orographic lift, which is created when air flows from a low elevation to a higher elevation."

"You're a genius, Byrd," Hutchins gushed. "I have faith in you."

"Maybe you're the genius, Hans," she replied. "To make sense of that parchment I gave you and pinpoint this canyon in Chiapas. But let's not waste time on compliments. Keep your eyes open and look out the window. If it's where you say it is, the demon rock may be getting close."

"It must be," Hutchins replied. "I just hope I can recognize—"

"—wait!" Candi interrupted. "There!"

"Certainly looks like a demon to me!" Byrd confirmed, looking across the canyon at a vast vertical rock face with crags and curves that presented a demonic appearance. Tufts of vegetation springing from the rock even looked like hairy horns. "It's a devil of a landing too," Byrd added. "That may be a touch of flat ground there to the right of it, but the turbulence is—"

On cue, the plane dropped suddenly, causing gasps from everyone except Byrd. It jolted left then right as if being tossed around by the demon itself.

"Brace for impact," Byrd commanded. "Just like you're shown on a commercial airline. I can't guarantee a good landing."

Byrd locked her gaze on the landing patch, but the plane did not feel like it was under control, dipping, rising, and tilting in the thermals.

"Abandon if you're unsure, even at the last second," Bourdell said. "Don't risk it."

And the last second was close.

With her knuckles white on the controls, Byrd narrowed her eyes and made her way in. The plane sped toward the landing site, its wings tilted at an awkward, potentially catastrophic angle.

"Straighten up," Bourdell demanded, agitation clear in his voice as he leaned forward. "Our wing could be torn right off."

Suddenly, the aircraft leveled out straight but was way too high to touch down, lifted by the force of the wind against the sides of the canyon: ridge lift. Byrd looked at the altimeter as it struggled to even find a reading, the plane bobbing in the air.

"Trust me on this, Bourdell," Byrd said, laser-focused as she extended both arms out stiff to hold the controls. "I've flown in currents like this before—dealt with ridge lift."

"Trying to read thermals is madness," Bourdell replied, turning to look at his old friend. "We're heading straight into a collision, and you're depending on natural lift to set the nose straight."

"You're a lifelong gambler, Bourdell. This is called rolling the dice."

Byrd aimed for the rock face below the landing area, seeing every nook and sharp edge on the jagged surface of the canyon side.

"Byrd, are you really sure?!" Candi shouted from the cabin.

"Trust her!" Hutchins shouted back.

The landscape became a blur of green and brown as the tip of the nose arrowed toward the rock. Out of the corner of her eye, Byrd saw Bourdell grip the bottom of his seat with both hands, looking more anxious than she had ever seen him. "Coming in hot!" he yelled.

The plane edged closer to solid stone. Blue sky disappeared from view, and only the rock face lay ahead, looming large and dangerous. Byrd rolled in just a touch of left rudder and applied forward pressure on the yoke to partially counter the ballooning effect of the updraft she was desperately hoping for. She kept her airspeed slightly above stall, using the rudder to stay aligned with the rocky slope.

"Flying the ridge, don't fight it," she said under her breath.

Then came the uplift, like the hand of God lifting the plane. More gasps filled Byrd's ears through the comms, including one from Bourdell.

Suddenly clear in the air, she saw the landing ground right beneath her. With steady hands, she guided the aircraft in and smoothly touched down.

A moment of stunned silence followed, then, "You did it, Byrd!" Hutchins said.

"I honestly don't know if it was me or not," Byrd replied. "I think I have some praying to catch up on."

"Well, we're alive, and we need to move," Hutchins said. "Lives are depending on us."

"Right," Byrd said, unbuckling herself and snatching three flashlights from their hooks. "Let's move."

Heat came in heavy, breezy bursts as Byrd, Hutchins, and Candi stepped down from the plane, and Byrd turned to Bourdell before he closed the door. "Prepare her for a quick takeoff, buddy," she said. "And whatever happens, stay inside the cockpit, ready to go. We may need to move at short notice. There's no one I'd rather be counting on than you."

Byrd flipped open the leather backpack and pulled out three compact pistols—sleek black Beretta 84s. She handed one to Hutchins, another to Candi, and kept the last for herself.

"Remember what I told you," she said quietly, locking eyes with each of them in turn. "Finger off the trigger until you're ready to fire. Always. You get jumpy, someone gets dead."

Hutchins and Candi looked at each other nervously.

"Either of you have experience with weapons?" Byrd asked as she hooked the Beretta inside her belt.

"What do you think?" Hutchins asked, looking down at the gun as it lay flat on his sweaty palm.

"I got some," Candi said confidently. "My dad built us a shooting range in the yard when we were kids. Neighbor didn't have much of a greenhouse left."

Byrd smiled, clipped the bag closed, and slung the worn leather backpack filled with dynamite over her shoulder.

Candi stepped forward and gently touched Byrd's arm. "Seeing as Hans found this place and you saved our lives, the least I can do is a little heavy lifting." She took the pack before Byrd could argue and settled it onto her back.

"Careful with that," Byrd said. "You slip and fall, we'll be scraping you off a cloud!"

They plunged into the long grass as insects immediately feasted on their sweat. Kicking aside dense vegetation, Byrd led her team toward the entrance of the cave beside the demon rock. A sheer drop lay just to her left, so deep that the bottom of the canyon remained obscured by heat haze. She kept her eyes fixed firmly on her path to avoid anything that might trip her up, turning just occasionally to check that her companions were okay. The calls of exotic birds rang out from somewhere in the distance, echoing around the canyon like warning sirens.

As the cave loomed like a hollow eye in the rock face, Hutchins stopped dead in his tracks. "Look," he said, pointing at long cracks in the rock around the entrance. "Earthquake damage. This really is the place, Byrd! We're really here!"

# 64

Byrd turned to look at Hutchins' happy countenance, wondering if delight was the right emotion right now. Candi interlocked arms with Hutchins and encouraged him to keep moving instead of simply staring in wonder.

They stepped up to the mouth of the cave. Moisture filled the air, and somewhere inside, water dripped against stone. Byrd shot the others a steely glance and then led the way inside.

"These cheap flashlights aren't really up to the job," Byrd said, her eyes following the beam up to the bubbled shapes of the cavern roof. "Just like our footwear and clothing aren't really made for caving, but we didn't have much time for shopping."

"Too busy buying dynamite to buy outdoor gear," Hutchins joked, his voice echoing in the cavern. As the party fell silent, the sound of water thumped onto limestone somewhere nearby, falling rhythmically like the ticking of a clock.

Byrd raised her flashlight and was greeted by the sight of stalactites, almost pure white, spread over a wide area in an intricate pattern. They appeared like a chandelier the greatest Schonbek masters could not craft. A natural work of art reflected in the perfectly clear pool that stretched on through the cave.

Averting her eyes to keep them focused on the path ahead, Byrd asked in a whisper, "So, what are we looking for first?"

"A dead end," Hutchins replied, his low voice echoing eerily off the limestone.

"Okay. Why, exactly?" Byrd asked.

"A small landslide, caused by an earthquake, brought rubble down and blocked the path—that's what Rodrigo told Wall. And that's what we're trying to blast through."

"Got it. And are you a demolitions expert, Hutchins?" Byrd's sarcasm carried in the echoes.

"I think you know the answer to that," Hutchins replied.

"I think I do. And demolitions ain't my area of expertise either. So, how do you know your explosion won't cause another landslide that buries us along with our hopes and dreams?"

Hutchins tilted his head to one side. "Because that's what Wall told me to do..." he said with a quiet lack of confidence.

Candi stepped across the moisture-slicked, stony ground and moved in close next to Hutchins. Stretching her legs slightly to reach his height, she planted a soft kiss on his cheek, letting it linger.

"That's for luck, Hans," the young blonde said. "I believe in you."

Hutchins straightened up, lifting his head and pushing his shoulders back. He set off, leading the way into the cave.

Byrd and Candi shared a grin.

The team pushed on deeper into the cavern, sweat dripping from their noses like moisture from the tips of stalactites. The walls closed in, turning this section of the cave into a passage with uneven ground and an abundance of shadows.

Candi suddenly gasped, and Byrd quickly turned to see the young woman lose her balance, her right foot slipping out from under her. Candi tipped backward, the bag filled with dynamite now falling toward hard stone. Byrd and Hutchins reached out and grabbed her at the same time, gripping an arm each just before Candi clattered to the ground.

Byrd looked at the leather backpack, then at Candi. Sierra Byrd reached out to take the backpack and then retracted her hand, deciding it would be bad for morale to relieve Candi of her duty.

"Be very careful," Byrd said, her tone carrying a warning. "An injury down here is a disaster. And I'm sure I don't need to warn you about unplanned explosions. Think about each step."

Candi nodded, and they made their way slowly down the natural passage, cutting deeper into the earth. Byrd felt a chill on her skin as the temperature dropped, and moisture in the air increased. She raised her flashlight again, then stopped in her tracks.

"Hutchins," she hissed in a whisper, grabbing the young man's forearm. "Surely that's it?"

Byrd swept her light beam from side to side, the glow washing across what appeared to be a wall of rubble towering slightly higher than head height.

"It must be," Hutchins agreed, brushing a curtain of floppy hair out of his eyes as he peered for a better look. Then, his eyes widened. "If Rodrigo was right about the landslide, he must have been right about the—"

Byrd squeezed his arm tighter. "You're almost there, Hans. Everything you have worked for. Now, let's make sure we get that dynamite right."

"Do you think we have enough to break through it?" Hutchins asked.

"It might be small as landslides go," Byrd said, swishing her light beam up and down, "but it looks pretty damn heavy."

Hutchins walked up and touched a few of the rocks as though he were a seasoned structural expert. He then looked at Byrd, offering no comment.

"Would you like me to place the charges for you?" Byrd asked, hands on hips. "Candi, pass me the backpack," she said with a sigh.

"No, wait. I can do it," Hutchins said, stepping toward Candi to take the backpack. "But any tips are welcome."

"Keep it shallow and spaced," Byrd told him. "You're trying to break the wall, not suffocate the blast. And when you light that last fuse, don't watch it like a firework. Get your ass back behind cover."

"I'm guessing we should *all* stand back," Candi said, raising her eyebrows.

"I think it would be a good idea," Hutchins agreed, taking one knee as he opened the backpack. "I saw some thick crevices back there. Get a good distance away and wedge yourself in somewhere. Don't come out until eight explosions are over."

"Save the coziest nook for me," Byrd said to Candi with a grin.

Byrd and Candi retraced their steps and quickly scanned for options among the shadowy crevices. Byrd backed into one, and Candi found another in the opposite wall.

Byrd peered out from her rock shelter as Hutchins knelt

by the wall of rubble, the backpack open beside him. He set up the rig with slow, cautious movements, placing the sticks of dynamite into dark crevices as the moisture on his pale face shone in the flickering light.

In one hand, he clutched a scrap of paper, smudged and folded, checking it obsessively between placements like he didn't quite trust his own memory. The fuse lengths had been pre-cut. *Short. Too short,* Byrd thought, her stomach tightening.

After placing all the charges, Hutchins took a lighter from his shirt pocket. His trembling fingers struck it against the rough cave wall. The sulfur flared to life, casting his face in a demonic orange glow that amplified the terror in his wide eyes. For a heartbeat, he hesitated, then stepped toward the first charge.

The flame bent and flickered as he moved. He cupped his hand around it, then offered it up to the first fuse. The fuse ignited with a vicious hiss. Hutchins moved frantically between the rest of the fuses, lighting each one quickly.

The final fuse lit, and Hutchins stood transfixed, mesmerized by the web of burning lines converging on the wall of rubble.

"Hans, get back here!" Byrd shouted.

Hutchins spun and lunged backward, but his heel caught on a jagged rock. He twisted in the air as he fell and crashed hard onto all fours.

"Get up!" Byrd shouted through clenched teeth, watching the fuses burning lower, crackling like dry leaves in a wildfire.

Hutchins scrambled, half-crawling for cover. He pulled himself into a narrow cleft in the wall as the first fuse burned down.

The first detonation came like the voice of a vengeful

God. The concussive force surged through the air, and the blast rushed over Byrd like a physical blow. The explosion sent a hammer of pressure into her chest, slamming her against the rock.

Byrd shoved her fingers deep into her ears, which already rang like church bells on a Sunday morning. Before she could recover, the second charge erupted, then the third. The rock convulsed, shuddering and heaving as though some titanic creature had awoken from a millennium of slumber. Small stones bounced and danced across the floor like popcorn in a hot pan. Larger stalactites broke free from the ceiling, smashing into the ground with enough force to shatter into deadly shrapnel.

She counted seven, then eight booms, each one echoing out. The final explosion punched the air from her lungs. And then—stillness, broken only by the slow patter of dust settling.

"Well, I'm still alive," Byrd said, her voice sounding tiny after the roaring blast. "Everyone else good?"

"Good!" Candi called out, her voice sounding strange, like a bass drum behind a wall.

"All good," Hutchins confirmed, though the quavering in his voice suggested otherwise.

Byrd emerged from the crevice, wincing as she straightened her spine. Each vertebra seemed to protest individually as though her backbone had been disassembled and needed manual realignment.

Candi appeared next, dust coating her blonde hair with a fine gray powder that caught the beam of the flashlight.

Hutchins followed last, his face streaked with sweat-carved channels through the layer of rock dust.

"Well," Byrd said, sweeping her flashlight across the

newly accessible passage, "let's see if that was worth nearly getting buried alive for."

The three stepped forward, then another explosion rattled through the cave.

Byrd dropped to the ground, covering her head with her hands. The others fell beside her. "Hutchins! What the—" Byrd yelled, when the reverberations died away. "I thought there were eight!"

"There were!"

The sound of another blast filled the cave, followed by a sharp clang like swords colliding. "Gunshots!" Byrd realized as the bullet hit the rock. "Behind us. Move!"

Byrd pulled Candi up by the wrist and sprinted toward the hole in the rubble. She pulled at a half-exposed boulder, yanking with all her strength. A bullet slammed into a boulder right next to her. More zipping sounds filled the cavern, and more bullets smashed into the rocks.

"Get down!" Byrd hissed. As they lay once again on the hard, wet ground, Byrd growled, "Start removing these rocks so we can get through. I'll hold them down."

As Hutchins and Candi tugged at the rocks, Byrd got herself steady on one knee. She drew her pistol and fired into the darkness. Shots came back hard and heavy, filling the cavern with appalling noise. Byrd moved forward in a crouch, drawing fire away from Hutchins and Candi.

She took a step forward but dropped to her knee again as a volley of bullets came, striking the rock surfaces all around her. Each impact sent fragments of stone exploding outward with high-pitched whines as the rounds ricocheted wildly.

Byrd waited for a momentary pause in the shooting, then darted behind a boulder. She peered around, searching for movement in the low light. A shadow moved further up the cave.

Byrd fired on the figure, aiming ahead of the movement. As the sound of the gunshots faded, she heard a grunt—maybe shock, maybe injury.

She squeezed off three more shots, then ejected the spent magazine and shoved a fresh one home. She waited, watching the cavern. When nothing moved, she stalked her way back toward the rubble.

Byrd tucked in beside a stack of rocks just as Hutchins pulled a large boulder aside.

"It's clear," Hutchins said, indicating the hole. "There's enough space to get through there now."

Byrd nodded, tucked the gun away, and ducked into the opening. With an anxious backward glance, Hutchins and Candi quickly followed.

## 65

Byrd emerged into a space that looked like a human-made tomb. She glanced up at a thick stone archway curving above her. She then focused the beam of her flashlight on a chunky, box-like object in the center of the space. Candi crawled through the opening and, brushing her knees, came to stand beside Byrd.

"It... it looks like a tomb," the young woman said.

"Well, actually..." Hutchins began, his voice echoing slightly as he pulled himself into the chamber behind them, "...a tomb is a space—it's the structure built to house the dead. A sarcophagus is a stone container that holds the body. You can have a sarcophagus without a tomb, but not the other way around."

He stood up straight and stepped closer, eyes gleaming with fascination. "And this one..." he trailed his fingers along the stone edge of the sarcophagus reverently, "this isn't just any coffin. Judging by the carvings, this was made for someone important. Royalty."

He ran the beam of his flashlight along the carved edges. "Look at these symbols," he said, crouching. "Tombs were meant to preserve memory. But sarcophagi... they were often designed to guard the body. Protect it—keep it sealed away."

Byrd nodded. "And in this case, to keep the Sunstone sealed away too?"

"Exactly. The symbols here aren't just decorative—they're warnings. You see the repetition of these spiral motifs? That's not ornamental. That's a binding mark. Ancient cultures used spirals to represent eternity, cycles, or traps. It's as if they were trying to tie something down... spiritually speaking."

Hutchins wiped sweat from his eyes, peering more closely into the sarcophagus. His mouth fell open as he laid eyes on the treasure he had finally unearthed.

Byrd stepped forward and saw that the stone tablet inside the sarcophagus was partially covered with bones.

"My god. I'm really here," Hutchins gasped, standing alongside her.

She glanced at him, catching his shimmering eyes in the flashlight's beam.

"We did it, Wall," Hutchins said quietly. "We did it, my friend."

"So you're sure we're in the right place?" Byrd asked matter-of-factly.

Ignoring or not even registering the sarcasm, Hutchins leaned into the sarcophagus and gently brushed aside the bones.

"This whole sorry mess is about that thing," Byrd said, training her flashlight on the artifact. "My aunt used to have something like that for birds to eat off."

The beam illuminated a circular stone tablet about the size of a laptop. At its center, a grotesque face stared back at them—mouth frozen in what could have been a scream or a snarl.

Hutchins leaned in, his fingers hovering over the surface.

"It's not just a *thing*," he whispered. "This is a ceremonial calendar, database of coordinates, astronomical guide, and pharmacological record all in one."

He traced the air above a series of spiraling patterns that radiated outward from the central face.

"These concentric rings represent celestial cycles. The Mayans were master astronomers. Each of these notches corresponds to specific celestial events—solstices, equinoxes, planetary alignments."

Byrd leaned closer, noticing how the stone's surface was crisscrossed with fine lines—some deliberate carvings, others the result of centuries of wear.

"What about these little figures?" Candi asked, pointing to tiny human forms positioned around the outer ring.

"Agricultural markers, I think," Hutchins said. "See this one with the raised arms? He's watching the stars. And here—" he pointed to another figure tending to plants, "—harvesting when the celestial alignments were optimal."

He moved his finger to a series of raised dots that resembled braille.

"These aren't random; they're mathematical notations indicating precise measurements—likely the ratios for creating medicinal compounds."

"So that's our antidote," Byrd said, running her flashlight across the artifact's surface again.

"And clearly, as we always thought, someone was appointed to protect it and hide it even in death," Hutchins said, looking at the bones that now surrounded the relic.

"It was never meant to be found?" Byrd asked.

"It was meant to be found by the Gods," Hutchins explained. "Proof that civilizations had taken advantage of the healthful gifts the Gods had provided."

Hutchins turned off his flashlight and placed it on the ground, then leaned in and hefted up the bulky tablet. He admired it for a moment, holding it up in front of him like a parent holds their infant.

While Hutchins was locked in a moment of reverie, Candi's light flickered once, twice, then died with a fading yellow whimper.

"Kid, we need to move," Byrd hissed. "These damn things were never going to last long. We need to get out of here while we still have light."

As Hutchins crouched to put the Sunstone in his backpack, a movement from behind the rubble made all three stop dead. Byrd heard voices from beyond the wall and whipped around to face the opening. Candi stepped toward the gap in the rubble, her gun raised.

"Get back," Byrd hissed. "Let me."

Crossing her hands at the wrist in the Harries Technique, the flashlight in one hand and her pistol in the other, she slowly craned her neck to get a view to the other side of the rubble. A sharp crack filled the tomb, then shocking vibrations traveled up Byrd's arm. What remained of her flashlight, destroyed by a bullet, fell to the ground. She gripped her Beretta with two hands, but in total darkness, there was nowhere to aim.

"Byrd!" Candi yelled from behind, panic wrestling with her voice. Clattering came from where Hutchins had been standing. Then, something rushed past Byrd with speed and force. As her eyes adjusted to the light, she saw a silhouette moving stealthily and rapidly.

The tomb illuminated just as the unmistakable figure of

The Thin Man disappeared around the wall of rocks and out into the cave. His distraught face glowing in the beam of the flashlight he had finally found on the ground, Hutchins cried, "He took the Sunstone!"

Byrd immediately darted around the rubble at the tomb entrance, but the crack of a bullet against stone next to her head drove her back. "Get down," Byrd yelled, dragging Candi by the arm and ducking in behind the sarcophagus.

"We have to get it back," Hutchins pleaded.

"Lives come first," Byrd hissed back.

Rocks scraped against each other on the other side of the wall as Byrd breathed hard, keeping low behind the stone box. She looked toward the opening and saw shadows shifting as men stacked boulders against the exit.

Byrd heard two men speaking in Spanish just beyond the rubble. The words were indistinguishable, and she only recognized the scratchy, gramophone voice of The Thin Man.

"They're sealing us in," Candi said, standing and moving around the sarcophagus despite Byrd's instructions.

"Dammit, girl," Byrd said and stood to follow. But the men moved quickly. Before Byrd reached the entrance, another boulder thudded into place, sealing them inside the ancient tomb.

## 66

"If we don't move now, they'll bury us alive," Hutchins whispered.

"If we fight, we'll be shot," Candi said.

"At least we'll die quickly," Byrd insisted, stepping up to the rebuilt wall of rocks as another boulder crashed into place from the other side.

"No!" she shouted, hurling herself against the wall. Her shoulder collided with solid stone, sending a jolt of pain through her body.

Byrd jammed her fingers into the narrowing gap and clawed at the boulders. Planting her feet wide on the uneven floor, she drove her full weight against the rock. The boulder shifted a fraction of an inch, then locked tight as more weight pressed from the other side.

Hutchins lunged forward, wedging himself beside her and adding his weight to the effort. Candi joined in, digging her heels into the ground as she pulled and twisted.

"Push!" Byrd commanded through gritted teeth.

They heaved as one, bones and muscles straining to

breaking point, but the boulders remained stubbornly in place.

"This is like trying to push over a damn cathedral," Byrd shouted, thumping the stone and assaulting her own knuckles. She wiped dirt from her hand, but the pain remained.

A mocking laugh drifted through the rubble wall—The Thin Man celebrating their entombment. Byrd slapped the stone again as rage surged through her body.

Hutchins raised his flashlight higher, its beam already dimming. The light wavered, casting frantic shadows across the walls.

"Not sure how long this one will last," he whispered, the beam noticeably fading even as he spoke.

"What are we gonna do?" Candi said, a whimper taking over her voice.

"We're gunna get out of here, that's what," Byrd said, sounding more confident than she felt. "Pick a section of wall and check it for any kind of weakness."

The three of them each took a different corner of the tomb. Working her way toward the back of the tomb, Byrd tuned into the muffled sound of trickling water.

Hutchins' flashlight faded, flickered, then surrendered to the darkness.

Byrd held a hand in front of her face but couldn't see it.

She took a deep, composing breath, then said, "Hutchins, how did you light the fuse for the explosives?"

"A lighter I picked up in Cancun. It won't throw out much light, though, maybe a few feet."

"Let me see," Byrd requested.

Hutchins struck the lighter, and a dancing orange glow filled the space.

"Okay, that's good. It's a real lighter. Not some cheap

garbage," Byrd said, crossing the tomb and taking the lighter. "Hutchins, gimme your shirt."

"What? Why?"

"Fuel," Byrd said. "You don't expect us ladies to undress, do you?"

Hutchins scowled, then, realizing Byrd was serious, pulled off his shirt.

Byrd shut off the lighter, removed the fuel pad, and rubbed fuel on the shirt. She set the fabric alight, then dropped it into the sarcophagus.

"Light!" she declared as flames licked higher. "Now, there's water behind the wall here." She beckoned her companions over to the rear wall. She picked up a whitish rock and marked a cross on the wall. "I can hear it somewhere back there. We just need to break through."

"Yeah, I am feeling a bit thirsty, but I think getting out of here should be our priority," Hutchins said.

"For a super-intelligent person, you really do say some stupid things," Byrd said, shaking her head.

"If there's water behind there, it means it's coming in from somewhere outside," Candi explained, with far more patience than Byrd could ever muster.

"And outside is where we want to be," Byrd added.

"That makes sense," Hutchins said, snagging up a large rock.

Candi and Byrd selected rocks too, and turned to the mark Byrd had made on the wall.

"I can't believe I'm damaging a precious historical site," Hutchins moaned.

"The damage to my existence if I'm buried alive is much more of a concern," Byrd said, preparing to strike.

"How do we know water won't flood in?" Candi said through gritted teeth as she struck the wall.

"We don't," Byrd replied. "But we need a way out. Or we die, and so do the people in the compound."

"That can't happen," Hutchins said, his voice rough with determination. He cracked the rock against the wall again, doubling his efforts.

"With any luck," Byrd said, "it's a sinkhole or natural well that'll lead straight back up to the top, but we'll need to swim underwater."

"Yeah, we've had *tons* of luck so far," Hutchins said, taking out his frustrations on the wall.

"Do you two have any freediving experience?" Byrd asked.

Candi and Hutchins stopped smashing the wall and looked at each other. "No," they said in unison.

"Just remember this," Byrd said, not breaking her rhythm. "Relaxation is the key. You'll feel like panicking, but don't. Stay calm. Expect to feel pain in your lungs. Expect your stomach to convulse. Let it happen and keep pushing upwards."

Candi and Hutchins exchanged a grave look, then nodded nervously.

"Let's get through," Byrd said, hefting her rock and driving it hard into the wall. The impact reverberated up her arms, but the ancient mortar surrendered—a spider's web of cracks spreading across the surface. Water trickled through in thin streams, gleaming like silver threads in the flickering light.

"Right there!" Hutchins pointed to where the cracks converged. "That's our weak point!"

He swung his rock, smashing it into the center of the web. Chunks of ancient brick crumbled away, some no larger than pebbles, others the size of a fist. Water gushed through the widening gaps, the pressure increasing with every strike.

"My turn!" Candi shouted, swinging for the wall. A slab the size of a head broke free, splashing into the water.

Water erupted through the breach, a horizontal waterfall that almost knocked Candi off her feet. The murky torrent sloshed across the tomb floor, swirling around their knees.

Byrd knocked away a few more chunks of rock, then studied the gap.

"That's enough," she said, dropping her stone and moving toward the opening. She positioned herself at the breach, bracing against the current that fought to push her back. "Remember, take a deep breath and hold it. Don't fight the water—move with it. And whatever you do, head for the light."

The water rose past their waists, then chests, the chamber filling like a bathtub with a broken faucet. Candi squealed as the cold liquid reached her chin.

"Follow me," Byrd said, sucking in a massive breath that expanded her lungs to their limit. The cold air burned in her chest as she forced herself to take in more than seemed possible.

She ducked beneath the surface and pulled herself through the jagged opening. Sharp edges raked across her shoulders as she squeezed through. The murky water sent a chill right through her like an electric current, stinging her skin and immediately numbing her fingers.

The void beyond the wall was dark and eerily silent except for the dull thud of her heartbeat. Byrd's military training took over. Stay calm. Find a reference point. Move with purpose.

She glanced back, hoping to signal to her companions, but saw nothing but dark and swirling sediment. She twisted, searching for direction in the disorienting darkness.

She looked up and saw the faintest glimmer of light, filtering down through the water. She pushed up, kicking toward the light with powerful strokes. Each movement felt like swimming through molasses as the pressure built in her chest. Her lungs burned, oxygen depleting faster than she'd anticipated.

The ache spread from her lungs to her diaphragm, muscles spasming as her body fought to breathe. Her mind started playing tricks—the light shifted further and further away, despite her efforts. Panic scratched at the edges of her consciousness like an animal trying to claw its way in. Her mouth wanted to open, to gasp, to draw in what would surely be a fatal breath of water.

Byrd kicked on, reminding herself to stay calm and focused.

The light grew larger, brighter. The murky green-black morphed into translucent blue. With one final, desperate surge, Byrd broke the surface. She exploded into glorious oxygen, her lungs expanding painfully as she gasped. She breathed deeply, once, twice, three times. The sun blinded her, an almost painful brightness after the subterranean darkness.

Realizing Candi and Hutchins had yet to emerge, Byrd took one more deep, fortifying breath, then plunged back beneath the surface. She opened her eyes, straining to see any movement, any sign of her friends in the murky depths.

Byrd reached out, flapping around in the dark water with both hands. Slimy sediment wrapped around her fingers, distorting her sense of touch. Every time her fingers landed on something thicker than liquid, it turned out just to be small stones or slimy vegetation floating in the water.

She thrashed around more frantically as she searched, knowing that every passing second was a moment closer to drowning for Hutchins and Candi.

Then, her hand landed on something more solid, like a branch. She grasped the object and realized it had a hand at the end of it. She pulled up, dragging whoever it was to the surface.

Hutchins emerged first, followed a moment later by Candi, the pair holding hands. They moved in spurts and splashes to the side of the sinkhole, then dragged themselves up and onto solid ground.

Byrd followed them, and all three lay on their backs, sucking in wonderous oxygen. Turning their heads to look at each other, they exploded into laughter.

The laughter ended as the first shot rang out, spraying dirt at their feet and sending them scrambling for cover.

## 67

Another bullet plunged into the turf right next to Byrd's head. She leapt to her feet, dragging Candi up with her. She glanced around, then sprinted in the direction of a large boulder. She slid down as she rounded it, coming to land on her thigh behind the rock.

Hutchins and Candi jumped in beside her as another strafe of bullets whizzed through the air.

Byrd reached for the gun she'd holstered at her hip. She felt nothing but sodden clothing.

"I must have lost it in the damn water," she spat, looking back toward the water hole. "One of you, pass me your gun." She held out her hand, but no one passed a gun across. She looked at Candi and then Hutchins. "Anyone still have their weapon with them?"

Candi and Hutchins both shook their heads.

"Who the hell's shooting at us?" Candi whispered, fingers interlocked at the top of her head.

"The corrupt cop. The Thin Man," Byrd replied. "He is likely well-trained, and he might not miss next time." Peering cautiously around the boulder, she narrowed her eyes and got a glimpse of The Thin Man. She could not see anyone else, despite having heard two voices in the cave.

"I'll get the Sunstone back even if I'm shot—if I have to crawl out of here with it," Hutchins said. "We finally found it, and now we need to find the plant."

"You're right," Byrd said, "but we're pinned down. We can't help anyone if we're dead."

Another bullet slammed into the rock.

Candi shuffled to the edge of the boulder and fixed her eyes in the direction from which the bullets were coming. "The backpack with the Sunstone inside is on the ground a few meters behind the skinny cop," she said. "Hutchins, get ready to grab it and run for the plane."

"No!" Hutchins hissed, clearly figuring out what she had in mind as she climbed to her feet.

"Yes!" Candi immediately sprang out from behind the rock and darted out into the open.

Hutchins watched her go, then sprinted in the opposite direction.

Sierra Byrd picked up a rock in each hand and followed Candi out of their hiding place. The Thin Man paced toward Candi and away from the backpack.

"Hey! Let's talk, officer," Candi shouted, walking toward the aggressors. "You wouldn't hurt an unarmed woman, would you?"

"Girl, you are something else," Byrd said under her breath.

The Thin Man strode further toward Candi, leaving the backpack unattended, and raised his weapon. After watching Hutchins slyly grab the backpack, Byrd raised her arm.

"Really? You're gonna shoot an unarmed girl?" Candi yelled.

The Thin Man closed one eye and took aim.

Byrd whipped her arm forward, launching the rock. The stone spun through the air. As she watched its trajectory, her sharp eyes could make out The Thin Man's finger squeezing on the trigger. A shot rang out at the exact moment the rock smashed into the officer's face. His head twisted sideways, a spray of crimson mist erupting from his mouth. He groaned and slumped to the ground.

Byrd spun toward Candi. The young woman stood twenty yards away, still upright, arms slightly outstretched like a statue in a pose of defiance. Then, Candi collapsed, her legs giving way beneath her.

Byrd ran to her, dropping to one knee. She scanned Candi's body and saw blood pouring from her upper arm. Byrd ran her trembling fingers along Candi's blood-soaked arm, desperately trying to find the entry wound to put pressure on it.

"Stay with me; it looks like a flesh wound," Byrd said, pushing down on the injury. "I think I disrupted his aim at the last second. But I wish I'd disrupted it more."

Candi's eyelids fluttered open, and she grimaced.

A shadow fell across Candi's bleeding body. Heavy footsteps approached from behind.

Byrd kept pressure on Candi's wound, unwilling to release it even as the hairs on her neck stood on end.

"Step away from her," came a voice, distorted and muffled.

Byrd slowly turned her head, keeping her body positioned protectively over Candi. A figure stood silhouetted against the harsh sunlight, his face obscured by a tactical black gaiter.

The man reached up and, with deliberate slowness—almost theatrical—pulled the gaiter from his face.

Byrd's blood froze as the face revealed itself inch by inch.

"Tom," she whispered, the name escaping like air from a punctured lung.

Keeping her eyes on her adversary, Sierra Byrd placed the young woman's hand on the wound and said, "Apply pressure here, darlin'"

Candi nodded once and did as she was told.

Byrd rose slowly to her feet. She barely had time to register the blur of movement before the first left hook swung her way. She raised her arm up to block, and Tom's fist collided with her forearm, the impact sending a shock through her body. He followed up with a right hook, cutting hard and fast through the air.

Byrd partially deflected it with her left hand, but it broke through and clipped her temple, a flash of light bursting behind her eyes.

Tom pressed in, throwing a tight uppercut toward her ribs.

Byrd shifted her stance, let it graze past, then clenched her fist and stiffened her right arm. She drove her elbow deep into his sternum, forcing him back a step. Before he could reset, Byrd twisted and slammed a knee into his stomach. He grunted as the hit landed solid, packed with every bit of hatred she had for him. Byrd followed it with a clean overhand right to his face, her knuckles cracking into his cheekbone.

Tom staggered backward. Byrd took a breath and planted her feet, ready to fight harder. Rage flashed in Tom's eyes. He stood tall and then barreled forward shoulder-first, slamming into her guard and knocking her off balance.

Byrd reeled, and before she could steady herself, Tom swung a brutal right hook into her ribs. The impact knocked her sideways. Another punch—left cross this time—clattered into her temple and spun her halfway around. Then a straight shot to her sternum sent her crashing to the ground on the small of her back. The scent of blood filled her airways.

"What do you want from all this, Tom?" Byrd said between heavy breaths, looking up at the man standing over her.

"To watch your life fade from your eyes," he said, his solid frame blocking out the sun. "Then to fly away into the sunset."

Byrd drew a long breath. She pushed herself upward, willing her legs to steady, but her knees betrayed her. She collapsed back to the ground, both palms flat against the dirt, fingers digging into the soil.

"Pathetic," Tom spat, circling slowly closer as if savoring the moment.

Byrd took another breath, allowing life to return to her limbs. She remained motionless, her head bowed as if defeated.

"Any last words?" Tom sneered, stepping closer still. "You usually have plenty to say."

In one explosive motion, Byrd slid her right hand beneath her leg and pivoted her entire body in a neat circular motion just inches from the ground, like a pencil compass drawing a perfect arc. She swung her heel around in a clean sweep, low and fast, driving it into the side of Tom's knee. The joint buckled with a sickening squelch of tearing ligaments.

Tom howled in agony, stumbling but not falling. He lunged forward, his fist aimed at her head.

Byrd rolled sideways, narrowly avoiding the blow. She kicked back and then sprang to her feet.

Clearly surprised by the speed of her movement, Tom attempted to raise his guard but wasn't quick enough.

Byrd swung her right forearm up into his chest, her elbow digging into his heart, then lunged forward with a powerful left hook.

Tom gasped and swung wildly before doubling over in pain. His knuckles grazed her temple as she twisted away, using his momentum against him. She hooked her foot behind his damaged knee and drove a fist up into his stomach.

Tom lurched backward, dazed.

Byrd unleashed a devastating uppercut that connected with his jaw. The impact smashed his teeth together and snapped his head back. Still, he remained standing, swaying like a tree in a hurricane.

Before he could recover, Byrd slipped behind him and delivered a precise open-palm strike to the base of his skull —not hard enough to kill, but with sufficient force to disrupt his brain's electrical signals. His body went instantly limp, and he fell to the ground.

"I don't think you'll be flying away into anything for a while, Tom," she said, wiping blood from her lip with the back of her hand. "Or walking, for that matter."

Byrd scooped Candi up quickly but gently and ran for the plane.

On a patch of flat ground nearby, The Thin Man crawled toward a Bell 525 Relentless helicopter.

As Byrd approached, the corrupt officer struggled to his feet. He held his severely broken jaw with one hand and raised his pistol in the other.

Byrd closed the distance, still holding Candi in her arms. When she was almost close enough to grab the weapon, she placed Candi on the ground and raised her hands in the air as the corrupt officer barked at her to stay back.

The Thin Man grinned, clearly pleased that the power was still his.

Byrd clicked her fingers, drawing his attention up. As his eyes rose, she ducked out of the line of the weapon, then sprang up into a kick. Her right leg extended like a missile on a launcher. She connected with his already damaged jaw, smashing the bone in several more places. The gun slipped out of the man's grasp as he collapsed, and Byrd kicked it far into the undergrowth.

"How did you find me?" Byrd growled, standing over the crumpled man. He held his jaw, wide-eyed and horrified at the extent of his injuries. She raised her fist and added, "You seem to be a big fan of pain?"

"Your old friend led us right to you," came the garbled response.

"Bourdell? Don't even try to tell me he's with you."

The Thin Man shook his head but said nothing.

Byrd only had to feint a blow while fixing her eyes on the shattered jaw.

"No," The Thin Man yelped, waving his right hand out in front of him in a pathetic attempt at defense. "But the drunk old fool didn't notice who was tailing him. Flight data did the rest."

"How many guards are at the compound?" Byrd hissed.

"Go to hell."

Byrd dropped and dug a knee into The Thin Man's chest. She clamped her right hand around his neck and squeezed. His eyes bulged.

"How many guards? What defenses, what weapons?" She eased her grip, allowing the man to speak.

"I don't know about guards, I swear." The Thin Man's

eyes darted nervously, his voice strained through his devastated jaw. He swallowed hard, then added, "But I do know this: Sallas has weapons that can take down planes." A gleam of malicious satisfaction crept into his gaze. "You'd be amazed at what gangs can get their hands on these days.

"What weapons?"

The Thin Man simply curled his lip, snarling. Byrd picked him up by the neck, then slammed his head into the ground, the occipital bone crunching as it connected with the sunbaked surface.

RPGs that fit—"

The officer suddenly stopped talking as he slipped into unconsciousness, his head rolling to one side.

"You look so adorable when you're sleeping," Byrd said, dusting off her hands and then gently picking up Candi again, cradling the young woman's head, her hand resting in soft blonde hair.

The familiar drone of aircraft engines cut through the air, rising from a distant hum to a roaring crescendo. Something in the sound's pitch sent a chill down Byrd's spine—the engines were accelerating, not idling.

The Pilatus PC-24 powered up, lurched into motion, and lifted off—climbing hard into the sky.

"Bourdell!" she shouted, disbelief warring with the evidence before her eyes.

The plane banked sharply, engines at full throttle.

Hutchins ran across the open ground toward Byrd. "I... I don't know what just happened," he shouted, pointing up at the plane. "Your friend just yelled at me to get out of the aircraft."

Sierra Byrd clasped her head in her hands.

"Did he really betray us?" Hutchins asked, breathless.

"It's not betrayal," Byrd said as she watched the aircraft

turn into a tiny silhouette. "It's trauma. He's suffering. I should never have gotten him involved."

"How could he do this?" Hutchins asked, throwing his arms into the air.

"It could happen to anyone, Hans. Anyone who went through what we did. I should have spotted the signs. The drinking, gambling."

"What are we going to do?" Hutchins asked, his voice shaky.

"Lucky our friend Tom brought us a new one," Byrd said, pointing up at the Bell 525. "Let's get out of here."

Byrd climbed inside the chopper and placed Candi into one of the seats.

"Will she survive?" Hutchins asked. "Please tell me she'll survive."

"It's a shoulder wound," Byrd replied. "The threat is loss of blood. Grab the medical kit, and we'll get her patched up."

Hutchins turned and did as he was told.

Byrd worked quickly to stem the bleeding, then adjusted the seatbelt and made sure Candi was secure. Hutchins took the seat next to Candi, then took her hand. Tears left dirty tracks as they streamed down his cheeks.

"Hutchins," Byrd said before she headed for the flight deck, "we got no time for emotions, buddy. I told you I'd save her. Now, get to work on the Sunstone."

## 68

As Byrd guided the chopper away from the canyon and into open skies, Hans Hutchins sat with his head in his hands, the Sunstone resting on his lap. Candi sat slumped in the chair beside him. "Think of it like a code," Hutchins muttered to himself, his voice just audible through Byrd's headset. "What did Wall say? Like coded coordinates."

"Are you okay there, Hans?" Byrd asked from the cockpit.

"I know the location of the plant is here somewhere," Hutchins said, running his finger across the stone. "The place where it grows in abundance, and it will surely be at least *somewhat* close to the canyon where the Sunstone was buried. But I can't decipher it. If only Wall were here."

"He's taught you well. Breathe. Relax. Let his teaching come flooding back to you."

Hutchins fell silent, leaving Byrd with only the sounds of static and the engine.

"I can't do it," Hutchins said, placing his head in his hands again. "I don't know what's happening. Damn brain fog. I just can't—"

*The Shadow of the Sunstone* 445

"You can do it, Hans," Candi said suddenly, her voice weak. Slowly, she leaned in toward Hutchins and planted another delicate kiss for luck on his cheek. "And one day, I promise we'll kiss for more than luck."

Hutchins' face lit up like a Caribbean sunrise.

Below, the rugged canyon dissolved into a sea of emerald jungle stretching to the horizon. Byrd scanned the shifting palette of greens—from the pale jade of new growth to the deep forest shadows—wondering what terrain would greet them at their next location, assuming Hutchins could decipher the Sunstone. She glanced down at the instrument panel, checking fuel consumption gauges and efficiency indicators. Every drop counted now, especially without knowing where they needed to go.

"I need your navigation system!" Hutchins shouted, bursting into the cockpit with such force that Byrd had to compensate for the helicopter's sudden weight shift.

"What the hell, Hutchins?" Byrd snapped, fighting to stabilize the aircraft. "You can't just—"

"The spiral patterns!" he interrupted, tracing a series of concentric circles carved into the ancient rock. "They're not just ceremonial—they're a coordinate system based on celestial alignments. Wall taught me this!"

He fumbled in his pocket and produced a crumpled piece of paper covered in scribbled equations and half-erased notes. "I need to convert these marker points to modern coordinates. The symbols at each spiral intersection represent numerical values—a latitude/longitude system predating Western cartography by centuries."

"That looks like a helluva mess," Byrd said, glancing at the paper—a junkyard of calculations, arrows, and crossed-out figures. "You sure about this?"

"The central figure isn't just the sun god—it's a fixed

reference point! Each spiral rotation represents a specific distance from that point. And these smaller markings?" His finger jabbed at tiny triangles on the edges of the sunstone. "They're cardinal directions!"

He leaned over Byrd's shoulder, invading her space to access the navigation display.

Byrd leaned to the left, accidentally sending the chopper off course. She corrected and shuffled over, letting Hutchins see the screen.

"I need to overlay this pattern onto your map—somewhere south of Chetumal, near the Guatemalan border."

Byrd zoomed in on the digital map, and Hutchins began tracing invisible lines across the screen with his finger, muttering calculations under his breath.

"Here!" he bellowed, stabbing at the screen. "Altamira! That's where linium grows!"

Byrd's eyes narrowed as the coordinates registered. "I don't suppose your ancient friends noted that that's inside a Mexican military airbase?"

Hutchins' triumphant expression faltered. "They weren't exactly worried about restricted airspace back then."

"That's a no-fly zone..." Byrd said, looking at the map.

"We have to try," Hutchins insisted. "You never bent a few rules, Byrd?"

"When the rules are enforced by precision-guided missiles..." Byrd thought for a moment. "It's suicide, Hans. The Mexican Air Force would be obligated to defend the base. The professor's safe. Maybe our priority should be to get Candi to a hospital."

"No. We need to get them all out," Candi said, straining to speak. "Get them treated."

"*You* need treatment," Hutchins insisted. "Very soon."

"He's right," Byrd said. "We did what we could. You're our priority now. We're taking you to get treatment."

"Then I will refuse it," Candi said solemnly.

"Candi..." Byrd said, shaking her head.

"I *will* refuse it," Candi said again.

"You know, you're a really difficult woman sometimes," Byrd said, shaking her head. "And that's why I like you."

"Plus, Wall said that one of the captives is carrying a child," Candi added. "Doing nothing is not an option."

Byrd looked at Hutchins, then glanced at the map. "You better sit down," she said, gripping the yoke. "And it's damn lucky our friend Tom provided us with a super-fast helicopter. You ready to have some fun, baby?" she asked the chopper.

Byrd's hands remained steady on the cyclic as she guided the helicopter over the patchwork of farmland that had replaced the jungle below. Mexico flew by in a blur beneath the fast, modern chopper as it headed toward the Guatemalan border. The sun bore down relentlessly, glinting off irrigation channels on the ground.

Surveying the landscape, Byrd took a deep breath. "The satellite images show a purple coloration just across the eastern boundary. We get in, get what we can, then get out again."

"Sounds good," Hutchins replied, sitting beside Candi. "Can you put it down just outside—"

"We've got no time to land. You're on the rope again. I know you can do this, buddy."

Silently, she noted that Hutchins had moved from *kid* to *buddy*—just like she called her old wingman, Bourdell.

"We're about five minutes out," Byrd said, her voice calm but carrying a note of urgency. "Hans, you ready?"

Hutchins adjusted his gloves, shifted nervously in his

seat, then nodded. Candi, sitting beside him, reached out and gave his arm a reassuring squeeze.

"Remember what I told you, fast-roping is all about control," Byrd said. "You grip the rope tight enough to keep yourself steady but loose enough to slide. Use your legs to stabilize and keep your descent smooth. Don't lock your knees when you land—bend them to absorb the impact. Got it?"

Hans gave a nervous thumbs-up. "Got it."

"Good," Byrd said, adjusting the collective to bring the 525 lower. The helicopter descended smoothly, the faint hum of the turboshaft engine filling the cabin. "I'll keep the bird as steady as I can. You'll have about three minutes on the ground. Get the cuttings, secure them in the pack, and get back on the rope. No heroics, no delays. Understood?"

"Understood," Hutchins said, though his voice wavered slightly.

"Don't worry, Hutchins," Byrd said. "The 525 was built for missions like this. Its lightweight structure and fly-by-wire controls make it easy to maneuver, and it hovers nice and steady. You're in safe hands."

As they neared the target zone, the patch of fabled purple plants loomed larger.

"There it is!" Hutchins said, almost pressing his face against the glass.

Byrd peered into the distance to get a better view of the vibrant purple patch—a striking contrast against the dusty beige fields.

"That's linium alright," Hutchins continued. "It's been right there all this time. I guess most people stay away from the area because of the base."

"I guess you're right," Byrd replied. "But we're going right into the heart of it."

A chain-link fence topped with razor wire came into view, surrounding the base on all sides.

Byrd tapped the screen of the 3D mapping system, which worked with the chopper's LIDAR and Synthetic Vision System, to scan for activity. For now, all looked quiet.

"Alright, we're entering the no-fly zone now," Byrd said. At that exact moment, the navigation system started beeping to inform them they were heading into danger. Clicking a switch, Byrd silenced the alarm. "Hans, get ready."

They soared over the chain-link fence, the helicopter's shadow racing beneath them across the purple linium fields. Byrd tilted the cyclic forward, the aircraft's nose dipping as she decelerated. The 525 settled into a hover above their target. She released the door latch and slid it open, unleashing a rush of warm air laden with the earthy perfume of sunbaked soil and wild vegetation. The powerful downdraft from the rotors created a perfect circle of bending plants below them, purple flowers and dust particles swirling in a miniature cyclone. Byrd held the 525 steady, compensating for minor air currents with precise adjustments to the cyclic.

"Hutchins, you're up," she called. "Rope's ready. Go!"

Hans shuffled to the open side door.

Byrd glanced back and gave him a quick nod of encouragement. He gripped the rope tightly and stepped off the skids. For a moment, he dangled awkwardly, his legs flailing, but then slid toward the ground.

"Good! That's it!" Byrd shouted, her voice cutting through the roar of the rotors. "Nice and easy!"

Hans landed with a stumble, but he quickly regained his footing. He unclipped himself from the rope and gave a quick wave up to Byrd. She responded with a thumbs-up and then shifted her focus back to the controls, keeping the 525 in position and stable.

On the exterior camera, she watched Hans move quickly, pulling the knife from his pack. The linium plants were clustered in dense patches, their legendary purple flowers buffeted by the downdraft. He knelt, cutting and carefully gathering each sample, then stuffing them into a bag.

Above, Byrd kept a watchful eye on the perimeter. A dust cloud kicked up by a patrol vehicle caught her attention, and she tensed, her fingers gripping the cyclic a little tighter.

"In the name of the Almighty, Hans, hurry up!" she hissed under her breath. She watched on the feed as Hans knelt amid the purple plants. "No time for reverence now, Hans. Clip and climb!"

Hutchins stuffed one more bunch into the bag and jogged back to the dangling line. He fumbled for a moment before clipping himself into the harness. He grabbed the rope with both hands and climbed, his movements slow but steady. Byrd adjusted the collective slightly to help counterbalance his weight as he ascended.

"Come on, Hans," she said under her breath. "Almost there."

With a final heave, Hans hauled himself back into the cabin, collapsing onto the floor. He puffed out an exhausted breath, his face flushed, but he held up the sealed bag triumphantly. "Got it!"

Candi clapped her hands weakly, her face lighting up despite her exhaustion.

"Nice work, rookie," Byrd said, a rare genuine smile lighting her face.

A stern, distorted voice burst through the comms, broadcasting on emergency frequencies: "You are in military airspace. Desist immediately and identify yourself. Final warning."

## 69

**Altamira Mexican Air Force Base.**

Byrd jabbed at the dashboard and shut off the comms, blocking any more communication from military air traffic control.

"What do we do?" Hans Hutchins asked, trepidation creeping into his voice.

Byrd didn't answer immediately—she was too busy eyeing the radar. A warning tone blared from the radar console as two dots appeared on the screen, rapidly closing in on their position.

"Strap in," she said. "We've got two bogeys—military jets. Looks like we've overstayed our welcome."

"M... military jets?" Hutchins stuttered. "Doesn't sound like something we can outrun?"

"Affirmative," Byrd said, her mind racing. "The 525 is fast for a helicopter but no match for fighter jets in a straight chase. If I can't outrun them, I'll have to outthink them—and outmaneuver them."

"Well, think fast!" Hutchins shouted.

"Just hang on tight," Byrd said, pulling back on the cyclic and banking the helicopter hard to the left. The 525 responded smoothly, its compact frame slicing through the air.

She dropped altitude quickly, skimming at high speed just feet above the dusty fields. The dry farmland provided minimal cover. Byrd headed for a series of tall irrigation sprinklers spaced out across the fields. Reaching the sprinklers, she weaved through the misty spray in an erratic pattern in an effort to confuse the radar readings.

The long jets of water struck the windshield in bursts, blurring her vision for a heartbeat at a time. The 525 jolted each time she cut through a spray arc. Soil and grit, kicked up by the rotors, rattled against the undercarriage.

The jets roared overhead with a deafening presence, their twin afterburners leaving parallel streaks in their wake. Byrd glanced up through the canopy, catching a glimpse of their delta wings and needle-nose profiles against the azure sky.

"F5 Tigers," she said, as the jets banked away in perfect unison, then dropped altitude and reduced speed.

"Come on, come on," Byrd muttered, zigzagging between the sprinklers. The 525's responsive controls and compact size gave her an edge, allowing her to fly where the jets couldn't—close to the ground.

Ahead, she spotted a shallow river running through the farmland. She dropped in close to the water, powering the helicopter just above the water's surface. The cyclic rattled in her hand as she pushed the 525 to its limits while using the reflections off the water to distort the chopper's heat signature.

The jets streaked past again, their afterburners glowing like raging suns as they circled back for another pass.

"If you fly this low, you're out of your mind," Byrd muttered.

The jets doubled back and roared up from behind, passing just above her, rocking the chopper with their wake. The helicopter's tail swayed dangerously before Byrd corrected, her fingers clamped tight around the cyclic.

"Did we lose them?" Hans asked, his voice quavering.

Byrd shook her head. "No, we only covered some ground to get away from the base. They're still on us—they now see us as a clear threat."

The jets streaked back into view, quickly flanking Byrd on both sides. She gritted her teeth and pushed the chopper harder, readings on the dashboard all racing to their maximum limit. The turbine's pitch climbed. Still, she kept it low, flat, and evasive.

She glanced at the jets either side, close enough to see the pilots clearly. One of the pilots tapped his headset, telling her to listen to the emergency channel she'd already shut off. While they were either side, Byrd realized, they weren't going to shoot her out of the sky.

Ahead, farmland suddenly gave way to dense jungle. Byrd's gaze darted across the terrain, seeking any advantage against the jets screaming alongside. Her pulse quickened as twin Mayan pyramids appeared, standing above the emerald canopy. The colossal structures stood proud, nearly kissing at their peaks, creating a sliver of sky between them not much wider than the 525's rotor span.

Byrd's hands deftly handled the controls as calculations flashed through her mind—rotor clearance, wind shear potential, possible downdrafts in the narrow passage.

"Brace!" Byrd shouted, suddenly banking the helicopter toward the stone corridor. The chopper raced toward the gap between the pyramids, stone walls blurring up ahead.

"Are you insane?" Hutchins shouted, pressing his face against the window. "We'll never—"

Byrd cut him off while narrowing her eyes to focus. "Watch me."

The jets stayed with her, their pilots clearly as determined as she was. Byrd eyed the glint of their canopies as they closed in.

"Are *you* insane?!" she screamed at them like they could hear her.

"Insanity saved our lives more than once already," Candi said calmly over the comms.

Byrd nodded and smiled.

The chopper tore toward the pyramids, the gap looking narrower with every passing second. Byrd adjusted the cyclic with razor-thin accuracy, ready to thread the 525 into the canyon created by the tips of the pyramids. She glanced again at the planes. If they continued on their course, they would slam into the ancient stone edifices.

The air pressure changed as Byrd approached the stone walls. Turbulence surged around the helicopter, bouncing it as if giant fists were slamming against the exterior.

Startled birds exploded from the pyramid terraces.

Byrd eyed the approaching structures—not smooth walls but treacherous surfaces with jutting corners and crumbling sections that could shred the rotor blades instantly. Her hands danced across the controls, making split-second adjustments as each new obstacle revealed itself through the windscreen.

The whole cockpit vibrated as Byrd surged on, taking another look left and right before attempting to slice between the pyramids. At the very last second, she saw the planes banking away, peeling off to avoid a catastrophic collision.

She'd shaken off her escorts, but she now had no choice other than to navigate the narrow gap.

She plunged into the gap, and the ancient stones rushed past on either side, close enough for her to see the cracks in the stone like wrinkles on an old sailor's skin. Byrd filled her lungs and held her breath as the rotor blades came within feet of clipping the edges.

"This is madness!" Hans shouted from the back.

"Shut up and hold on!" Byrd barked, sweat dripping into her eyes as she focused on the herculean task of keeping the helicopter level. She flew straight and true, battling with the forces of nature that tried to push her chopper left and right. Then it hit—a gust of crosswind like a slap across the fuselage. The helicopter pitched, then yawed. Byrd corrected hard, but too late.

The helicopter swung to the left, and a blade clipped the stone with a sharp crack. Sparks shot out in all directions as if from a blade cutting through metal. Byrd growled with exertion as she wrestled to bring the chopper back under control, desperate to avoid any more collisions.

Warning lights lit up across the dash like a Christmas tree. The main rotor torque reading spiked, and a vibration warning buzzed through her headset. Her fingers moved swiftly across the panel, checking system gauges and monitoring for pressure drops in the hydraulics.

"Come on, come on," she muttered. "Stay with me."

She brought the helicopter back level, but the gap between the pyramids seemed to grow even smaller. Byrd tightened up as she braced for impact with the stone walls. She kept her focus, guiding the machine straight as a tightrope. Then, the 525 cleared the gap and soared into the open sky.

"Yes!" Byrd shouted, punching the air.

The cabin erupted in a mix of laughter and relieved sighs. Hans clutched the sealed bag of linium like a trophy, his face pale but triumphant. Candi leaned back in her seat, her eyes closed, a faint smile on her lips.

"We haven't escaped this unscathed," Byrd said, the smile falling from her face. She scanned the instrument panel. Rotor RPM was stable, but just barely—still ticking in the green, but flirting with the yellow. A diagnostic alert blinked from the vibration sensor. She adjusted the trim slightly and eased up on the throttle, coaxing stability back into the airframe.

The cyclic still shivered in her grip, a constant reminder of how close they'd come. She gave the overhead panel a quick once-over—hydraulics holding, engine temp spiking but not yet critical.

"She's still flying, but she's not happy," Byrd announced.

"Will we make it?" Hutchins asked.

"One last push," Byrd said. "For anyone who has been poisoned, time is running out."

## 70

**Mexican desert north of Cabo San Lucas.**

"Hutchins, you need to decipher that thing a little more," Byrd said as they sped across the desert in the direction of the compound. "How do we use the plant?"

Hutchins knelt on the floor of the cabin, the revered stone tablet in front of him. He ran his finger over the carved indents of the words one more time.

"You can really read all that?" Byrd asked, pushing as much speed out of the 525 as possible. The chopper whined and rumbled, cutting through the air.

"It's ancient Nahuatl. I can read some, but without books to help me, it's damn hard." He leaned forward, focusing on one particular section. "The key to life is in the blood of the plant..." he read quietly. "The *blood* of the plant. I may be translating it wrongly."

"Could it...could it be the sap?" Candi said, her voice just a whisper. She looked down at Hutchins. Although her expression was one of pain, she hadn't issued a single complaint.

"The sap! I always assumed it would be dried and ground leaves, but maybe. Maybe." Hutchins continued to read. "It should be dried for a quarter *tonalpohualli*, or day count, to avoid the...unpleasant scent."

"How long is that?" Byrd asked.

"A long time. Much longer than we have."

"So it's no use?" Byrd said.

Hutchins muttered as he continued reading.

"The details say the drying process is to avoid the scent," Hutchins said. "But the health-giving properties may be contained in the *fluid* sap."

"Let's try it," Byrd said. "It's all we have."

Hutchins stood and took a sample of the large linium plant from the bag. He cut into the stalk and then ripped it apart. "I need water."

"Cooler at the back," Byrd said.

Hutchins dug out a bottle of water. He unscrewed the top, then scraped away the sap from an entire stem and dropped it inside. He screwed the top back on and shook the bottle viciously. The sap dissolved into the water, coloring the water purple.

"Man, that smells like a bag full of diapers on a warm morning," Byrd said, crinkling her nose.

"Well, it's purple, and it's drinkable," Hutchins said. "And it probably smells better than I do right now."

"It will have to do," Byrd confirmed. "Gather every drop of water you can find. We're approaching the compound now."

Through the windshield, the compound appeared on the horizon.

Byrd sped toward the chain link fence, slowing the chopper as they neared.

"Collective down, collective down," she muttered

through gritted teeth, easing the aircraft toward a patch of relatively flat ground just outside the perimeter fence. The damaged helicopter descended in a slight corkscrew, forcing her to counter with opposite cyclic.

Twenty feet from touchdown, a sudden crosswind sent them lurching sideways.

Byrd instantly compensated, her boots skipping on the pedals.

The skids hit the sand with a bone-jarring thud that sent shock waves through the airframe. The Bell 525 bounced several feet, kicking up a cloud of sand and dust before coming to rest at an awkward angle, one skid slightly higher than the other.

"Sorry, not my best work," Byrd said, shutting down the engine, then unbuckling.

"We're here, that's all that counts," Hutchins said, already on his feet. "We're going to end this." Hutchins placed his hand on Candi's. "We'll be back soon."

"You're a hero, Hans," Candi said, meeting Hutchins' gaze.

Hutchins nodded once and then followed Byrd out of the chopper. The pair ducked through a convenient gap in the wire fence and ran inside.

"This is weird," Hutchins said, looking around. While the place appeared to be deserted, broken wood, glass, and ceramics littered the sand.

"It looks like they had a brawl," Byrd said, eying a patch of what looked like blood.

"And this, look." Hutchins pointed at a reddish-purple patch. "It looks like that stuff we recovered from the island. The stuff that made the girl sick."

Byrd heard groaning, then the sound of thunderous vomiting from inside a white building. Side by side with

Hutchins, they ran toward the building. Byrd reached the door and pushed down on the handle, but the door was locked. Another groan drifted from someone inside. Sierra Byrd put her shoulder against the door and was about to shove when the door opened. A young woman wearing a stained white tank top looked out at them.

"We saw you land," the woman said. "I hope you're here to help because we're getting desperate."

"How many people need treatment?" Byrd said immediately.

"Some are almost gone," the woman replied sadly.

Byrd pushed through the door, followed by Hutchins. "Your name?"

"Briony."

"Yes, Briony, we are here to help. To save lives, you need to do exactly what I say." Byrd's gaze riveted Briony to the spot. "Understood?"

Briony nodded.

Byrd turned her attention to what resembled a military field hospital, the filth and pain caused by a combination of fighting and poisoning. People lay either on simple camp cots or slumped on the floor. Some writhed with agony, clutching their stomachs. Others lay still, their skin pale and eyes closed.

"Hutchins, this way," Byrd said, stepping over to a young man slumped against a crate, his skin sallow and his lips cracked and dry. "We deal with the quiet ones first. If they've got energy to complain, then they're alright for now."

Byrd braced the young man's head with one hand and uncapped one of the water bottles containing the linium infusion Hutchins had prepared.

"Small sips," she said firmly, supporting his jaw and

tipping a stream of the liquid into his mouth. The man gagged once, then drank.

"Briony, get this wound cleaned up a little more," Byrd said, pointing to the deep gash across the man's temple, then to the medical kit. "I'll dress it when everyone has the antidote."

Byrd and Hutchins worked quickly. Hutchins poured doses of the linium into cups while Byrd assessed triage priorities, focusing on anyone with signs of dehydration, high fever, or disorientation. One woman lay curled beneath a broken window, her breathing shallow. Byrd pressed the back of her hand to the woman's forehead and felt it burning. She used a rag soaked in water to cool her face, then gently pried open her mouth and coaxed in the medicine.

As the woman swallowed, her breathing hitched, then steadied. Byrd felt for abdominal rigidity or signs of internal bleeding, but it looked like poison was the main culprit. She folded a rolled blanket beneath the woman's head and turned to the next patient, already reaching for the linium.

Now able to prioritize those still on their feet, Byrd passed the medicine to Briony, and Briony drank deeply.

"Is anyone outside or in other buildings?" Byrd asked when everyone inside had been given the antidote.

"Yes, the devotees of The Mentor," Briony told her. "The evil ones."

"But there was no movement. Have they been poisoned too?"

"They have," Briony confirmed. "They unwittingly poisoned themselves."

"Then they will also need help," Byrd said.

After a pause, Briony nodded. They headed outside with a container of purple liquid in each hand. Byrd stopped at the first young woman she saw, tied up behind the stage.

She knelt beside her and immediately helped her to drink the antidote.

"What's your name, young lady?" Byrd asked after the woman had taken the antidote.

"Tammy," came the weak reply.

"And you are a follower of Sallas?"

Tammy shook her head. "Not anymore. He had us under his spell. All of us. And look what happened. I just want to go home."

"Well, it's over now," Byrd said, placing a reassuring hand on the woman's bony shoulder. "There's a helicopter waiting to take you where you need to go. Hospital. Families. Freedom."

Suddenly, Tammy's eyes rolled back, and her body went limp. Byrd gently tilted the young woman's head back to open her airways.

"Byrd, I think it's working!" Hutchins said, rushing out of the white building.

"Not for everyone, Hans. Some of them are too far gone. This girl's recovery was momentary."

"No, it *has* to work!" Hutchins said, resting his hands on his knees as he stared at Tammy.

"The antidote may only buy time for her," Byrd said, standing. "She needs a hospital, and so do some of the others. Get everyone to the chopper."

As the last people boarded, Briony stood beside Byrd at the doorway. "There's one man still here," Briony said. "The Mentor's enforcer. An evil beast of a man. I hate to say it, but he should be left to rot."

"That's not how we do things," Byrd said solemnly. "He's coming too."

"You're military?" Briony asked.

"Not any longer. But my soul still is."

Byrd scanned the compound and saw the vast outline of the man's body as he lay injured on the ground beside a charred wooden fence that still smouldered. She then realized it must be the same man who had fallen from her chopper during the rescue of Wall. Sierra Byrd strode across the sand and stood over the large creature as he lay on the ground, his eyes closed. Byrd saw his barrel chest rising and falling and knew he was still alive.

"Gonna be a workout session just carrying you to the chopper, buddy," she said as she leaned down to lift The Ogre. Hutchins rushed over to help, along with a couple of cult members who still had the strength to move freely. Together, they carried the beast across the compound like they were carrying a small car.

Inside the chopper, Byrd climbed into the cockpit, flipped the battery master switch, and began the start-up sequence. The turbine whined to life—but just as she engaged the starter, a caution light blinked red on the panel: "ROTOR IMBALANCE – ABORT." The engine spooled down with a defeated whirr.

# 71

Byrd muttered under her breath and scanned the diagnostics. "Damn blade strike at the pyramids has knocked the rotor system out of alignment." With the torque readings running all over the lot and the vibration sensor peaking in the red, it didn't look good. She shut the systems down and rebooted them, but got the same result.

"Byrd, it's Candi," Hutchins said, rushing into the cockpit. "She's lost consciousness, and I can't revive her. She's going downhill fast."

"Damn it," Byrd spat, running through one of the troubleshooting systems. "The rotor system isn't starting properly. I'll check the rotors." She climbed from her seat, quickly checked Candi's pulse and airways, then exited the chopper.

"Do whatever it takes," Hutchins said, returning to Candi's side. "We don't have much time."

Byrd circled the aircraft methodically, scanning for damage. The desert heat radiated up from the sand in visible waves as sweat trickled down her spine. She started with the tail boom, running her fingers along the metal surface, feeling for structural weaknesses.

"How bad is it?" Hutchins called from the doorway.

"Keep checking on Candi," Byrd replied, not looking up as she carefully inspected the tail rotor. The gearbox housing showed signs of impact. She wiggled the blade assembly and felt the unmistakable looseness of damaged bearings.

Byrd climbed onto the skid to reach the engine compartment, the metal hot enough to cause pain through her gloves. She moved onto the main rotor, noticing the damage even before touching the blade. The tip of the leading edge warped where it had struck the ancient stone. She grabbed the rotor tip and tried to move it through its normal arc, feeling the grinding resistance of damaged bearings in the swashplate.

"It's a miracle we even got here," Byrd said, looking out at the horizon. Heat currents danced in the baking desert. "We could keep the aircon running a couple of hours at least. If that runs out, they'll die in the heat before the poison takes them."

Standing back on the sand with her hands planted firmly on her hips, Byrd stared down at the desert beneath her feet. A single bead of sweat broke free from her brow, tracing a path down her nose before falling to the parched desert floor. The droplet vanished instantly into the earth, leaving no trace—much like their chances of survival. She scanned the empty horizon, feeling the crushing weight of all those lives pushing down on her shoulders. With help so far away, they might as well be stranded on Mars.

"I'm so sorry," Byrd said quietly to no one and everyone. "This thing isn't going anywhere. Even if by some miracle we get it in the air, flying a damaged and overloaded chopper is suicide."

Sierra Byrd paced back around the outside of the chopper. Her shoulders slumped as hollow despair gnawed at her insides. With each labored breath, darkness crept further into her thoughts, suffocating hope like a smothering blanket. Memories of Afghanistan passed like storm clouds over her mind.

She thought of Bourdell and his fleeing from the conflict; maybe she, too, was not yet over the ghosts of the past. She shouldn't have put herself in a situation like this, which she clearly wasn't up to. And now, because of her recklessness, people would die.

Then, from somewhere in the distance, a sound drifted across the desert. Instinctively, Byrd recognized the noise. She would recognize that sound anywhere—to her, it was like the music of the great composers, just in mechanical form. She narrowed her eyes, assuming that the heat and stress were playing tricks on her.

Peering out at the horizon, Byrd saw something. Just a dot flying above the point where sand met sky. The noise came again, more distinctive this time.

"Is it really…" Byrd muttered in disbelief, cupping a hand above her eyes against the harsh desert glare. "I'd recognize those Twin Wasps anywhere." She sprinted into the chopper, nearly colliding with Hutchins as she grabbed a pair of binoculars from the cockpit.

"What is it?" Hutchins asked as she rushed back outside.

Byrd didn't reply. She raised the binoculars with trembling hands, adjusting the focus wheel as she scanned the horizon. The magnified image transformed the distant dot into one of the most beautiful sights she could imagine—the unmistakable silhouette of a C-47 Skytrain. Sunlight glinted off its polished aluminum fuselage like diamonds scattered across flowing water.

The aircraft descended gradually, the Twin Wasps thundering with increasing volume. Black exhaust fumes streaked behind the cowlings as the pilot throttled back for final approach.

The C-47 seemed to hang suspended for a moment—twenty tons of engineering mastery defying gravity through sheer aerodynamic will. Then, with the grace of a temple dancer, the wheels touched down, sending twin plumes of sand spiraling upward like miniature dust devils.

Byrd stood open-mouthed, the binoculars forgotten in her limp hands.

The Skytrain's propellers slowed to a stop, the sudden silence somehow more overwhelming than the engine's roar had been.

The magnificent machine rolled toward her, the desert bringing the aircraft to a halt perfectly, as though designed just for that purpose. With a gentle screech of brakes, the C-47 stopped, and the pilot's door opened.

"Bourdell!" Byrd yelped as her friend waved from the cockpit.

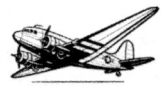

Mexican desert north of Cabo San Lucas

Sallas barreled across the desert on his heavy-framed Harley-Davidson motorcycle, its knobby tires tearing into the sunbaked dirt, the engine roaring like the furnaces of hell. Dust curled up behind him as he leaned into the throttle, squinting toward the horizon. On his back, the RPG-7 launcher he'd recently acquired moved up and down, sliding across his white shirt.

Looking ahead toward his former base, he suddenly saw the smoke—thin but rising steadily from within the compound. A fresh plume joined it, dark and curling.

Sallas yanked the handlebars to a stop, fishtailing the bike into a skid.

"Dammit!" He punched the handlebar hard enough to make his knuckles throb. With a low growl, he reached into his jacket, pulled out a battered phone, and jabbed at the screen with his thumb. "You'd better pick up if you want your face to remain recognizable."

He scrolled to a contact labeled Dr. Garcia and hit call. The line rang several times before Garcia finally answered.

"Doctor," Sallas said the moment it connected, "why the hell haven't you called me?"

"I was just about to," Garcia said, his tone rising with clearly feigned innocence.

"Don't lie to me," Sallas snapped. "You always put patient safety above your own neck. So noble. But remember what will happen to you if you hide anything from me. Stop protecting random patients at the risk of losing your own family. Is it really worth it, good doctor?"

On the other end, Garcia cleared his throat nervously.

"I found him in a regional hospital," Garcia said. "Professor Wall. He's alive."

Sallas raised an eyebrow. He stepped off the bike and began pacing, boots kicking up little puffs of red sand. "Where?"

"Armação dos Búzios. He checked in under a false name. Took time to trace him."

Sallas slowly ran a hand over his face. "Of course he did."

Garcia paused before finally saying, "What do you want me to do?"

Sallas gripped his phone tightly, pinning it to his ear. "I want you to prep something for me... final. Paralytic and cardiac arrest combo. Succinylcholine to drop him. Potassium chloride to finish the job. No mess. No delays."

Garcia paused. "Prep it? You're coming to do it yourself?"

"Damn right, I am. I want to see the life drain from his eyes."

"Good," Garcia muttered. "Because I don't want to do this disgusting deed for you."

Sallas barked a joyless laugh, then hung up without another word. He tucked the phone away, threw his leg back over the bike, and twisted the throttle. The engine snarled back to life.

He didn't look back at the compound, instead focusing straight ahead. He indulged his imagination and pictured the needle sinking into Wall's wrinkled skin.

Then, despite the noise of the Harley's engine, something even more powerful caught his attention. He glanced up, squinting against the sun. A vintage C-47 Skytrain, wings wide and unmistakably military, was ascending away from the compound. He yanked off his goggles and stared up at the plane, jaw clenched.

"Did you just take off from my damn compound," he growled. He stepped off the bike and reached around to his back.

## 72

**Mexican desert, Cabo San Lucas.**

"Truly a plane of the Gods," Byrd purred as the C-47 Skytrain banked away from the compound, the Twin Wasps rumbling with majestic power as they gained altitude.

Byrd looked around the cockpit, its dark metal fixtures worn smooth by human touch over decades. Her hand rested on the bright red mixture control lever regulating how much fuel was added to the airflow. The RPM, manifold pressure, and fuel pressure readings looked good, and the plane's musty, metallic scent smelled even better. Bourdell sat next to her in the co-pilot's seat.

"You okay, buddy?" Byrd asked, throwing her friend a glance. "When you left me at the canyon, I thought you were losing your mind."

"Can't lose what you don't have," Bourdell said, barking out a laugh. "Honestly, I've been losing my mind for years, Byrd. Don't worry about that." Bourdell turned to her and smiled through the white-yellow stubble on his top lip.

"But why did you bail at the canyon?"

"I didn't bail, Byrd," Bourdell said. "I noticed a heat spike under the avionics bay—right beneath the main instrument stack. It wasn't engine-related. Wasn't supposed to be there. Those cut-throats attached a magnetic thermal charge to the exterior—on a timer to take us all out at the same time."

"So you ran?"

"No—I flew out to try to save your damn life." Bourdell scrunched up his bushy eyebrows as he looked Byrd in the eye. "I knew you'd get on top of them and take the chopper. But if that thing had gone off while I was sitting there, they'd be picking up pieces of you in Guatemala. I've seen it before in cartel jobs. I landed a safe distance away and disarmed it."

Byrd nodded, feeling soft warmth settling in her stomach. "I should have known you wouldn't let me down."

"Right," Bourdell said, running his eyes across the C-47's displays. "I just hope this old plane doesn't let us down!"

"She'll be grand," Byrd reassured him. "I was only planning a few tweaks."

"Sure. *Sure* you were."

"You were the one who got it in the air, Bourdell." Byrd smiled. "What happened to *Nope. Negative. Nein. Non. One-hundred-percent that's never, ever going to happen?*" Bourdell simply responded with a knowing nod of the head.

Byrd's eyes swept the horizon methodically as they flew, old habits from combat missions never quite fading. The endless beige-and-brown landscape stretched toward infinity, broken only by the occasional rock formation or sparse vegetation.

Then, something caught her eye—movement where it shouldn't be. A dark speck trailed a thin plume of dust, moving like a bullet across the desert floor.

She blinked hard, focusing her vision. The speck

resolved into a more definite shape, cutting a diagonal path away from the compound. She reached for the binoculars and focused on the object.

"See that, Bourdell?" Byrd said, passing the binoculars to him. "It's a motorcycle, all the way out here."

Bourdell put the binos to his eyes and peered down. "Too fast for casual travel, and there's no good reason for someone to be out here in the desert."

Byrd straightened her back and tensed every muscle, adrenaline and alertness kicking in.

The motorcycle kicked up a distinctive trail of dust. The black dot grew larger as the C-47 approached.

"Get Briony up here, would you?"

"Sure thing." Bourdell climbed to his feet and returned a moment later with the young woman.

"Hey, Briony," Byrd said. "See that bike down there? You think that's Sallas? I didn't get great visuals on the guy back on the island."

"That's him, for sure. The long hair and that Harley. And who else would be out this way alone?"

"Wait a second," Byrd said, her voice filled with a quiet dread. "He's holding something. Is that a goddamn RPG?" Visions of Afghanistan flashed through her mind.

"Just like a terrorist," Bourdell said grimly, "he knows the biggest threat to his compound is from the air. Byrd, get to work before he wipes us all out."

"Bourdell, take the controls," Byrd said, climbing to her feet.

"Where are you going?" Briony asked.

"This thing has been retrofitted with side-mounted miniguns, and we need them right now."

"Aim for the wheels. He should live to face justice," Bourdell said with cold calmness.

"I know that, buddy. I'm not a big fan of head shots myself," Byrd replied, already moving toward the cabin where the weapons systems had been installed.

She slid into the gunner's position—a reinforced seat bolted to the aircraft's frame with a clear field of fire through a modified window in the fuselage. The M134 Minigun sat on a custom-mounted gimbal system, its six rotating barrels gleaming.

Byrd flipped the protective covers off the optical sight and activated the power system. The targeting computer hummed to life, green status indicators lighting up across the control panel as the weapon's electric motor engaged with a high-pitched whine.

Sierra Byrd adjusted the headset comms before gripping the handles—the twin pistol grips that provided stability and trigger control. She felt the familiar texture of the metal beneath her fingers.

"Weapon hot," she announced into her mic, flipping the arming switch. "7.62mm NATO rounds, four thousand per minute cyclic rate. Tracer ratio one-to-five."

"It better be hot—he's taking aim," Bourdell said with urgent volume. "Now, Byrd. Now!"

Her eyes quickly scanned the digital ammunition counter: 2,000 rounds available, enough for thirty seconds of sustained fire—or just a few precise bursts if she was careful. It only took one bullet.

The stabilization system compensated for the aircraft's movement, gyroscopes whirring as they kept the barrel assembly level despite the plane's gentle banking turns.

"Take your shot, Byrd," Bourdell said through Byrd's headset. "Before he does."

"Roger that," Byrd replied, her eyes never leaving the targeting system. Her left hand made a slight adjustment to the elevation control as the targeting computer calculated bullet drop over distance.

Through the digital sight, she tracked Sallas, the crosshairs showing both the current point of aim and the projected impact point, accounting for the aircraft's movement, target velocity, and environmental factors. The rangefinder laser bounced back a reading of 380 meters—well within effective range. Wind drift indicators showed a 12-knot crosswind from the east.

Her finger settled on the trigger, taking up the first stage of pressure until she felt the mechanical resistance that preceded firing. The familiar tension matched the tightening in her chest as traumatic memories of older missions in a faraway land surfaced.

She shook her head, defying her own doubt. "No hesitation today," she said under her breath.

Through the crosshairs, Byrd saw Sallas take aim, the RPG-7 launcher steady on his shoulder. Death for everyone who had been saved was suddenly seconds away.

Byrd fired. The minigun barked repeatedly, the vibration humming through her arms and chest like a living thing. She kept her eyes locked through the sight, watching the desert as the rounds screamed toward their target.

Plumes of sand and dust rose into the air as the shot struck the front tire, kicking up violent bursts of sand and shrapnel. The explosion lifted the bike off its axis. Sallas flew horizontally like a javelin, the RPG torn from his shoulder before he hit the ground. The motorcycle flipped end over end, its rear wheel spinning wildly as it somersaulted through the air.

Sallas' body bounced twice on the sand before he slammed into the earth in a contorted heap. Dust swallowed the scene again, and for a breathless moment, nothing moved.

When Byrd got visuals again, she saw the bike lying meters away, wheels still spinning. Sallas tried to lift himself, then flopped down, clutching his bloodied face. From high up in the air, Byrd gave The Mentor a wink.

"Don't worry, Sallas. Looks aren't everything," she told him from a distance.

At the same time, Bourdell wobbled the C-47's wings by way of salute, then straightened up and headed for civilization.

# EPILOGUE

**Isla de la Fortuna, Caribbean Sea. Two weeks later.**

The island heat softened with the late afternoon, and a breeze curled through the open hangar like the tide creeping into a forgotten cove. Sierra Byrd stood near the tail section of her trusty C-47, her arms streaked with grease up to the elbow. She squinted up at a sun-bleached flap hinge, adjusted a bolt with the smooth twist of a spanner, and gave the metal a satisfied tap. The aircraft had saved lives, and today she was giving it the love it deserved—a light inspection and a polish. It had been out into the world and done its duty, but now, it was hers. Everything around her was. The open hangar, the coral-dusted runway, the little flight school she'd once thought impossible.

She heard the slow crunch of footsteps outside. Bourdell's silhouette appeared in the doorway, backlit by late sunlight.

"You've been at it for hours, Byrd. Time for a drink."

She turned, wiping her hands on a rag already too dirty to help much. "That an order, Commander?"

"Call it friendly advice," he replied. "Hopefully, your plane won't need to see any action for a while."

"With Sallas and Tom going to trial, and that creepy thin guy arrested by his own police force, you're probably right," Byrd agreed as she stepped down off the inspection stand.

"You didn't feel like just leaving Sallas to wilt in the sun after you dealt with him?" Bourdell asked.

"I can't say I didn't think about it," Byrd replied, wiping oil from her face, "but I called for a medevac the same time I called law enforcement. After we rescued so many victims who were willing to testify, I decided he'd be better off rotting in a correctional facility. Same with Tom."

"You must be getting soft in your old a—" Bourdell stopped himself and tilted his head to beckon Byrd outside.

Byrd followed Bourdell out, shielding her eyes as she emerged into the glow. The bar sat just off the beach, shaded by a palm-thatched roof and open on all sides to the sea breeze. They set up behind it like it was second nature—Byrd pulled two metal cups down from a shelf and reached for the ice bucket. Bourdell sliced the top off a fresh coconut with a single, swift motion. A squeeze of lime, a dash of dark rum, and the cocktail cried out to be sipped.

"This is a little more refreshing than bourbon," Byrd said, taking her first drink and letting the flavor sit on her tongue. "Smoother. I've had enough of the rough stuff for a while."

Bourdell raised his cup. "To smooth flights."

They sat with their seats angled toward the surf. The beach curved away in either direction, empty but for the occasional seabird gliding low over the sand. Waves lapped the shore with the rhythm of an easy heartbeat.

"So," Bourdell said, leaning back, "you done with ghostbustin'?"

Byrd gave a soft laugh. "Mostly. This place helps. Every day feels a little less like I'm running from something."

"Good. I like seeing you like this."

Before Byrd could reply, a pair of familiar figures emerged from the leafy path that cut between the squat bungalows of the accommodation block. Hutchins and Candi walked in step, their hands intertwined. Candi's hair caught the light in a shimmer, and Hutchins looked relaxed in a way Byrd had rarely seen—tanned, loose-shouldered, genuinely happy.

"Evening, lovebirds," Bourdell called.

"Evening," Hutchins replied, flashing a grin as he led Candi to the bar. "You might like to know," the young academic said as Bourell handed him a drink, "that I spoke to Wall this morning."

Byrd raised her eyebrows. "Yeah? How is he?"

"He's home. Says he's enjoying his wife's cooking and pottering around in the garden."

"No treasure huntin'?" Byrd asked.

"Nope," Hutchins said with a smirk. "He said he's just looking at the flowers and drinking tea. No digging. But he'll have to put his black tie on soon—he's getting an award for finding the Sunstone and the miracle plant."

"No award for you, Hans?" Bourdell asked, placing a hand on the younger man's shoulder. "After everything you did?"

Hutchins shook his head. "I wanted him to get the glory."

Candi laughed and snuggled up closer to Hutchins.

"I think Hans got all the reward he needs," Byrd said, glancing at Candi and bringing smiles all round.

They sat in companionable quiet for a moment. Byrd glanced at Hutchins and Candi, their hands linked on the bar between their drinks. She nodded and smiled to herself—before her keen ears picked up on something in the distance.

A small rumble carried through the stillness. Not thunder. Not distant surf. Byrd tilted her head, listening.

The rising whine of helicopter rotors cut through the evening air. A familiar shape swung around the curve of the beach, racing close to the water like a metallic seabird.

"If I'm not mistaken, that's a Eurocopter," Byrd said, watching the chopper power their way.

"You expectin' someone?" Bourdell said, followed by a sip of the drink.

"I'm always expectin' something," Byrd said, placing her drink down and walking back around the hangar to the apron. She arrived just as the chopper thundered overhead and then touched down.

Byrd cupped a hand over her eyes, protecting them from the spirals of sand and dust thrown into the air by the rotors. The engines powered down, and the door slid open.

Sierra Byrd planted her hands on her hips as a woman stepped down. The newcomer raised a hand in a wave and started across toward Byrd. The pilot hopped out a moment later.

"Eden Black," Byrd said as the woman approached. "As ever, your timing is impeccable." The pair merged into a hug. "Have you been workin' out?" Byrd said, glancing down at Eden's trim figure.

"We've been stuck on the Balonia for weeks," Eden replied, meeting Byrd's gaze. "Training is my solace."

"You know what they say about all work and no play," Byrd said, turning her attention to the approaching man. "And Captain Baxter. It sure is a pleasure to see you." Byrd pulled the young man into a hug before he could resist.

"And what brings you both to my lil' corner of the planet?" Byrd turned and led the way back toward the beach bar.

"After what feels like months at sea, we wondered if we might hole up here for a while," Eden said, keeping in step with Byrd. "The Balonia's about a hundred miles away—"

"Eighty-seven nautical miles," Baxter said, speaking for the first time.

Eden shrugged. "We thought we'd come in early and get the party started. Got room for two more?"

Byrd led the way to the beach bar and pulled out two more chairs. She made the introductions, and Eden and Baxter took their places. Bourdell set about fixing everyone's drinks.

"It's a beautiful place you've got here," Eden said, looking up at the sinking sun.

"It ain't bad at all," Byrd replied, taking a sip. "Would be even better if all these people would just leave me alone to enjoy it."

"Now that's certainly somethin' you don't mean," Bourdell said, retaking his seat.

As drinks flowed and the sun slid away behind the horizon, Hutchins dragged Byrd's old boombox down onto the sand.

"You know you can get these speakers now that connect to your phone," he said, sifting through Byrd's collection of CDs.

"I'm sure you can, darlin', but that's not the way we do things out here."

Hutchins selected a CD and pushed it into the player. A Latin pop beat boomed from the speakers.

"How in the name of all things holy did that get in there?" Byrd said, shooting to her feet in mock outrage. "Get some Little Richard on, or Bill Haley, Chuck Berry, or even Elvis!"

Candi leapt to her feet and, taking Hutchins by the hand, spun into a Latin dance.

"I think you're overruled, Captain," Bourdell said, meeting Byrd's gaze.

The last gold of sunlight scattered across the water in a serene shimmer.

"You're all tasteless," she muttered, settling back into her seat.

Beside her, Bourdell tapped his foot and swayed to the beat. Byrd took another sip of her coconut cocktail and let her eyes wander.

Off to the side, she spotted Candi and Hutchins swing into a turn. Candi leaned in, her voice quiet but clear enough to carry to Byrd.

"Come on," she whispered to Hutchins. "Let's find a private spot on the beach."

Hutchins smiled, clearly caught off guard. "Of course. Sure. But why now?"

"Because of this," Candi said, sweeping her arm across the scene. "It's all about timing. Sunsets, soulful music... and not getting shot at."

Hutchins laughed, kissed her forehead, and took her hand. They slipped away into the darkening stretch of sand, leaving behind only a soft trail of footprints. Byrd watched them go from her seat at the bar, her chin resting in one palm.

"I'll have to make sure they visit often," Byrd said.

"I thought you didn't want *anyone* to visit often," Bourdell said, leaning across.

"Well, I changed my mind," she replied, watching the

last hint of Candi's silhouette disappear behind the curve of palm trees. "For now."

Eden and Baxter laughed and raised their glasses.

"Maybe," Bourdell said, raising his glass with a smirk, "you're just not meant to drink alone."

Byrd clinked her drink against his.

"You know," she said, "I think you're right."

"You know what," Eden said, leaning over and clinking glasses with Byrd, "I think Nora Byrd finally found her place."

"Don't call me No—" Byrd shouted, but at that moment Bourdell jumped to his feet and cranked the volume to the max. "Oh, fine. Call me whatever you want!"

The moon rose huge and slow over the horizon, and in that moment, with no ghosts pressing at the edge of her vision, Sierra Byrd breathed in the warm Caribbean air and smiled.

## BYRD IS BACK!

**Reserve your seat in the cockpit for Nora "Sierra" Byrd's next adventure.**

By pre-ordering the next book, you'll be among the very first to dive into the next high-stakes mission—and you'll be giving us a much-needed nudge to keep writing!

We're aiming to have Book Two in your hands by the end of 2025. But as you've probably gathered from this story... things don't always go exactly to plan.

**Secure your spot now!**
**Search your local Amazon store, scan the QR, or:**
**http://www.lukerichardsonauthor.com/byrdisback**

*Byrd is back!*

# A NOTE FROM THE AUTHORS

**Thank you so much for joining us on Nora "Sierra" Byrd's first adventure.**

It's been a real pleasure to entertain you over the last few hours. We hope you enjoyed spending time with Byrd and her crew as much as we did.

Collaborating on this book has been a unique and rewarding experience. It brought together our different writing styles, creative ideas, love of exotic settings, and given a character from Luke's *Eden Black* series a chance at her own adventure.

In case you didn't know, Nora "Sierra" Byrd first made her entrance in *The Atlantis Agenda*, when Eden, Baxter, and Athena lose their helicopter in Mexico City. Stranded and in need of a way out, they search the area and stumble across Byrd's Flight and Parachute School, a few miles north of the city. With no better option, they break in under cover of darkness. They head for the hangar, planning to "borrow" a plane when something unexpected happens.

"At least someone thinks what's inside is worth protecting," Athena said, stepping alongside Eden. The beams of their lights swayed through the gloom.

"That shouldn't be an issue," Baxter said. "We've got a tire iron in the truck. We'll be in there in a few seconds."

"You'll do no such thing," came a voice from behind them. "Now turn around really slowly. I wouldn't want you to get shot accidentally."

Eden gritted her teeth. She looked up at the large hangar doors in front of them, blocking their path. She glanced left and then right. The voice sounded close behind them, trapping them against the doors.

As though reading Eden's thoughts, the voice came again. "I've got the business end of this Remington 870 pointing right at your backs." The mystery assailant pumped the gun, as though proving the threat. "I won't tell you again. Turn around now."

Eden glanced quickly at Baxter and Athena, then nodded almost imperceptibly. Together, slowly, the three turned around.

The sight of their aggressor took Eden by surprise. A woman in her early middle age looked the three of them up and down. She had a great beehive of black hair tied up on her head. She wore the overalls of an Air Force pilot, open at the front with a red tank top beneath. There was something strangely glamorous about the woman, Eden decided. Her large, brown eyes darted from Eden, to Athena, and then to Baxter.

"Now then, I think you had better tell me why you're breaking into my airfield in the middle of the night," the woman said, raising the gun to impress upon the three the fact that she wasn't asking.

And the character of Nora "Sierra" Byrd was born.

Some of you sharp-eyed readers may have noticed that the "Sierra" part of her name is new. That was John's idea—he felt that just calling her "Nora" didn't quite have the punch you want in an action story. He was right, of course. At some point, Luke plans to go back and sprinkle a few "Sierras" into the earlier books. Until then, chalk it up to one of those quirks that come with spin-offs and long-running series.

**Now comes one of our favourite parts of the book, telling you the truth behind the story.**

**The Shadow of the Sunstone** is, as you now know, a story about the search for eternal life. It's a quest as old as human history—and though ours may involve vintage aircraft and a quick-witted pilot, the subject matter is anything but lighthearted.

Humanity has chased immortality for centuries, often with grim consequences. From sacred springs to deadly elixirs, the pursuit has always demanded a steep price.

In 16th-century Hungary, Countess Elizabeth Báthory reportedly bathed in the blood of young women, believing it would preserve her youth. Chinese emperors ingested mercury in the hope of becoming immortal—only to find an early grave. Across medieval Europe, alchemists obsessed over gold-laced tonics that promised eternal life, but delivered only slow, painful deaths.

The idea that eternal life might come from a plant isn't

new either. In ancient Greece, the mysterious herb known as *silphium* was famed for its near-miraculous properties. Used as everything from a cooking spice to a fever remedy—and even as a contraceptive—it was so valuable that Julius Caesar is said to have stored a thousand pounds of it in Rome's treasury alongside gold.

But *silphium* resisted cultivation and by the first century C.E., it was so rare that Pliny the Elder wrote of a single stalk being discovered—promptly delivered to Emperor Nero as a gift. For centuries it was believed extinct. Only recently has a researcher in Turkey claimed to have discovered a plant that's strikingly similar, growing in the Anatolian highlands.

Of course, no legend of eternal life looms larger than the Philosopher's Stone. Said to transmute base metals into gold and produce the fabled Elixir of Life, the Stone promised both wealth and immortality. Among its most famous seekers was Nicolas Flamel, a 14th-century Parisian scribe whose name later became synonymous with alchemical success. Did he truly unlock the secret? Historians say no. But the myth persists—in dusty manuscripts, whispered conspiracies, and the occasional burned laboratory notebook. Some stories are simply too alluring to die—which is, we suppose, the immortality us writers hope for!

The ancient Egyptians took a more engineered approach. They didn't merely hope for life after death—they designed for it. Through the art of mummification and the construction of mathematically precise pyramids, they sought to secure the soul's journey into the afterlife. Pharaohs consumed rare herbs and minerals believed to prolong life, including the sacred blue lotus—thought to expand consciousness and open the mind to the divine.

Their *Book of the Dead* was a manual for the soul's passage, filled with incantations, rituals, and passwords meant to guide the departed through the perils of the underworld. For the Egyptians, death wasn't the end. It was a doorway—and preparation was everything.

So, has anyone ever truly found the secret? We doubt it. But some places do seem to come close.

On the Greek island of Ikaria people live remarkably long and healthy lives. Here, longevity isn't rare, it's expected. Locals climb steep hills well into their nineties. Their diet is rich in wild greens, legumes, olive oil, and herbal teas made from native plants—some of which may have echoes of the ancient *silphium*. Whether it's biology, environment, or something more elusive, people on Ikaria simply live longer.

Maybe the real secret isn't locked in a tomb or hidden in an elixir. Maybe it's in the hills, the herbs, and the pace of a simpler life. Tempting, isn't it?

The idea of the Mentor and his shadowy cult was a fascinating one to explore in this story. While fictional, the group draws heavily on real-world influences—especially some of the more bizarre spiritual movements of the 20th century. One such inspiration was *The Source Family*, a Los Angeles-based commune that emerged in the 1970s.

They wore flowing robes, practiced esoteric rituals, chanted in invented tongues—and ran a health food restaurant on Sunset Boulevard. At the center of it all was a man named Father Yod: a former jujitsu instructor who reinvented himself as a spiritual leader and self-declared prophet.

Charismatic and deeply unconventional, Father Yod married more than a dozen of his female followers, presided over daily meditations from a throne, and led the group's psychedelic rock band, *YaHoWha 13*. They lived communally in a mansion in the Hollywood Hills, where spiritual enlightenment mixed freely with countercultural experimentation.

The story took a darker turn when the group abruptly relocated to Hawaii, hoping to build a utopian society. Things unraveled quickly when Father Yod attempted to hang-glide off a cliff—without any training—and died. He claimed he "knew it was his time to ascend." It's strange history. But it's real.

And as we crafted our fictional cult, we kept coming back to this unsettling truth: people can be drawn into the orbit of a powerful leader when they're desperate for meaning. Sometimes, that search leads to beauty and healing. Other times, it leads straight off a cliff.

### A note on the aircraft featured in this book

Every plane that appears in these pages is real, drawn from aviation history—but we've taken liberties. Some flight paths, maneuvers, or mechanical feats may stretch the bounds of what's technically possible. For the aviation purists reading, we offer a sincere apology—and a thank you for your patience. Story sometimes takes the stick.

The real star of the skies, though, is Byrd's aircraft: a lovingly restored Douglas C-47 Skytrain. Originally designed as the DC-3, this twin-engine, all-metal transport first took flight in the 1930s and revolutionized civilian air travel. When war broke out, the U.S. military adapted the design for combat operations, reinforcing the airframe, adding cargo doors, and equipping it for rugged conditions. Thus, the C-47 was born.

She could carry 6,000 pounds of cargo or 28 fully equipped troops. She wasn't built for speed, but for resilience. Pilots came to trust her without question—she was tough, dependable, and forgiving in a crisis. Even when riddled with bullet holes or battered by weather, the C-47 had a reputation for bringing her crew home. Affectionately known as "The Gooney Bird," she might have looked awkward on the runway, but in the air she was a workhorse—steady, capable, and essential.

Her resume is remarkable: dropping paratroopers on D-Day, flying treacherous supply routes over the Himalayas to support Chinese forces in World War II, and running missions during the Berlin Airlift, where she helped sustain an entire city during the Soviet blockade. Today, she still flies in private hands and museums around the world—a living symbol of endurance, craftsmanship, and courage.

This book also incorporates our love of travel. Both of us have spent years travelling all over the globe, and love putting that into our stories. Set in the Caribbean with action across Mexico, this story is a combination of real settings and fictional ones. The island on which Byrd's flight school *the Isla de la Fortuna*, and the island on which Hutchins and Wall first discovered the ancient human remains the *Isla de la Vida Eterna,* are both fictional. The Mexican towns, of course, are real and we've done our best to capture the vibrancy of these places.

As for what comes next—well, Byrd's just getting started. There are more secrets buried in forgotten places, more myths waiting to be cracked open, and more flights into danger than she'd probably like. At that time of writing we're already plotting the next chapter in her story, and if you've enjoyed this mix of legend, history, and high-stakes adventure, we think you'll want to be there when the wheels leave the ground again. Until then, keep your eyes on the horizon—and never stop chasing adventure.

Thanks for your company, see you on the next one!

Luke and John

May, 2025.

**Join the Adventure Society TODAY!**

WANTED: Readers for a hazardous journey. Expect ancient secrets, exotic locations, and danger around every corner. Safe return? Doubtful.

This is your invitation to join Luke's Adventure Society. You'll get exclusive updates of all upcoming twisty adventure books, behind-the-scenes secrets, correspondence from his real-world travels, and your first look at new books inspired by real-world mysteries.

If you like your fiction fast, fun, and full of intrigue, you're in the right place.

**To sign up now visit:
https://www.lukerichardsonauthor.com/
adventuresociety**

**Your next adventure starts here...**

## BOOK REVIEWS

**If you enjoyed this book, we'd be incredibly grateful if you left a review.**

Reviews matter more than most people realize. First, they help new readers take a chance on authors they haven't heard of. Second, they influence the mysterious algorithms that decide which books get recommended. And third—we just really love hearing what you think.

Good reviews can make a huge difference for writers like us, especially as we build a new series from the ground up. It only takes a couple of minutes, but it means the world to us.

Just head to the place where you bought the book, scroll down, and click *'Write a review.'*

Thank you so much.

# HAVE YOU MET EDEN BLACK?

**Meet Eden Black—the archaeologist who fights back.**

Nora "Sierra" Byrd made her first appearance in one of Luke's Eden Black archaeological thrillers. If you enjoyed the action in this story, the *Eden Black* series is your next stop.

**A secret society.**
**An ancient manuscript.**
**One woman to stop a deadly conspiracy.**

Professional treasure hunter **Eden Black** isn't afraid of danger. The relics she recovers don't exactly come with easy access—or polite company. But when her father dies in a mysterious plane crash, the stakes get personal.

Grief turns to suspicion as Eden discovers a deadly pattern: everyone connected to a long-buried archaeological dig is dying. Everyone except her. She was only ten at the time—but now, someone wants her silenced too.

When her father's home is burned to the ground, Eden is forced to act. To survive—and uncover the truth—she must track down a lost manuscript tied to an ancient secret... and bring a powerful cabal out of the shadows.

Perfect for fans of Dan Brown, Clive Cussler, and Ernest Dempsey, the *Eden Black* series delivers globetrotting mystery, cinematic action, and page-turning suspense. Start the adventure today—and see where the trail leads.

**Start this best-selling series with THE ARK FILES today. Search your local Amazon store, scan the QR, or visit: http://www.lukerichardsonauthor.com/meetedentoday**

# ABOUT THE AUTHORS

**Luke Richardson**

Luke Richardson is a British thriller author whose stories blend high-stakes adventure with real-world intrigue. With a background in education and a lifelong love of travel, Luke has visited over 40 countries—and brings each destination vividly to life on the page.

Before becoming an Amazon bestselling author, Luke was already hooked on travel. It was, in fact, a trip to Mumbai, India, that pushed him to start writing seriously— he remembers watching the city unfold through a taxi window and realizing he didn't just want to see the world; he wanted to write it.

Luke's books take readers from the pyramids of Egypt to the neon chaos of Hong Kong, weaving together fast-paced plots, atmospheric settings, and characters you'll root for (and sometimes against). His stories are perfect for fans of mystery, history, and edge-of-your-seat adventure.

When he's not writing, Luke can be found planning his

next trip, walking in nature, or enjoying a strong coffee and stronger plot twists.

https://www.lukerichardsonauthor.com/

**John Hopton**

John Hopton is a Yorkshire-born thriller writer now living in Japan. He writes international adventures with a sharp edge and a global scope, inspired by years of travel across India, the Middle East, East Asia, and beyond.

Before turning to fiction, John wrote a well-received travel memoir, drawing from his journeys through some of the world's most dynamic and unpredictable regions. That real-world experience now fuels his thrillers—stories packed with pace, danger, and unexpected detours.

When he's not writing, John enjoys exploring the lesser-seen corners of Japan, discovering obscure local legends, and reading books that make him miss his train stop.

**Copyright © 2025 by Richa Creative**

All rights reserved. No part of this book may be reproduced, distributed, or transmitted in any form or by any means, including photocopying, recording, or other electronic or mechanical methods, without the prior written permission of the publisher, except in the case of brief quotations embodied in critical reviews and certain other non-commercial uses permitted by copyright law. For permission requests, write to the publisher at the address below.

Richa Books

Hello@LukeRichardsonAuthor.com

This is a work of fiction. Names, characters, places, and incidents either are products of the author's imagination or are used fictitiously. Any resemblance to actual persons, living or dead, events, or locales is entirely coincidental.

Cover Design: http://toullacreative.com/

❦ Formatted with Vellum

Printed in Dunstable, United Kingdom